THE FALL OF JERICHO

THE FALL OF JERICHO

This book is a work of fiction. Character names and descriptions are the product of the author's imagination. Any resemblance to actual persons, living or dead, is entirely coincidental.

Copyright © 2024 Sydney Applegate

Edited by Caitlin Lengerich
Cover by Bianca Bordianu

ISBN 979-8-9895332-0-6

Published by Sydney Applegate
Learn more at www.booksbysydney.com

To Corinne, my dream girl

And to all the girls that prefer their prince charmings with questionable morals.
This one's for you.

Content Warning

The Fall of Jericho is an electric romance-fantasy jointly narrated by two enemies, both of whom have behaviors that should be advised to all readers before proceeding. Subject matters in their story contain interrogation, murder, graphic language, mentions and near-acts of suicide, discussions on the death of loved ones and domestic violence, and references to sexual content. Readers who may be sensitive to this kind of material, please be advised. Otherwise, brace yourself for what can *really* happen when you meet someone once upon a dream…

THE FALL OF JERICHO

PART I
CLAIRVOYANCE

1
Jericho

I'm getting sick and tired of everyone swearing up and down that they are innocent.

Each member of the family, that the guards brought in an hour ago, comes to terms with their imprisonment differently. Four children, three of which are boys, and two parents.

"You're wrong about us!" the middle son shouts. Kurt—if I heard his sister correctly, when she pleaded with him to stop yelling—remains the only one in his sorry family that insists on saving his tears. Even his weakling father descends into hysterics. "You have no proof."

Scattered candlelight provides a dim, haunting glow over the interrogation room that some would go as far as to call a torture chamber—bouncing off the mirrored walls and marbled floors. Were it not for the multiple sets of chains bolted to the floor, and the cluster of people in my custody pleading their futile case, this room could eclipse the beauty of any arts rehearsal hall. Where a skylight once allowed prisoners to decipher the time of day, a black-lidded ceiling now shuts the rotating inhabitants of this room within the harsh reality of what this place truly is: a tomb.

"You think my dreams deceive me?" I sneer, stalking towards the boy, my robe scraping against the floor.

"I think your dreams are a bunch of horseshit," he says spitefully.

The insult makes my lips curl into a devious smile. "I see. Well then, if you are so bold, why don't you select who dies first?"

His mother desperately tries to break from her chains to comfort her daughter, who has now become sick to her stomach with the realization that this is the end—and when she cannot gain much ground, she looks at me with hopelessness. "What are the charges against my family? How is this possibly fair?"

I mean to respond, if only because she asked somewhat nicely. But now, Kurt's nameless brothers are looking at me with a fury I know well.

"You're a monster," one of them says, his shaggy hair falling over his sweaty forehead. "But you're only half the king your lousy father was—"

Knowing he cannot move his chained hands to protect himself, I sink my hunting knife straight into his vulnerable, traitorous heart. His body drops onto the hard floor with a single thud, and his mother wails loud enough to make me reach for my ears in an effort to cover them.

"It's very noble of you to protect your son—your

brother," I say. "But you're all fools, because in doing so, you have chosen to die for his decisions."

My Head Councilman, Ardian, hobbles out of the shadows, with a bored yet dismayed look on his face, and tosses a burlap sack of coins in front of the ill-fated family.

Kurt's eyes darken in horror. "What the hell is that?"

"Your mother asked what the charges against you all were, and I'm answering her. So, tell me," I say, angling my eyes specifically towards the patriarch of the condemned family, "how long have you known your son is a thief?"

The father stumbles over his own tongue, unable to form a complete sentence—his guilt evident. His efforts are so pathetic, it makes his daughter feel the need to speak for him. "He didn't. None of us did."

"But you all suspected," I cut in, eyeing the girl and her family.

"That's not fair—"

"Isn't it? There are strict rules and consequences, as you know, for sheltering fugitives and resisting arrests. Your brother is no different, and according to the testimony of my guards, you each fought against them when it came time to take your brother away."

"That's what families do, you bastard," Kurt shouts. "They *fight* for each other. But perhaps I should cut you some slack—you wouldn't know what that's like, considering your own mother couldn't even fight for herself."

Ardian doesn't have time to look away from the carnage that ensues.

"Was all of that truly necessary?"

A grumble vibrates through my chest as I finish scrubbing the blood off of me in one of the designated washrooms. I look towards him in the mirror and realize that, in the heat of the moment, I wound up with Kurt's blood splattered along my jaw. "Once they come in, they do not come back. You know this. It establishes consistency."

"Your subjects will not consider you soft for sparing the family members of a guilty party, Jericho," my Head Councilman argues, his voice thinning out the further into his sentence he gets.

I slam my hands onto the counter. "Did you not hear what that boy said about her? Did you not hear him slander the greatest queen to ever grace this earth? Because if my memory serves me well, you stood there, like a coward, and now you're judging me for defending her honor?"

Ardian eyes me with a disgusting amount of pity, and I'm inclined to tear into him next.

"I get that blood makes you woozy, but if you're so put off, stop lingering in the cells when I go to finish things off. Your presence won't change my mind on what needs to be done."

He shakes his head. "Innocent blood . . . I wonder if one day it will have that same effect on you that it does me—"

"Oh, go pray to the Saints that I'll see the light and repent from my wicked ways or something," I chide, swiping a white hand towel across my chin, staining it red, and letting a sly smile cross over my features when Ardian's attention skirts towards it. "You knew what you were walking into when the crown passed over to me. I even gave you the chance to jump ship. So, tell me right now, have you had enough?"

Perhaps it's because I'm pointing my knife at him in questioning, rather than appealing to his integrity as my Head Councilman—either way, he responds with, "No, Your Majesty. May the Saints bless your dreams."

He departs without another sound, and I brace myself before the mirror. I look over myself one last time—searching for any semblance of regret, remorse, or conviction.

I find nothing.

The green marshes jutting south of the Royal Domain have withered away into a naked, brown realm of twigs and toiled branches. The windstorms have likely damaged a few of the nearby villages, too, but something in my gut tells me that I've been beckoned here for reasons other than possible repair initiatives.

It's chillingly quiet outside, and while I don't remember consciously walking to this location, I do not sense any danger nearby.

Upon further recollection, I remember this place from when Father and I had visited to recruit new staff. The Makers District was chock-full of well-trained craftsmen from carpenters to blacksmiths, topiaries to architects. Talented people, now all nestled in their beds to recharge for another day's work, line these woods.

So, why am I out here alone?

It's peaceful, yet it's reminiscent of the kind of peace you only receive in moments where you're truly alone. The thought makes a tinge of sorrow well up in my throat.

A rustle from a hedge nearby startles me more than I should allow it to. Still, I decide to dismiss it for a rabbit or another creature that often mulls about these lands—maybe a rodent. Straightening out my slacks and examining my riding boots, I glance about the area in hopes of finding my means of getting here—my footwear suggesting the existence of a horse. I click my tongue, hoping to hear a "neigh" or hooves clipping on leaves in response, but am only met with silence.

What the hell am I doing here?

And that's when a woman appears from the shrubbery I heard move moments ago.

Her skin resembles the sweet caramels the royal bakers created for the winter holiday parties my mother used to host, and her hair is the color of how I take my coffee: undiluted and dark. She stands yards away from me, but something about her presence convinces me she smells like pine trees and jasmine. Maybe it's the shadows, but her face tells me enough about her day to know that it was probably exhausting—and yet, that darkness frames her hazel eyes well.

She looks at me head-on, our gaze unbroken, and her only tell regarding how she feels about this interaction comes from the small gesture of tucking part of her hair behind her ear, which I see now to be pierced through, several times, with small, silver hoops.

I silently beg her to say something.

Anything.

Intrigued, I step forward—

"Come find me," she whispers—a challenge.

And then, she disappears behind the trimmed hedges she first floated in from.

2
Venus

The bite behind the winter morning air wakes me before the sun does, and though it peeks over the horizon with an enticing, subtle glow, it provides no additional warmth. I hear Geneva shiver from across the room, and when she hides her face beneath her covers, I can't tell if it's to better diffuse the cold or to keep the daylight from coming into view. But her efforts amount to nothing when our bedroom door swings open and knocks into our shared, rickety dresser.

"Look alive, ladies!" Calliope announces, just as she does every morning.

My little sister groans at the sound of her voice, refusing to accept that it's morning. "Would it kill you to sleep in just once?"

"First out of the womb, first out of bed," she chimes, all too cheery for the early hours of the day. She's already primped and primed her face and hair for the day, touching up her lips and lashes with what pitiful excuses for cosmetics we can afford, and tying her hair into an updo that makes her look more like a milkmaid than a musician. The sun shines kindly on her skin, which is lighter than Genny's and mine. I always figured it was a distinguishing trademark, gifted to her from the Saints or some shit—likely for being the painfully optimistic oldest daughter.

Sluggishly, I set my feet on the floor, still sore from the day before, but when Genny doesn't give any indication that she'll get out of bed, Calliope asks me, "Do you smell that, Venus?"

I'm not entirely sure how to play along until she shoves her elbow into the soft part of my arm. "Maybe," I lie, a feigned brightness in my voice. "It smells . . ." I wait for any nonverbal hints my sister can give me, and I'm offered nothing. ". . . fresh?" I guess reluctantly. "What do you smell, Cali?"

"Only the district's best companion for my morning hotcakes," she says, a smile so wide and proud on her lips that I hear it in her words. "Of course, Venus and I are more than happy to use all the syrup—"

That's what gets her. Hope dances in her brown, sleepy eyes as she nearly explodes out of her bed. "The maple kind?"

Before Cali can even answer, Geneva wraps her arms tightly around her in gratitude. "Traded it for some commission work later tonight—a gig in the Noble Lands. With that in mind, you'll both need to fend for yourselves for supper."

"Shouldn't be much trouble," I assure her, and with that, Genny leads the way, stomping down the uneven stairs without a care for being quiet.

Despite our social status, I've always been perfectly content with our home—the quaintness of it in the sense of housing three women within the body of a tree, but the grandness of knowing that us girls managed to purchase it without aid.

Men in the marshes were always eager to hear of any ladies in need of a loan, because where money was given, much more was returned. I had been on the sour end of a deal like that when Genny had gotten a stomach infection last year. Antibiotics from the local physician cost me two weeks of laying mulch for his wife's garden in the blazing sun. If even medical professionals knew to search for leverage in that way, I determined that none of my sisters and I ought to be seeking help from anyone, even if it meant residing in the least desirable part of the Makers District, and living amidst the disarray of home improvement projects we couldn't afford to take on.

Geneva is already shoveling hot cakes in her mouth by the time I make it downstairs. "I can cook tonight if you're willing to clean up after me."

I nod, knowing that dealing with the leftover scraps and plates is worth avoiding any horrendous meal I would attempt. "What do we have from the shelf?"

Calliope hands Geneva the bottle of syrup from the rusty countertop. "Use sparingly," she warns. "I want Venus to have some, too." Then she moves back to examine the cupboards and the shelves of spices. Cali hums in speculation. "Some pasta, garlic, herbs . . . no vegetables at the moment, though. Maybe Venus can trade an extra hour for some of the carrots in the Carrowers' yard," she suggests, her eyes on Genny.

I try to smother my grimace. "Excellent idea, Cali."

"Ooh! Maybe I can sneak some chocolates from work, as well!" Geneva offers, hoping to settle the slight frustration she can read in my eyes. But as soon as the words are spoken, she regrets them.

"The staff may forgive you if they catch you, but not King Jericho." Calliope almost laughs, shaking her head. "What if Jericho dreams about you smuggling food? Then what?"

Geneva's face falls flat. "What . . . why would you say something like that?"

I desperately try to use my eyes to signal Calliope to *stop talking*.

"Isn't that what happened with the Prokium boy two roads down?" Calliope asks, only looking me in the eyes after the words are out.

Kurt Prokium had been seized from his home two hours before Genny got home from work a few nights ago, supposedly on charges of theft from noble property. He, his two brothers, sister, and parents were all taken into palace custody and haven't been seen since. It's been days, and I hadn't heard news of their release. But in those situations, release is unheard of—I just didn't have confirmation of their killings. That is, until Calliope.

A cloud of sadness invisibly hovers over Genny, and I watch her set her fork down on her plate. "Wait . . . Kurt's dead?"

To her credit, Cali's sudden realization crashes over her like a wave of color finally seeping into her skin. "How insensitive of me. I'm sorry, Genny," she mutters shortly before closing the cupboards and reaching for her shawl and cramming her feet into her walking boots. I expect her to say her apologies again, but she appears too embarrassed to try. The wind slams the door behind her once she disappears into the morning outside.

Though my appetite suddenly feels reduced, I still reach for one of the hotcakes stacked in the middle of the kitchen table, stabbing it with my fork and dropping it on a plate that Geneva passes to me. I'll need all the energy I can get today. "She didn't realize you and Kurt were close," I say, trying to remedy Calliope's misstep.

"I barely knew him," she whispers, disheartened. "He was just a boy I knew from our schooling days."

That could not be further from the truth—at least not entirely. When she and I went to barter for Calliope's birthday cake ingredients a few months prior, she ran into Kurt just outside the Trading Block, and conversed with him for some time, leaving me to negotiate with the stingy bakers and cooks of the town. Most days following their reconnection, I took note of the flush in Geneva's cheeks when she'd come home late, silently putting together the reason she'd be so worn out when her job required little of her in regard to physical labor. My heart shatters for her, but I know there's no use in wounding her more by confessing what I secretly understand.

"But that's still"—I try to find the right words—"startling, to have someone you've known be murdered. And for what? Some dream?"

Geneva winces. "Messengers from the palace say that the Saints blessed Jericho with night visions that were meant to help guide him and his Council toward producing new policies. Some say his dreams even helped his father draw up plans for paved roads leading to Cheratowe." Then, her fury starts to bleed through. "But now, all they do is line up people for slaughter," she says, the strength in her voice buckling. "Kurt was innocent."

"I'm sure he was," I try to say, consoling her, but realizing that my use of past tense finally is enough to snap her hold on her tears. They flow, but they do so in silence. After dabbing at her eyes with her sleeve, she takes one final bite of her hotcake, drowned in syrup. It seems that even maple sweetness can't revive her spirits.

"I hate him," Genny murmurs under her breath before collapsing into my arms, searching for some reassurance.

Her response is totally appropriate. Everyone has their reasons to hate King Jericho, and while I have my own list, things that hurt my sisters will always rise to the top. And, there's always been a soft spot in my heart for Geneva. Despite being the baby of the family, she's had to grow up sooner than any of us—having to take on a job at twelve to help make the monthly rent on our home, never knowing her mother, while Calliope and I got to properly mourn her, not to mention losing the only parent she had when King Jericho had Father executed for something he saw in one of his infamous, idiotic visions.

Within three years of Jericho's inherited reign, Geneva had seen two people she once knew personally die for the dreams of a coward.

"Believe me, Genny," I say softly to her, stroking her hair as we embrace. "If that Morgan Dynasty monster ever comes within arm's length of me, I will kill him myself."

3
Jericho

"A rdian, it *surely* was a sign."

"Sir," my Head Councilman begins, a cross expression on his wrinkled face. He hasn't even bothered to hear the details, and I can already feel the way he tries to shut me down. "Perhaps some dreams ought to be left in the night."

Steam heats within my skull. "*What* did you say?"

True fear settles deep into his system. "M-m-my apologies," Ardian stutters clumsily. "I just mean . . . I am well aware," he phrases in a manner that implies careful calculation, "of your blessed mind and the dreams that the Saints give you. But what if those dreams are . . . not in favor of the kingdom long term?"

I smile, even as my fury begins to boil over. "Do I sense distrust in you, Head Councilman?"

Ardian Asticova hides a frown beneath his long, graying beard. He shakes his head curtly, just once, as if trying to erase his misstep, and he puts his index finger to his temple. "No," he finally responds. "Forgive me, sir. Your wisdom exceeds no bounds."

"Indeed," I agree, satisfied.

Ardian concedes, and the sadness in his eyes is pathetic. It's the same expression I witnessed the night before. As I readjust in my chair, I notice that Ardian hasn't sat down. "Do relax, old friend," I say, casually.

He shakes his head. "Sir, forgive me, but . . . a whole family? For one man's crimes?"

"Not forgiven." My temper begins to escalate. *Are we really still hung up on this?* "I do not stand for traitors. They would've protected him, bought him time to run if they knew we were coming for them—"

"That's what families do, my king," he says coldly, using my title as an insult. "Last night, that was too far. My heart has grown weary of useless killings, and it brings me deep anxiety to know it has only set your heart aflame. Think of your mother—"

"Precisely," I say congenially. "She was innocent. But the pests we exterminated yesterday evening? They are no more than the dust beneath my boots, now."

Something about the sight of terror coursing through someone with only the threat of words to trouble them makes me sit up straighter in my seat. "So, I shall not ask you again, Head Councilman. *Sit down.*"

As if bracing himself for an onslaught, Ardian slowly settles into the cushioned seat diagonally from me at the breakfast table. A female servant casually enters and drops off my morning coffee along with a plate of eggs and sausage links. We both pretend as if she isn't there.

Only once she strolls out of earshot do I hear Ardian

speak again, snapping back into his normal, mild-mannered spirits. "Do share, then. What did this dream entail? Overtime pay for contracted castle staff, maybe some education reform for outliers along the Damocles River?"

"None," I begin. "I saw . . . a woman—"

I see Ardian wince, and while it takes strength to keep from sneering, I still allow him to interrupt once more. "I cannot condone more bloodshed if it is the path your dream has led you down today."

I raise a hand towards him, motioning him to pause his lamenting. "While I . . . value your honesty, that is not the point of this discussion. I only speak on the notion of her presence startling me."

Ardian seems perplexed at that. "A nightmare?"

"A challenge," I clarify, beginning to cut at my eggs. "This woman was playing a game with me. Testing my authority and my ability to track her down. But what startled me—no, I misspoke, what *captured* my attention was how real everything felt."

Every vision I'm bestowed in my sleep transports me to places I've never been, or have rarely visited. Last night, I felt the cold air beat into my clothing, I heard the branches around me bend and groan to the sound of the harsh wind. I sensed the mysterious girl approach my location all while I was left to scan the area alone.

"The woman?" Ardian asks again.

"She prompted me to come find her."

The same servant wordlessly returns, bringing all that Ardian ever asks for in the morning: a cup of herbal tea and three medication tablets for whatever condition seems to make him look ten years older than he is. She disappears just as quietly and quickly as before.

"Ought we look into its meaning?" Ardian suggests after a momentary silence. "There are men that study holy communication in our realm. We can inquire, if you wish, about the meaning of this woman's task, or why you dream that a common woman is trying to tell you—Urovia's King—what you ought to pursue. They may also have answers in regard to *how* detailed your dreams have become, especially with being able to feel the physical atmosphere in those visions."

I take a bite of food—it's too cold. I dump the contents of the plate onto the table before throwing the cleared saucer into the wall past Ardian's head. As if used to my distaste, he covers his head from any pieces that fall.

"The only answers I desire will come from her mouth and hers alone." I crane my neck towards the door to the room and bellow, *"Clean this shit up!"*

The servant comes into the room, this time with a hustle in her step.

"Tell the chef he gets one more attempt to make me a decent breakfast. Same food, but with cut up fruit on the side. Have him personally bring it to my chambers exactly fifteen minutes from now. And please inform him that if I do not enjoy what he provides me, I'll sink my knife and fork into something else."

The servant girl nods. "Yes, Majesty." One final time, she retreats from our presence.

Ardian hums to himself to ease the tension he seems to feel in the room. When his song surpasses my patience, I smack my palm against the table and stand to my feet.

"We will retrieve the girl. Today."

"Your enthusiasm is understood, Majesty," Ardian agrees. "But with what backing? What motivations?"

"Can a king not be supplied the object of his wishes?"

"Of course, but you mentioned her presenting a challenge to you. Is she any threat to our guards, could she harm any of our company?"

A smile melts along my lips. "It should not be of any issue, as I plan to accompany you in the pursuit of the girl myself."

Stunned, Ardian remarks aloud, "It must be of great importance to have you join us in this event firsthand." And then, something like distant hope burns in Ardian's weary, old eyes. "Majesty, might you be implying a . . . romantic fascination?"

While I do not answer him affirmatively—more so because I'm outright appalled by the inquisition rather than anything else—my hesitance appears to be enough for Ardian to rejoice. "Saints bless you both!" he cries out. Then, angling his head towards the door the servant left through, he shouts, "Delta! Do come quickly, child!"

"Head Council—" I interject, meaning to set the record straight.

But moments later, Delta Navarro arrives. Her rich, brown hair and sun-toned skin take on an amplified hue in the morning light that streams through the grand windows along the wall. Small strands fall along the sides of her face while the rest is pinned back, though the length of it just barely brushes against the slope of her shoulders.

"Uncle," she says respectfully to Ardian, though the

tone in her voice implies that she finds this setting vaguely unsettling. Then, she turns to me. "Majesty."

The order of whom she addresses is incorrect, but I let it go uncorrected, seeing old Ardian smile towards his niece wider than he has in some time. "King Jericho's visions predict that—"

"A lady will be joining the palace grounds," I interject, helping Ardian understand that he overstepped. "She will need her own apartments, and given where we're claiming her from, certainly a bath."

Ardian lets a scowl bloom across his features, coming to terms with the fact that he must make another trip back to the area the doomed Prokium family came from. "Ardian believes you'd accept the role of a lady's maid. Unless he's mistaken."

"He is not," Delta replies calmly, her lashes casting a shadow over eyes of magnificent teal. "I am grateful, my king. I shall also make for honest company when she arrives."

"Which should be sometime early tomorrow morning," I say, noting the grandfather clock against the wall, as the minute hand ticks, ever so slightly, to showcase forty-seven minutes past the ninth hour of the day. "You are dismissed to attend to those requirements."

Delta leaves without a sound. I don't think I even hear her shoes kiss the floor as she saunters off. So quiet, so simple, so bearable—one of my few hidden mercies in this Saints-forsaken castle. "So, it's settled, then." I exhale.

"It appears so," Ardian says with renewed confidence, rising to his feet after swallowing his medication and washing it down with the remnants of his tea. His face scrunches up for a moment before clarity returns to his features. He sighs in relief. "Best of luck to your chef. I shall reconvene with you here this afternoon, gather our team, and review your explicit instructions on extracting the girl."

Just when he seems informed enough to exit the room, he pauses, a flicker of confusion appearing on his features. "You didn't mention her name."

And I suddenly realize this may be quite an endeavor after all. "I never got it."

4
Venus

The extra hour spent on my blistering feet was brutal. Over my many years in the agricultural scene, especially in its design and upkeep, I had come to understand my limits: an eight-hour workday, an hour at home to lay down before dinner, a simple meal, and then maybe an hour or so to read if I'm lucky. So when Calliope volunteered me to work another hour, not to mention when she threw Geneva's emotional well-being off its axis, I knew bringing home something extra for dinner was the least I could do—but it didn't make my feet ache any less.

Cramming all my tools back into my compartmentalized box after cleaning off the stray weeds and sticks, I take note of my commission once more. While the weather remains too cold and unpredictable for me to do any unique hedge work, Mrs. Carrower wanted a fresh start for her garden for when spring arrives, which meant laying mulch, reviving her flower beds, and changing the soil to account for the hopeful change in outdoor temperatures. Hands braced on my hips, I realize that my work is much more rewarding when the final product produces a design or an array of colorful flowers.

Spring is my favorite season for work, by far. Sure, the pollen borderline suffocates me, but every flower is in bloom, the sun has not reached its summer cruelty, and I'm not tempted to jump into any of my commissioners' pools yet—which has gotten me into trouble a time or two before.

I hear a skidding noise and turn to find the Carrowers' eldest son, Drue, stepping out from the sliding back door. My promised carrots hang from his strong grasp, and he carefully steps down from the ledge. "Wow, it looks . . ." he comments, scanning the dirt wasteland, "barren."

"When the leaves return and the temperature becomes more bearable, I'll be back to plant whatever technicolor imaginings your mother has stored up in her head. Then you'll see why my work is so essential."

He smiles playfully, glancing down at the carrots in his hand. "Yes, Mother does enjoy your catalog of abilities. I just happen to know more of what skills you possess in . . . other manners."

Something warms in my middle, and, backpedaling slowly, I angle my movements to carry me along the cobblestone path that wraps around the side of the Carrowers' house. This part of our routine may have lost the element of surprise and newness long ago, but once Drue and I reach the shadow-covered part of the path, free from the surveillance his parents could have by peering through the windows, we fly into each other.

Mouths collide, hands grapple at clothing, and tensions unwind. He undoes the buttons that keep my cotton overalls fastened, and as the fabric begins to fall, I groan at the feel of his calloused hands sliding across my now bare thighs.

I ought to feel guilty for taking comfort in Drue's touch when Genny just lost the first man she ever loved, but there's something cathartic about being with someone like this when I'm angry at the world. It makes me feel comforted—but twistedly, it makes the experience fun.

Which is probably why I look forward to these odd jobs. Not just with the Carrowers, but with any families that happen to have opportunistic children. I've met a few like-minded employers in my day, but none as faithful and true as Drue. He has little money to squander, but if he had more, I am certain that my time would be his first and favorite purchase.

Which is the other part of this arrangement that must remain essential—the trade. A woman's touch for the price of feeding her. Some lousy vegetables for his name to be further etched into my bedpost—because nothing good ever came from sexual touch with no ulterior motives.

Drue carries me further down the path to a darker alcove before laying me down on a bench I helped install into the stony ground months before, leaving my discarded overalls behind. He reaches for my shirt, but I place a hand over his own. "The cold," I rasp, and only then does he remember I've been outside for hours. Understandingly, Drue presses one final kiss to my chapped lips before slinking over to me.

"Don't make a sound," he orders, as if he were my authority. "Or the neighbors will ask questions."

But as his mouth moves along my neck, I remember the carrots. I remember the grime and sweat from today's job, feel it gathering beneath my nailbeds and dirtying my skin. Then, I remember Genny, who may have spent her entire day sobbing into chocolate melt, trying to hide her anguish from her employers.

No, Drue was not the boss of me. Hurt, frustration—that was my true master. But to curb its appetite, I needed Drue, in this moment, to feed it.

"Take me away from here," I say.

I find peace in knowing Drue doesn't read the sadness in those words—only the desperation.

Geneva beats me to the house by an hour.

The pasta was completely boiled already, and Genny was in the middle of stirring the spices together in a large mixing bowl when I tried to slip in soundlessly.

A creak in the floorboard gave me away.

Now, I've been dodging her questions, lying my ass off about my whereabouts, what happened, and how my day went so that she doesn't think about Kurt and his family. Still, my efforts seem to fulfill their purpose, as Genny appears to be in much better spirits since this morning.

I continue to run the carrots I brought home under the sink water as I ponder aloud, "I wonder what lovely repertoire Calliope graced the nobles with this evening."

Genny's responding laugh is a snort. "Probably another aria or two. Maybe something operatic if her guests have requested it after a few drinks."

"What I wouldn't do for a whiskey right now." I sigh, placing the carrots on the only clean cutting board we have. Genny hands me a knife before walking the bowl of pasta to the table. "How was your day, though?"

"Not terrible," she says plainly. "Although, this one lady apparently heard a rumor that palace guards were riding into the Noble Lands and paid double to override our scheduled orders. Flattery and sweets in exchange for her family's protection, I'd assume."

Another dream, I realize in slight horror. *That's two back-to-back. They're getting closer together.*

"I bet that helped the shoppe greatly," I say in an attempt to keep her from noticing the apprehension on my face.

"Oh!" She grins mischievously. "I was the only one in when she came by. The woman was so frantic that she gave me all the money herself." And then, she pulls out a small bag stuffed full of coins.

My jaw falls onto the table. "Holy *Saints*!" I snatch the sack of money, as if seeing it with my eyes wasn't enough to prove her testimony. I gasp at the coldness I feel between the material, as if this woman Genny mentioned yanked the money straight from her lockbox. "And your employer has no idea you took home such a large sum?"

Embarrassment paints her cheeks a rosy color. "I confessed what I had received when my employer returned. But he let me keep it since I kept the shoppe afloat in his absence," she gushes.

"Glad to know the nobles treat you well."

"Not all those with money and status are cruel, sister,"

she remarks quietly.

I bite my tongue, knowing that any quip that could fly out of my mouth would make me sound bitter about her prosperous working conditions. And if any of the Deragon girls deserve a break, it was Genny.

Still, it didn't make me desire one any less.

I return the money to her, placing it in the palm of her hand. "You hold onto it. I made fair wages today. Hide it from Calliope, though, or she might volunteer you to happily pay the next four months' worth of rent."

"Am I not permitted to do so?"

"Well," I debate, ". . . maybe two months' worth. But pocket the rest. See if you can barter any of your old garments for a heavier coat. It'll make your rides to work more tolerable in the cold."

Her approving nod tells me that we have come to an agreement, and, thundering up the stairs, she goes to search for a proper hiding spot for her loot. Wordlessly, I scoop out my desired portion of noodles onto a dish and ponder on what poor soul will meet Jericho's stony gaze tonight at the palace.

Then, a newer, perhaps more unsettling thought occurs to me.

"Something the matter?" Genny asks. I hadn't even heard her reenter the kitchen.

"Have you ever wondered about Jericho's physical appearance?" I inquire. "King Ronan's face remains on our coin, not having undergone an update after he passed away. There also hasn't been an issue of the *U. Herald* that has documented his face. Ever. Only royal staff and affiliates know what he truly looks like."

Genny serves herself and finally sits next to me. "I prefer not to dwell on it. It's like how people theorize that giving a street animal a name fosters attachment to it. If I assign King Jericho a face, suddenly, I have a distinct picture of what I fear the most."

"You may do as you please, but I shall imagine him as a swine, nonetheless."

The statement draws out a genuine giggle from deep in her belly, and we both pick up our bowls, clinking them together since we have no fine wine goblets to toast with. Three cautious bites later, as if I needed to assure myself that I did not go overboard on the herbs, I begin shoveling my dinner into my mouth, gnawing on a carrot before musing aloud, "It's getting late, don't you suppose? I wonder when Calliope—"

The distant blare of a low-tone horn steals away my breath. I nearly choke on my food from the startle it brings me. Then the cold sweats arrive, the kind that I always strive to fight off before I physically become ill.

Genny shoots me an alarmed expression. "Venus?"

"Grab your coat," I croak, forcing myself to regain bodily composure. "And stay behind me, understand?"

I do not desire to see her nod in obedience, nor can I bear any devastation or fearful realization that may take over her in the following moments. All I know to do is drag us into the street and follow the stream of bodies journeying up the road towards an unknown fate. But the more I try to push my apprehension beneath the surface, an unrelenting, private intuition creeps in—warning me about what exactly this outburst entails.

The deadly King's Guard has arrived in the Makers

District again, only this time, they're here to make a public spectacle of someone's impending doom.

5
Venus

The marsh is littered with people who first poke their heads out into the street to see what the fuss is about, but instantly regret their decision to do so when they see Urovia's colors stitched into banners that blow from the masts of three grand carriages. When their wheels stop thundering over the dirt trail, and seven or so guards hop out of the bookending carriages, the night seems to grow thin, like none of us can breathe deeply enough.

"On behalf of King Jericho," one of the men begins, although he's vastly different from most of the guards here. In fact, he appears out of uniform and much older than those that arrived with him. A fleeced, hooded cape adorns his slender frame, hiding most of his noticeable features, save for a long beard and the center of his face. I can barely make out the color of his eyes. "We are in pursuit of a young woman."

At his words, the guards begin to spread out amongst the cluster of bodies, still petrified and motionless. The men gathered in the streets, however, move out of the way. I hear their not-so stifled gasps of relief—that is, until their wives, sisters, and daughters start being manhandled by members of the King's Guard.

King Jericho's lackeys take the time to individually note people, and in their silent evaluations, they either yank people forward or shove them back. "If you are brought forward," the aging man continues, "we will need a further word with you. If you are prompted to step back, consider yourselves dismissed and free to return to your previous activities."

None of those already dismissed dare to leave the general area. They're too terrified. Too intrigued.

Geneva's nails sink into the skin on my arm in worry, and while the pain is immediate, I swallow the urge to screech. Instead, we watch as the women around us are all evaluated, and quietly pushed back. They look through everyone closely, but I know it's a farce for some people. Jericho wouldn't send his men into the marshes blind.

They know exactly *what* they are searching for, if not whom.

Hidden by a herd of people, I finally catch a guard glancing back to what must be his superiors before bringing someone forward, their first victim.

As if not wanting to be associated with the girl, the crowd begins to back away, finally giving us a fair chance to see what kind of woman they are searching for—what physical traits they are trying to match per the king's orders. But before I can brace myself, Geneva screams, her grip on my arm tightening hard enough to bruise me.

Calliope.

The guards flagged *Calliope* as a potential suspect.

Genny's reaction draws unwanted attention from the other guards nearby. Two of them immediately approach my sister and I, one guard examining each of us. As she tries to tear herself away from them, the guards grab Genny's hand and raise her arm, taking her skin tone into account. Meanwhile, my guard doesn't bother with formalities. He simply yanks me towards Calliope.

Geneva's guard soon follows, dragging my sister along with him. "No," she gasps. "No . . . no, please . . . *no!*"

"It's okay," I lie, trying to ignore my internal panic when my guard refuses to let me turn my head towards Genny. "We just happen to look the part. We're going to be okay. Take a deep breath—"

"I didn't do anything!" Geneva wails relentlessly. Her guard, finally fed up with her hyperventilation, throws her into the dirt.

"Don't you *dare* hurt her!" Calliope shouts, her voice guttural, and when she fights the hold another King's Guard member has on her, she breaks free. But only for a second. Just before her fingers can reach out to touch Genny, to reassure her or hold her, the guard traps her back in his hold. "Take me! Not her!" Cali almost screams.

It's a bold proclamation, and it's one that I know would never be offered if I were the one in trouble. But it brings me no offense. Agreeingly, I flash Calliope a knowing look, and our silent statement is understood, just as it always has since Father died.

Genny will not be harmed, even if it costs us our lives.

Still, if only to maintain control of the situation, I

sternly snarl, "Shut up. Both of you."

Then, a new sound cuts through the open air like a knife, and I see a door to the middle carriage fling open, which I realize had not opened earlier. I assumed that particular carriage was designed to transport Jericho's newest victim—that it arrived here empty.

I discover how wrong I am when a glamorous boot finds purchase on the uneven ground, then another. The world goes frigidly quiet as its passenger disembarks, looking to the surrounding guards for answers to his silent questioning. Unlike the other guards, this new figure wears the opposite arrangement of colors. The guards don black garments with red accents, but this man wears a crimson officer's uniform with midnight-black, shiny detailing, including luxury lapels and fine aiguillettes. A sword sits in a sheath on his hip, and I take note of how it rests on his left side. He must be left-handed, or perhaps he is well trained on both sides, able to fend off his foes with his nondominant hand until needing to switch to his more powerful one. All I know is that I have never seen this man before, nor have I seen any man quite like him—and I probably never will again.

Despite wanting to peel my eyes away from this stranger—like someone caught in the snare of a traumatic event that cannot help but keenly watch continue—there is something about this man's gait that commands my attention, something about his composure that draws my eye. He has a head of brown hair so dark that even in the daylight, I might mistake it to be black, and his eyes remind me of the hottest flame coursing from a gas stove. The slight softness of his otherwise angular features, to any ordinary woman in the marsh, would be spoken of as swoon worthy. Still, I sense something deeper, perhaps something lethal in his face.

"Why such a commotion?" he asks, a wry taunt in his tone.

It is only once this man speaks that I begin to understand just how precarious this situation has become for my sisters and I, because every guard and every citizen here to witness this moment firsthand folds at the waist, bowing deeply in his direction. I then hear the rustling of Calliope's skirts and the shifting of Geneva's posture as she picks herself up from the earth just to lower her body in recognition as well.

"Your Majesty," Geneva's guard acknowledges.

Jericho Morgan never comes to collect the vermin he eradicates himself—and yet, here he is, matching my curious gaze so intensely that I fear he may blind me.

Though I have never seen a portrait of Jericho before, he turns out to be far more handsome than I anticipated, but not in a good way.

He bears the kind of handsomeness one may dread most in their worst enemy—intoxicating in a foul way. Even now, despite resenting him for the death of my father, I cannot look away from him—and it seems he cannot peel his eyes from mine either.

The sea of dipped bodies slowly lengthens back to its normal, varied heights . . . and only then do I realize that I never bowed before him.

"Sir, this young lady is causing quite a disturbance," one of the guards declares after a suspended period of tense silence.

Though his attention mentally switches back to the guards and to Geneva, his eyes still linger over me. Not on my sisters, not towards the crowd—*me*. I think Calliope picks up on the notion, too, and steps towards me ever so slowly.

"Well," Jericho drawls quietly, "she must believe that she is being wrongly accused."

When no guard speaks in return, the king paces about the area, finally looking somewhere else. I expect to feel relieved in a way, like the unknown weight in my chest would lessen. But I discover that it only swells when he turns his focus elsewhere, and I do not know why.

Jericho saunters over to where Calliope stands, smothering a frazzled expression. The wind rips through her hair, and even as it covers her face, she does not move to adjust it. "My king," she says gently, and I silently hate her for not being snide towards him.

To which Jericho only shakes his head, and though his sights remain on her, he says to the guards that begin to gather around him. "This is not the one."

Calliope steps back calmly, but I watch her lip quiver in dread—her only tell that the king's directions seal a most unfortunate fate. Geneva and I are the only remaining people that the guards found a dark curiosity in.

The young king quickly surveys me again, then Genny, as if looking at her were more of an afterthought. His eyes rove over me with absolutely no regard for manners, flagrant and insulting, and I long to wrap my hands around his royal throat.

Genny reaches for my hand, slowly sinking behind me in efforts to hide herself from him.

"Sisters," Jericho finally comprehends. Then he turns his attention to Geneva, nearing her with a dangerous smile. "And you must be the baby."

"Piss off," I sneer.

The words may as well have struck him across the face.

"Oh, do say that again," he hisses like a snake, as if daring me that I won't.

Genny trembles against me, Calliope continues to fight the urge to say something to defend our honor, and I'm too far gone to exhibit any kind of restraint. Hatred builds in my core, and it makes me feel invincible. "I said"—I take one step towards him—"Piss. *Off.*"

Jericho stands statuesquely still, as if waiting for more. And so, without another thought, I give it to him, drawing filth from my nose and the back of my throat before spitting it out onto his shiny, obsidian shoes.

Genny stops shivering, and I can hear Calliope's thoughts without having to look at her.

Jericho closes the gap between us, terrifyingly calm.

The king stands so closely that he would barely need to lift his arms to strangle me, and his height forces me to raise my chin to him in acknowledgement—if I wouldn't bow to him, he'd force me to gaze up at him like he was a Saint.

After the gasps of the bystanders around us fizzle out, I discover that my damned heartbeat is skyrocketing, and Jericho hears it, too.

Then, with his face mere inches away from touching mine, Jericho reveals a special, sinister smile. "I knew I'd find you."

6
Jericho

The girl is a fighter.

Despite the fact that she now rests slumped across from me in the carriage, it took four of my best guards several minutes to get her inside. The girl seemed insistent on not being separated from her younger sister, considering she refused to let me see her whole frame when I simply wanted to introduce myself. Another girl among the lot, the one that I dismissed previously, managed to restrain the sister so we could get a better hold on . . . *well, come to think of it, I do not know her name.*

To say that the girl went out kicking and screaming is an understatement. She put on quite a show, more so than most of the people my guards collect, according to the frustrated looks that adorned their faces as one by one, guards took each of her limbs. They had practically splayed her body out into the letter X before they realized she was, by the Saints, too powerful. Ardian eventually had to inject her with a sedation dart.

Still, amidst all that fight, all that resistance, she never seemed hopeless. No, this girl wanted to be annoying—and she succeeded.

After three hours in the royal carriage, it appears as though she is finally coming to. I watch as she rubs at her smoky, hazel eyes, accidentally pulling out a few lashes in the process and smudging unwashed eyeliner from who knows how many days ago. Upon further examination, I fill in the gaps about her that my dreams did not pick up on originally.

A soft birthmark graces the slope of her neck, and an additional piercing at her cartilage turns the edge of her ear red, as if it were fresh. There are several, small scrapes that appear to have turned to scars lining her hands, and then, I note the many bruises bringing unwanted color to her otherwise flawless, brown skin, from where her blouse slackened off.

Her clothes are worn and grubby, but her smell is relatively tolerable. Even though I confronted her in the marshes, I was so overcome by the notion of her being real—and far more stubborn than I imagined—to really care about it on the whole. The look on her face tells me that she finds my scent to be far beyond any measure of cleanliness she's ever known, and it infuriates her.

"Morning," I say to her. Praying to the Saints that she doesn't immediately notice my hand on my weapon, I feel the intensity of her responding stare. It is not threatening, but it is certainly icy.

She greets me only with a certain, raised finger.

"Might you have a name?" I ask as courteously as I can manage.

Though I do not expect her to reply, she maintains her gaze when she tells me, "Venus."

I roll my eyes. "Like the goddess?"

"Like the flytrap," she corrects me, a bite behind the words. I watch her finally give up a smile when the comment makes me scowl.

"How old are you, Venus?"

She rolls her eyes at me. "Is this your idea of small talk?"

"Answer me!"

Frightened, she jolts in her seat. She blinks once, twice. "Twenty-three, Majesty."

Despite her horrid behavior, she is not so tone-deaf to where she forgets the customary ways of addressing me. "And what of your family name?" I inquire.

"Deragon," she replies, making her brewing anger evident.

The name is distantly familiar, but not enough to bring up any distinct memories or faces. I pretend to try and recollect before giving her a look that says I'm stumped, if only to eradicate that stupid grin of hers—it works.

"You murdered my father," she says simply.

"I murder plenty."

Her expression turns vividly sour. "He was *innocent*," she snaps back.

That, too, I want to fling back at her in spite. But I opt for another response instead. "Ah, I remember, now. Brought in alone . . . at the indication of another."

Fire burns behind her eyes. It's a lucky conjecture, I suppose.

"He made a compelling case for himself, so much

that I almost considered hearing him out." The lingering mention of almost sends Venus into an internal fit of wrath, despite keeping her body unnaturally still. I sense it boiling behind her eyes. "When he understood that his chances of release were slim, he resorted to vowing my ruin. But I knew he'd fold. When the executioner arrived, he begged—"

"So are you going to kill me or not?" Venus interrupts, and while I anticipate the words to be expressed dauntlessly, the sound of her voice indicates genuine curiosity, perhaps even dread.

"Why? Care to prepare your final words?"

"Words are useless when there are no ears around to hear them," Venus says plainly. "I'm more concerned with what the gossip will circulate."

Her subtle mention of a lasting reputation intrigues me. "How would you want to be remembered, Miss Deragon?"

Venus pauses then, finally demonstrating that she is, in fact, afraid of something. If not of me or even death, then at least the world's mass perception of her. For a moment, I was concerned that Venus had been a curse sent from the Saints in disguise, meant to disarm me and bring endless frustration rather than test my ability to face a challenge that excited me.

But as it turns out, despite her defiance, Venus buckles just like the rest of them. She remains alive at my mercy, and the revelation is nothing short of satisfying to see sink in.

"I'd want them to know . . . that I tried my best," she states quietly.

Before I get to say anything more, the floodgate Venus holds on her composure flies open and she erupts into hard, broken sobs.

A strange sensation falls over me seeing Venus like this all of a sudden. It's nothing I haven't seen out of guilty captives before, but she truly seems to believe she is done for, despite not being chained, gagged, or kneeling before an executioner. She continues to cry, but not for mercy, which I find odd. Her eyes leak hot tears as she observes the world beyond the carriage window as if this moment were the last time she'd ever get to do so.

"I'm going to miss them," she chokes out.

Saints above, she's quite the sob story.

"You'll miss whom?"

"My sisters, you *dick*!" Venus snarls, reaching for something in the pocket sewn into her overalls before launching herself at me.

I dodge her outright, and the full force of her body weight crashes into the sitting bench. Had it not been cushioned, Venus surely would have chipped one of her teeth. No bother, her stumble provides me the perfect window needed to draw my sword and point it in her direction.

"You think you can kill a king with a pocketknife?"

Venus laughs, and only then do I realize that she's stopped crying. *That little faker.* "Move your sword and find out."

I do no such thing.

"Do it, you coward," Venus says in a way that implies an invitation. And while I first assume she means having me lay down my weapon, I am proven wrong as I watch her chuck the small, pathetic knife into the carriage's wall. Now defenseless, Venus stretches out her arms in rebellion, wanting to see if I will commit to my typical behaviors and kill her.

"Begging. Just like your father," I drawl.

"Don't make me spit on you again," she warns.

And it's that sentence alone—the way she chides me like a disobedient child and not a rightful king—that sends me over the edge; that has me crossing my line of tolerance into a territory of hatred. Her spirit is impressive, I'll say. But the realization is undeniable: I've never loathed another person more than I loathe her right now.

I despise her defiance and the way she looks at me like I'm not a threat to her. I resent the way she thinks fighting me is fun and that she can ultimately get away with it. I cannot predict her movements or adequately prepare myself for what heinous things will fly out of her mouth, and I surely do not see myself growing fond of her foul spitting habit.

And yet, above all else, I hate Venus for still being the most fascinating person I've come across in this lifetime. She is, without a shadow of a doubt, my most perfect nightmare.

Somehow, I know it was the right call, going after her.

"I'm afraid I have other plans for you." I exhale. "But for now, I will not tolerate your insubordination."

Her eyes go wide, but I'm already moving swiftly. I flip my sword through the air, catching it on the bladed end as I firmly jam the hilt into the side of her head. Venus flops to the ground without another sound.

Once her frame goes completely still, aside from the rise and fall of her chest, I cast my sword aside and look at my bleeding palm, irritated. I stoop down with intent to wipe my blood on her clothes, knowing damn well they will be thrown out as soon as we reach the castle. But the carriage meets a bump in the road, knocking me off my balance and back into my seat. With no patience left, I brush my bleeding hand on the wall behind me.

This would indisputably go down in history as the carriage ride from hell.

7
Venus

His Majesty abandoned our carriage sometime after he knocked me unconscious again, but his absence is a small mercy—no need for maddening small talk or formalities like *"my king"* or *"Majesty."*

Still bitter from the night before, I groan as the soreness in my head pulsates. I bet money on there being a bruise or a knot, but I have no time to dwell on my anger when I remember that the pain means I'm alive. Unable to believe it, though, I drag my worn body across the carriage floor and peer out the window to see the dawn with fresh eyes.

The early morning haze covers our location like woolen blankets draped on unseen clotheslines; we may as well be crossing through the clouds. I vaguely see spots of pinks breaking beyond the thinner parts of the fogbank, and I smile knowing that there's a chance it might be warmer outside if we are, indeed, far from the marshes.

Then my stomach groans. It prods at me viciously, and, merged with the pain in my head, it immediately becomes an unbearable sensation. Desperately, I yank at the door handle, but it doesn't budge. Bile bubbles up in my throat, and with no other options, I clench my hands into a fist and smash through the glass. The fresh air immediately hits me, but not enough to ward off the inevitable.

Avoiding the shards as best as I can, I hang my head out the jagged, broken window and expel everything I've ever eaten out of my stomach.

When the final waves of sickness end, the horses come to a slow halt and one of the men steps down from their seat to attend to me. To my solemn surprise, it's the older nobleman I had picked out from the ensemble the night before, perhaps one of Jericho's advisors. "Are you quite alright?"

Weakly, I glance towards him, knowing he may be the only one that cares to extend a small measure of grace to me. I wipe the side of my mouth in hopes of salvaging my disheveled appearance, though there may not be much hope for the condition of my hair. "Might there be water—"

He brings two fingers to his cracked lip and blows sharply into them before I can finish my question, signaling another guard to stand before him. This new person salutes. "Your orders, Asticova?"

"This young lady has signs of a concussion and requires refreshments. Might you have any water to spare for her?"

That's when the guard looks at me in my sickly state,

and rather than recoiling in distaste, his eyes flare ever so slightly. He already begins his retreat when he replies, "Of course, Head Councilman."

Head Councilman.

"You mustn't strain yourself for the next few days, Miss Deragon. Do you understand?" His words are firm, but his tone implies an underlying gentleness.

"No," I say, my head still fuzzy. "No, I do not understand. How am I being granted more days beyond this one? I can assure you, the king will be happier to know I'm dead, rather than injured, though I'm still rather confused as to why he didn't kill me last night."

If I had ever gotten to have a relationship with my grandparents, I might best be able to compare this Asticova character to them and their role. His outgrown hair, both from his head and along his face, makes him appear older than he must be. A man of his complexion and generosity couldn't be too far into his fifties, but knowing most Urovians in the marshes rarely live to see the age of sixty, I silently find solace knowing he likely has a long life of keeping Jericho level-headed in front of him. The king's Head Councilman seems to be the nicest of the lot.

"Oh, child." He sighs. "Must you expect the worst in His Majesty?"

I offer him a look that tells him, *Yes, yes I must.*

The summoned guard returns with a canteen, likely his own, and hands it over to me. Then, from a knapsack behind him, he pulls out a rolled-up piece of parchment, with scarlet ribbon wrapped around the middle to maintain its curled shape. "The king veered off-course an hour ago when we stopped to feed the horses. He asked if I could pass this off to you."

"Thank you, Tolcher," he remarks passively, taking the document into both hands before untying the thread and opening it. By the time Mr. Asticova sprawls it out completely, the soldier disappears fully into the haze.

Etched in almost violent penmanship, King Jericho writes:

Rumors report that the doves are set to flock eastern, and while I'm not craving dove, I have the growing urge to shoot something. Given your previous grumblings, I figured you'd rather not have me shoot the girl, so I have gone to hunt.

Speaking of which, the girl will need to see a physician once you get back Broadcove, if she even wakes up. Good riddance either way. If she survives the ride, have Delta give her a bath, or three—

He promptly shuts the scroll before I can read any further, and the action makes me wonder what other offensive material Jericho penned regarding me. Embarrassment leeches the blood from Mr. Asticova's already pale skin. "I do apologize, Miss Deragon." He sighs, vividly upset. "He's better than this, I promise."

The man seems so appalled by the king's letter that I don't bother adding fuel to the fire. But then again, why tell me so ardently that King Jericho possesses the means to not be so monstrous?

It doesn't matter, not when my head still aches so fervently. I turn to the Head Councilman and introduce myself formally. "I'm Venus," I mutter, offering my extended hand.

Though I anticipate him to shake it in greeting, he stoops over and places a kiss against the skin on my hands. It's a hard press, squishing bone with only his lips—and it makes me fear that my reasons for being stolen away from the marshes branch into deeper, hidden intentions. "Ardian Asticova."

I smile once more, a gesture of understanding and respect, before I quickly excuse myself behind the carriage and continue to be sick.

To my great appreciation, Ardian had a sleeping tonic with him for the journey to retrieve me, and while he originally brought it for his own needs, he took pity on me and offered it for my own use. The Head Councilman's kindness was borderline devastating as he additionally offered me a thick blanket to keep warm now that my smashed window let in the cold air, and led me back to the carriage. I eventually allowed my muddied brain to turn off and find sleep again.

I try to imagine happier things, if only to ward off the misery of being awake and fully conscious. So, as the carriage rumbles across the beaten paths and I'm lulled deeper into my dreams, I find myself in a barren portion of the Makers District, maybe a mile or so between the trolley station and my home. Night cloaks the world in darkness, and no sound stirs throughout the village, not even a swamp critter near the marsh banks.

I'd almost consider the setting around me to be peaceful were it not for the unknown prompting in my gut somewhere, a voice whispering, *"There's someone looking for you."*

Willing to heed the voice's warning, I wander down the empty, unpaved lane, sticks breaking underneath my feet. The sounds set me on edge amidst the silent dreamscape, and the air is clear, as if to reflect the clarity of what I'm seeing—

Footsteps.

My first thought is to hide, so I crouch behind a patchwork of bushes. Peeking through weeds and hedges, I listen as the steps grow louder, more frantic. The person approaching must be nervous, too, stumbling over themselves in a location unknown and precarious to them. Distant rattling makes me assume that the mysterious being is wearing something ornate, like a decorated serviceman. The closer the sound gets, the colder my skin feels, as if the fabric on my sleeved shirt gradually thins out.

Well, I'll be damned, I think as the lost individual comes into view.

My captor king dons the very same uniform he wore when he stole me away from the marshes. Three shimmering medals hang from the slit over his left pectoral, and I wonder to myself how many throats he slit for those honors. He probably did it himself, given he's not opposed to killing families at a time. My stomach knots up, but the moonlight reveals the genuine curiosity of being in a foreign area on his features. For a moment, Jericho seems . . . human. Like he undergoes fear just as the rest of us do.

I wonder if he'll jump in surprise if I give the bushes

a rustle.

I do so, but rather than becoming spooked by the noise, the king's interest heightens. His examination of the surrounding marshes intensifies, and though his eyes blare straight into the hedge I take cover behind, I appear to blend into the night too well to be seen.

His head cranes further away, his weight shifting, and as I start to release myself from my crouched position, I wonder if I can sneak up on him. Scare him as payback for my throbbing head and weak stomach. Tenderly, I begin to step towards him, his back facing me. I force my growing smile to stay subdued—

King Jericho sharply turns back in my direction, and when he sees me, he looks as though I may have hit a nerve. Still, once the initial shock wears off, he glances me over with blatant confusion—almost in a way that appears as if he doesn't know who I am. But that certainly cannot be the case. He picked me out amidst a throng of other people without even knowing my name. He knows my face.

Doesn't he?

No, I realize. *The moment I told him to piss off, his attention snapped. It was my voice that made me recognizable.*

I gather enough venom behind my words before I tell Jericho, "Come find me," and traipse off behind the bushes I first took shelter behind. Not too far down the path, there's a cluster of sharp sticks. Maybe, if he gets close enough, I can pick one up and aim—

The moment I mean to grab one and evaluate its sharper end, my body wakes me up again.

I first note Ardian slumped across from me, sleeping

sitting up, his head tipped back and mouth slightly agape. He snores quietly, somehow on rhythm with the carriage wheels tumbling over the rural, gravel path. Then, to his immediate right, King Jericho's scroll rests untouched, tempting me.

Eager to add to my, *"Why Jericho Morgan is a Piece of Shit"* list, I unfurl the document once more and pick up where I left off:

Truthfully, she does not reek half as horridly as I anticipated. Perhaps she has decent hygiene habits despite living in the bloody marshes.

I daresay you may grow to like the girl. You're disastrously soft in that way, but rest assured, the moment I figure out why she compelled me to come find her in the first place, we'll see if that changes. Report to the boardroom when you arrive home. And for Saint's sake, try and act like I know what I'm doing with her.

No outgoing signature or royal seal rounds out the catty letter, but what I notice about the note, more so than anything else, is the lack of my name, despite being heavily referenced. I'm just *"the girl"* or *"her."* It makes my blood simmer beneath my flesh, and yet, I believe that I just won the first round of, what I can only imagine, will be an ongoing war with Jericho.

I read the lines again, the only ones that matters:

The moment I figure out why she compelled me to come find her in the first place, we'll see if that changes.

And for Saint's sake, try and act like I know what I'm doing with her.

The dream I just had . . . it didn't belong to me at all.

Somehow . . . I think I just encountered *Jericho's* dream. And knowing that he remains clueless in how to proceed with me coming into his castle, I plan on taking full advantage of what little control his confession has given me.

8
Venus

Another hour or so in the carriage passes, and eventually Ardian wakes up. The first thing he notices is his throat—dry from breathing through his mouth. He puts a hand to the skin there. "Pardon me," he murmurs, although the noise is almost a croak. "I am not the most elegant sleeper."

"Considering you saw me projectile vomit earlier," I counter, and an earnest smile meets me in return, "you could snore as loud as a train engine for all I care."

Ardian begins to form something lighthearted in his mouth, as if to ease my supposed embarrassment, but he pleasingly sighs before inching towards the carriage door. With a flick of his wrist, he pulls back the curtains that shaded the light breaking through the fogbank, revealing a world unlike anything in my wildest dreams.

The flatlands of the Makers District are a long-forgotten memory as I behold the watercolor masterpiece the Saints themselves must have painted up for the wealthy citizens of Urovia. Sweeping hues of lush green and vibrant blues, sloping hills lead into crystal ponds or don perfectly paved cobblestone and wooden roads, and rounded bridges connect the different peaks together, as if uniting miniature islands over the distant carriages, crossing closer to sea level—though none as finely furnished as the one I abide in.

As other vehicles pass by, friendly passengers stick out of their windows and wave, meaning these carriages must belong to individuals and their families. In the Makers District, my sisters and I considered ourselves profusely lucky if more than two public, cramped trolleys came by our village to transport us to our employers each day. In fact, I'd never seen a carriage in person until Jericho and the King's Guard came to the marshes yesterday. I only ever heard about them in stories Genny and Cali would tell me about what they've seen in the Noble Lands.

Amidst all the splendor, the harsh winter also doesn't appear to exist here, with hordes of flourishing trees lining the civilian pathways in assortments of greens with slowly budding pinks and lavenders. Technicolored plants thrive in the absence of weeds, distant harbors contain several fleets of cargo and passenger vessels, and poised conveniently above the sprawl of extravagant homes—likely belonging to members of Jericho's court of influence—lies the heart of Jericho's territory.

Nearly twenty grand archways create a makeshift barricade, but upon further examination, I discover tracks along the top bars—more passageways. Some even run through the inside of the castle itself. The individual housing quarters, at the base of the grand estate, are painted all different shades of warm-toned colors, amplifying the hues of the shifting trees surrounding us. The monstrous castle stretches high, as if reaching for the sun, along a rounded hill. Grand spires top off every tower in sight like arrowheads, perhaps to fend off attacks from the skies. Two ginormous, twin statues of wild beasts stand at the grand entryway, watching over the city, frozen in a posture of preparation and promising violence. Above their heads, rows and rows of observation balconies criss cross over top of one another.

Something tells me that no matter where one stands, the view would still be magnificent.

"I trust that you will feel at home here in Broadcove Castle," Ardian says hospitably, and while I still glance out at the splendor of the city, I hear a hopeful smile in his voice.

"Comfortable, yes," I answer, trying not to think about my sisters shivering in the cold and wondering if I'm dead or alive.

But I don't think I could ever call this place my home.

Not when King Jericho seized the one man that kept my family in balance, brought him to this beautiful place, and uncaringly took his life.

By the time the carriage finishes its uphill climb towards the main gate of the palace grounds, I almost worry I will suffer from altitude sickness. My head throbs, my eyes feel sore within their tired sockets, and my mouth has become insufferably dry. The sensation ebbs once the wheels stop rolling, though, and a guard from the carriage in front of us opens the door. Instantly, a heavier dose of fresh air courses through the boxed area I began to feel entombed in, and, as if new energy courses through my bloodstream, I promptly exit before Ardian gets the chance.

Already, I hear mumbling, fascinated voices from beyond the entrance, and while I anticipate them to stream from court members, benefactors, or politicians, the welcoming committee for my arrival seems to be the kitchen staff. It's a small mercy—to be greeted by people similar to my own economic rank—and it helps restore confidence in my steps as I approach my lavish prison cell.

Ardian flanks my back, right side, and the set of guards Jericho commissioned for my capture create a perimeter around us, hands resting on their swords in case something charges at us—or in case I draw my own weapon. They're wise to fear me, but the moment I cross the threshold of Broadcove Castle, the illusion of fearlessness dissipates.

Gut instinct tells me that, despite the entryway being five times the size of my family home in the marshes, this would be considered a quaint little foyer. Knowing the king that occupies this castle, though, I must admit, I was expecting black interiors, the absence of natural light, and maybe even a rusty moat around the property. Instead, the walls look as though they were soaked in gold, with widespread tapestries of ancient artwork adorning the walls if cream and crimson swirls don't already branch along them. High above us, a crystal chandelier curls inward, as if trying to claw the paint from the ceiling, with countless candles burning from each pointed end, and to my immediate right, a curved set of stairs widely runs along the wall and stretches to the second floor.

On the first floor, behind the staff members that gather around to look at me in awe for having come here without chains or an immediate death sentence, I spot a spectacular dining room table, with oval-bodied chairs and plush cushions where guests would sit. A more humble light fixture looms overhead, and I can just make out the shimmering silverware on the table before one staff member in particular—a girl far too pretty to be taking orders from the likes of Jericho—steps in front of my view pocket.

"They're just fascinated by you," she tells me, her thick brows lifting in equal interest. "They've never seen one of us be welcomed so openly like this."

"If you consider kidnapping a warm welcome, then yes."

The girl finds my spirit intriguing, and her smile swells in an almost mischievous way. "Perhaps," she merely replies, evaluating me silently before agreeably saying, "I'm Delta, and for the duration of your stay, I'll be your lady-in-waiting."

Something sinks in my stomach. "Aren't those kinds of ladies in charge of tending to the needs of . . . royalty?"

"Normally, yes," Delta answers. "But given your circumstances, I'm your lady-in-waiting-for-Jericho-to-make-up-his-mind, wouldn't you say?"

I almost chuckle at her bluntness. Delta and I might just become friends. "I'm Venus," I finally introduce myself.

Her skin has a refined, deeper warmth about it, but with a signature cream overcoat. Her brown hair appears faintly yellowed in the gleam of the golden foyer, and there's something truly remarkable about the way her dark auburn eyes glimmer—how they reflect compassion for some and a heartless stare for others. I consider myself lucky, at least presently, to be a recipient of the former.

A signaled look from Delta assures the guards that I'm not a threat to her, and I watch as Ardian follows suit as all the men saunter off somewhere else. "Would you care to see your rooms?" Delta offers.

"Rooms?" I ask pointedly. "Plural?"

Delta finds my shock hilarious. "A guest of the king will not be housed inadequately."

But I'm not a guest at all. I'm a prisoner, and while the word on my final sentencing isn't set just yet, I am here strictly on borrowed time—the message for Ardian justified as much.

Even so, I allow Delta to whisk me up the stairs and lead me towards the eastern wing. Along the way, we pass through decadent hallways and artistic corridors that are so magnificent, I fear I may get lost in this liminal space forever. Three more turns—two lefts and a right—and I discover that Delta guides us through one of several observation balconies, and as we begin to cross into the daylight once more, I wonder if she meant to take us through this one on purpose.

As if she knew we'd run into King Jericho on our tour.

Despite stiffening at our arrival, he admittedly looks more relaxed than before, merely donning dark slacks and a knitted, black sweater. The sweater in particular seems to stir something in my chest, though. I first assume this given the way his hands take shelter in the fabric, as if to keep warm, but I grasp a deeper understanding having caught him inhaling the sweater's scent before being alerted to my presence.

In fact, his sweater looks like an article of clothing a woman must have stitched for him with love. Perhaps his mother.

The *U. Herald* never reaches the marshes unless something significant occurs these days, but I remember when the paper's bold headline spread tragedy across the front page: *Merrie Morgan, Queen Consort of Urovia, Dead at Forty-Five*

The news emerged a little over two years ago, and considering King Ronan went soon after, it must have been a devastating affair. Sadness knows how to leech the life out of people, so if the death of Queen Merrie ultimately took the life of King Ronan as well, how come it didn't claim Jericho, too? The Morgan Dynasty nearly vanished at the loss of a single woman, and reasonably so. To lose a wife or a mother . . . that kind of loss is incomprehensible. I certainly lost my own way when both of my parents met their end.

But how twistedly resilient must a person be to live on behalf of their beloved dead if only to bring suffering to others?

"Welcome back, *my king*," I sneer, dropping into a mocking bow.

Embers crackle within his frost-blue eyes, shading them a touch. "Just call me Jericho if you're going to be a bitch about it," he instructs flatly.

He moves to turn his back on me, but I manage to call

out, "Have a successful hunt?"

As if in disbelief that I'm still running my mouth, or that I intercepted his bad-mouthed letter to Ardian, Jericho glances at Delta with a crazed expression, who in turn grins at the fussy king like a cat. It's nice to see that she remains thoroughly entertained by our irritable dynamic.

"Ardian was much more delightful than you," I muse aloud, roaming my eyes over the landscape beyond. The balcony seems to overlook the side of the castle, towards the roads we originally traversed to arrive here. From such a high vantage point, I can almost see the land's dividing line between lush greenery and barren pathways that lead into dreary, malnourished woods. "Despite all your atrocities, I suppose you inherited one good man on your Council."

His grimace is a sweet victory, but it is rather short-lived as Jericho says to Delta, without entirely looking her way, "Ready the bathing room that overlooks the south lawn. I'll show Venus to her apartments myself."

"Of course," Delta responds agreeably, and while I'm above groveling, I debate insisting that she stay. But I have no power here—not yet at least—and I watch with smothered anxiety as she retreats down the hall.

9
Venus

In utter silence, Jericho leads me through the balcony's seamlessly ending path. In the distance, birds chirp, flowers bloom, and the sun slowly begins to reach the crest of the distant, sloping hills.

"I trust that the grounds are to your liking," I hear him ask through my distracted glances.

Though I doubt he'd take my opinions into thought, I remark that, "The gardens could use some love. But otherwise, yes. I find Broadcove to be rather charming," I admit, though my heart secretly longs for the familiar creaking stairs, the stiff mattresses, and my sisters back home.

Jericho proceeds quietly for a moment or two, still marching forward, his hands clasped behind his back. Then, as if fully soaking in my sentences, he turns on a heel and stops us just before we cross into another main sector of the castle. "The gardens are your only drawback?"

"Are you displeased that I find your home to be fine-looking?"

"No," he states firmly. "You just . . . tend to have more venom in you than this. I expected you to tell me the decorations are horrid, the colors are repugnant, and that the staff is completely insufferable." Jericho pauses to look beyond the ledge that guards us from plunging to the ground below. "What about the gardens pulls your attention negatively?"

I furrow my brow. "Are you serious?"

"Despite your preconceived notions, Venus, I do care about the state of the imperial city, even if it's in regard to its general maintenance. So, out with it."

Humoring him in his request, I evaluate the lackluster grounds once more. I wonder if the issue is simply due to understaffing—if Jericho hasn't butchered any of them already—or maybe the employed personnel aren't given the king's full attention. "It's manicured well, it just lacks vision."

The edge of Jericho's mouth crooks upward. "Funny. I wouldn't have pegged you for the artistic kind."

"It comes with the job."

"You work?"

I try not to bristle at his question. "In the marshes, you work a job or you die."

Jericho lets up a little bit, nodding in false understanding. "Estate design?" He guesses, assuming I hold a job within the higher ranks of the Makers District, employed by the wealthy nobles who can afford to not only dwell in a home of their own, but create proper decoration flow and intentional patterning.

"A topiary," I tell him flatly. "I used to work in the Noble District," I say, but stop short, unwilling to admit to Jericho that, when his dreams took my father's life, no one in the upper ranks wanted a Deragon touching their gardens. "But I mainly do rudimentary gardening work, now—sowing, pruning, helping people with their harvesting." I realize once the words are out of my mouth that none of my skill sets are something of true merit to him.

Shame walks at my side as we proceed through the vast castle in stifled silence. The only sound bouncing against the magnificent, ornate walls is that of his fine shoes clicking across the floor. Internally, I try to estimate what I could earn from bartering those damned shoes down in the Makers District. Better yet, if I sold them to either of my sisters' employers . . . the money seems insurmountable, even as I stroll through a golden, towering mausoleum.

One final turn and Jericho stops before a door with minimal embellishments along the mantle. Turning the knob in a single jolt, he swings the door open wide to reveal the largest bedroom I've ever laid eyes on—even larger than the rooms I've seen in the Noble District.

The first thing that catches my eye is the wall, which isn't necessarily a wall at all. No, it's a widespread row of windows that overlook what must be the Damocles Sea. White hexagonal flooring sprawls across the ground like snow, the only reminder of the harsh cold the marshes are likely experiencing this time of the year. Fleur de Lis in cream paint are scattered across golden wallpaper behind a bed that's so large, my sisters and I could all sleep comfortably, side by side. I know this because three satin accent pillows divide the bed into perfect, equal thirds, and it's almost as if I can picture us all together again—Calliope on the left as her and I sandwich Genny in the middle. I imagine pressing a kiss to her forehead and having her giggle through a reluctant groan.

It hurts to think about for too long.

"Jericho?"

"Yes, Venom?" he asks plainly, and the moment my responding look turns sour, he grins. Shit, I have a bad feeling that name is going to stick.

Even so I try my hand at asking him nicely while he remains in good spirits, "Would you be willing to send a letter to my sisters back in the marshes telling them I'm alive?"

Jericho looks at me with a stale expression on his face. "I present you with one of the grandest rooms in the entire castle, and you think you can ask me for more favors?"

"You're right. You know what? Forget I asked. How about you just tell me why I'm here, why I deserve to be in a room this exquisite. Or do you even know that yourself?"

Hell itself boils within his blood. "What the hell is that supposed to mean?"

"It means that I may not exert any power over you in reality, but I have a foothold in your mind. It means that I know how to boss you around in your own fantasies, which I find infinitely hilarious. But best of all, it means that for the first time in your sorry, spoiled life, you obey someone other than yourself. And you hate me for it."

Jericho hisses at me, fists clenched at his sides. "You're going to regret mouthing off to me," he warns—his hands locking down around my wrist before yanking me out of the room.

10
Jericho

Venus goes into shock the moment I kick open the interrogation room door.

I've never seen anything like it. Typically, if prisoners are awake, or conscious, for this part of the process, *this* is the moment they start kicking and screaming and swearing at me. But not Venus.

No, the only thing about her that moves are her eyes, rapidly skipping back and forth between the door, the chains, the floor, and the mirrored walls. She sees herself in four different places and cannot seem to make out which version of her is real, but in some twisted way, the illusions fascinate her, grasping her attention long enough for me to lock her wrists within the steel manacles with minimal resistance.

Venus gives the cuffs a jerk, the chains holding true. "Kinky," she murmurs, if only to make it seem like her current state of affairs doesn't absolutely petrify her.

"This isn't some pleasure dungeon," I sneer. "Do you

have any idea how many people have died in the same spot you're in right now?"

Her eyes narrow in defiance. "I may not know how many, but I can certainly name a few of them."

"And you'll be one of them in a few minutes if you don't tell me what you were insinuating back there," I tell her—a warning.

"I don't know what you're talking—"

I yank my knife out of its hidden holster within my pant pocket, clenching a fist around the smooth hilt.

Venus merely peers up at me from the top of her eyes. "Oh, please. You think you're the first man to threaten me at knifepoint?"

I drop it on the floor, the clattering sound hanging in the air. "Fine. I don't need a weapon to get to you. All I have to do is leave you chained up here, take a carriage back to your slum of a homeland, and go find your sister—the little one."

That gets her. She doesn't fight against the chains, but her hazel eyes promise violence, blackening by the second. Venus knows better than to assume my threats are empty.

"Start talking." I hiss.

Her face is completely neutral as she tells me, "I don't know how it happened."

"Bullshit."

"I'm not above lying to your face." She almost chuckles. "But I mean it when I tell you that. I. Don't. Know."

"You said you have a foothold in my mind, that you boss me around in my fantasies. Start there. Tell me exactly what you mean by that."

Venus grins like a cat. "Back in the marshes, you had told me that you found me. Well, after you went to go shoot birds, I realized that you only came after me because I told you to."

"So, why did you?"

She pauses, ransacking her brain for an answer she cannot quite seem to find. "I don't know that either."

"You're a lousy prisoner, you know that?"

"I know you want answers, and trust me, I'd be happy to supply them for you. But the fact is, neither of us know shit. You can't torture a lie out of me, and considering your current desperation," she adds pointedly, yanking against her chains to prove her point and drawing a deep frown across my face, "I know better than to badger you about it. Now, will you let me out of—"

"No," I say, my skin turning hot. "You're going to sit here until you figure it out."

She merely pouts her lip, eyes glinting with malice. "Did the almighty King Jericho just put me in a timeout?"

In the span of two seconds, my knife is back within my grasp, angled against Venus's exposed throat. I take secret pride in the gasp that escapes her, as she was unable to prepare for my sudden movement. Her eyes burn through mine, and I realize that threats won't work on her. In order for her to open up, she needs to know that she's gained equal ground.

"Don't make me kill you, Venus," I say, offering her an inch of leverage.

True fear meets her eyes as her throat bobbles, and the blade gently cuts the surface of her skin there. "You hurt everyone, I don't understand why you wouldn't want to hurt me."

I pull her closer to me—fighting the growing worry that she may pierce my soul with only her gaze—and her denial rushes out, replaced by the tension of us sharing the same breath. Venus is . . . so warm. So soft, despite her harsh lines and coarse inner resilience, the absence of her goading smile is an almost haunting sight, because in its stead, her parted mouth nearly grazes my own. The rise and fall of her chest pushes against my own, and I worry that I'm about to do, or say, something incredibly stupid.

"I think . . . I think I'm supposed to trust you."

Venus blanches. "What?"

"The Saints always show me bad people. But you haven't done anything wrong, you invited me into your world . . ."

I draw back my knife, sliding it across the floor far away from her—a silent apology. Then, I let go of her altogether, and she sinks to the floor, as if all her energy had been depleted. Scrambling, I fetch the key to the chains and free her, telling myself that letting her go, when I would rather shake the information out of her, will help gain her trust.

And the first thing she does is shove me backward, hard—her teeth gritted like an animal ready to shred me into pieces.

She probably planned to swing at me, too, but my feet trip over themselves and I barely manage to brace a hand onto the ground before I fall like a log. Venus laughs darkly at the sight. "Let's get one thing straight, *you* dreamed of *me*, not the other way around. Which means what you saw was *not* an invitation, especially not one to touch me like you just did."

"Venus, it wasn't like that—"

"You chained me up in the same spot you killed my father, you threatened the safety of my sisters after you already separated me from them, you prepared to *torture* me for information, and yet, you expect me to think that we're supposed to, what . . . trust each other? *Work together?*"

"I don't know," I say flatly, steam building within me.

Venus has certainly had enough, and turns to go, leaving me in the darkness. But just then, something hits a nerve that I nearly forgot about. "Wait. Yes, I do. Meet me at North Star tomorrow morning."

Her eyes cut back towards me like daggers. "What the hell is North Star?"

"Delta will tell you. Just be there at nine."

Ten minutes past nine the next morning, I stroll into the greenhouse I affectionately call North Star, which remains so expansive that no matter which door I coast through, I descend upon an entirely new view.

Amidst the tumultuous moments and relationships in my life, I'd always found this secluded place to be my center—my sole comforter—even more so than the boardroom. And while this greenhouse started as an anniversary gift from my father, his neglect for something Merrie grew to treasure, became my ultimate gain.

Mother could never be seen gardening herself, but

she'd spend hours here, just staring at it all. She loved her lilies, violets, irises, and hyacinths. Her world was composed of every flower imaginable, but more than any other, my mother adored her peonies. The soft pinks reminded her of the hopeful blush she first held for my father when they met, of the idealistic image of a romance turned to permanence.

What a load of shit.

Still, I knew what transpired behind the curtain of my parents' public relationship. Urovian monarchs were afforded several luxuries, but the option of divorce was never one of them. My father's heart had hardened long ago, so in efforts to avoid his growing wrath, I took up the private hobby of keeping Mother's greenhouse alive. Tending to this greenhouse had become so habitual already that, when she died, I decided to keep at it. Not because I found any joy in it, but because I couldn't handle watching her previous flowers wither away just as my memory of her was beginning to.

So it is awfully fitting to find Venus Deragon at the center of the greenhouse, stooped over to smell the peonies, of all things. "You're late," she tells me with her back turned.

"You're lucky I didn't stand you up."

"You make it sound like this is a date or something," she says tauntingly, spinning to look over at me for the first time since yesterday.

Surely not, I think to myself, *because I'd never court a woman whose daily attire consisted of denim, let alone long-since starched, plain blouses.*

As I step closer, I catch her bracing her hands firmer

along the stoned planter. "Why are you looking at me like I'm going to hurt you, Venus?"

Venus forces a crafty smile onto her lips. "Because I know you could."

She's not as invincible as she pretends to be, I think to myself.

Still, if only to reassure her for the moment, I leisurely raise my hands and murmur, "You can check my pockets if you want, but I'm not armed. I'm giving you the benefit of the doubt today."

"How kind," she murmurs with false sweetness, and while I give her free rein to pat me down or search my clothes for the knife that I held against her throat yesterday, she seems inclined to not touch me—another instinct adapted from yesterday's confrontation. Instead, Venus looks around North Star with a neutral sort of expression. "Delta told me Queen Merrie loved this place."

"Yes," I say, trying not to dwell too long on how the pink peonies at Venus's back brings out a richness in her coffee-toned skin. "It's a calming area, don't you think?"

Her head dips to one side. "You're asking me how I feel about flowers?"

Saints above, must she ruin everything? "Whatever," I mutter. "I asked you to meet me here because I've figured out what you're here to do."

"Oh, really?"

"The gardens—you commented on their current state, and I'm willing to hear you out. As of today, you're the new groundskeeper."

She smiles with vicious intent. "What are my wages?"

I'm more surprised that she does not care to pick a

fight with me about taking up such a grueling, demanding job than I am about her asking for money. "You're pretty greedy for a guest," I remind her.

"You've got the funds to spare," she merely returns.

"Fine. Give me a number tomorrow and it's settled. I've never seen your work in the field, but the only thing you need to know is that I manage this greenhouse on my own. You are not to touch this place with your tools. Are we clear?"

"Crystal," Venus replies shortly, glancing around the room as if she were looking for the nearest exit, like she's ready to run as far as she can from me.

I bid a silent farewell to one of my favorite spots on Broadcove's property, and Venus follows me out of North Star and into the fair morning light, undiluted by greenhouse glass and tall shrubbery.

With the front of the castle looking out towards the great scope of buildings, entertainment establishments, and the well-paved roads for trade and travel, the back of Broadcove acts as a landscape of tranquility. The expansive gardens illustrate the antithesis of the hustle and bustle of life below the castle, and while I see an empty valley of sprawling green, the look in Venus's eyes when I shift back to her tells me she sees her something more—a blank canvas that she soon can fill however she wants.

We descend the slope of a hill that drops us off at the front of a fountain. Beyond it, well-nourished hedges boxed in grand, carved planters create a pathway for us to walk through. "Why did you become a topiary?" I find myself asking her, suddenly nauseated by the silence between us.

"My dad used to be one," she says, sourly. "He wanted at least one of his daughters to understand his career, but he sustained a back injury and couldn't get the treatment that he needed to continue his work. I, eventually, took over for him."

Of course, it's about the girl's father, I think to myself.

"Look, we both know what I did to him." I groan. "But for your sake, and mine, I'm going to need you to let that go. Keeping a record of wrongs with me won't end well for you."

"It already hasn't, Jericho," she counters, raising her voice. "You've got some nerve to tell me to move on when I know damn well you lash out on others because you're not over what happened to Merrie."

The last time someone dared to bring my mother's death into conversation, especially one designed to enrage me, died moments after the words left their lips. Venus ought to consider herself lucky that I left my knife in my room this morning.

Then, Venus's eyes cast downwards in pensive thought. "I don't know what he did, Jericho," she says quietly. "And I know he's been gone for some time, but not knowing what he did, or what your visions accused him of . . . kills me."

I consider the admission to be her attempt at giving me some ground of my own, but still feel the need to throw it back in her face. "Can't you accept that your father likely died for my simple leisure?"

But Venus seems undeterred in her personal quest for the facts. "No, I cannot. Because you told me that the Saints always show you bad people. If I'm supposed to believe that your crackpot visions are real, and that you're a man of your word, which is certainly a stretch, that means that my father was a bad man. I'd even go as far as to consider you being a smart individual," she adds, and while fawning and flattery is sometimes known to soften my defenses, I sense the backhanded aspect of the compliment. "Which means that you wouldn't just conveniently forget his face, his name, or better yet, his crime. It's why I didn't buy that shit you said in the carriage about how he pleaded for his life. My dad was not that kind of man, and not even in death would he resort to begging *you* for mercy—"

"Maybe it did happen a little differently. But you know what?" I yank Venus closer by the softer part of her upper arm. "I'm going to let you figure that out for yourself. Because, like you said, *you* came into *my* dream, Venus," I snap, a vein popping out along my neck. "Perhaps, if you try hard enough, you'll finally get to see your father's mistakes through my eyes."

Knowing better than to barter with me for answers or even small hints at what his flaws were, Venus stares out at the expansive land surrounding us. The distant pine trees towards the edge of Broadcove's property create a separate horizon line, one that separates her from a whole other domain she knows nothing about. Still, her eyes glean over the forests like they are full of opportunity.

"Pay me whatever you paid the person before me, but send my wages to my sisters," she says, her eyes still lingering over the emerald pastures. "Otherwise, the deal is off, and I'll go back to making your days miserable and have a marvelous time doing so."

To Venus's credit, I find it honorable that she's willing to give up such a sum of money to her sisters when, by the looks of her, she's never seen the amount of money her services earn her here in her entire life.

"Done," I say, offering my hand to shake on it in agreement, and while she flashes a revolted look at me, she still dares to make the contact and clasp her hand within mine. "And whatever you want to do with the grounds, it's all yours. Form a team, do it yourself, I don't care."

As long as you're out of my hair.

A ghost of a smile starts to creep along her lips, which appear chapped from the cold weather. "Are there markets that I can visit? Places I can barter for resources in order to start my work?"

I'm almost physically struck by the word. "Barter?"

"Yes, barter," Venus says plainly. "Like . . . trading services for a small good—"

"I know what bartering is, Venom," I say, grinning at the disgust on her face. "I'm not a halfwit. And anyways, no one in Broadcove barters, and royalty never pay. Make a list of what you'd like. I'll have one of my guards go—"

"*I* would like to go into town," she presses. "Even if it means I'm accompanied by the guard you were planning on sending. I'd like to explore the territory."

The marshes were always a devastating place to do business in, but had I known bartering became a more reliable and thorough currency than coins, perhaps I could've come to understand her demeanor better at an earlier convenience. "Fine. Tolcher can take you tomorrow."

"Great," I hear her say just before the wind picks up. Her dark hair flies in a wave of shadows, and with us still standing close, it soon catches in my face. I mean to swat her locks away, but . . . her hair is rather soft. Probably in part to the bath she took yesterday, but there must be a natural sort of quality about it that feels so silky. It also smells nice—not like the castle soaps, but like the pine trees out in the distance. Maybe even firewood.

Finally, Venus realizes that her hair is borderline choking me, and she rapidly gathers it up in her hands. "My apologies," she seems to say sincerely. "Delta recommended I have it braided back today, but I resisted."

"Sounds like you," I say through a chuckle.

But the sound makes Venus step back, as if I've frightened her again. "Have Tolcher send for me in the morning," she merely returns, and without another word, she drifts off towards the gardens to get an accurate assessment of what she's in for.

11
Jericho

Venus receives dinner in her room tonight, just as she did yesterday—at least according to Ardian, who stares me down at the table upon noting her absence aloud.

Normally, if someone recommended an old bat to bother me with agenda points, or become weepy for people he doesn't know personally, when I find merit to eliminate them, I'd tell them to butt out of my business. In fact, I hadn't been fond of the man as he served my parents. Not to mention my father always bitched about him and his need for friendly delegation with our opposing territory, Mosacia, from which he hailed.

But when I inherited Ardian, through my father's untimely death, I discovered a special liking towards him—although my definition of "like" can be rather convoluted.

While Father had employed Ardian as our Mosacian ambassador, I eventually expanded his job responsibilities—partnering with him to keep tensions easy as I found my footing in my new role as King. I just needed him long enough to keep them from attacking us while I was at my weakest.

But now, at my most formidable, my most precarious threat is not across the sea, but two wings down from me.

"From what I know about Lady Venus"—Ardian sighs in pointed aggravation—"she doesn't seem to scare easily, and yet, this is the second night in a row she hasn't come to dine with us. Can I ask what you did to make this situation so uncomfortable for her?"

I merely cut at my steak. "Have you ever considered that she just doesn't care for me?"

"That much is obvious," he retorts. "But there's something more. Something you're not telling me."

"You're not going to like it."

To my surprise, Ardian doesn't push further, not wanting the real answer to outweigh whatever mental horrors he begins envisioning. "Whatever it was, Jericho, maybe you should consider . . . apologizing. Even if it's not entirely truthful. It's the thought that counts."

Two hours later, as if haunted by my Head Council's supposedly sage advice, I rip my body out of bed, after my private bath, and hobble across the sweeping halls of Broadcove to pay Venus a visit. I have my lines rehearsed in my head:

Venus, I am regretful of how I spoke to you during the grounds tour this morning. I shouldn't have kept your father's death to myself, rather, I should have rubbed it in your face and surely set you off on a personal mission to murder me yourself. Do forgive me.

Truthfully, since Ardian and my sobering discussion about asking for forgiveness, I've been feeling unlike myself, so maybe a little flare of hatred from her before bed might be just what the doctor ordered.

I knock on the door to her room and silence answers back. Knowing Venus is likely ignoring me, I don't bother knocking again before throwing her door open and—

Venus isn't in bed.

In fact, the sheets and the pillows seem to lay perfectly untouched. She came with no luggage—like there'd be much for her to pack anyways—so she hasn't laid anything out over the furniture, and as I stroll in to assess the view of the sea, no fingerprints mark the windows.

It's like Venus never even set foot in this place.

Tiptoeing out of the empty space, I catch wind of a peculiar sound this time of night. Brisk footsteps pitter patter down the stuffy hallway, and from the typical patterns I've observed over the years, Ardian always takes to his bed early, while the guards remain stationed in unmoving positions, and most of the servants finish their chores and regimens before the end of daylight. So when I turn to look at the sound's source, I'm not surprised to find my Head Councilman's niece walking the halls alone.

Lately, I've started remembering the sound of Delta's steps, how she crosses through Broadcove Castle at a faster pace in the nighttime. I wonder if she's afraid of the dark and she guides herself through the grounds like this to quell the nerves.

"I'm just making a final round before bed," she tells me hastily, then curtly dips into a half bow in acknowledgement.

I never grew to like her, per se, but Delta is a fairly tolerable woman. Though my appreciation for her isn't nearly as high as it is for her uncle, I understand the likeness of them. She remains one of the few ladies in this castle that is neither fussy nor dull—my one exception to speaking to women of different social classes—until recently.

"Might you be able to point me in the direction of where Venus is currently? I . . . wanted to apologize for making her feel unable to attend dinner this evening," I force out.

Delta's eyes bug out in surprise at my efforts of extending an olive branch, but I find solace in how she doesn't mention it aloud. "Forgive me, sir," she begins, a slightly panicked look in her eyes. "I tried to get her to stay in the rooms you gave her, but I found her this morning in the same spot she is now—"

"What spot?" I ask stiffly.

Delta doesn't respond, opting to simply start walking back down the hall she originally intercepted me from. We move in silence, my form following hers like a shadow. Moonlight vaguely streams in through the windows diagonally from us, shining on the other side of the castle. Having assigned Venus in the East Wing of Broadcove, I've managed to keep my respective distance from her, but the nearer we draw towards her new location, the more unnerved I begin to feel.

Careening to the right, Delta stands before the door to one of the studies, an office previously occupied by my mother. "She's in there," Delta whispers, as if not to draw Venus's attention to our arrival.

I nod in quiet understanding, twisting the knob and opening the door.

Her eyes gently rest shut, dark lashes brushing soft, hazelnut skin. A low, vibrating hum comes from her body with each inhale and exhale pattern, her mouth slightly agape. The tip of her nose, or what I can see of it before it smothers itself in the carpeted ground, almost glows red—like she's been in the chilly weather too long and she's catching a cold. Or perhaps she's been crying in secret.

To my greatest intrigue, however, sleep allows the anger in her face to soften. Now, Venus looks kind. Peaceful, even. Yes, Venus Deragon may be disquieting at best, but seeing her completely vulnerable like this begins to scare me more than anything else in this life.

Even unconscious, she somehow disarms me.

"I tried to get her to stay in her rooms," Delta whispers again, her hushed voice dancing over the edge of my shoulder. "But Lady Venus was relentless. I figured you wouldn't mind, though, given you put her in the wing furthest from your personal rooms. It'd be different if she set up camp towards the West Wing."

I backpedal my way out of the room, unsure how to respond to Delta verbally, while still looking at Venus's sleeping frame. She's curled up with a blanket she took from another room, nestled in a posture that reminds me of someone shielding themselves from danger, and when I finally click the door shut and block her out of my sight, I instantly feel my bones relax within my body. "It's . . . fine," I resolve.

Soft snoring flutters beneath the crack of the door, and there's something intrinsically frightening about watching her sleep. Because in this state, she's not thinking of new ways to rile me up, or how she can uproot my own inner peace. Here, her body has no choice but to shut down in order to gather enough resilience for what tomorrow morning may bring her.

And it deeply unnerves me.

Ice runs up my spine, and I finish my statement by telling Delta, "Have her in her rooms again tomorrow. I think I'd like to use this space again."

Delta glares at me blatantly enough to be jailed for it. "No one has taken any papers in this room in two years, and suddenly, when Venus finds enough comfort to sleep somewhere, you're just going to take it from her?"

It's not just a room, I want to spit back at her.

"I am King," I say instead.

"And you have *nine* other offices to pick from." She lets out a frustrated sigh, slowly comprehending the way she spoke to me just then, and while she does not retract her statement, she dips her head ever so slightly. "She wasn't going to tell you, you know."

I crook my head at her. "Tell me what?"

"That she was sleeping here, or rather why she isn't sleeping in the rooms you had me prepare for her."

Instinct tells me I shouldn't care regardless of the answer. But Delta shakes her head in a disheartened manner and reveals, "She said the mattress was too comforting, and that the floor felt more like home."

12
Venus

I wake up to a rather unsettling, scribbled letter:

Venus,

If you don't wish to share your dinners with me, fine. But I get your breakfasts. I'll even allow Ardian to join if it would bring you a sense of security. If we're supposed to make this work, we need an open dialogue to occur in a setting where you cannot just walk off in the middle of it like you did in the gardens. Consider all I've said.

— Jericho

My skin crawls the longer I look at the note. Who dropped this off here? Did Jericho know I abandoned the room he gave me? Did he bring the letter here? And if so, did he contemplate killing me where I lay? I mean, I wouldn't have put up a fight.

Now, unable to hyper fixate on anything other than

Jericho murdering me in my sleep, I toss the note as far away from me as I can throw it and scramble to my feet. Snatching up the blanket I stole from one of the spare sitting rooms, I stash it away, in a lower cabinet towards the edge of the wall and glance over at myself in the faded reflection the window provides me. My hair seems less static-ridden than anticipated, but the carpet fragments leave marks along my face like small splatters or pin-needle pricks.

Shuffling out of the office and carefully closing the door behind me, I work my way back to my original rooms, knowing Delta has probably laid out clothes for the day ahead of me. I had requested new overalls, not sure if women in Broadcove were even allowed to wear something other than dresses, and as I peek at the garments set aside for me, I'm happy to see buttery-soft, chestnut pant legs draping from a connecting top piece. Elegant gold stitching in the shape of olive branches and budding flowers curl in the middle of the garment, and a cream, linen blouse reaches its invisible arms to either side.

But, more beautiful than the hand-tailored clothes, a sharpened dagger with a ruby prism structured into the hilt's middle glimmers back at me in greeting. Another note rests beneath the blade, which I delicately take into my fingers.

The verbiage in this note is far more alluring than Jericho's letter. And it is brief.

If you're smart, you'll start sleeping with this.
— Delta

"Lady Venus—"

I sharply turn on a heel to allow my body to shield the damning note and the beautiful dagger. And, while I expect to see Ardian or perhaps even Jericho, I'm thrown for a loop when I see one of the guards that accompanied Jericho in the marshes. The one who gave me his canteen. Golden hair pairs interestingly well with his light brown skin. I cannot tell if he simply spends his days in the warm sun or if he shares a similar, yet distant, heritage with me.

"Oh goodness," he stutters, his cheeks flushing pink as he looks me over in the most doily-looking nightgown Delta forced me to wear for bed. "I apologize. I should've knocked, but the door was left ajar, and . . ."

"No worries, whatsoever. I should only be another minute or two . . . Tolcher," I say sheepishly, hoping I remembered his name correctly.

"No need for formalities," he returns, a boyish grin on his soft face. "You may call me Henry."

My nose scrunches up at the name. "You don't look like a Henry."

"Then just . . . call me, whenever you're ready to depart. I'll be right outside the door."

As suddenly as he entered, he leaves without a sound and fully shuts the door behind him. Considering he's a guard, I can picture him leaning against the wall in waiting, and I wonder if catching a lady undressing makes him blush from the other side. It's the mental image the thought creates that has me deciding this outing might be enjoyable after all.

No Jericho? No judgment? I know a new standard of heaven.

I dress in eagerness, and just before folding the note up and stuffing it between the mattress, I safely tuck away Delta's gifted dagger into one of the deep pockets of my overalls.

I'm relieved to learn that the marketplace is cluttered with potential materials for my biggest maintenance job yet, but I'm, perhaps, even more at ease knowing that Jericho assigned me a watchman that may tend to hover, but is nonetheless kind.

Henry Tolcher faithfully trails after me down every outdoor aisle in the goods and services square, which is a noble feat considering my growing excitement for all that the marketplace holds. There's everything from fine mulch and ceramic planters, to healthy vegetation and seed packages organized by the type of bloom. My main distraction, of course, comes from the stunning fruits that cultivators hold up boastfully at their individual tables—and considering the likes of the food supply in the Makers District, their gloating is well deserved. There's a cantaloupe with my name on it if I had the means of carrying it.

Still, I peel my eyes away from the massive melon and angle my attention towards what I came here for. Beneath a makeshift canopy of stray cloths and textiles, a middle-aged woman with a worn, white face catches my eye and waves me over. "Pretty young lady, might I interest you in a catalog of Earth's loveliest colors?"

Flattery, where I come from, always came with an additional cost—an ulterior motive. And while this woman's toadyism reaches out towards me for the sake of Tolcher's coins, it works on me as well. I'm no fool—the people in Broadcove, and in the surrounding village, are sure to be some of the craftiest people in Urovia. But the technicolor glow I catch within the shadows of her tent draws me in like a magnetic force—my feet closing the gap between her and I without my brain realizing I've left Tolcher behind.

"Hi there," I say to the woman, a stupid, giddy grin on my face as I behold small packets with colorized denotations of the different flowers I could grow in the gardens.

"Hello," she returns. "I'm Ivana. What's your name, Miss?"

"Venus," I tell her, my voice drifting as I catch a passing glance over the color coordinated tabs. "I quite admire your inventory." I sigh. "You have a great eye."

Ivana's brows raise in subtle intrigue. "My inventory, you say? What seems to be my most impressive product?"

Needing to feel sure of my decision, I scan her humble tent once more, my eyes roving over drawstring pouches of seeds containing the means to grow looming sunflowers, electric tulips, and bright daisies. But a lady of any class—especially the wealthy and dim-witted—could think the popular sellouts are lovely. No, my fixation remains on the pouch with an indigo indication ribbon. "The *Echium vulgare*," I finally answer, naturally sophisticating my tone as I enunciate the root name for the stunning plant.

"Exquisite taste!" Ivana rejoices, clapping her hands quietly. As she removes the small parcel from its hook, Tolcher draws nearer, and like a wave of cold air, his presence and natural musk barrels into me. I don't need to glance behind me to know his stance is both authoritative and protective at the same time. "And who is this fine gentleman?" Ivana comically drawls.

It's only when he begins to relax and look more like a young man I'd meet in the markets back home, rather than in the militia, that I realize the two already know one another. "It's always a pleasure, Ivana. What a coincidence that Venus intuitively felt drawn to your station."

"Indeed, though my heart does hope you would've stopped to say hello no matter where her feet wandered, Henry."

He gives the lady a reassuring smile. "Of course, I would." He blushes, looking over the seed package I selected. Tolcher turns his attention towards me this time. "What kind of flowers did you pick?"

"Well," I begin while Ivanna starts a purchase sack for me in case I get carried away and need to buy more, which I certainly will, "it's commonly called blueweed. The chemicals in the flower are said to neutralize the poison in viper bites. When fully bloomed, they are dark blue with purple pistils, one of my favorites. But I haven't seen one in my homeland in years, maybe even a decade."

Instantly, a pitiful expression crosses Ivanna's worn features, aging her in a way. Sure, her white hair suggests that she's past her prime, but up until she started feeling bad for my lack of living alongside an abundance of blueweed, she seemed like she could fall around Ardian's age. "Where are you from, dearie?"

"The marshes. Within the Makers District," I say shortly, knowing that even more pity is probably headed my way.

To my great surprise, though, a wide-eyed sort of excitement falls over her. "How wonderful! That's where Henry is from." She beams. "I'm from the Noble District, but up until I recommended him for the King's Guard, he worked as a carpenter in my township. An older lady like myself cannot possibly do years' worth of home repairs on her own."

Henry shakes his head with a meek smile on his lips. It strikes me then that he's quite handsome. I try to quell the butterflies stirring in my stomach as he bashfully replies, "Yes, but she's conveniently forgetting about the part where she set me up with her daughter."

Ivanna laughs to herself. "Ah yes, my finest endeavor to this day. The moment you married my Nadine, I earned free repair work for the rest of my life."

Son of a bitch, why are the good men always taken?

Amidst my imagination creating an unknown, and probably far-from accurate depiction of Tolcher's mystery girl, Ivanna positions herself to face me and asks me, "Now, how do you know my son-in-law?"

"Oh, I'm Jericho's newest nightmare," I joke, but the words happen to work out in the literal sense as well. "I mean"—I try and recover, shaking my head at myself—"I'm his new groundskeeper. Quite the promotion from tending lawns and yards in the marshes."

Ivanna's eyes flare. "Your work must be astounding!

Well then, can I get you anything else, Lady Venus?" She inquires kindly, tipping her head in acknowledgement of how even without a rank or a title, being a guest of Jericho's garners a great deal of respect. She then gestures to her entire supply, desperately hoping she can sell me more of her inventory.

I glance around Ivanna's mobile station and wonder to myself if she's been left to lug this heavy cart and all its contents into the public marketplace every day she wishes to sell. Noticing my mental observation, Tolcher secretly hands off the pouch of glimmering coins from the Broadcove Treasury to me, and in turn, I set it on the lip of the wooden dividing counter.

Fireworks seem to sparkle in the depth of Ivanna's eyes.

"I'll take everything."

Tolcher had to commission three additional guardsmen to bring wheelbarrows for what we walked away with. He assured me that the castle had plenty of equipment—such as plows, gloves, rakes, and shovels, and he additionally informed me that Broadcove possessed a magnificent tractor automotive—a machine that he explained to me on the carriage ride home.

I mean . . . to Broadcove.

"Why did you leave the marshes, anyway?" I find myself asking him just as the wheels stop their circling and we reach the castle entry underneath the awning.

"Well," he says, stopping himself from the natural flow of exiting the carriage, "the money, truthfully. Ivanna grew fond of me and my work, and I daresay that she was my salvation out of a hard financial situation. But once Nadine and I tied the knot, I didn't want my mother-in-law to bear the burden of funding our lives. That's when I applied for the King's Guard."

I nod to myself, but his answer seems to lack the weight I was hoping it would hold. "No, I think I mean . . . how did you know that leaving the marshes was the best thing for you?"

His returning smile is polite but devastating. "A life in the marshes is the worst thing for a person. It doesn't matter who you are."

For perhaps the first time since encountering Jericho, I feel an internal conviction to do something out of desperation rather than spite. "My sisters—they're dying out there," I add pleadingly. "You and I, of all people, know that women on their own only have so many years to survive. Henry . . ." I say, hoping to seem more genuine, personable. "What can I do in exchange for—"

But Tolcher places a finger over his lips, instructing me to lower my voice, and reaches into his uniform coat where he's stashed another pouch of golden coins. "Didn't Jericho tell you? There's no need to barter in Broadcove. Now go." He pockets the money once more before insisting I go back inside the castle.

The moment my feet reach the cobblestone path, and the door closes behind me, the carriage takes off again, with Tolcher inside. The speed at which they depart tells me all I need to know about how he thinks my sisters are currently faring.

"How was the marketplace?" a voice, almost kind,

says to me, and while my instincts tell me that it's Ardian, my eyes descend on Jericho in disbelief.

"Just fine."

"Did you have fun spending my money?"

"Loads," I sneer, already striding towards the gardens.

13
Venus

All throughout my work today, I've been thinking about one thing and one thing only: finding a way to make Jericho pay for the hell my heart has been through.

But the moment Tolcher comes back to Broadcove this morning—four days since I'd seen him last—I know he plans on hiding information from me. Mainly, vital details about my sisters' health, updates on the amount of food they had by the time he arrived, and, of course, an assessment of whether or not they had chosen to assume the worst and start grieving me.

"What *can* you tell me?" I grumble.

"It's hard to explain, Venus," he starts off, his voice wobbly. "They're just happy to know you're alive. Confused, of course, but happy, nonetheless."

"Tell me they accepted the money you brought them." I heave a heavy, nervous sigh.

"With gratitude," Tolcher assures me. "And they wish you well, it's just . . . they asked about why you were taken into our custody, and considering King Jericho doesn't show his hand of cards to anyone, I couldn't give them an answer. Even some of our highest-ranking men do not have a solid explanation as to why you're still here."

Once more, I am reminded of that odious letter Jericho left in the office for me, because as much as I want to think of myself as a glitch in Jericho's system, that note, and my own intuition, tells me that Jericho may not be so far away from figuring me out if we start spending time together.

"Are you okay?" Tolcher asks, mentally assessing me.

"What's it to you?" I snap back. "If you're not going to give me more than a basic summary, then leave. I have shit to do and dirt to shovel."

While offended by my tone, Tolcher manages to find enough understanding in his heart to leave me be and not press on. From where I stand, I let the rake in my hand clatter to the ground and look despondently down at the clippers and tools beside me.

I find my weary feet abandoning my tasks and treading over to a familiar spot—the greenhouse Jericho insisted I *do not* tamper with. Something about the place was enchanting, and the closer I move towards its tall, yawning glass doors, the more distinctly I hear, what I imagine, are whisperings from the flowery sanctuary.

Come forward.

Come unguarded.

Take refuge among the flora.

No guards appear stationed at any of the entrances, and I slip through one of the translucent doors undetected. Vibrancy practically punches me in the face when I first step inside. It's something I shouldn't have forgotten about from the first time I entered this unique little haven. I'd never seen such intense, overbearing color. The stone fountain sputters to life suddenly, as if detecting my arrival, and water splays in several perfect arches. The serenity that envelops me within these green, polished walls is almost hypnotic, and if I'm not careful, I fear I may wind up trapped in here.

This place is everything I desire my work to amount to. Blaring colors, lush petals, healthy and sustained greenery—yet, it exudes the more peculiar energy on the castle grounds.

"Are you even real?" I ask the air around me.

"Are you?" I almost think I hear something mysterious ask in return.

"I did not expect to find you here," a soothing male voice surprises me.

My head snaps to attention, but when my eyes meet Ardian's, my fight-or-flight instinct quickly disengages. His posture remains non-threatening, and his body moves along at ease as he continues his steps forwards. "It's a nice little spot, don't you think?" he muses.

I glance around the room, assessing the state of the flowers that slowly begin to overwhelm me. They seem to almost bow in my direction. "Lovely," I force out, my throat dry. "Jericho insisted I not alter the place, and by the looks of it, I wouldn't want to anyway."

Ardian smiles sadly. "Yes, the king is quite protective of his mother's greenh—"

"His *mother's?*"

"Of course," he returns simply. "Or did you have

Jericho pegged as the gardening type?"

"Not entirely, it's just . . ." I drift off into thought. I mean, it makes a lot more sense that his mother had her own little sanctuary, but if she's been gone for more than two years, that means that he's been the one keeping it alive, keeping her alive to an extent. "What happened to her?"

Ardian seems threatened by my inquiry.

I try and soften the expression on my face. "I don't wish to pry, but the *U. Herald* stopped getting delivered to my district after Queen Merrie and King Ronan passed. The papers never pointed out a cause of death, which had a lot of people thinking . . ."

"Merrie Morgan was a wonderful ruler," Ardian carefully answers before I can finish my statement. "But there were moments that the true colors of her territory oversaturated the joyous life she had built . . . and the day she left us was one that, perhaps, detrimentally altered the way many people saw the world."

My stomach lurches at Ardian's strategic diction regarding Merrie.

She *left*.

"I understand what it feels like to miss home, Venus," Ardian cuts in. "When I left mine and brought Delta here with me, I experienced several different emotions at first, much like you are. But rest assured, I believe Broadcove will grow on you."

"Like it did for Merrie?" I return flatly, not letting him avoid the darker truth I now knew to be true.

Ardian doesn't meet my stare, and it tells me all that I care to know about the questions swirling silently in my brain. "Broadcove may be bursting with beauty, but even with the food, and the shelter, and the ability to continue working," I say as enunciated as humanly possible, in hopes that Ardian can read the helplessness in my voice, "I still cannot trust a word that Jericho says." When he tries to say something else, perhaps to inform me that he's an ally I can rely on, I add, "I do not feel safe here."

Mentally fixating on the dagger Delta left for me, that currently burns a hole in my side pocket, I wonder if placing my hand there would make me look suspicious. Ardian tries to find something comforting to say among the flowers, and as his attention diverts from me, I do just that—my fingertips grazing cool steel. When there's clearly no avail to Ardian's pursuits, he turns back to me and asks, "Is there anything that I can do to change your mind about how you feel?"

I merely shrug. "Give me your word that I have not come here to die."

But Ardian and I both know that there's only one way out of Broadcove. Jericho is too controlling to let me walk free, and even if he and I do work together to figure out why I called out to him in his dreams, who's to say that the true answer wouldn't enrage him? Who's to say that he unravels the very thing that links us, and it threatens his throne or even his life? I mean, Saints, he hates me as it is. And in his most natural state, he proves to be incredibly volatile.

I'm doomed.

I head for the door I entered through, turning my back on Ardian and his empathetic expression. I hear the words, *"I'm sorry"* come from somewhere behind me, but when the tone doesn't match the timbre of Ardian's voice, my feet swiftly whisk me away from the stunning flowers and mysterious, sweet aroma of North Star.

I skipped out on lunch, opting to work through my intrusive thoughts and hopefully escape the North Star haze that seemed to have descended over me.

It felt like trying to break a fever, to swipe blindly at invisible cobwebs that covered my face and seeped into my mouth—unproductive and silly. Eventually, I delegated a few tasks to the already established groundskeeping staff including: using the tractor to plow a new plot of soil so we can start planting the blueweed next week, watering the crops—given the lack of rain in recent months—and correcting the overgrowth along the walled, hedge passages.

Once that was in order, I straightened myself out and began my walk towards Jericho's section of the castle as inconspicuous as possible.

According to Delta's gathered observations she had shared with me over breakfast this morning, Jericho typically confines himself to one of his offices from two in the afternoon all the way until six in the evening, but usually he can be found in the one in the West Wing that overlooks the traveler's paths. When I pressed further and asked what it is he does in there, Delta promptly responded with, "Probably stares at himself in the mirror or some shit," to which we both doubled over in laughter

The West Wing of the palace, I take note as I peruse the hallways, is far larger and considerably more protected by members of the King's Guard. Despite knowing I won't bump into Tolcher, who is stationed along the southern edge of the castle, I find that the further I roam from my side of Broadcove, the smaller I feel. This place makes me feel like an insect likely to be crushed under Jericho's shiny boot.

In fact, from where I'm standing, this appears to be far larger than a hallway, and not even three steps later, the path gives way to six scattered chandeliers hanging from high above, and the most spectacular mural I've ever beheld spans the entire length of the lavishly long ceiling. With fresco details of naked babies with wings playing harps, and beautiful, curvy women bidding rosy-cheeked smiles to sophisticated men.

No furniture clutters the open space, and with each proceeding step, the floor echoes the sound of my working shoes. In the vast silence, the sound seems almost distortedly loud, and it makes me lighten my movements. Just another twenty paces or so, and I'll reach the grand, carpeted stairs that creates a whale tail sort of shape, creating two diverging paths for hypothetical guests to ascend—

Guests, I realize.

This is a ballroom.

A surreal sort of glamor seems to descend over me like snow as I find myself too far from any of the sides of the room. Floating alone in a sea of empty air that people ought to be breathing in beside me, I imagine what this place must look like with a gathered crowd. What fine music must sound like when someone strikes up a band. If only Calliope could see this place—if she could sing a measure or a stanza of lyrics to learn what the acoustics must be like here. I wonder how different hues of luxurious dress fabrics would contrast with the extravagant gold of Broadcove's walls, and as my eyes carefully trace their way up splendid columns and follow every swirling embellishment, I picture Geneva smiling down at me from one of the several empty balcony ledges. Eyes wide open, I visualize her wearing a beautiful yellow gown with tacky ribbons for straps—childlike and lovely as she ought to be at her age.

Not what she has been forced to become.

And standing in the middle of the imaginary commotion, I envision myself in a dress that took three ladies' maids to tie me up in, donning jewelry heavy enough to sink a ship, arm in arm with someone equally as dashing and bejeweled. I think of draping my leg around their body, exposing skin through the slit of my dress, perhaps even saying something risky and sensual in their ear—the fantasy of it all sounds so fascinating in my head.

But no daydream fully separates me from the reality of this cavernous room. Truthfully, knowing what I do about Queen Merrie's passing, I would not be surprised if there haven't been any parties since, and if there was any sliver of hope left for entertainment and social life here after her death, that flame was promptly snuffed out when King Ronan followed her to the grave not long afterwards.

Still, I scan the room once more, ensuring that no unwanted eyes linger nearby. Once I feel it's safe to proceed, it's all too easy to shut my eyes and imagine I'm in the middle of a marvelous gathering. A feast, perhaps, but before the guests have grown too full to leave their chairs. I was never taught the proper technique, but from Calliope's stories, I had committed the distinct timing of the partner dances to memory. 1-2-3, turn, 1-2-3. I scale the space in a sweeping waltz turn, picturing the skirts of my gown billowing through the air, and as I rise on relevé—

Footsteps sound from one of the distant pathways, and, as I instantly break my ballerina's composure, I sprint for the closest hiding place—a burgundy curtain slung against either side of the lower-level entrance. Like a bat out of hell, I go flying across the vacant dance floor and, just before the mysterious being enters the room, the thick, maroon velvet covers me so only one of my eyes peers out and investigates.

Ardian appears alone, strolling aimlessly through, not just this room, but probably many rooms beforehand. From my limited vantage point, I see him rubbing his fingers over each other as if in slight distress, and his eyes randomly track the room. Eventually, his gaze lands upon the portrait high above him. He sighs, releasing the tension in his shoulders. "Not a day goes by—"

"That you don't miss her?" a firm voice I hadn't deigned to look for cuts in from the stairs. In the same moment that I realize the woman in the mural must be Queen Merrie, I also recognize the voice's owner without bothering to look. If Jericho's specific timbre hadn't given his arrival away already, the clunking of his designer shoes would have done the trick.

"I thought you had records to attend to in your office,"

Ardian hints pointedly.

"I thought you had gossip to quiet," the king counters. From where I stand, I can only see the edges of his profile—dark hair nearly covering his eyes, the first bit of red fabric along his officer coat, and typical dark pants. "Your niece gave me a funny look this morning before informing me that no one has been brought in for questioning since Venus arrived."

Ardian seems thrilled. "Well, sir, have you had any new visions? You and I usually converse about them, but since you haven't brought any to my attention, I just assumed—"

"No," Jericho interrupts him, clear disdain in his voice. "I haven't had any new visions."

Ardian looks like he could burst into song. "Oh, Jericho! How wonderful!"

"Not *wonderful*," Jericho whines back at him, rudely mimicking his Head Council's enthusiasm. "My own servants think I'm weak."

"On the contrary," Ardian challenges, running a hand through his beard. "They don't think you're weak. It's just strange for them to see you . . . at bay, given your usual standard of one weekly prisoner. Venus has been here for longer than that, now, and not only have you not convicted an outsider, but you've also spared and housed her. And as far as my niece is concerned, Delta merely implies to me that you sound more like yourself these days, the version of you she met when both of your parents were still alive."

I hear a counterargument die in Jericho's throat, and the next time he speaks, the modulation in his voice is different. "The *only* difference," Jericho states through what sounds like gritted teeth, "between the man I was while my mother lived, and the man I am now is that back then, at least one person believed that my visions were real. That they were truthful, helpful. I admire you a great deal, Head Councilman, but let's not pretend that you think I am of sound mind."

Ardian says nothing.

"You think I've gone off my rocker. That I'm some heartless murderer who has unknowingly convinced his own staff that he couldn't possibly possess a merciful heart for a poor girl like Venus," he spits out. "But you're wrong. I killed those people . . ." Jericho says, finally stepping into my full line of sight from behind the curtain and squaring up to Ardian, "because my visions left me no choice. Thieves, murderers, outstanding debtors, but most of all, I've killed traitors—people that traded chatter and information about Broadcove and about Urovia to the very people you left behind to be here."

The Mosacians.

I try not to let a chill skitter down my spine at the thought of the rivaled territory out east, past the Damocles Sea that creates a permanent boundary—the dividing line that lies right beyond my room's windows.

"Venus is a lovely distraction and all," he adds bitterly, a forced laugh in his throat, "but I have a feeling that my visions will return from their unknown respite, stronger and more vivid. And when they do, I will not hesitate to slay people by the hundreds."

I force my body to hold its breath, a shaky sensation coursing through my bones.

Watching as Ardian straightens his posture so as to not stand down from the king's accusation, he asks him warily, "Are you suggesting there's a breach of trust here in the castle, Jericho?"

"They may not reside here, but I know, beyond a shadow of a doubt, that they exist somewhere—it's why I've stopped the *U. Herald's* spread. It helps narrow down who could possibly be spreading false intel about our territory. I know what I've seen in my visions before, and I know exactly what I'll do if there's even the slightest chance at shutting down the fugitive forever. I don't care what you, my staff, or the pompous Holymen have to say about it."

I hear the gulp go down in Ardian's throat. "Yes, Your Majesty."

"You're dismissed," Jericho bellows, and while his Head Council doesn't run off scared, he does make haste in the opposite direction of Jericho.

Standing alone, amongst the ballroom's grandeur, I watch as his head tilts upward, silently acknowledging his mother's mural. Then, he makes his way back to where he came from, and just before I step out from my concealed place, Jericho's steps halt, as if some force had startled him.

A sinister chuckle echoes faintly. "To whomever is stalking me from behind the curtain," he calls out somewhere out of my line of sight, "if I catch you eavesdropping on my conversations again, I'll see to it that you won't have eyes or ears to spy on me with."

He then strolls off towards the depths of the West Wing without another word, two ginormous doors slamming shut behind him.

Untangling myself from my lackluster hiding spot, I suddenly feel a complete loss of control. I still don't know my full way around Broadcove without getting lost or needing to have a servant point me in the direction of where I'm trying to go. I work a grueling job—albeit self-afflicting—that depletes my energy to fight back, and even when I do my best to remain invisible, I still stick out like a sore thumb.

Saints, how am I supposed to kill this man?

When I get to my rooms, I choke down my dinner of quail and stew, nodding my head and feigning interest as Delta rambles on about court intrigue and who she finds the most attractive out of the waitstaff. Typically, the conversation flows naturally, but since the moment I stepped into North Star—since I felt some otherworldly, lingering presence in that place—nothing in my body or soul has been right. I don't feel like myself, nor can I remember how to retrace my steps and get the old me back.

I supposed the intense scrubbing I put myself through is a start. The moment Delta boils enough water for me, I promptly kick her out of the bathing room, get my hands on the rough sponge and nail brush, and go to town. I relentlessly scrape the dead skin, sweat, grime, and lingering spirits of North Star off me, my motions so ferocious and rough that I fear I may draw blood.

And what if I do? Perhaps the sting would do me some good, too.

I soak my hair in the eventually murky water, submerging myself in my own filth if only to contemplate the feeling of drowning. The heated water burns my face, but I welcome the discomfort of it as I clench my eyes shut even tighter than the second before. I allow my pores to open, my reflexes to relax, and my will to carry on disintegrate around me.

I'm just too tired to fight anymore.

Once I'm dried off and dressed in cozier pajamas that the seamstress in the lower sector commissioned for me, Delta encourages me to at least climb under the covers and see how I like the feel of satin on my skin rather than automatically walk myself to the quaint, corner office. I flash her a toothy smile as the initially cold kiss of the material caresses my freshly shaved legs, forcing my head to nuzzle itself within the plush pillow. When my contentment is to Delta's liking, she blows out the lit candles across the expanse of my room and bids me goodnight.

Everything about abiding here upsets me—the uncanny atmosphere of North Star, the overabundance of luxury, and Jericho always being one step ahead of me—pushing my buttons, avoiding the answers to my questions, even sensing my presence when I'm trying to remain invisible. It's so crippling to my common sense, I begin to wonder if Merrie felt this helpless before the end.

And that's when an almost evil idea creeps into my mind.

I'm once more an unknown, and unseen, observer of a quiet night in the marshes. This time, my scope settles a little closer towards the border of the marshes and the main hub of the Makers District, not far from the trolley station that Genny and Cali take to work every day.

Half-covered dining spots lie scattered here and there, minimal shops filling in the gaps, and in the center, there's a greasy-looking pub I don't think I've ever noticed before—mainly because I tended to gravitate towards the louder establishments that lined the swampy coastline, over the ones that curved inland. Upon closer examination, and despite not knowing just how late in the evening it is, I catch sight of two gentlemen at the pub, identical drinks on the rusty countertop. Their backs remain turned to me, but I can vaguely hear their conversation.

"It's a damn shame . . . 'bout Her Majesty." The larger of the two gripes to the other, fidgeting in his chair to the right of his companion.

"Your sullenness makes my drink taste bad," the leaner man mumbles, taking a violent swig of his cloudy beverage. I almost wince looking at it.

"Beer's shit anyway," the big one counters. "Besides, Merrie is all there is to talk about anymore. Why not mull it over for a while, huh?"

"Because, Parson," the nameless one replies, his irritation vivid, "it's maddening."

Parson turns towards his companion with an unsettling smirk on his scraggly bearded face. "You know something."

"I'd be a fool to go sniffing around for conspiracies," his companion scoffs, but his response is no denial.

"Oh, but I can certainly see you being that fool," Parson challenges, a sudden revived energy taking root in his movements.

He adjusts himself in his chair. "I am only going to ask you this once, Tristan. Tell me what you know."

That name—Tristan.

My father's name.

Father drops the hooded cape onto the back of his neck and turns to face Parson fully, giving away his side profile to reveal the truth. Yes, this is a moment from the past—and it's a defining one. I comprehend as much when my father's mouth gives way to a secret smile, and he whispers, "It'll cost ya—"

That's when a third character in this dream reveals themself, although I do not see them directly before they shove their cold hand over my mouth.

They come from behind me, their grip forceful as they shove a sack over my head and drag my body somewhere away from their sight. As the world turns pitch black around me, burlap cutting across my cheeks and nose, I know better than to kick and scream and fight this stranger for control.

All I need to understand about this dream is that it's not mine, because my consciousness would keep me there, glued to their conversation.

No, this is another one of Jericho's visions.

And he doesn't want me to see what happens next.

14
Jericho

I haven't deigned to speak to Venus in over a week, and after the cold, bitter way she spoke to me at the castle entrance, I suppose that it's better that way.

As I let my icy rage melt over the following days, I also secretly watched her at work, evaluated how she began to reconstruct the aesthetic of the Broadcove gardens. As vibrancy and health slowly returned to the outdoor scenery beyond the castle walls, my instinct to make Venus suffer faded into the quiet realization that she was right. She is talented . . . and it makes my skin crawl.

Every now and then, when I cross the open terraces throughout the different wings of the castle, I passively glance over which faction of the grounds Venus fusses with at that given moment. In only a week, Venus has created the beginnings of something spectacular. Even in the night's dreary shadow, I see the splendor she's planted, and trimmed, and smoothened out.

And it's beginning to haunt me how easily she slipped

her grubby little fingers into my home. Ardian and Delta love her, the staff adores her—given her arrival has altered the dynamics of the castle—and I'm starting to wonder if I haven't foreseen anything out of fear that Venus will intercept what the Saints long to show me.

Fear . . . for *her*? It's preposterous. And it ends right now.

The next thing I know, I'm lying on the floor next to Venus in my mother's abandoned office—her eyes are wide open, searching mine.

"What are you doing in here?" she asks.

"I don't know," I answer truthfully, startled by how fast sleep must have found me, but more so startled by the fact that she doesn't balk from our close proximity.

"I'm not sleeping in the rooms you picked out for me," she remarks stubbornly.

There's a childlike disposition about the way she speaks those words. Like she's a little girl who'd stomp her foot on the floor in defiance if she weren't already laying down beside me. "I'm not asking you to."

Venus rubs the skin along the side of her face that rests against the carpet, but says nothing more. It makes the silence feel suffocating, drawing the question, "What would you do if you had the chance?" from my mouth.

Venus stares at me. "Huh?"

Of course, out of all the things that my subconscious could focus on, or think to ask her about, it's this.

"If you could do anything, I mean," I restate. "Not for the money, not as a personal burden your father passed onto you, but

something to give your life fulfillment . . . what would you do?"

She's quiet for a moment, not as if to debate her answer, but to rationalize whether it's safe to share her intended answer with me.

Then, Venus murmurs, "I've always wanted to have the chance to train as a performer. My older sister, Calliope, is a beautiful musician and has a near-hypnotic voice, but I could never carry a tune or harmonize with her to save my life. So I think if I was given the opportunity, I'd want to be a dancer."

A dancer?

It's a shocking answer, truthfully, one that I certainly wasn't expecting out of her. Part of me thought that she would want to do something more violent and athletic if offered the luxury of free time. But the arts? I suppose on some level, considering the way she tends to the castle gardens and creates beautiful landscapes, she would be good at it—but for the length of time that I've known her, expressing joy in the form of dancing has never been something I considered Venus would think about, let alone secretly dream of.

There's a faint blush in her cheeks as she continues through her fantasy. "From Calliope's stories, when she would perform for wealthier crowds, I've always envied the noblewomen and how they dance hand in hand with fine gentlemen, or the ballerinas that travel in revered companies across the territory."

"The winter ballets are my favorite," I muse aloud, and when I meet her eyes again, there's something new swirling within that hazel pool—something foreign and soft.

"In another life," Venus whispers sadly, "I would've loved to try my hand at the art in some way or another."

I can't do it—I can't look at her face, at the brewing heartbreak rising from beneath her usual, tough exterior. It's too much to bear at once. "My mother loved to paint," I offer up as some sort of relatable connection.

Venus nods, but the ghost of dreams that never came to be still haunt the air around us. "I bet her works were magnificent."

That's when I feel her calloused hand creep across my own, having deftly inched away from the spot it rested before. Her touch . . . is comforting. Perhaps the direct antithesis of what I imagined it would feel like. But more than that, it's consoling. Venus's fingers begin to curve around mine one by one, as if understanding my loss, somehow.

Of course, she understands. This version of her is a figment of my imagination.

But if that's the case, why haven't I dropped her hand yet?

What the fuck is wrong with me?

"You do not like her," I remind myself in the mirror. "Not even a little bit. And she *certainly* does not like you."

But even as I say the words aloud, and commit myself to hold true to their meanings, I find myself straightening the lapels of my jacket and tidying my hair. I catch myself looking at my jawline and wondering if I need to shave or if my five o'clock shadow will not come off too aggressive. I check to see that my pants aren't wrinkled, my shoes are tied, and that—most importantly—my emergency pocket knife is tucked away in an accessible pocket. I may be feeling uncharacteristically generous, but I'm not stupid.

"You are not afraid of her," I add for good measure, though the mental note is still somewhat embarrassing to voice aloud. "She does not pose a real threat to you. You are simply a king that is approaching a situation with no exterior protection. It's simply a precaution, and a wise one."

There's a knock on the door, but before I can get to the knob and turn it, I already hear the person's footsteps receding down the vast hallway. Cook staff, I realize, bringing me exactly what I called in from the kitchen when I first awoke this morning. Carefully opening my bathroom door outward, I see that said servant had the brains to put my requests out of the way from the door's path.

Before my bed, a tray of food presents two separate orders: steak, eggs, and crispy morning hash on a steaming plate—obviously mine. The other isn't even on a plate, but rather a bowl of vibrant color and fruits. No protein adorns the second dish. Instead, a pool of purple, berried mush decorated by blueberries, cut up bananas, and slivers of lush strawberries stare back up at me. Granola peppers the top of it along with coconut shavings.

Picking up the tray in my hands, I feel the temperature seep through the glass and wood—heat in my left and cold in my right.

Hot and cold. Just like us.

Without making it look like I'm in too much of a hurry to any passersby, I quickly trod out of my expansive rooms, allowing the guards to close the door behind me—although, they do extend me a bashfully confused glance or two as I disappear towards the direction of the East Wing.

I've never carried my food anywhere, let alone carried someone else's food to them, but as the gardens have begun to bloom and my resentment has begun to wither, I've found myself more willing to make a decent effort in communicating with Venus. As long as she does the same.

Here's to hoping she feels receptive today.

After five minutes of walking, I knock on the small office door with the edge of my shoe three times.

Silence.

The longer I hold these trays at a tabletop level, the more my arms start to ache, but I know she's in there. I knock again, harder this time.

"Five more minutes, Delta," I hear her voice say sleepily.

Keep your voice gentle, I remind myself. *You need this to work.*

"Venus. It's me. Can you open the door?"

15
Venus

Panic roars in my blood as I jolt fully-awake to the sound of Jericho's voice.

What time is it?

Am I late to my work?

Did I sleep through breakfast?

What the hell is Jericho doing here?

"Um . . ." I try to scan the room for a stray comb or a breath mint on the desk, or anything to make myself look less appalling and tousled from sleep, but I fear there's not much to help my case. "I just need a minute to straighten up."

"I don't care if you've just rolled out of bed," he returns through the closed door. I don't have it locked, so I'm surprised that, at the very least, Jericho hasn't tried his hand at the doorknob. "We should talk."

At his words, I find my footing and stand up. A clock on the fireplace mantle, which reads an hour before my shift, ticks another minute onward, as if telling me not to keep the king waiting. Loosening a breath, I trudge over to the entry door and open towards me, figuring Jericho would be cross-armed and frowning at me first thing in the morning.

Instead, he presents a tray of food to me, my breakfast order and, it seems, a plate for himself, too. The awkward look on his face only confirms my theory, and though his tone is rugged, his voice is soft. "I just want to speak with you."

Want, I realize he said, not *need*.

Well, maybe need, as well, but the word choice doesn't go unnoticed. Trying to flatten my static-ridden hair, I nod. "Come in, then. I'll pull one of the chairs over to the desk," I say, already moving—

"No, let me," Jericho says, a gentleman's disposition in him for a change.

Saints above, what has gotten into him?

Jericho quickly strolls over to the small sitting area across the room from the singular desk, setting the trays down at a spot where he and I will sit next to each other, but also diagonally. The silverware clatters on impact, but even as the metal sound rings out, Jericho steps aside and pulls out a chair. *My* chair.

Neither of us speak for a long, suspended while.

"You may sit," he motions to the chair gently.

Cautiously, I proceed to my designated spot, and once I'm seated, Jericho pushes me towards the table with ease. Then, he takes his place beside me, divvying up our breakfasts accordingly. Setting my bowl before me, then my spoon, he offers up a weary smile before grabbing his knife and fork. He's already cutting into his steak when I impulsively blurt out, "Shouldn't we bless the food?"

Jericho's brow pops upward, as if trying to figure out if I'm joking or not. "Bless the food?"

"Yes," I insist. "Like . . . give thanks to the Saints."

"You do this every day?" he asks.

I try not to let my face look pained. "Well, I don't always get food every day, but the days I do, yes. I thank them."

Despite whatever confusion riddles his face, Jericho shrugs and decides to go along with my request anyways. "I wouldn't have pegged you as the religious type, but sure."

I wonder if I'm testing my luck by doing so, but, curious about his recent change of attitude, I choose to lay my hand over his own. His pulse quickens, but to his credit, whatever repulsion or gut instinct he has to rip his hand away, he doesn't give into it. I close my eyes, and say my piece.

"Blessed Saints, we thank you for the provision of this meal and all meals we may be granted today. Watch over our families and keep them safe. May your praises ring amongst the stars," I say, and, with a single, tight squeeze against Jericho's hand to let him know it's over, I open my eyes once more and prepare to pick up my spoon.

In practically the blink of an eye, Jericho is cutting into his food again as if he's been starved out, desperate to shovel the food in his mouth—and while I assumed it is in an attempt to avoid conversation, he opens his full mouth and says, "So . . . what the hell are you eating?"

"I'm not sure. Delta recommended I have one. She loves these things, but the damn seeds always get stuck in my teeth," I add, chuckling to myself.

Suddenly, Jericho's judgment falls somewhere between predatory and observational. I can instantly tell that he's assessing my teeth, and while I've never had much access to dental care, or similar advanced hygienic resources, he doesn't seem too off-put by them. Nonetheless, I start to feel self-conscious about my smile, by how my teeth aren't pearly white or perfectly straight. "What are you looking at?" I demand, though I already know the answer.

"Nothing," he brushes off unsuccessfully. "Just . . . curious about the taste of it."

"Here," I volunteer quickly, collecting a spoonful of fruit and sweetness and handing him the loaded utensil. "You can have some."

Jericho's eyes widen, though I cannot place if they are rageful or struck with ghastly shock. "I can't possibly eat after you."

I suddenly feel exposed by the gesture and retract the spoon, eating the portion instead. Along with it, I swallow down secret shame.

Still, despite his excuse for why he won't take the spoon for himself, I cannot help but think back on how he had written to Ardian and ordered I bathe thrice. Like I was some feral animal. It's something that I might not forget for a long while. "What did you want to speak with me about?" I ask him outright, knowing that if he attempts small talk any longer, we'll both be miserable.

Jericho clears his throat, fist covering his mouth, and then says, "I wanted to commend you for your work so far on the gardens."

"Oh?"

"Yes," he says, eyes on his full plate. "I must admit, I never got to see much of your previous work before hiring you on, but it's . . . quite honestly, breathtaking."

Nothing in his tone makes me think he's flattering me in order to ask me something heinous and wildly offensive—although, I figure every ruler ought to be a stellar actor in their moments of need. *Does he need me for something?*

"Well, thank you. Professionalism and creativity are what I strive to uphold in my work."

"Indeed," he says, sipping on a mug of dark, steaming liquid—coffee, I assume. "And you do well . . . but I want to reduce your workdays."

"What?"

"And your hours," he adds.

Mild panic begins to creep down my spine. "Have I done something wrong?"

"Not in the slightest," Jericho clarifies, his tone unusually reassuring. Truthfully, he sounds nothing like the spoiled king that first took me from my homeland. "Delta tells me you come here in the first part of the late evening and crash. If you end up overexerting yourself, it'll be my fault."

"Since when do you care if something negative is your fault?"

"You know what, fine. I deserve that," he snarls. "But you deserve a break."

"I just started."

"Well . . . stop."

"And what would I do on the days I don't work?"

Jericho dares a soft look in my direction. "Whatever

you'd like, Venus," he whispers.

Something in his words spark a vague memory.

He's playing me. Baiting me to relax and be vulnerable with him just before he pulls the rug out from under me and kills me. Well, I'm not falling for his shit.

"I don't want time. I want answers."

Jericho smiles. "You're not getting any."

"Then you're not getting answers either."

And just as he begins to connect the dots, I throw my food in the air and run from the room as the bowl shatters on the floor.

Without wanting to make the existence of Delta's ruby dagger known outright, I figure the easiest outlet for a near-suicide would be threatening to leap from one of the high terraces.

In the depths of my soul, part of me longs for my theatrics to be genuine. No more nights feeling guilty for being offered a luxurious bed, no more mornings consumed by how much I miss sharing a room with Genny, or even being woken up by Calliope. No more evenings avoiding Jericho at supper, and above all, no more chance encounters with Jericho's deadly visions.

But if I'm going to pull this off—if I'm going to play the long game and kill King Jericho myself—I must come out of this alive.

And if I guessed correctly about the manner of his mother's death, Jericho is sure to come barreling after me—

"No! Venus!" Jericho shouts, but his voice is distant,

meaning I've gained enough ground to start bounding towards my own destruction, and he knows it. "Wait!"

Oddly enough, running away from a man who's had so many people killed for crimes I'm not entirely sure they committed, at full-speed and approaching a steep, fatal fall has never made me feel more alive. My feet kick up behind me faster and faster, sleepwear rippling through the air as I cross into the canopy of one of the balconies.

With enough of a lead in front of him, I hoist myself onto the ledge, my hands grappling onto one of the pillars at my side. The wind has picked up today, and if I'm not careful, one misstep is sure to—

"*WAIT!*" Jericho finally screams out. "*VENUS, PLEASE!*"

I've never heard Jericho use the word please.

His voice is so raw and guttural that it floods me with guilt.

Stumbling out of the hallway and drinking in the sight of me standing at the edge of death, Jericho gasps— genuinely gasps—as if choking on the ghost of air he no longer understands how to breathe. Compassion suddenly takes ownership of him, I hear him say to me, just barely over the sound of the wind, "I need to apologize to you."

Resentment roils around in the depths of my core, but I force myself to turn my head and meet his gaze with a pitiful look. There's distance between us, and while each step Jericho takes towards me to close that gap is labored, seeing him stare me down with unknown desperation begins to cue me in on the most startling possibility of all.

Jericho Morgan is about to bargain with me.

"I thought a king doesn't owe anyone anything," I spit back.

"I was furious when I discovered Tolcher was taking the carriage back to the marshes the day you and him visited the marketplace. But I soon realized that it could've been different—you could've been the one to make a break for it. You could've knocked Tolcher unconscious and blindly rode your way back to your rickety village and to your sisters—"

"That's what you think this is about?"

"No, Venus. I know what this is about, it's about your dad. About me. And I'm sorry, but I cannot give you the answers you're looking for. What I can tell you is, somehow, I think your presence here is . . . making me better."

"*Better*? What a sick joke, Jericho."

But Jericho appears relentless to prove his confession sincere. "I haven't brought anyone in since you got here."

"I know that."

A smile creeps along his mouth. "You were the one hiding behind the curtain—"

"And you know what that little conversation told me about you?" I snarl. "It told me that you do not want to be better, or even decent. You just want to keep living wastefully, pointing your pitchforks and pitting your guards against people that are not even a fraction as appalling as you are."

"*Watch your fucking tone, Venus,*" he sneers.

"You insult me in a letter to your Head Councilman, and yet you think I ought to dine with you? You're the last person I'd want to lay eyes on, let alone share a meal with. And despite your track record for bloodshed, you choose to prolong my death so that you can try and solve me like some puzzle. So I'm taking my death into my own hands," I say. "Unless you can give me one good reason why I shouldn't jump."

Something grisly and feral rumbles to life within Jericho's chest.

For good measure, I lift one foot up off the ground and dangle it just over the ledge.

"Because you *confuse* me!" Jericho almost shouts, eyes wide and breath uneven. "Since the moment I discovered you, I cannot get you out of my head. It's downright maddening. When I'm awake, and have every opportunity to expel you from Broadcove, or be rid of you forever, there's something in my soul that refuses to allow an alternative arrangement. You belong here, and yet, you anger me, you purposely mean to hurt me, and you cause problems for my sanity every day."

"Don't say another word," I demand, though the sound of my words in the open air between us sound frantic.

"But nothing wounds me more than comprehending the possibility of losing you," he forces out, his knuckles white from how hard he makes fists at his side. "It riles me to realize that you'd rather die in poverty than spend another day with me if you were given the choice."

"You just want your control," I counter.

"Obviously," he admits in an almost entitled manner. "But more than that, I think . . . I want to know why you and I seem to be linked. My dreams do not deceive me—ever. They always guide me in the right direction.

And if you jump off that ledge, I will likely tear myself apart never knowing what you and I were supposed to accomplish . . . together."

Something swells within me at the final word.

Together.

For the first time, Jericho begins to scare me. "You're full of shit," I still manage to say.

"No one believes that my visions are real. But not only do you know they're real, you've experienced them. And I want to know why. Why you?"

"Trust me, I don't want any part of it anymore."

"Maybe I've put you in countless positions to hate me, but I want to fix it. All of it." He stops for a moment, positioning his thumb on the edge of his bottom lip. "Venus, I want you to stay here. To live here, to help me."

"*Help* you? But we clearly cannot stand each other—"

"I want you," he interjects with perfect enunciation, as if to carefully make sure I catch every word of his request, "to be a member of my Council."

"Holy *shit*—"

"Would that . . . make you happy?" he asks almost frantically.

"Since when have you cared about my happiness?" I ask, a hesitant challenge to see if his words are truthful.

"Since the moment I realized you were about to jump off that balcony," he instantly replies. "I just . . . I thought all that we were doing to one another was in good fun. I didn't think that—"

"I'd commit to it?" I finish for him.

He nods, and rather than pry at the king's vulnerability more, I choose to absorb his truth instead.

I roll my fingers over my thigh in a repeating pattern as I debate some sort of counteroffer, a bartering chip from deep within my arsenal. "If I'm here, I want my sisters here, too. In the castle. I want you to invite them to Broadcove yourself, and if they decline, I want you to buy them out of their debt and put them somewhere they feel secure."

Jericho blows out a breath that's ragged enough to cue me in on the fact that he'd been holding it in. "You drive a hard bargain, Venom," he says with a sly smile on his face, regaining his usual demeanor.

"Oh, please," I chide, casually jumping down from the ledge, knowing that my job here is done. "You and I both know I'm not asking for much in comparison to what I could."

"And what would that be?"

I try to keep my face from giving away my deep-rooted desires. "I could make you beg me to stay here, to do as you ask of me."

Jericho's returning grin is heart-stoppingly wicked. "Already had it in mind."

Suddenly, Jericho lowers himself to the ground, his left knee tucking underneath him, then his right. He sinks into the floor as he looks up at me. "Is this what you want to see?" Jericho taunts, his blue eyes burning holes into mine. "A king on his knees for a girl from the marshes."

The word *"yes"* must be shimmering within the reflection pool of my eyes because the returning look on my face makes him grimace through a hoarse laugh. "Well, even though you are quite possibly the most frustrating and persistent woman I've ever met, you may be the only one that has a shot at understanding me, and my visions. And for that reason, I can't let you go, despite every instinct within me yelling at me to run as far from you as I can."

Unsure what else to say, he stays there, lowered beneath me. Still kneeling, he traces the path of my legs with his fingers up until my sleepwear covers the rest of me.

My blood heats with something other than wrath when I track his gaze, even more as he breathes out, "Stay, Venus. I don't know how to do this without you."

I find myself crouching down to meet him at an equal level. "Do what, Jericho?" I ask, knowing that there's a critical piece of information I'm missing here.

The look on Jericho's face tells me he refuses to give an inch, but there's a deeper, underlying hopelessness he holds within himself. "Okay." I sigh. "You keep your word about my sisters, and you have a deal. Now tell me, what don't you know how to do without my help?"

He uses his hands to brace himself on the floor, standing to his feet once he feels he has the strength to. Jericho's smirk is a sight of the past, now replaced by a hollow vacancy. No rage, no annoyance, no grin. Nothing at all.

"I leave for Mosacia in two weeks."

Mosacia, my mind screams. *Dangerous. Cold. Conniving.*

"Saints, Jericho, why would you go over there?"

"Diplomacy," he says quickly, though his words don't necessarily convince himself that he's confident about it. "But my reasons for going aren't what I'm concerned about. I'm concerned about you—about preparing you for court relations, personal etiquette, Mosacian customs, and catching you up on Urovian history, of course."

I know better than to ask why.

"As a member of my Council," Jericho continues, "you are to accompany me."

16
Jericho

Bloody Saints, I got Venus to stay.

Not just that, I managed to convince her to join my Council.

Which I suppose isn't so extraordinary after all, given Ardian was its only member, but a win is a win.

And yes, it came at the cost of a little groveling, but I can be quite the actor if I need to, and it is certainly what I'll be telling myself in order to sleep at night and forget that I literally sank to my knees for her—and while on the ground, I traced the lines of her body . . .

Begging aside, though, it also came with the mention of quite a few agenda items.

The problem of her sisters seemed to resolve itself quite easily. Considering Tolcher already paid them a visit—and likely smuggled them some money—I suppose I have nothing to worry about. Was it enough money to maintain livable conditions? Who knows. Let's just hope her sisters are at least half as crafty and diligent as Venus, because otherwise, I'll have to pull some more strings.

There were, of course, other means of busywork, such as commissioning a wardrobe for Venus's needs beyond work. But the biggest predicament of all still remained at large—her father.

Cleverly enough, I've stalled on answering any questions in those regards for the last four days, but now, I'm potentially cornered. I try not to look at Venus, or the way she's desperately fidgeting with her fingers as she sits across from me at the boardroom desk. Instead, I focus my attention onto Ardian, who funnels through his pile of documentations and correspondence letters with a wide, unbreakable smile on his face.

"Jericho, might you like to hear the latest news from our friends across the sea?"

I shut my eyes as he retrieves a piece of parchment from the stack of files. "Just don't do your Victor impression again," I warn him.

Regardless of the tone in my voice, Ardian giggles to himself and clears his throat. Across from me, Venus appears massively intrigued by the first dose of insight on the Mosacian Empire, and, knowing our territories' long-term history, I don't blame her. I'd be quite curious, myself.

"Dearest Jericho," Ardian begins with a newfound lilt in his voice. Ah, yes, his *Harriet* impersonation—I ought to have made a clearer distinction that I despised both. "We are overjoyed to host you, your ambassador, and, as you've informed us, your newest Council member. Apart from whatever distinguished uniforms you feel compelled to pack, our tailors and seamstresses are working around the clock to provide a trousseau for the duration of your stay. As agreed, your company shall remain in Mosacia for the month, and in turn, we shall be delighted to convene for diplomatic engagement on your lands come this time next year. We additionally thank you for providing flexibility to our current circumstances."

"Circumstances?" Venus pops in.

"Harriet's likely with child," I mumble. "And too far along to travel, at that. I figured they'd have stopped making babies by now, but I fear that she's got her poor husband on a leash."

"Hmm," Venus muses, eyes hinting at deeper mischief. "Sounds fun."

Ardian coughs but manages to press on through the end of the letter. "If there are any other modifications for your stay that we need an updated detail on, do write back. Otherwise, we shall see you come the first day of April. Honorable regards, King Victor and Queen Harriet." And with that over and done with, Ardian theatrically lays it face down on the hard surface in front of him. "Well"—he sighs in relief—"where shall we start?"

"What all can you teach me in the next week and a half?" Venus blurts out, her eyes finally drifting in my direction. "I want to know what I'm up against."

"I can assure you," Ardian cuts in, but Venus doesn't break her gaze, "Mosacia is not an enemy. Victor and Harriet are good people. Victor's father passed him the throne willingly when the time came, not through death. The happy couple was right around your ages back then," he feels the need to include, and I watch as Venus's face contorts into something sour.

At least we're spick and span on one thing—*this* alliance is not a happy, romantic union.

"Rest assured, you can trust them and their hospitality," my Head Councilman insists. "And you are not to take their generosity for granted. Are we understood?"

Though I figure he poses the question for Venus, the suffocating silence in response reveals that the sentiment is designed strictly for me—as he and I both secretly know the track record of my bitterness towards their perky little family. "Yes," I force myself to answer.

"Excellent!" Ardian collects himself. "The first thing you should know is that the Seagrave Family is a force to be reckoned with. Good people, yes, but if anyone in Urovia thinks that they stand a chance against the power of the Seagrave Family, they are ignorant fools."

"How so," Venus inquires, and I watch her lean forward in her seat.

Ardian smiles. "Because their dynasty is formidable. The traditional means of passing the throne to the oldest in the bloodline has been a seamless transition of power for the last seven generations. Not only that, but with how many kids they have, even if someone were to take one member out, another one would follow—and trust me, they raise all their children as if they are the true heir."

"You mean with so many kids in competition with one another, there's never been a bloodbath over it? Not even a fistfight or something?" Venus grumbles, though her eyes reveal a humorous sort of curiosity.

I try not to chuckle at the question, because boy, wouldn't that be a sight to see. "No," Ardian replies smoothly, his tone neutral. "The Seagraves uphold a loving household. There's never been any need for violence."

Venus grins like a cat. "I don't buy it for a second."

Though Ardian appears put out by her personal opinion, I find myself unable to keep the laugh buried away in my chest. It bubbles up, tugging the corners of my lips upward, and I try to cover my face with my hand. Then my eyes dare a glance at Venus, and as I regain my composure, I watch her try to fight the slipping grip she has on her own restraint. "Neither do I," I tell her, a reflection of the smile on my face gradually appearing on her own.

Look away, something tells me.

"The fact remains"—Ardian tries roping us back in—"that without just cause, there's no reason that we ought to impose threats on Mosacia, or the Seagrave Family. If the two of you keep relations with them in good form, then the only other main objective you ought to understand," he says, eyes focused on Venus once more, "is that our two territories are divided by wounds from our forefathers and foremothers, not because of recent events. In order to keep from resurrecting those past conflicts that were laid to rest, it is our job, collectively, to preserve peace, dependability, and friendship between their empire and our land. Do you think you can do that?"

Ardian has a soft spot for his homeland, but a secret part of me thinks that his assessment of our territories' division is quite tone-deaf. Meanwhile, Venus stops to mull his question over in her mind. "That depends, what will that require me to do?"

"Play nice with Harriet, for starters," I tell Venus, not bothering to sugarcoat it like Ardian certainly would. "Saints—the moment you walk in, she'll probably have a conniption that I brought a girl with me."

Venus's expression darkens. "Do the Seagraves believe that I'm your lover?" Her eyes sear into mine like bolts of blazing flame. "I would certainly hope you did not give either of them any reason to presume so, considering you and I can barely function well together in a workplace environment."

"I hate to break it to you," I return, "but *this*"—I gesture to the room and to the vast lands beyond the spectator window—"is not your typical work environment. And no, I even went as far as implying you were a male companion as to avoid the rabble. You're welcome."

Venus doesn't appear too thankful, though.

Ardian does not leave room for another word to be said on those arrangements, stating that, "We should briefly discuss our itinerary. First and foremost, Harriet and Victor will want a full update on our territory's status: financials, climate conditions, any unrest, and so forth. We, in turn, will be able to evaluate their empire's strengths and weaknesses, and discuss means of further cooperation. From there, Venus will likely be introduced to the Seagrave children and spend time learning Mosacian customs, culture, and history."

Before she can speak her mind on her profound disinterest on the matter, Ardian holds up a distinguished finger and says, "As Jericho and every other guest allowed into Sevensberg Palace has had to endure."

She groans like a child nearing the edge of throwing

a tantrum, but she resigns herself to crossing her arms and pouting. "Whatever." She sighs. "How many kids are there?"

It brings me great joy to deliver the punchline. "Six. Seven if you count the one she's growing."

Venus practically stomps her feet in agony, knocking her head down into the table and letting it rest there, as if to try and shield Ardian from the exasperation on her face, which fails incredibly. Still, my Head Councilman states that, "Additionally, there's the matter of the dinners and, of course, Harriet will feel particularly obliged to throw some sort of celebration together before we depart back for Broadcove."

Suddenly, Venus's griping mellows out into a chilling sense of quiet. She peels the skin of her face off the hardwood table. "There's . . . a party?" My peripheral vision checks on her, noting that neither one of us dares a full, blatant glance at once another—but knowing what I do about her love for dance, I watch as hope begins to glimmer within her eyes.

"Yes," Ardian answers almost sweetly. "But Her Majesty prefers to surprise her guests of honor with what the party entails. There's always something . . . relatively unique about her gatherings."

"*Odd* is what Ardian means to say," I correct, picking at my nails as I say it.

Venus snickers. "Alright, I'd like to propose a compromise—"

"It doesn't work like that," I try to tell her.

But she unabashedly prepares her offer. "I'll go along with whatever you need me to for this visit, no questions asked, and I'll do so with a smile on my face. In fact, I will *guarantee* good relations with the Seagraves." That little detail seems to draw Ardian in—stupid idiot. I only peer deeper into her eyes, searching for her one condition before she speaks it aloud. "But it'll cost you."

Time stills, and the way she voices that final, contingent phrase strikes a nerve.

She sounds just like her father.

If I thought one Deragon girl was a handful to have in Broadcove, two more sounded like my personal hell.

But my hands were tied since those were the only terms she'd agree to: a docile Venus that would play nice, and not cause problems, in exchange for the extraction of her sisters. She'd explained Tolcher's bare-bones account of her sisters' statuses and expressed concern. And while I didn't necessarily feel her pain, I remember how hard she fought off my men to stay with them—to protect them. It inspired me to at least try and start our makeshift alliance on a high note and reunite the remaining pieces of her family.

Venus had drafted a written list of instructions for the other groundskeepers about what she hopes to see implemented when we return from our brief excursion. Apart from that, along with tasking Delta to throw together a few sets of clothes into a bag, she'd practically sprinted for the carriages out front once I agreed to her conditions.

In the grand foyer, I fasten the buttons of my coat together and tightly wrap a knitted scarf around my neck. While Broadcove is often the warmest part of Urovia, today, it snows, meaning the weather will only grow more violent the farther we travel. It takes all my strength to peel my eyes from Venus as tiny, crystal flakes found a home in the darkness of her hair, but even more strength to tolerate what's likely to be a few sarcastic comments from my Head Councilman as he approaches from behind me.

He sighs happily to himself. "Back to the marshes again?"

"The price I pay for diplomacy, I'm afraid."

Ardian grins with pure, unhinged delight. "I'm not so sure. You didn't put up much of a fight when Venus—"

"If you are meaning to imply," I scoff, "that Venus's role in my Council stems from anything more than a rocky partnership, or my secret means to get what I want from her, I'm afraid you'll be gravely disappointed."

His eyebrows flick upwards, as if to say, *"You keep telling yourself that."*

Still, Ardian finds enough good nature in him to pat me on the back. "Safe travels, my king. I trust you'll be more hospitable to Miss Deragon's sisters than you were to our newest Council member, originally."

I huff a short laugh, already walking towards the carriage as I answer with, "The portrait of charity and innocence."

No more than twenty paces separate me from Venus, now nestled within the cushioned shield of a blanket Delta sent her on board with. Her cheek rests against the frozen window, and her eyes flick towards me as I climb in and shut the door behind me. "Ready?" she asks.

A significant amount of trust has grown between Venus and I since the last time we shared a carriage. Now, there is no need for secret knives, foul words, or physical altercations. So, I tell her, "Let's just hope your sisters aren't nearly as insufferable as you are."

Venus smacks me across the arm for the smile my words draw out of both of us.

17
Jericho

After almost ten hours on the road, I'm offended that our final destination is such a dump.

I wouldn't even go as far as to classify Venus's house as a house at all. Their family home is more like a treehouse—a rectangle box turned vertically that starts at the base of a tree and spans up its grand, jagged trunk. An indented room pokes forward, casting a solid shadow over Venus and I upon the sparse doorstep, and my gut instinct says that Venus doesn't barge through the door because it was left unlocked. It's because they cannot afford such a small security measure.

The first step into the shadowy entry room makes the floorboards creak and groan like an old man, and with the harsh wind blowing outside, I faintly hear the windows along the side of the house bend and bow. A dingy table with four, splintered, wooden seats rests untouched from whenever their last meal was, and only one cramped room rests on the first floor before brittle stairs spiral up towards the second floor.

"Take a seat," Venus instructs me, her strained voice barely reaching my ears. "Over in the shadows. I need them to see me before they see you."

Retreating closer to the vacant fireplace, the used firewood still faintly smoking, I do as she asks of me. Her sisters likely aren't terrifying creatures, but from what Venus detailed about them on the ride over—specifically on how her and Calliope are extremely protective of the younger one—Geneva—if my presence threatens either of them before Venus can explain our presence, it'll be a headache.

"Genny? Cali?" Venus calls out, her hands cupping around her mouth in hopes of amplifying her voice. "It's me. It's Venus. I know it's late, but I'm here. Come downst—"

From what little I remember outside of Venus that initial night, the first figure that comes pounding down the stairs is not the one that clung relentlessly to her side. While Venus stands in the main room, where light reveals half of her frame, I linger in the darkness, observing the first reunion from slightly afar.

"Venus!" she cries out.

She barely has, *"Cal,"* out of her mouth before their bodies smash together in the tightest embrace I've ever witnessed in my life. Her older sister clings to Venus as if they'd been pasted together.

"Saints, Venus! We were so worried about you!"

"Me?" she cries out. "I feared that the two of you weren't eating, that you were working yourselves to death—" Suddenly, Venus becomes aware of her other sister's absence. "Where's Genny?"

"Sleeping," Calliope replies. "Long day at the shoppe, work keeps her mind at bay."

"To avoid dwelling on what? Me?"

"Sure," she answers unconvincingly. "Oh, Venus, I'm so glad you're back. When that guard came and told us what happened, we were so relieved. We were worried sick that King Jericho had claimed your life, too—"

I shift my body weight to try and sit more comfortably on the stone lip, but the scuffling sound gives me away, and just as Calliope angles her head towards the darkness I take shelter within, Venus steps in front of her line of vision. "Don't scream," she whispers with an intensity that almost jolts me.

"What do you mean—"

And when Venus steps aside and reveals my presence, Calliope goes ghastly still.

"You *bastard*," she sneers, and from the way Venus spoke of Calliope as cheery and harmless, she certainly has the ability to bite back.

"It's good to formally meet you, too, Calliope," I remark plainly, running a hand through my hair in efforts to charm her into submission. "Venus was right. You are rather lovely."

Venus glares at me in a way that promises a beating later, and a secret part of me hopes that it stems from jealousy and not from flattering her older sister. Especially when Calliope begins to blush in silent response.

"I do apologize," I continue, taking careful steps towards the pair of ladies, "for the last time we saw one another. I could've made my intentions with your sister clearer. That is my error."

Calliope levels out her face, as if sobering herself enough to fully receive the answer to her question of, "And those intentions are?"

"Oh." I sigh with simmering joy. "Only the worst things you can imagine."

Venus does not find my joke hilarious in any measure, and neither does Calliope.

"So, why are you two really here?" Calliope further interrogates, crossing her arms and pursing her lips. "As happy as I am to know you're safe, I hold true to my promise. Nothing harmful comes to Genny, even if that means I kick you both out of this house."

I expect Venus to square her shoulders and stare down Calliope with the fire of a thousand suns—but Venus appears impressed. Pleased, even. Deragon women are strange.

"That won't be necessary," Venus answers with a smile. "Because we're here to get you out."

Calliope means to ask more, thoroughly intrigued and hopeful for what this conversation entails specifically, but a faint, unsettling sound distantly catches all of our attention—the sound of retching.

Geneva must be awake, after all.

Venus starts running, but Calliope hightails it in front of her, blocking her path as much as she can manage before Venus ultimately overpowers her. She grips Calliope by the wrist that stretches out towards the railing and with both hands, and she twists the skin in opposite directions. Calliope howls in pain, but Venus proceeds, practically stepping over her older sister now slumped on the floor.

Deciding to follow after her, I figure this new development ought to be good.

Then, Calliope stands up, bracing a hand out in front of me. "Don't go up there."

I've always liked a challenge, always taking slight, secret pleasure in the midst of drama. Everybody does, and I don't bother to feel guilty about it as I once more press forward, navigating around Calliope's lackluster body blockade and praying I don't get an atrocious splinter from the wooden handrail, muttering, "You certainly are not in a position to tell me what to do."

Offended, Calliope begins trudging up the stairs behind me, our shared steps creaking beneath our shoes. Luckily, by the time I reach the top floor and my eyes find the bathroom door left ajar, the sound of vomit hitting the toilet bowl has temporarily ceased, replaced by heaved tears and hushed words of compassion—both sounds setting me on edge. I mean, Saints, I think I'd rather hear the vomit again.

"Venus!" Calliope calls out behind me. "I couldn't stop him—"

"Stop who?" Geneva's weak voice flutters down the hall.

"*No one*," Venus hisses loudly, providing one last warning if I wish to heed it.

Which, of course, I don't. To hell with manners and personal space, I'm not their villain anymore. If anything, I'm here to be heroic and get them out of this rundown hellhole. Geneva will have to see me again one way or another, so what's the harm in now?

Two seconds of staring into that depressing, tattered

bathroom tells me that I should've listened to Calliope after all.

Stomach acid drips in a line off Geneva's bottom lip, and her eyes are ringed in red. She senses my stature between the doorframe of the room, and while Venus continues to rub a consoling circle along her back, the expression on Geneva's face—the pure contemplation of rage and ruin there—tells me that no amount of time or comfort will ease her pain.

And immediately, I know why.

"We begged the guard not to say anything when he came," Calliope tells Venus calmly. "Genny wanted to tell you herself. She had told me you knew about the boy already, the one you told me to shut up about the morning you were taken, and—"

Venus's eyes go wide, and she flashes me a concerned look that tells me, *"You've stepped in it, now."* Still, even in the heat of the moment, the stress vividly showing on her face, she presses a tender kiss on her little sister's shoulder. "Genny," she croons, dropping into a seated position at her side with calculated slowness. "Are you—"

Geneva, still poised over the toilet, begins to sob, nodding in confirmation.

"Don't cry," Venus begs, wrapping her arms around Geneva as she begins to wail hopelessly. "Genny, please. It's going to be alright. The sickness means you're healthy." I begin to backpedal out of the room, unsure of how much longer I can stand the anguish enveloping the room. "It means that the baby is, too—"

"But he's not here to do this with me!" Geneva cries out, spitting into the toilet as if to cap off her statement with an exclamation mark. "I'm to mother a child that will never get to know the light and love of their father. And I never even got to tell him," she says, attempting to cradle herself for an extra layer of emotional support. "Kurt will never know that he was in line to be such a wonderful father . . ."

Kurt.

That name . . .

Oh, fuck me.

I know where a grieving woman's thought process wanders off to next; I've seen it many times before, and knowing Venus's natural tendency towards vengeance, I can only imagine the frightful depths of Geneva's despair. I'm almost out of the bathroom completely when Geneva's identifying finger points right in line with me, convicting me to where I cannot peel my feet off the floor to take another step. And even if I could, Calliope has me boxed in.

"And *you* took him from me!" Geneva roars.

All three Deragon sisters angle their eyes towards me, fury and fixation barreling into me.

You see, this is why I choose to eliminate the entire family of the guilty, so no mourners are left behind.

But even as the thought creeps in, something new and unsettling also finds its way into my bloodstream. The nerves in my arms pulse and tighten as if I were going into cardiac arrest, and then, it filters into my chest, weighing over my lungs. Drawing breath becomes labored, and I hate myself for how it feels.

To experience remorse.

18
Jericho

After picking herself off the bathroom floor, Geneva requested a private conversation with Venus in their shared room—likely to rip her a new one about why I'm here with her, and then promptly explain the details Venus missed since she came to Broadcove—so she obliged. Worse, however, is that her departure leaves me alone with Calliope.

Not that Calliope even holds a candle to Venus's bitterness, but blood often runs true. I've seen it in the way I've slowly transformed into my father.

Unsure of what to do with me hanging around, Calliope busies herself by making me a cup of coffee, which she'll likely spit in if I don't keep watching her every move. She's conventionally beautiful, with a pretty, round face and skin that I'd describe as golden. Men in the Noble District likely hire Calliope for her face rather than her voice, but my instant drawbacks hold true.

First of all, I could never maintain a romance with

a singer. My voice ought to always be the loudest and most widely received. And secondly, when women know they're beautiful, they either develop a softer disposition to pair with their looks or they begin to think too highly of themselves. Calliope belongs to the former category, and it dulls the fun in teasing her. Whereas someone with more of a bite, like Venus—

Jericho, were you seriously about to rationalize why Venus might secretly be the more attractive sister? Get a grip.

After three minutes of silence, that feels more like twenty, I watch Calliope pour the stark liquid out of the coffee pot and into a cracked pottery mug. Considering the state of the house, and how my drink doesn't steam, I know better than to ask for sugar or cream—they likely don't have any.

Now, forced to sit across from her at their pitiful excuse for a dining table, sipping cold coffee and hating every second of it, I say to her if only to combat the dismal quiet, "Calliope. That's a rather lovely name. Never heard one like it."

"It means beautiful voice," she murmurs, her dirty fingers clinking against her own cup. "I don't suppose you've heard of me throughout the Noble District."

"I regret to inform you that I haven't," I remark. "But perhaps your talents will be much more appreciated in Broadcove."

Calliope seems agreeable, or she's at least mellowed out since I let Venus and Geneva isolate themselves from me for a while. "The guard that came by never mentioned we'd have to leave."

"Believe me, if I had my way, I'd gladly leave you

both here. One Deragon girl is enough already." Calliope smiles at that, and the human gesture makes me reassess my initial perception of her. "But . . . Venus has a point. Especially knowing what we do now about the little one."

Something about how I reference Geneva in that way makes Calliope cringe—as if I wasn't mentioning her at all, but rather the babe growing within her. "I'm glad we're leaving the marshes, and I'm a little surprised that us leaving is Venus's decision. This house . . ."

"Is a piece of shit?"

Calliope giggles. "Yes. It really is. But that's not what I meant to say. I just mean . . . as glamorous as it may sound for me to work as a hired singer for Noble parties, or Genny as a chocolatier uptown—we only managed to keep this home because of Venus. After our parents died, her employment was always the most regular. But it was also the most grueling."

Without letting my face show it, I think back on the vision I had where Venus confessed her hidden desire to dance—to perform. Then, I remember the time she shared how she'd taken up the skills of a topiary when her father had become too weak to continue. And it makes me secretly wonder if Venus ever resented Calliope over the years for it—for getting to take up the arts and not be forced into the role of carrying on her father's legacy before he even went to the grave.

"She'd subject herself to such hell for us. The extreme weather, her demanding employers, but worst of all, her high standards for taking care of us. Though I keep it to myself, I think it's because the moment she took over for Father's workload, and then we lost him," Calliope whispers, her attention darting vaguely in my direction without truly looking into my eyes. "Venus convinced herself that she had to *become* him to save us. So she did."

I don't remember the last moment I breathed since Calliope began talking.

Sadness swims in her brown eyes. "I just worry that she's lost touch with herself because of it."

Finally, sensing her window of opportunity to keep conversing about Venus, Calliope clasps her hands together and settles deeper into her uncomfortable kitchen chair. "Alright, King," she drawls. "How about we have a chat about what's *really* going on here?"

Ah, here we are. The typical eldest sibling lecture to a perspective mate. "You mustn't worry about me," I assure her. "I'm no threat to her heart or her virtue."

Calliope frowns at that, the first sign of confusion or distaste I've yet to see from her. "Her virtue," she phrases as a statement, but I know that there's a secret search for clarification beneath.

Saints, this is not what I wish to be discussing with another woman, let alone Venus's sister.

"Yes, her virtue," I repeat. "You know, her chastity, her . . . maidenhood?"

That's when Calliope starts laughing. Although snorting is the better description. "Ha! You must be joking," she nearly howls, slamming her hands down on the table in hysterics. "Look, I don't know how things work in whatever fancy schmancy land you're from, but here in the marshes, a woman's body is her greatest bartering tool."

Suddenly, I remember the precise instant Venus had

first mentioned bartering to me, just before visiting the royal marketplace. My stomach tightens at the memory.

"Do we hope for love?" Calliope continues. "Sure! But believe me, a woman like Venus is a hot commodity to everyone in the marshes and the Makers District, supposed *virtue* intact or not," she finishes.

A sudden predatory sensation courses through my bloodstream. "Everyone?"

"Oh yes," she drawls, as if this is the juiciest gossip in the territory and she's sitting on a gold mine. "Venus never talks to us about it, but Genny and I know. Most of what we consider luxury that Venus brings home typically comes at a price that only Venus has been brave enough to pay. And for that, we're thankful. She'll never catch any judgment from us about it, whatsoever. We just hope she's not prey to any violence or presumptuous people who've heard about her reputation."

I find myself leaning in closer to Calliope, my hands curling until my nails dig into the wooden table. "Are there any people she frequents that you're concerned about?"

"Genny mentioned that Venus had previously worked extra hours for the Carrowers. In fact, the day you arrived, I had volunteered her for an extra hour in their garden in exchange for some carrots, which she brought home for Genny after we learned about the death of her . . . Kurt," she says carefully. "The couple has a son around Venus's age, Drue. He's a simple man and all, but Venus could do better. Truthfully, intuition tells me that Venus settles for people like Drue in romantic situations so that she can remain in control. She's certainly the facilitator out of us girls." She chuckles, as if her statement hadn't just shot an arrow through my chest.

Venus . . . reduced to the worth of carrots from yards she helped cultivate?

I want to set this house on fire—

"King Jericho?" Calliope interrupts.

I try to shake off the righteous anger from my mind. "Yes?"

"Was Kurt innocent?"

Embarrassed and convicted by my answer, I sigh. "I'm afraid so."

I figure that our conversation is over, until Calliope adds, "Was our father?"

The pain on Calliope's face drains the strength from my bones. She deserves to know the truth—Venus and Geneva, too. But the cost of telling the truth is too steep. Instead, I offer her what I can for now.

"It's complicated."

19
Venus

Two minutes ago, I heard Calliope laughing her head off, and considering her one job was to distract Jericho from further upsetting Genny, it doesn't exactly thrill me to know he's likely charming the skirts off her.

"I'm sorry about him," I say to Genny as I tuck her back into bed. "Had I known you were awake, I would have warned you."

I remember the way my sister cowered behind my frame when he arrived in our town, and rightfully so. The man killed our father—my own dreams have confirmed that much—and when Jericho's attention poised fully on her that fateful, first meeting, he knew nothing about the lovestruck girl who'd lost the man who meant everything to her the night before.

No, all Jericho saw in her—in any of us—was poverty and weakness.

"Venus," Genny whimpers.

I reach for the empty bucket I stashed by the side of

her bed, raising it up towards her mouth. But she shakes her head. My next, knee-jerk reaction is to grab a cold washcloth and lay it along her head, or retrieve a glass of water for her from the kitchen—

But Genny places a sweat-glistened hand over mine. "How can you work with him?"

As I helped transition Genny from the grimy bathroom to her bed once the worst of her sickness leveled out, I explained to her our arrival and schedule for the trek back to Broadcove. After whittling down Jericho's strength, he assured me that Genny and Cali would have their own living quarters, plenty of food, and would no longer need to worry about finding employment.

Then, I explained that, despite this brief family reunion, Jericho and I would be leaving for Mosacia in less than two weeks' time. I knew nothing about the land, the royal Seagrave Family, or their subjects—all I knew going into it was I'm supposed to play nice.

So long as my service in Jericho's Council held true, his arrangement to provide for my sisters would remain as well.

"To be truthful with you, Genny," I confess, stroking her hair tenderly, "I don't know. It's still new, but there are some days where he's driven me so mad, I've contemplated putting myself out of the misery of dealing with him. And yet, no matter how irritated we are with each other, I at least have the reassurance of knowing my work protects you and Calliope. That's worth every sacrifice in the world."

"What do you have to do?" she asks, her gentle voice lowering as if she fears that the walls have ears of their own. "Do you . . . I mean, you don't . . . kill for him, right?"

My eyes flare and my heart sinks into my stomach. "Saints, no! I would never kill anyone, Genny." I scoff.

"Not even Jericho?" she challenges, her precious face contorting into a dark sense of disbelief.

"If that Morgan Dynasty monster ever comes within arm's length of me, I will kill him myself," I had told Genny once.

Stronger than almost any other morale in my bones, my primary objective in life has always been to shield my baby sister from the horrors of the world Calliope and I had to navigate once both of our parents were gone. For Calliope, that meant playing house and being the optimistic, makeshift mother figure that woke us up in the morning, cooked breakfasts, and sang prettily to herself. If the wildlife here hadn't already died out from the horrid weather conditions and sparse harvests, I'd consider Calliope cheery enough to befriend bluebirds and communicate with cows and horses like they were her closest companions.

Which left me to continue taking up my father's passed torch in every remaining aspect of my life.

I became the family grump that wanted ten more minutes of sleep in the mornings because my body ached so badly. That glowered at Calliope when she volunteered me to do more work that would bring home more food and resources when we needed it. I was forced to get my hands dirty, to deal with snobby employers and blistering temperatures, and submitted myself to the earth day in and day out. Once that work was done, I'd then partake in whatever physical intimacy I could find in the Makers

District to convince myself I didn't hate my life.

But I did. I hated my life.

Although, I never hated my sisters, especially not Genny. If anything, they were what kept me alive. So, when Jericho and the King's Guard came to find me, I did not fight back against his guards because I feared death for myself, but because I refused to let death come for Geneva and Calliope, too.

"Only if I have to," I finally answer.

That's when I let Genny's eyes catch sight of my pocketed blade from Delta just before I bury it into the folds of my coat again.

But we both know that's a lie—I'd keep my promise to her, and I'd do it gladly. All in due time. We just don't say so aloud.

20
Jericho

Despite my efforts to lure the Deragon sisters into the carriage and have our coachman carry us through the night, Venus insisted that I spend one night in her shack of a home—an equalizer for how I had insensitively barged in on Geneva. She'd already put her sister to bed, and at any rate, Venus had discretely bid our escort and the horses goodnight before we even entered the house, directing them to a rest area back in the District that would provide them food, water, and a place to sleep.

Calliope eventually came up with a lame excuse for why she needed to dismiss herself from our conversation and go to bed, but I was already tiring of our exchange anyhow, so I certainly wasn't offended. But then, Venus descended the stairs, not to tell me to have sweet dreams, or to apologize for the drama this evening brought, but to say that *she* was going to sleep and to make myself comfortable on the couch.

The cushions may as well have been cotton sacks full

of cement.

I tried to sleep, believe me. But the longer I laid there, something began to eat away at my skin—and to my great surprise, it wasn't bed bugs.

It was a vision with no voices, no dialogue, no context. Just a mental picture of a plain house I'd never seen before, but one that my body felt a gravitational pull towards the moment I set my feet on the cold floor and walked out the door of the Deragon household.

After a fifteen-minute hike uphill, and two humiliating spills from stepping on patches of black ice on the paved road, I laid eyes on the house in question, with a satisfactory grin I cannot seem to smother.

The Carrowers' place is quaint and quiet this time of the night. I am unaware of just how much this family accumulates in wealth, and while the size of this place is smaller than my typical enjoyment, anything is better than hearing my teeth chatter in the tiny icebox that Venus calls home.

Searching for an easy access point, knowing their front door is bound to be locked, I notice the faint indentation of a door within their back fence, the lines peeking out at me amidst the dim moonlight. Twigs snap and dead leaves crunch under my feet, splitting as my rage begins to fester and my fists clench.

A bold, black latch waits for me, and when I cross the space needed to get there, I lift it up and push the wood slowly, as if to not incite any bothersome creaking that would give away my whereabouts to anyone, street rodents included. Once in the yard, I find myself in the middle of a dark, cobblestone pathway that runs along the side of the house, and my foot knocks painfully into one of the iron legs of what appears to be a park bench in the patchy shadows. A swear escapes my lips, and I crouch down to console what will certainly be a bruise on my toe by morning.

I force myself to continue onward. As the grassy knoll enters my view, I take a gander at what Venus's services earned the Carrowers family, which looks to be nothing but fresh mulch, padded dirt, and the slow resurgence of weeds Venus probably spent hours pulling. Looking at all that she did for them, despite her recent absence and her new residency in Broadcove, I can only imagine what the inside of her hands feels like: calloused, hard, worn. Everything that a fine lady's hands shouldn't have to be. It just feels . . . wrong.

The patio door unlocks when I go to slide it open, giving me no struggle. *Idiots.*

Pleased with my good fortune, I step inside their home with no fear for my safety, given I hear the head of the household snoring heavily from two rooms away. No domestic animals seem to take residence here, thank the Saints, because a rabid dog or a mewling cat would certainly convict me for being here at such a miserably late hour. Failure wouldn't be getting caught by the Carrowers, though. True failure would mean word about this getting back to Venus.

Interior wise, the Carrowers' place is a slate of stony gray with light undertones. Modern furniture sits staged in a sort of precision that feels like the house hosts no one at all—cold, in a way—and the only burst of color comes from a potted plant that wilts pathetically on their kitchen countertop.

I snicker to myself. *Moronic fools can't even water a damned plant without Venus's help.*

There lies a set of stairs with one isolated room that I make out from the kitchen's vantage point, and, not bothering to make additional observations about the rest of the unassuming house, I cross the first floor and ascend the steps with a tiptoed urgency, approaching what must be Drue's bedroom with an electrifying rush of adrenaline.

Unlike the back sliding door, Drue's door is locked. At least someone in this house isn't irredeemably stupid. Assessing the simple mechanism within the silver knob, however, I merely reach into my coat pocket for Venus's travel-size utility knife she first threatened me with—the one I had quietly taken ownership of once I knocked her out—and pick the lock. I slither into the room with no need for hushed movements or careful footsteps, and the young man sits straight up at the sound of my intrusion. In the dark, I hear him stumble for something to protect himself, and before I entertain the idea of him grabbing a weapon or reaching for something comical like a nightside lamp, I flick on the light switch.

I almost laugh aloud.

Saints, he's absolutely ordinary looking.

What was Venus thinking?

"Who the hell are you?" this Drue character bellows, puffing himself up to look like he could take me in a fight. Not a chance.

Despite not being in my royal uniform, I forget that the *U. Herald* doesn't reach the Makers District anymore, so aside from eyewitnesses the night I brought Venus to Broadcove with me, no one knows what I look like, including Drue—and I suppose that's a good thing.

Because in masterful silence, I stroll towards him, forcing my demeanor to appear as nonthreatening as humanly possible, even offering him a dashing smile.

And then, with all my might, I punch Drue Carrowers square in the mouth.

21
Venus

As much as I love Calliope, she never fails to be insufferably happy in the mornings. Some days, it's a saving grace, like on mornings when I'd be running late for work. But today, her liveliness may land her in hot water not only with me, but with Jericho, who I hear grumbling viciously back at Calliope downstairs.

"Do you hear them, too?" I ask Genny, trying not to laugh when Calliope counters a verbal blow he hurls at her by calling him a *"pretentious, grumpy bastard."*

Genny laughs, guarding her stomach with a protective hand. "Yes, and that's *Calliope* talking," she points out. "I can't even imagine the vile arguments you two get into."

We fall into giggles at that, trying to stifle the sound enough to keep our laughter from fluttering down the stairs and into their ears. But it's to no avail, and I hear Jericho's heavy, thundering footsteps come trudging up the stairs—a deaf man could hear the way he marches. I almost expect him to kick the door in or something dramatic enough to command our attention and prove himself to be a strong, inescapable force; but he merely stops before the bedroom door. I picture him putting fisted hands on his hips like an irritated parent.

"You won't be laughing when I leave your sorry asses here. The carriage leaves in ten."

I chuckle, whispering to Genny just loud enough for Jericho to hear me, "He's just as pushy as Calliope. I bet our driver is still snoring away—"

With almost comedic timing, I hear the horses that pulled our carriage neigh at each other out in the street before the coachman says something muffled and offers them an apple each.

Dammit. Jericho likely flips me off from the other side of the door for my distrust, then retreats back into the main den towards Calliope.

Only once our surroundings make no sound does Geneva dare a brave glance in my direction. "What will you do?"

"What do you mean?" I ask her, untangling myself from my bed quilts for what may very well be the last time. The movement prompts a distant guilt within me for some reason.

"When you kill King Jericho," Genny finishes, speaking softer than before. "What will you do afterwards? What will become of us?"

Secretly, I take note of the way Genny says *when*, not *if*. As serious as the subject may be, her faith in my capabilities comforts me. Still, I try not to allow the lack of definitive answers show so obviously on my face. "I won't be killing *anyone* until I know that, after he's out of the way, you and Calliope will be secure. The baby, too."

Geneva blushes at that, and the gesture cuts deep into my soul, my memories. In this moment, Genny becomes the perfect replica of our mother—nurturing and selfless and . . . happy. Despite our declining wealth and the growing, negative circumstances, she was happy.

But even as she looks at her womb with love and adoration, Genny sighs. "And you? Who makes sure that you're safe?"

I walk over to her bed, pressing a kiss on her temple. "I do."

By the time we reach Broadcove, the servants have been dismissed from their daily duties, but that does not keep them from welcoming us back.

With far more charity and giddy smiles than what they greeted me with when I first arrived here nearly a month ago, the culinary workers and ladies' maids beam with delight as my sisters disembark the carriage. Calliope matches their warm hospitality with a wide grin and a sing-songy, "Hello! Hello!"

Behind them, Ardian and Delta stand arm in arm, the former politely introducing himself to my sisters as they pass by him and venture off to their allocated apartments along the East Wing, and the latter winking wryly at me—just once.

My dagger burns a hole in my pocket.

"Lovely kin, Madam Council," Ardian murmurs sweetly as I go to shake his hand.

"Madam *Council*?" Delta blurts beside him.

"New development, yes," Jericho cuts in curtly.

Delta snorts, pointing between Jericho and me. "But you loathe one another."

"Which means when they *do* agree on something, it's quite the achievement," Ardian returns.

Jericho's suppressed, conniving smile awakens something in my chest, and I feel it faintly stir. Like a fish swimming in circles.

I almost go as far as to consider the look on his face to be handsome. Dreadfully so.

But I smile back at him, letting fresh color flush within my cheeks—letting him know that I see him that way, albeit in his rare moments of generosity. People I've known in life have told me before that when I smile, without restraint, a dimple pearls on one side of my mouth. I feel it, now, and I feel Jericho's attention dart towards it. He suddenly stills, uncertainty shimmering in his blue eyes.

"I know you think the marshes are my home," I dare to tell Jericho, but only loud enough for him to hear. "Or that it's a place back there in the winter night. But my home . . . my home is with my sisters. And I cannot thank you enough for letting me go back for them." Then, before I allow myself to drink in his reaction, I pull back and turn to Ardian. "Goodnight, gentlemen," I bid with a frantic nod, moving swiftly and gracefully up the crescent-bent staircase and through the expanse of dark hallways.

Delta arrives at my door no more than ten minutes after

my rapid exit, briefly knocking before practically diving into the room and shutting the door behind her as if she were being chased by a monster.

Panting against the door, Delta stares at me, teal eyes wide. "What the hell was *that*?"

"I don't know what you're talking about," I lie.

Delta wipes imaginary sweat from her forehead. "The look you gave him, the smile he gave you. The deliberate eye-banging you two were forcing my uncle and I to endure—"

"The *what*—"

"Please, Venus." Delta groans, sloppily running over to me and jumping on the bed in flamboyant despair. "Please tell me that you are not falling for his bait."

To say that I did not find Jericho's smile briefly enchanting would be regrettably false. However, one little smile will certainly not sink my mental resilience— no way. Yet, her comment implies something deeper— that Delta has either personally experienced the sour end of humoring Jericho's charms, or that she has seen how his wiles bewitch other women of his interest. "What are you trying to ask me, truly?"

Delta eyes me in a way that makes her wonder if I'm genuinely not connecting the dots.

I roll my eyes and groan. "Because I'm not screwing him, if that's what you're afraid of."

"Thank the Saints," she says, releasing a ragged breath. She sits up for a moment, looking around the room and debating with the walls whether or not she should speak her mind further. "I guess what I'm getting at is . . . you're going to be gone for an entire month. Just you and Jericho."

"Correct."

"Perhaps you need someone to keep you company, and to keep you two in line—"

Oh, I see what's going on here. "You want to tag along."

"I know they have servants that can care for you just as wonderfully over there, but for what it's worth, no one knows you like I do," she says, her hands lingering over top of mine. "Well, maybe your sisters. But we've spent the last month together, becoming close and all."

It's a sweet sentiment, really, but I flash her a knowing look and she sulks. "Alright, *and* I'd love to see my homeland. I haven't been there since Ardian moved us out here when I was seven, and I haven't seen the Seagraves since the last time they visited Urovia. I've never been allowed to go overseas and see them, so it would mean the *world* to me if—"

"No one ever let you cross the Damocles?"

Delta shakes her head. "Merrie would always offer, but Jericho always made a stink about sharing the boat with a girl."

"Then you can come with me out of spite. Besides, I haven't the slightest idea how to dress myself up to royal standards, so you'll certainly come in handy."

Delta immediately kicks off her celebrations, full of dancing and thrashing and leaping around the room like a madwoman. Kicking off her shoes in different directions and undoing the tie wrapped around her dark hair, she flies around me like a bird who's been freed from its cage—and I wonder, in that moment, just how much of a gift this trip truly is for her. Spinning and twirling and catapulting herself onto the furniture, just to stand and cheer and thank the Saints for a *damn jailbreak*, in her words. When the intensity of her revelry catches up with her tired body, she travels back to her previous spot beside me, and I hear her heartbeat pound violently within her chest. "Do you still have the dagger I gave you?"

"Yes."

"Good. You're going to need it."

"Are the Mosacians that bad?"

Delta guffaws. "Not a chance. They'll love you! In fact, I almost worry how much they're going to love you."

"Why's that?"

Delta closes the space between us, her legs grazing mine and our foreheads touching in an almost sisterly embrace. She looks down at the blade again, intentionally avoiding my eyes as she speaks. "Because Jericho is a jealous man."

I feel my blood turn cold in my veins. "What?"

"His compulsion for bloodshed may have mellowed out, but I promise you, his obsessive nature will soon fixate on something else—like lust." She faintly drags an indolent finger along my jaw. "And considering how I caught Jericho smiling at you," she finishes. "I have no doubt in my mind that you will be his next target."

22
Venus

Departure day sneaks up on me like a thief in the night.

Delta finished packing our trunks early this morning and fetched Tolcher from his post to load our luggage onto our designated vessel in Honeycomb Harbor. The first thing she said to me when I woke up was, "Tolcher says we're sailing on a ship called *Crystal Wrath*. Isn't that epic?"

Meanwhile, Tolcher's way of saying "hello" first thing in the morning, as I drift towards the boardroom for one last Council meeting is, "Your little friend packed as if she were going away for a year, not a month."

"Travel jitters," I return. "She and Ardian migrated here from Mosacia, so that makes this her first time visiting her homeland in . . ."—I do the math—"wow, around fifteen years."

Tolcher's poor hands bear grip marks from where he clutched the handles of our heavy luggage, and just as

I attempt to apologize for the discomfort, he wipes his hands along his dark slacks—as if realizing that hauling all our baggage was the least he could do for Delta. "Well, good for her. And good for you, you know, finally wearing something other than overalls."

Delta lent me one of her day gowns: a black, tea-length dress that reminds me of the dark fairies from childhood storybooks, cinched at the bodice and flowing from the waist downward. Although, this piece was certainly built to hug thicker curves than what I currently possess. Sure, it falls off my bones in a natural pleating, but it is evident that it does not fit completely. The squared-off neckline covers the point where my cleavage begins to dip downward, and the sleeves cover my shoulders, stretching all the way to my wrists in a tailed trim. Delta attempted to pair the dress with scarlet heels, but having insisted that my first time wearing high heels not be on a rocking boat, Delta begrudgingly let me get away with ordinary, onyx flats. However, she insisted on some sort of red accent, applying paint to my lips before I could give my consent and sending me on my way.

"I feel like a noblewoman," I find myself saying like it's a bad thing.

"The red lip is a nice touch," Tolcher points out. "Jericho will like it."

My stomach lurches. "What's that supposed to mean?"

"Only that he'll be pleased with you for wearing Urovian colors," he assures me, already reading the unease in my posture. "Ardian, too. Nothing . . . romantic."

Which reminds me. "When will I get to meet that wife of yours? I am starting to believe that she isn't real."

Henry laughs at that. "Nadine writes for the *U. Herald*, meaning she never has to leave the house until it's delivery day for one of her articles. I've tried bringing her here—her and Ivanna both—but they find this place to be far too high maintenance for their individual endurance. I don't particularly blame them."

I file that detail about the *U. Herald* under my mental category of things to inquire about later, offering Tolcher a delicate smile. "I shall come to your house then," I suggest, though now that I'm hearing the words aloud, I seem to have rudely invited myself over. "If you'll have me, of course," I amend. "I'd love to meet her."

Tolcher nods. "First thing when you return home next month?"

"I promise," I reply.

We both wave to one another in farewell, turning opposite of each other to go return to our own, delegated business. But I allow my steps to loiter, soaking up Henry's presence for as long as I'm allotted until his warmth no longer hangs over the hallway.

Two hallways down, the boardroom door rests cracked, just enough to catch the daylight streaming through the glass windows. I lightly press my weight into it before revealing myself fully. I say, "Hello" to Ardian, who simply murmurs my name back in a quiet welcome.

When I brave a glance at Jericho, he stares me down with perplexment—angling his attention to the dress Delta gave me.

It only occurs to me now that this is the first time I've worn a dress in front of him.

"Please," Ardian cuts in, his voice unusually

congenial and upbeat, "have a seat, Lady Venus. We have important business to attend to before the two of you leave Broadcove."

I seem to have been so focused on avoiding eye-contact with Jericho that I didn't care to fully observe the boardroom's most noticeable change. Normally, the eight chairs that typically adorn half of the expansive desk we convene at remain empty.

But today, they're all filled with people I've never laid eyes on, all of whom wear religious robes and the Saints' emblem on a chain around their necks.

"First of all," Ardian says by way of greeting, carrying a small stack of paperwork in his hands as he takes his seat at the boardroom meeting table. "I shall miss you both dearly. Secondly, I'm under the impression that my niece is venturing with you both," he remarks in a manner that appears questionable, unaware of the statement's factuality.

"I'm afraid your niece is quite the beggar," I joke.

"And, it seems, *you're* quite the doormat," Jericho interjects.

"You are the most insufferable person to have a conversation with, sometimes," I quip, unbothered by the presence of the surrounding Holymen as I say it.

Jericho grins. "Respectfully, I couldn't give a—"

I make a *zip* sound through my teeth, sharply gesturing my hand to mimic a zipper in the middle of his rude counterstatement. Jericho's responding glare makes my toes curl in an almost sensual sort of joy, and our nameless guests raise their brows at one another in surprise. "As I was saying," I begin again, my voice stiff in my throat, "Delta is coming with us. If I'm supposed to embark into enemy lines, I could use at least *one* ally."

Ardian shakes his head in dismay as I send a pointed look towards Jericho. "No, no, *no*," he says as calmly as he can manage while still informing me that he's upset. "That is not how Urovia needs to present itself, and again, Mosacia is *not* our enemy."

"Maybe not," Jericho murmurs under his breath. "But maybe *I* do not wish to present a false union alongside someone who spends every waking moment trying to exasperate me."

"It doesn't *matter*," Ardian snarls, eyes wild and face tense with fury. "You two—whatever this partnership may be—are the face of this territory the moment you cross the Damocles. On Urovian soil, you two can bicker and bitch at each other all you like, but if you're to stay in the palace of people who could've wiped out the Morgan Dynasty the moment Merrie died, you will behave."

I dare not look at Jericho, but something in my gut tells me that at the mention of his mother's name, he tenses up. His muscles brace for some invisible attack or accusation, and despite my revolving distaste for the man sometimes, my heart secretly hurts for Jericho. I've never seen Ardian stoop to the level of bringing up the dead just to make a point.

I almost anticipate an apology from him, but Ardian seems far from through. "More so, you will be diplomatic. You will smile, uphold proper court manners, and if the King and Queen so much as ask you to twirl for them, you will obey—humbly," Ardian adds pointedly. "They are kind people, but if you cross them, there will be consequences. From them and from me."

All of Ardian's cards are on the table, and while I prefer not to meet the Head Councilman's eyes directly, Jericho confronts him with a steady glare. "I don't appreciate your tone with me," he says quietly, in a way that reminds me that people who yell are scariest when their words are hushed.

"Well, as you so kindly tried to say to Venus," Ardian says, inching closer to Jericho's electric blue stare, "I don't give a—"

"*Mr. Asticova*," one of the men interjects, aghast.

Ardian quickly reverts to the show-boat stature he first received me with, straightening himself out and beginning a patterned pace about the boardroom. "Gentlemen, thank you for meeting with us. As I've shared with you in our previous correspondences, Jericho recently extended Lady Venus a personal invitation to serve on his Council. So, as requested, I've provided you all with the means for an open discussion."

Had I known I was going to be interrogated today, I would've brushed up on the Saints' history. Frankly, all I knew about them was that they were, conveniently, the first people I'd find myself swearing to when life went into the gutter—but their uniformed dress makes me fear they'll quiz me on the proceedings of a church service, or my perspective on sexual purity as a young woman.

Suddenly, I'm grateful Delta dressed me in a gown I'd normally deem matronly.

"Miss Deragon," their ringleader, I presume,

enunciates sophisticatedly. "It's a pleasure to finally put a face to the name. My name is Octavian, and we are the Urovian Holymen."

Jericho scoffs from his seat just before standing up and dismissing himself. "I'm not doing this," he mutters halfway out the door.

"Jericho!" Ardian barks, madder than I've ever seen him.

"It's alright, Mr. Asticova," another Holyman murmurs soothingly. "We do not require Jericho's presence in this conversation, nor yours. You're dismissed."

If the statement hurts his feelings, the only sign of it lies within the way he blinks back at them. In a near robotic motion, Ardian finds his footing and uncomfortably sees himself out, shutting the door behind him.

Eight pairs of old, weary eyes meet mine, observing my clothes, my hair, and my skin—the last one in particular being a facet about me a few of them seem hung up on. "So, Venus," Octavian starts up again. His worn, pale skin and shiny bald head pairs well with the snow-white robes he and the other Holymen wear. "How are you fairing in the Royal Domain?"

The hairs on my neck stand on end. "Better than when I first arrived, certainly."

No one speaks, nor chuckles. The silence is palpable, and I hate it more than sharing meals with Jericho—and that says a lot. Four of the men, who haven't said a single word so far—not even their names—continue to glower at me like I've offended them. My patience wears thin. "What are you all looking at?"

Octavian smiles pleasantly before saying, "We just

want to know how a woman of your background manages to transcend society's divisions and wind up on the king's Council."

I flash him and his pack of bigots a villain's smile. "Being the star of the king's wet dream can get you almost anything you want."

The moment the other Holymen contort their faces in disgust, I decide I was right to speak obscenely, to stretch the only knowledge I have on why Jericho found me in the first place. Saints forbid someone tell Jericho Morgan what to do in his own damned dreams, but considering the haste he made in hunting me down . . . I could have very well excited Jericho in a sexual context. The notion makes my insides recoil.

"She can't be serious," a member of the gallery comments under his breath.

"What'd you expect?" I laugh, narrowing my eyes at them. "That I was some charity case Jericho brought on to make the people trust that he wasn't dangerous? That I happily left my sisters in the marshes?"

Secretly, I wonder what Jericho would do if he remained in the room. I know better than to hope he or Ardian would have come to my aid—I can certainly defend myself against some elderly, prejudiced men—but it'd be a small help to have at least one person on my side. "Well, spit it out. What did they tell you about me?" I press.

Octavian looks at his fellow Holymen, as if needing approval to provide me with an answer. But before he can say a word, another man—three chairs down from Octavian and with a much friendlier face—looks at me with respect when he responds with, "Our sources tell us that you are in line to become Queen Consort."

My jaw nearly falls into my lap.

"Who told you *that*?"

The nameless man who bothered to clue me in on why his associates felt the need to glare daggers at me reaches into his robe and pulls out a rolled-up copy of the *U. Herald*. As my fingers graze parchment I haven't touched in almost two years, I wonder how bad this could really be:

Written by Nadine Tolcher   27 MARCH

THE MORGAN DYNASTY: SET TO EXPAND?

King Jericho Morgan has been through the wringer following the tragic passing of his parents, Queen Merrie and King Ronan— may they rest in peace. However, it looks as though the Saints have brought a source of new, unfamiliar joy into his life: a young lady by the name of Venus Deragon.

Urovia's newest darling is not what you'd expect Jericho to be drawn to, though. Born and raised in the marshes to a poor family, Venus previously worked as a topiary for different families in the Makers and Noble Districts, and did not receive formal education past the age of fifteen. Despite the odds stacked against her, it seems as though Venus has truly captured the king's heart.

> An anonymous source additionally shared exclusive details on the lengths our young king has gone to appease his beloved. They said, "Not only has he offered her a spot on his coveted Council, but he has even allowed the lady's sisters to make Broadcove Castle their permanent home."
>
> There's been no mention of a ring, nor any public statement by Venus or Jericho personally. But if our sources are to be trusted, Urovia can expect an extravagant wedding and a new Queen Consort soon, perhaps even by the end of the year!

"The edition was published two days ago," the kinder man whispers, nervous to approach me in the middle of reading. "And when we learned that you and Jericho were set to travel across the Damocles—"

"We had to know for certain," Octavian interjects, gesturing to his counterpart to take his seat once more. "If these accounts held any truth in them, or if it was merely rumors and playful conjecture."

My sense of calm has officially dwindled into nonexistent, first with this antagonizing group of Holymen, and now with Nadine, whose husband could have warned me about *marriage rumors* during our conversation *minutes* ago. "I am not one typically romanced by cruelty, so what kind of person would it make me to forever link myself to a man who murders recreationally?"

"Does he?" Octavian asks, testing me. "Or, as twisted as you've come to view it, does he kill for the right reasons?"

"*Never*—"

"Oh!" Octavian smiles pleasantly, which feels a hell of a lot more taunting than any of Jericho's cat-like grins when we're toying with one another. "This is personal," he realizes. "Gentlemen, leave us. I'd like to partake in a private conversation with Lady Venus."

The six silent observers wordlessly obey, filing out in an orderly fashion, but the one Holyman that dared to come to my defense fights his instincts to follow suit. "You too, Clemence," Octavian growls, and the grit in his voice sends chills spiraling down my spine. To my dismay, Clemence darts out the door at a quicker pace than the others at his demand.

The moment the door shuts, I expect Octavian to slap me or insensitively throw a slur in my face. But to my greatest surprise, he relaxes his posture and releases a labored breath. "Care to know a secret, Miss Deragon?"

I simply stand there stupidly and wait for him to speak.

"Nadine did not write this edition of the *U. Herald*. Well, at least not the part about you two being lovers." He chuckles. "I did."

"*You?*" my voice cracks. "But you clearly cannot stand me. Why would you ever—"

He waves his hands out towards me, as if calling for a ceasefire. "Do forgive me. I must apologize for my crude portrayal earlier. I swear to you, I take no offense in the least to your background, your status, or your bold manner of speech. In fact, the only thing that you could do to insult me, my dear, is fail."

Anxiety leaks into my stomach in a slow drip. "Fail at what, sir?"

"Killing Jericho, of course," he answers as if the notion were obvious.

Before I can even stutter over the beginnings of an excuse—a lie to clear my name and convince him that my true motives for being in Jericho's realm are pure—Octavian raises a finger to his lips, insisting that he speak first.

"Before any new editions of the *U. Herald* become published, they all must go through approval by the Holymen Convention. After that, we have the final say on whether the story dies with us, if it reaches the press, or if we want to add commentary and quotes to the piece before submission. So the moment I learned through Nadine's original piece that Jericho had been hosting a woman he'd envisioned in his sleep, that she had been abiding there unharmed . . ." he lets out a breath, still blown away by the notion. "I knew you were smart, that you'd use your time to seek revenge rather than fall prey to the luxuries of Jericho's lifestyle. And I needed to create a narrative that disguised that." A scheming smile blooms across his lips. "But I do wonder if my little fib might just be the push Jericho needs to clearly see the possibility of what the *U. Herald* insinuates. Happiness anew, a woman there to support him in diplomacy and in private, even a sense of family with the arrival of your sisters. Don't you see, Venus?" he says all too seriously. "Jericho doesn't have to be alone anymore."

Something cold and long-since hardened begins to melt within me, and guilt reigns where empathy ought to reside. My thoughts had always been to plant seeds of bad advice in his ear and then watch him destroy himself from the inside out. Then, once he was distracted, I'd bring out Delta's dagger.

But this alternative feels much more punishing, for both Jericho and me. For this to work, my manipulation tactics would need to be so air-tight, that I'd likely have to convince myself that a marriage to Jericho is what I really want—the exact opposite of what Delta warned me about.

If Jericho truly was coming after me in a passionate way . . . I'd have to let him.

"Why do you want Jericho dead?" I ask Octavian.

"Why do *you*?" he challenges.

I dare not say a word.

Octavian momentarily surrenders his power over our exchange, if only to gain my trust. "The Holymen Committee is split down the middle. Clemence and three others think that you are exactly the change we need in Urovia, specifically to help buff out Jericho's sharp edges and seek positive reinventions for the land. But the other half of us believe that the Morgan Dynasty is disastrous for the territory, and that if we never had the chance to spare Merrie or Ronan, that Jericho should've gone with them soon after. Until Urovia could hold a free election and cultivate a new dynasty, Mr. Asticova would govern. As the Mosacian Ambassador, he knows how to keep his homeland from attacking us while also sustaining Urovia long enough to find a replacement."

"Did Ardian know about this plan?"

Octavian no longer smiles. "Your turn. What would you get out of killing Jericho?"

I bite my lip, hating myself for sharing the truth. "One of his dreams condemned my father to death, and if he won't grant me his reasons for killing him, I'll at least have the satisfaction of avenging him."

"I see," Octavian muses. "I guess that brings us back to the question I posed earlier. Considering Jericho is reminded that he murdered your father every time he looks you in the face, wouldn't you say that the only way Jericho morally tolerates your presence is by convincing himself that he was right for killing him?"

"No," I reply flatly. "Jericho does as he pleases with whomever he pleases."

"Wrong," Octavian counters, his voice growing louder as a vein rises along his shiny forehead. "Jericho holds power, which means he has more liberties, but that does not mean that he can exercise his will in the absence of morals. Yes, murder is a dark act, one that can cause a rift in a person's very soul . . . but when the Saints urge you to do something, you obey. No matter how ugly the instructions are."

I cannot believe this. "You defend Jericho's violence, yet you stand against his rule?"

"Wrong again. I believe," Octavian stammers, "that Jericho is undoubtedly Blessed by the Saints with divine, prophetic visions—the entire Convention does. It remains our only plausible explanation as to how Jericho remains steadfast to the treacherous intimacy that murder creates within the living and the fallen. The key difference in our division, regarding Jericho, however, is that one side believes that *you* can influence him for the better, and therefore, you might alter the kind of messages the Saints provide him within his dreams. That when the dust settles, you and Jericho will rule together and revive this present dynasty."

It is a pretty picture; I'll give him that.

"But as formidable and strong as I trust you are, my half of the Convention knows the truth: that even if Jericho loved you, and you begged and pleaded with him to defy his violent visions, the control that the Saints have over him and his gifts remains unstoppable."

When Octavian approaches me, I watch his Saints' emblem clatter against his robes as he walks. It's a peculiar little design—a kite-shaped symbol cut into fourths by a cross with arrowheads on each end—and for a moment, I think I even hear it thrum, as if I awoke a living creature. "The only way that you're protected if Jericho dies—especially by your own hand—is through marriage, and with my interference with the *U. Herald*, I've set you up for the seamless path to success."

That's when Octavian gradually leans in towards my ear. "So, for the sake of your sisters if not for yourself," he murmurs, and only then do I realize that this statement hovers over the line between urging and threatening, "turn on your charm. Be prepared to build a romance so foolproof that even you won't be able to distinguish the lies from the truth."

Octavian goes still for a moment, as if wanting to hear the blood pulsing through me. He smiles at the sound I try hard to smother.

"And when all is said and done," he finishes, "make sure that King Jericho never sees his killing blow coming."

23
Jericho

Nestled beneath the valleys of the sloping hills, the glittering Damocles Sea remains the crowning jewel of Honeycomb Harbor as it stretches out towards an unknown fate and reflects sunlight onto the cobblestone boardwalks and the arches that bend beneath pedestrian bridges. Thank the Saints the weather remains promising, because there's no way in hell I would ever allow myself to exist in a universe that would allow Venus to see me getting seasick from rocky currents or choppy, storm-ridden waves.

Cargo ships are the only boats that ever leave Honeycomb Harbor these days, delivering agreed-upon livestock, crops, and other resources as laid out in whatever revised version of Urovia's and Mosacia's trade treatises remain in practice. Old habits die hard, I suppose—as no one from Mosacia nor Urovia has shipped out to pay a visit to the other continent except for the royals. Our annual diplomatic gatherings have been on hold since

Mother passed, but Ardian seemed ready to wring my neck if I stalled another year, even when I claimed it was due to prolonged grief.

He didn't buy it for a second.

The ladies' trunks lay where Tolcher stashed them this morning, staring me in the face within the open room across from mine. Delta's luggage practically covers the entire bed, while Venus's quaint duffel bag—

"Happy travel day!" Delta pops in from the worn, wooden stairs that deliver her to the lower levels, her voice dipped in sugar and delight. "I cannot believe this is happening, that I get to go back and see everyone! I've missed them more than I can express! I wonder how they've all changed." Suddenly, she gasps, a hand over her mouth and her eyes unblinking. "I wonder if they know I'm coming . . ."

I need a tonic for the headache Delta is currently giving me. "It's nine in the morning."

Delta giggles like a child, her cheeks rosy as they pinch together in a smile. "You have the servants up at dawn every day. Your nine in the morning is my noon, practically."

Her bothersome presence aside, I feel the need to clarify something about the comment she just made. "Delta, you do know that, despite the role I've provided for you with Venus, you're not technically a servant, right? As Ardian's niece, what you choose to do with your time . . . that's your business—including when we get to Mosacia."

"As long as Venus's needs are met first."

"Of course," I reply, and I wonder instinctively if I

rattle off the words far too swiftly. "Now, if you'll excuse me"—I straighten up—"I'll just be . . . resting." The lie is pitiful, unconvincing at best—but Delta gives me the benefit of the doubt and excitedly stomps up the stairs again to the main deck. The moment she vanishes, I shut my door to all other noise and disturbances and splay out on my designated bed with a deep sigh of relief.

Just as quickly, however, a faint gallop sounds off down the road and I nearly catapult off the bed and peer out the port window.

Riding sidesaddle, despite likely never having ridden a horse before, Venus gracefully makes her way to *Crystal Wrath*, hazel eyes glinting and wide as she beholds the ship. She now dons a fur coat and what looks like faintly sparkling tights beneath her dress, and a sick, twisted part of me longs to view her bare legs again. The more I think about it, I've only ever seen her legs unguarded the moment I begged her not to jump—well, shit, now *that* is all that I can picture in my brain.

Ardian helps her down from the dutiful mare, extending his hands out to her brace for the impact of her full weight, and appearing surprised by her lightness. I watch from a hidden vantage point as Venus floats to the ground like a feather in the wind, and she thanks my Head Councilman for his assistance with a brief kiss upon his cheek. Something burns within me at the sight, more so when Ardian smiles bashfully and bids her safe travels. The bastard nearly blushes as he indicates the gangway to her.

Suddenly, Venus dips her eyes downward, right in the direction of the window where I'm currently spying on her—and against my better judgment, I duck just before she can spot me.

I *duck* . . . from *her*.

As if further tallying my many embarrassments of the day, I try not to relive it—the moment those self-important Holymen drove me out of my own boardroom. Sure, I run on a short fuse, but knowing how pretentious they can be, especially towards poorer women . . . I can only imagine the scene they caused with Venus in the room, and I certainly didn't need to be there to witness it firsthand. I knew it was going to get ugly once I noticed that, not long after I stormed out, Ardian caught up with me in the hallways, having been dismissed from the Convention's conversation.

Delta's giddy squeals are muffled by the wooden floorboards that make up my ceiling, and drowning out the sound completely, thank the Saints, comes the bellowing of the boat's commanding horn. It nearly shakes the entire ship, and supposing I ought to make good on my word of going to sleep once more, I situate myself back on the bed provided for me and force myself to unwind.

We'll likely reach Sevensberg by breakfast if the waters prove to be smooth, which means I only have to stomach two meals with Venus's and Delta's respective moods—one if I manage to sleep through lunch. Just shut your eyes and pray that your body blocks out the sounds of the sailing crew and the two women clambering about.

No more than five minutes after I hear the heavy, rusted anchor being drawn up to the bow and feel *Crystal Wrath* begin to coast freely, my mind gives way to dreams.

Unfortunately, the first thing I see behind my eyelids is someone I thought my conscience had laid to rest a long time ago.

Father has forsaken his usual crimson uniforms for all-black dress clothes, save for a single, white tulip boutonniere pinned to his suit coat. The emerging gray that washes over his once-brown hair adds the signature touch to his storm cloud disposition, paired with weathered eyes and a neutral expression.

I'm twenty-two again—it's two weeks following Mother's death and I'm still choked up about it. But not Father, and he's certainly not sharing in my grief today. "If the Herald *captures a picture of you shedding even one tear, consider yourself disowned."*

"Had you no love for her? Ever?"

"Your mother was a selfish woman from start to finish," my father spits, saliva flying out from his mouth and landing on the side of my face. "She lived selfishly, she raised you selfishly, and she died selfishly—too caught up in her emotions to control herself. Merrie had decades of life still in store for her, and she threw them all away. And for what?"

That's one thing I hadn't come to know yet—why. I was desperate to figure it out one way or another. So much of how Mother died remained shrouded in mystery and secrecy, as if even mentioning the manner of her death would contaminate the person speaking of it. Suicide certainly wasn't the most lovely of conversation topics, but it just . . . didn't feel right associating the act with someone as resilient as my mother.

"What do you need from me, Father?"

He merely looks down at me in disdain, as if the question was the stupidest thing to ever be said. That infamous, fatherly glare never fails to remind me that while I am nothing like him, being like Mother was perhaps the greatest insult to him of all. "Need? From you?"

"Yes," I press on. "I do not mean to allow my thoughts to spiral so intrusively, but . . . we are weak without her."

"We are the Morgans, dammit!" Father roars. "We are stronger than ever—"

"We are about to bury a woman that not only the public adored, but one that the Seagraves saw as family. I've observed your meager rapport with the royal family, and if you're not careful, Father, they could use our moment of weakness to attack—"

He hits me, hot and unrestrained. Frankly, I expected him to smack me sooner, and I'm quietly impressed with myself for getting in what words I could up until this point. My eyes water reflexively, not out of sadness—but he strikes me harder for it. "You're no better than an infant."

"Perhaps I ought to settle down here in Broadcove, for good. Maybe it would help our case if I became more involved in how we produce policies and maintain order." Then, a new suggestion glimmers to life, and while it remains the antithesis of what I want in this stage of life, I say to him, "Or . . . if I marry, I can introduce Urovia to an endearing Princess that can capture the hearts of—"

Father scoffs, tickled by the idea. "Don't be ridiculous. You don't need to worry about finding a wife. Take a lover, Jericho. Take six for all I care. Do something worthwhile with yourself or drive yourself into your own ruin. Either way, I'm not going anywhere, and you're certainly not getting my crown."

Truthfully, I never envied his riches, or his cruelty, or his position as King. I knew I'd assume the role eventually, likely when I was in my forties or fifties and Father finally kicked the bucket. So for now, I possessed every rhyme and reason to go out into the depths of Urovia, get drunk, get laid, and get out of my father's way. But as I come to terms with what life will be like in the absence of Merrie Morgan, I decide that I need to stay in Broadcove—to make sure that my mother's part in keeping Urovia afloat does not dwindle beneath the flame of my Father's rage.

I force my dreams to fast forward, to skip the funeral entirely. I hate watching the moment they laid Mother's casket in the ground behind Zayanya Cathedral—how, as the world wailed and sobbed for her, I stood there like stone and masked my grief so convincingly, I could've been a stranger to her. Her only son refused to mourn her publicly, and to this day, it feels like an eternal act of disrespect I'll never make up to her.

Once we returned to Broadcove Castle, Father drank himself into a stupor, and I cried so hard I made myself sick. Mother was the only one that ever believed my visions held divinity and discernment, the only one I confided in when my dreams resulted in physical side-effects. Bruises on my limbs after battling what I thought was a fictional monster, sore muscles after imagining I trekked through the shadowed forests between the Royal Domain and the Noble Lands. Even when I told her that I had dreamed of a conversation she and my father had—one that ended with him shouting profanities at her and pulling her out of the room by her hair—she told me that my visions were true. She believed in my gifts enough to share her deepest vulnerabilities.

And now, she was gone, and there was no one left to believe in me but myself.

With all that remained of my emotional and physical strength, I found my way into North Star, fell to my knees before the last round of peonies I planted for her, and prayed to the Saints so hard I began screaming.

"If any of you are real and I'm not truly crazy, give me a sign! Some way of knowing that she did not die in vain and that I will not be left to make do with only the ashes of a family!"

Relentless banging on the other side of my bedroom door threatens to knock the wooden slab off its hinges, and I wake with a start.

Beyond the nearest port window, the seawater teeters our boat and the afternoon sun hangs over the horizon in its usual four o'clock position.

"Who is it?" I inquire sweetly, desperately hoping that I'm not about to be forced to make small talk with Delta again, especially right after waking up from a long span of sleep.

"Open the damn door, Jericho!"

Despite her sour tone, Venus's presence, compared to anyone else's, is a small mercy. I run my hand over my hair, doing my best to flatten any frazzled pieces from sleep. "Delta driving you up a wall yet?"

"I need to talk to you. *Now.*"

The deeper and grittier her voice gets, the more I must fight the urge to crack a smile. Still, I force my feet onto the floor and begin the short walk to the door. "If this is about the herd of Holymen that crashed our meeting this morning, I had nothing to do with it."

When Venus maintains her silence, I realize all too late that she's likely turned red with rage from behind the door. Disengaging the lock and turning the door's handle, I swing my arm wide—

And before I fully drink in Venus standing in front of

me, she's swatting me across the head with a rolled-up sheet of parchment.

"Venus," I try to call her off calmly, but she proves to be relentless. "Venus, what's the matter?"

Her blows get harder, more frantic. They ding me on the top of my head, swipe across my face, and harshly dot the tip of my nose. None of them hurt, necessarily, but the fire in Venus's eyes warns me that if I do not put a stop to her persistent swinging and help make sense of what set her off in the first place, she may very well drop the parchment and bring out her fists.

"Venus *stop*—"

I'm right about one thing: Venus finally releases the thick paper. But the moment she gets rid of it, hurling it into my grasp, she steps away from me and catches her breath. Color slowly leaves her face, dulling the redness of her previous fury—and against my better judgment, I find myself fixating on the sound and rhythm of her ragged breathing, the way her shoulders shrug as she calms her body down. I try not to imagine it in other contexts.

"Well?" Venus barks, pointing out that I have yet to unravel the papers.

Saints, what is going on with me?

And so I unfurl what I realize is an edition of the *U. Herald*. One, I discover, that only recently reached the press and went out for public distribution. All I need to see before my heart falls into my stomach is the title.

"When were you going to tell me that you were in love with me, Jericho?"

PART II
CONNECTION

24
Venus

The moment *Crystal Wrath* reaches the Mosacian coastline, I understand why Delta longed to return here.

The first glimpse of the morning sun winks at us from the horizon's rim, and while it casts an orange haze over the dockyards, the first step onto the main deck proves that it only offers the ruse of warmth. Not only that, but the sun appears to be the only flare of color in sight—because beyond where our vessel drops its anchor, Sevensberg Palace's pure white architecture might just blind me.

Wincing, I squint my eyes at the massive estate, filtering just how much of its intense shine I can bear at once, and I find that my new home base for the month portrays the opposite of what Broadcove encapsulates. Where Broadcove's golden, towering walls stand as a centerpiece amidst a technicolor fantasy, the clean structure of Mosacia's grand palace lets me know enough about how wealthy the royals are. The roofs are coated in silver, and metallic flags wave in the wind above white brick chimneys, and steep, double-paned windows lie sprinkled across the palace's stunning exterior. Unlike how I typically maintain outdoor property, the Mosacian royals appear to favor a tidied look, with pine trees trimmed and planted in line so perfectly, I wonder if they're fake. No flowers bloom here, and the murky waters on this side of the Damocles ripple with every swayed movement. Seven hedged paths direct travelers towards seven, different doors along the front wall, the largest of the lot centered before a fountain massive enough to be considered a pool, and behind it, a cavernous, pentagonal entryway whose doors stretch nearly four stories high.

Sevensberg Palace could swallow Broadcove whole.

In the solace of standing here alone, my body braced on the ledge of *Crystal Wrath*, I quietly thank Calliope for all the mornings she riled Geneva and I up from bed earlier than we appreciated. Moments like this— beholding a foreign, porcelain palace on the heels of a month-long adventure—only come around once in a lifetime for people like me. I ought to reach out and grab it.

I disembark without bothering to wake Delta or Jericho.

Having firmly denied my accusations of affection yesterday, Jericho then proceeded to scold me about falling prey to gossip—especially from sources as insubstantial and contrived as what gets obtained in the *U. Herald*— and warned me about the *real* dangers of Mosacia. If I already had become swept away by the lies of a simple newspaper, Jericho made it all too evident that I wouldn't survive a week in Sevensberg. I believe his exact words were, *"Residing on the opposing side of the Seagrave family is no better than walking into a den of hungry lions."* But halfway down the gangway, no one has come to welcome me. No humble servant hurries over to gather my luggage or direct me anywhere specific. So yes, perhaps the hospitality isn't stellar.

But I have my dagger, the company of a friend, and a mission to put Jericho in his grave. The last thing on my mind is whether a rich couple, in a land I'll likely never visit again, likes me or not.

The layout of Mosacia's port appears simpler than the elaborate trails and stunning water archways back in Honeycomb Harbor. The Seagraves must inherit fewer visitors than Urovia, because only four docking slots—three for trade vessels and the other for visitors, in which *Crystal Wrath* currently occupies—have residency here, divided along a straight line. From there, a set of sleek, cream stairs provide direct passage straight onto Sevensberg Palace's vast front patio.

Lucky for me, Delta snored all while I rummaged through her travel-packed trunks earlier this morning, and I managed to spritz her floral perfume along my neck and slip into a dress that faired better than the dismal, black frock she stuffed me in the day before. Now clothed in satin, cerulean blue that brings out the green in my eyes, with frilly sleeves and a sweeping tiered skirt, I feel like I belong here. More than that, I feel free here. Something amidst the dawn—or perhaps in the way that no strings seem to tether me back to Jericho, Delta, or

Crystal Wrath in this present moment—promises change.

Promises possibility.

Not even halfway up the connecting stairs, I catch a glimpse of a handsome stranger spying on me from behind a planted pine tree.

"Excuse me!" I call out, unafraid of being forward with my passive observer.

The stranger—a man no more than five years my senior—defies my expectations and comes out from his cover. Stepping into the light fully, I notice that he wears dark riding leathers, and yet, no horse lies within sight. Perhaps he's merely out for a morning stroll. Politely, the nameless man raises a feeble hand and waves once. The smile he pairs with it stirs something in me, and I find myself drawing closer. "Hello, there."

"What's a pretty lady like you doing down by the docks, and all by your lonesome?" he croons, his accent ringing clear as day.

The sound of his voice gives me all I need to understand just who I am dealing with—that, and the recollection of Jericho's painstaking Seagrave family debrief over dinner last night.

Slater Seagrave matches Jericho's description perfectly: curly, golden hair spiraling just to the point of his shoulders, and eyes that pierce a person's gaze so deeply, I can hardly make out their true color. Framed by thick brows and finely shaped facial hair, Slater stands before me in a way I can only describe as statuesque—the epitome of male beauty and confidence. And yet . . . he doesn't strike me as the prideful type. Merely flirtatious.

"Waiting for someone to show me where I'm supposed

to be," I return, adapting the role of a lost damsel.

As I ascend the remaining steps and surpass the distance between us, I immediately note the differences between the two heirs of the disputing lands; where Jericho is sadness and fury personified, Slater reminds me of the sun—radiant and warm. He looks like someone whose touch would quell the coldness in my weathered hands, and the impenetrable light he carries within him almost makes me believe that he is naïve.

Almost.

I know better than to assume the eldest child of the royal family is gullible, or perhaps, maybe I'm the one at the end of a joke that he's playing on me. One key difference that really stands out, however, is that he looks far more rugged and torn up by the world than Jericho does. Maybe it's the leathers, or maybe it's the fact that Slater woke up before the sun and is not snoozing away the morning—but much like me, Slater looks to have obtained fruits of tiresome labor, while Jericho likely spent his whole life indoors with other people left to do his grunt work at his beck and call.

"You haven't told me your name," Slater murmurs. "No doubt, you must know mine."

"Venus," I return, and extend my hand towards his own.

His vibrant eyes sparkle with intrigue. "Like the goddess."

Funny, that was the exact same phrase Jericho had mused aloud when I first, begrudgingly introduced myself. However, Slater seals this first interaction with a gentle kiss along the back of my hand, a far greater start than Jericho ever had. "I suppose so," I whisper.

"And how did you end up in Sevensberg, Venus?"

"Fate," I tell him, and the blush that forms in my cheeks then is real. Smiling, my eyes drift back to the coastline one last time, and I mentally abandon my Urovian identity in favor of this new, spontaneous person I'm portraying to Slater. "And how fortunate am I, running into the dashing Heir Apparent?"

"You find me . . . dashing?"

"Of course. After all, you certainly look the part of a royal."

Slater reaches for a piece of my dark hair and strokes the softness between two of his fingers. I gave Delta so much heat for insisting I wrap my entire head in rollers after washing it in a basin last night, but the next time I catch up with her, I ought to thank her tremendously for the suggestion. Slater appears absolutely bewitched. "Would you like a tour of the grounds, Lady Venus?"

"She most certainly would not."

Jericho's voice takes both Slater and I by surprise, his tone grave and his eyes bloodshot. Neither of us heard his footsteps on the gangway or the groaning wood signal his incoming arrival, but here he stands. His hands likely fisted in his plaid trouser pockets, I instantly see the beginnings of his pectoral muscles beneath a dark, emerald sweater. Oddly enough, Jericho's choice of dress feels out of character—casual, yet academic.

"Well, I'll be damned," Slater exhales, an implied humor beneath his words. "I haven't seen you, Jericho, in nearly three years."

"Would've been longer if I had any choice in the

matter," Jericho returns snidely, scaling the remaining steps and squaring off his body equally to both of us.

"I thought Mr. Asticova would've leashed you by now. Did you forget that my parents' policy with these visits *requires* a Council member to keep your lot in line." I try hard to ignore how Slater makes himself sound like a snobbish, tattletale child, but my body cringes instinctively. The gesture gives me away.

"Venus"—Jericho indicates with a chipper smile—"is his replacement."

Slater's eyes flare, his mouth falling slightly agape. "*She* is on your Council?"

"What seems to be the matter, Slater? Do I not look the part?" I ask innocently.

To which Slater instantly reverts into his previous flattery, looking over me with a new perspective as he says to Jericho, "I see why you chose her. If she manages to charm Victor and Harriet, perhaps there's more that can be accomplished from your visit than I anticipated."

I wink at Slater playfully knowing damn well Jericho sees me do it. "Shame. I only wished to charm you."

Slater lets his laugh overtake him. "Don't worry, darling. You've succeeded."

Jericho looks sick of our shit already, and it's not even eight o'clock. "We ought to be going, now—"

"*Slater?*" Delta's shrill voice pierces through the morning air. "Holy Saints! Is that you?"

For the first moment since I stumbled upon Slater, he breaks eye contact and glances towards her direction. Already, Delta sprints for him, and he only gets a few seconds to brace his body for the full weight of her. With all her strength, she slams into him, leaping into the air and wrapping her legs around Slater like he's her long-distance lover. "Gods, kid, I thought I'd never see you again!"

"So you missed me?" she asks, her heart so full I fear it could sing. Her eyes well up with tears, and she fights to wipe them away before Jericho notices them glistening. "Really?"

"Not more than Diana, but damn close," he answers, his smile blatant and childlike. "Those first two years, I think we all expected the arrangement to fail and for you and Mr. Asticova to return. But alas, cranky old Chumley still remains the sourest trade Father's ever made."

Thatcher Chumley, I remind myself, raking through my retentions of Jericho's dinner conversation last night, which covered enough Urovian and Mosacian history to have it spill out of my ears. The Urovian counterpart to the ambassador trade that Ronan and Merrie agreed upon when Jericho was around the age of eight. One native of each territory would assume a permanent residency in the land foreign to them, be appointed to that ruler's advisory board—which Jericho rebranded as his Council—and send monthly feedback and informational updates to their homeland. Everything that happened within Broadcove's walls became the Seagrave's business and vice versa; although now that I'm dwelling on it, wouldn't Slater have recognized who I was the moment I shared my name? Perhaps his parents are the private type.

A bright, enthusiastic trumpet rattles off a cheerful rhythm, and Slater cocks his head towards the single musician hidden amongst the silver spires. "Come along, everyone," Slater instructs, straightening himself out before leading us onward. "My parents have been made aware of your arrival, and they'll expect to address you formally in the throne room."

Delta happily clips at Slater's heels, and Jericho pretends that he doesn't take orders from anyone while following along anyway. But the closer we move to the heart of Sevensberg, the more unsettled I feel, like there is a prisoner within my blood pounding their fists against my bones, desperately hoping to escape. A warning, I realize.

Two monarchs, six heirs, an ambassador, and the king I crossed the Damocles with.

Somewhere in this assortment of supposed allies, I fear an enemy conceals their true intent and waits patiently for the right moment to strike.

25
Venus

Unlike Broadcove, whose receiving room slowly expands in size the further you drift down the hall, and is adorned with a lavish, side stairway, Sevensberg diminishes your stature the moment you step through the doorway. One moment, you approach porcelain splendor amidst a constellation of evergreens, thinking that the majesty of the place will erupt in profound color the moment you cross the threshold. The next, you become dwarfed by ancient architecture, monochrome-tiled floors that would likely freeze your bare feet, and barren walkways everywhere you turn.

It's easily one of the great wonders of this known world, and yet, it also reminds me of a tomb.

"This way," Slater directs, leading our group down a diagonal hallway.

My gut begins to twist inside of me with each additional step. It forces my pace to slow, and eventually, Jericho notices. He stalls for a moment, too, as if yanked backwards by an invisible force—and a heartbeat later, Jericho seems to understand my sudden change in confidence and motions me to his side, the gesture not domineering, but almost compassionate.

Then, in an uncharacteristic moment of weakness, Jericho loops my hand around his arm and guides us forward, a kind expression on his face.

My heartbeat quickens, and I loathe myself for it. I'm here on strict orders to find a way to kill Jericho, yet, when he gives me one millisecond of decency and chivalry, my heart flutters like a damn hummingbird.

Telling my girlish nervousness to fuck off, I say to Jericho, "You don't have to do that."

"Yes, I do."

Delta begins chatting Slater's ear off again, catching him up on life in Broadcove—what her Uncle Ardian is up to these days, and how she and I have become "fast friends." Meanwhile, I find myself lingering over the sight of my dress sleeves draped over Jericho's pale hand, his littlest finger covertly stroking the end of the lace trim. It's comforting enough to settle my anxieties long enough to ask him, "Are they nice? The Seagraves?"

He does not immediately answer me, but in time, he nods affirmatively. "They're decent people. But these visits tend to reopen old wounds."

"Such as?"

"My father never bothered to be kind to the people he convened with," he replies, and I'm pleasantly surprised by his sudden forwardness. "But he was especially brutal when dealing with the Seagraves. In fact, Mother and Harriet were dear companions, always writing to the other when they could, and Father hated them both for it. He'd start fights over it with Victor, and curse my mother out in front of guests and staff whenever he'd intercept her letters from Harriet—it was a nightmare."

I nearly trip over my own feet turning a corner behind Slater and Delta, too wrapped up in what Jericho is saying. "Why would he be so up in arms about Merrie being on good terms with their political allies?"

"Because Father felt like less of a man when Mother had her way. He couldn't stand being the submissive one, so when Merrie got along swimmingly with Harriet, he never viewed their friendship as something conducive for Urovia, but detrimental. Father feared . . ." He leans into my ear, whispering, "that Harriet would take advantage of Mother's kindness and betray her."

We approach another towering set of double doors— these ones coated top to bottom in liquid silver with pearly white swirls looping rhythmically through one another. Ahead of us, Slater reaches for the curved handle—Delta giggling idly by—and just before the doors open, Jericho says, so quietly that his lips brush the edge of my ear, right along my highest piercing, "I hope that, as daunting as it may feel to face the family behind these doors, you know . . . you were the right person to come to Mosacia with me. Not Ardian."

A cold blast of air hits me when Slater swings open the throne room doors, masking the shockwave that runs through my bloodstream.

My ear burns at the absence of Jericho's sudden touch as he quickly pulls away.

If I ever felt intimidated by Sevensberg Palace's

entryway, the throne room makes the memory of it feel like a stuffy coat closet. Ivory floors bleed upward into moonstone gray walls. Sculptures of beautiful, unknown people with laurels draped over their brows observe our distant figures from the rafters, heads tilted in curiosity and their bodies stretching down to melt into the walls. Oval screens stand vertically against the back wall, holed out and replaced by translucent glass, with a faint rainbow sheen radiating within each carved shape.

Beneath the technicolor luster, sitting on twin, oak thrones with gracious expressions on their faces, the King and Queen of Mosacia strike me as exactly what Ardian assured me of: kind people. When they rise from their seats in their initial greeting, Harriet looks as though she may surpass her husband by a few inches, but it doesn't dim his overall grandeur. While her face appears plain from this distance, there's a unique, strawberry undertone that streaks through her honey blonde hair. Still, Harriet's presence carries a personal warmth that fights off the colder interior of the palace. No heavy cosmetics adorn her face, only the simplistic additions needed to make her eyes look larger and her lashes longer. Perhaps she cares less for appearances and niceties of that nature, or I at least guess so as I consider the apparent bump indenting the front of her dress.

Just as Jericho had assumed—another heir.

The king, on the other hand, possesses the handsomeness that Slater clearly inherited, the kind that I've only ever found in the types of people I ultimately never end up with. Gray streaks faintly cut across his dark scalp, and his eyes appear as devoid of color as the walls boxing us in—but if I could rewind the clock and witness him at my age . . . *Saints.*

"Why are you staring at him like that?" Jericho mutters out the side of his mouth, refusing to look me in the eye.

I smile to myself. "I think you know why."

To his credit, Jericho says nothing, maintaining his calm and collected façade, especially considering that this makes two Seagrave men that I've fawned over in the last hour. Still, I suppose the age gap—not to mention their literal marriage—is necessary when I see King Victor smile at his bride as she runs a supporting hand along the base of her pregnant belly. Painfully enough, the two of them prove to be rather adorable.

"Welcome," Victor calls out as he leads his wife towards Jericho and me. "I trust that your journey here went smoothly."

"Indeed," Jericho replies, his tone more diplomatic than I've heard from him. "Though do give my guest some time to recuperate. I'm afraid she's not used to this sort of traveling."

The queen finally turns to look upon me more intently. "Guest," she muses, noting the indication. Still, she manages an earnest smile. "Of course, you must be Lady Venus! You're the new Council member."

"Yes, Your Highness."

"Please, do call me Harriet," she requests sweetly, to the point where it almost sounds as though she coos. The words arrive as I am in the middle of a curtsey. "We'll be spending most of your stay together, so no need for formalities."

And then, as if cued by someone hidden from sight,

a door on the left side of the room, up near the elevated dais where Harriet's and Victor's thrones rest, their five remaining children file into the room.

Delta screams with joy.

The littlest children—two boys, no older than the age of eight—appear terrified of her joy. I realize it's because they likely weren't born when Delta and Ardian migrated to Urovia. But the eldest of the children, lined up next to one another, barely manages to contain her excitement, matching Delta's elation and racing at the speed of light to crash into her. Their limbs tangle up within each other's hold, and eventually, I cannot make out whose arm is whose or how they are managing to breathe when they are so tightly embraced.

"That's Diana," Jericho points out, then whispering privately to me, "Slater's failsafe."

When I'm afforded a better look at her once Delta pulls back, I find that, like Slater, she is borderline alluring. A curtain of golden hair sweeps across her eyebrows and down past her shoulders. A stern nose frames her angular face, but it is only once I peer deep into her misty green eyes that I finally take a true liking to her. Even as she looks at Delta with joy and optimism, there rests a quality about her eyes that tells me she possesses an unruly strength that few have seen, that burns beneath her skin because she came second to her older brother.

She reminds me so much of myself.

"Lady Venus," Victor addresses me with a pleasing smile, "meet my children. I trust that you've already spoken with Slater, my eldest, and now you know my oldest daughter, Diana. My two little boys"—he indicates the twins—"Kellan and Madden. And lastly, my girls, Greer and Annabelle."

The boys bow towards me, thinking I hold a monumental rank that they must honor publicly—but I must admit, the gesture is charming. Worse, for as much as I loathe children and the idea of having any of my own, they are irresistibly adorable. To the right of them, however, as I poise my attention on the two girls, I realize something unique about each of them. The older one, Greer, bears a set of three parallel scars along the side of her face, the middle one crossing faintly over her right eye. Maybe an animal attack? I'll have to inquire with Jericho later this evening.

And then, there is Annabelle.

Children like Annabelle, back in the marshes, never stand a chance against the harsh elements, the lack of resources needed for their individualized needs, and certainly not the cruel whispers about why they ended up the way they did. To gaze upon a child of her condition back home was to experience heartbreak, knowing their life would never be anything beyond constant struggle.

But here, in Sevensberg Palace, Annabelle smiles wider than I ever have, the epitome of unbothered, unbridled joy. Dare I say it, Annabelle is the crowning jewel of the Seagrave family.

With hazelnut hair cropped just above her neck, and eyes that glimmer like aquamarines in the light of the massive windowpanes, Annabelle certainly steals the show. Her cheeks have this permanent fullness about them, as if she never stops smiling—and I find myself unable to keep my own grin down below the surface when she looks my way.

"It's a pleasure to meet you all," I say, unable to tear my eyes away from Annabelle in particular.

The twin boys giggle at each other, and when Harriet asks what they find so hilarious, Kellan reports loud enough for the whole room to hear, "Madden said he thinks the girl is pretty!"

Diana *"oohs"* playfully, as if convicting her little brother of a dirty act, and Annabelle cackles—it's the best belly laugh I've ever heard. Poor Madden blushes to the point of turning red altogether, and Kellan points at me so that there's no mistaking which girl in the room his brother finds pleasing to the eye. All the while, I find my feet carrying me towards my not-so secret admirer, crouching down to meet his level. "I bet you'll be the most handsome man in Mosacia when you get to be my age," I tell him, squeezing his small hand in my own reassuringly.

"Wait for me?" Madden hopes aloud.

Jericho's genuine laugh from behind my back nearly knocks me over.

"Something tells me," I hear Slater's voice answer on my behalf, "that Venus isn't the type to be tied down, little man."

I stand to my full height again, craning my head towards Slater's cocky, crooked smile. My comeback is already preloaded, but a set of soft hands run along my shoulders and direct me back down the carpeted walkway we first entered through. "I shall show Lady Venus to her rooms, now," Harriet announces to the entire throne room. "Kids, back to your studies. You'll see our Urovian friends at dinner later this evening."

"May I sit by Venus at dinner?" Annabelle's soft voice pipes in.

Madden groans and stomps his foot.

"Of course," Harriet answers, and while she flashes me an apologetic look, I am more than willing to go along with the arrangement.

"It'd be an honor, Princess," I curtsey. Cherub cheeks fill with color and delight, and she squeals as she follows Greer into the hallway. Even after she disappears, I hear the distant sounds of joyful clapping. Then, turning to Madden, I add, "You can have my other side, if you'd like."

He nearly bulldozes Kellan as he sprints out, suddenly embarrassed, yet ecstatic, for tonight.

I clear my throat awkwardly as I pass by Jericho, still managing a smile for propriety's sake. Rather than responding in any manner, he greets Victor stalely, and the sound of their hands clasping briefly echoes before Harriet and I walk out of earshot.

Beyond the massive doors, Harriet leads me through the throne room, approaching a hall that careens towards, what must be, the residential quarters deeper into the palace. Two guards—one manned at each looming door and donning silver armor—politely tip their heads in recognition and let us pass through. The moment the train of my dress crosses the grand doorframe, the guards close us off from the rest of the world.

And Harriet falls into a chuckling fit.

Good heavens, she's practically snorting.

"I'm—Ha!" she hoots, trying to restrain herself by

covering her mouth, but hilarity dances in her eyes. "I'm so sorry. I just . . . I mean, I just don't believe it!"

I raise an inquisitive brow. "Believe what?"

"That Jericho brought a girl with him!" She beams. "And aren't you a stunning young thing?" she marvels, twirling me around so that she can scan me all over. She seems even more satisfied than before when she takes in the backside of my gown. "Bless the Gods, our communications were quite dull when Jericho came along companionless. You, my dear, are practically our saving grace this time around."

I desperately long to correct her, to tell her that Jericho and I are not a romantic pair, but by this point, there's a great chance she and Victor have obtained a copy of the most recent *U. Herald* publication. Perhaps she got it from her Urovian ambassador, or one of their spies that I am not supposed to know about. Regardless, I force myself to let her presumption slide. Worse, I go along with it. "He hasn't proposed yet," I murmur, "but I suppose being asked to serve on his Council is a step in the right direction."

Harriet's laugh is like a soothing hum. "Be patient with him. Jericho takes time."

Tell me about it, I want to say. But I hold my tongue, opting to follow Queen Harriet deeper into the labyrinth of Sevensberg.

26
Jericho

I chuck the nightside lamp into the stony walls of my private suite the moment I'm left to my own devices. "Son of a *bitch*!" I scream, kicking my foot into the ottoman at the end of my bed for good measure.

Annabelle is always wary of strangers, yet right off the bat, she wants to sit by Venus at dinner. And do not even get me started on Slater, who looked at Venus like he'd give away his entire inheritance to have her—not to mention Venus looking at Victor in a similar manner. And shit, even the *seven-year-old* has the hots for her—

"And you do not?" a voice whispers from an invisible hiding spot.

I stop in my tracks.

"I can't do this right now," I say by way of dismissal to the cursed conscience that has recently begun plaguing my waking hours, in addition to those that I spend trying to get some sleep.

Since Venus's arrival, word around Broadcove was

true: my visions had stopped flooding so rapidly—perhaps entirely—and, in the most hidden parts of my soul, I began to think that her presence was perhaps the key. Then, on the boat ride here, I relived a moment I had suppressed for years, one where I demanded the Saints prove themselves and their existence. Mother's death reduced my life to one of loneliness, especially in navigating visions that were growing stronger every day and I was still so unaware as to why they were coming about.

Why my mind bothered to bring me back to that moment, I didn't know, at least not until Venus banged on my door and demanded to know why I was in love with her.

Me? In love with *Venus?*

It took great strength not to spew laughter in her face right then and there.

But now, my chest grows heavy, my head starts to swirl, and suddenly, all I know how to focus on is Slater's sensual fascination. Saints, I could practically *smell* his growing obsession for her. In a matter of moments, she was beloved. Dare I say it, even with Delta back amongst her childhood friends—people she saw as family—Venus still eclipsed her. She garnered all the attention.

And now, that *voice.* One that I know with haunting certainty belongs to—

A knock sounds at my bedroom door, and before I can tell the hopeful guest to scram, the knob turns, and the stranger exposes themselves.

"Chumley," I muse, not entirely put off by his arrival. "To what do I owe the pleasure?"

My parents traded Thatcher Chumley to the Seagraves in exchange for Ardian when I was around the age of ten. I had been devastated to see him go, given that he always stuck out his neck for me when Father grew cross with me. In time, Ardian became somewhat of an advocate for me, too, but nowhere near Chumley's caliber of kindness. But assessing him, now . . . he looks haggardly, like weight has been leached out of him. His only mercy lies in the fact that he hasn't gone bald. But his copper hair has certainly dulled into a dreary, ashy brown.

"I'm afraid I have nothing of great importance to discuss, no pressing matters. Only that, well, it's nice to see you again."

"I must admit, you look as though you've seen better days."

Chumley chuckles. "Do you want children, Jericho?"

The question feels as surprising as if he were to have pulled a weapon on me.

"*This*," Chumley gestures to his depleted disposition, "is what children do to you. And I'm not even the parent!"

Glancing around my generous suite, I notice a ceramic bar cart stationed between the lavish bathroom and the sitting room. Quickly cutting across the space, I grab Chumley a bottle of green liquor and an iridescent shot glass.

"Although," he calls out from his side of the room, "being King and all, you could always pass along your offspring to wet nurses and nannies, or in the Seagrave's case, your trusty advisor."

Something about the comment stops me mid-pour, and I nearly spill alcohol on the cream, carpeted floor.

Recovering just in time to catch the excess in my own glass, I walk the liquid over to Chumley and offer it up in silent understanding. In turn, he sniffs the drink and instantly begins to relax. "To the Saints who allow us to survive each day."

"Indeed," I remark, clinking our glassware together before shooting it down our throats.

I never paid much attention to Chumley's drinking habits when I was young, but if he drank even half as often as Father did, he certainly knew how to handle his liquor. Even now, he barely even blinks at the green substance that begins to make my eyes burn. "I've been wondering," he begins, all the while I'm trying not to choke out a miserable cough, fighting for my life against the vile drink, "have more positions opened up on your Council? Or are they limited to beautiful women?"

Finally in control of myself, I merely say, "That's an awfully loaded question."

"We can keep this conversation off the record, if you wish."

Chumley gestures to the seating area, and the hearth crackles in invitation. But I'm not so easily persuaded. "You may bear Urovian blood, but you live with these people, Chumley. You'll surely share every detail I give you—"

"I'm resigning," he blurts suddenly.

My eyes dart frantically to the door he entered through, grateful to see it closed yet jolted by the statement. "What are you talking about?"

"Well," he clarifies, "more like . . . escaping with you back on *Crystal Wrath* when you set sail for Honeycomb

Harbor."

Okay, I'm convinced.

We forgo the bedroom in favor of the sitting area, as he previously suggested. My footsteps rapidly take me to a plush, chaise lounge while Chumley opts for the edge of the posh, leather couch. The charming fireplace winks with the quiet recognition of guests, and I almost instantly feel its responding warmth settle over my exposed skin. "What happened?" I ask, knowing that a man as sacrificial and tolerant as Chumley wouldn't just abandon his post casually—especially not when this sort of departure could potentially cause great discord between our territories.

He shakes his head repeatedly, as if his answer is too taboo to share with me.

"Sir," I say in a manner of respect rather than frustration. "I know that you've only ever seen me as a young, unassuming prince, but things are different now. I am King, and while it gives me the right to demand you tell me why you'd be willing to risk so much to leave Sevensberg, it more so provides you with the understanding that I *have* to know what the hell is going on. So, out with it."

Chumley stares daggers into my soul, as if hanging onto one, final shred of denial.

"Do not make me sell you out to Harriet and Victor. Do not force me to trap you here or provide the means for your rightful imprisonment, or worse. Just . . . tell me why. Tell me everything, so that I can understand."

Poor Chumley fights to keep the tears from falling, maintaining the strength in his voice as he tells me,

"Greer's scars."

Yes, I instantly noticed the harsh marks the moment she strolled in. She didn't look like that the last time I saw her. "What about them?"

"The manner in which they were obtained," he whispers, "was not an accident."

I read between the lines as analytically as possible, even as a part of heart wilts for the girl. "Does Harriet know?"

"No." He exhales, wiping fiercely at his eyes. "Victor insisted that she got severely scratched up after a steep fall from climbing trees."

"Has Greer confided in anyone besides you?"

"She never disclosed anything to me," Chumley clarifies sadly. "I . . . witnessed the event. And aside from screaming in pain immediately after, she hasn't spoken a word about it to anyone, nor has she spoken in general—"

He disappears into a chasm of sobs, and despite the ghastly sight and the sick feeling in my stomach crying always creates, I let him. My list of questions begins piling sky-high, however.

When was this?

Were there any other possible witnesses?

Are any of the other children at risk of similar treatment?

Shouldn't Harriet be made aware of this?

How long has this sort of behavior, on Victor's part, been going on?

Are any resources being provided to Greer in attempts to reverse her muteness?

But for now, my most burning inquiry stands as follows:

"What good does leaving Sevensberg do for Greer, or for anyone, rather? And your answer better be a damn good one."

Chumley doesn't know what to say, his eyes still raining tears that drip onto the floor or seep into the sofa. For a minute, I almost believe that he will relinquish his hold on the subject and move onto something else. But after a suspended moment of anguish, he peels his face away from his hands and whispers, "It allows me to help you raise an army when we come home."

"*Excuse* me?" Ardian's relentless assurances that claimed *Mosacia is not our enemy* replay in my mind at a shrill, inexorable volume, as if an invisible being is screaming in my ear for only me to hear. "You want me to attack a territory twice our size because you suspect its king abuses one of his children?"

"Did you not see her face, Jericho? It's *torture*—"

"*Damn the girl, Chumley,*" I snarl, standing from the chaise. "Where was your fury for me when I was hurting? You could see what was going on—to me and to Mother. And what did you do about it? I never saw Mosacia come to my aid when Father was still alive."

That certainly shuts him up.

I release a labored breath. "The answer is no. Urovia does not have enough manpower nor resources for an attack based on rage rather than reason. Besides, the way Urovian policy functions—in case you have forgotten—is that adjustments involving our militia must be a unanimous agreement within my entire Council. I cannot evade Ardian—whose answer will be a resounding *no*—and I certainly will be unsuccessful in explaining justifiable violence to Venus. Frankly, given our history, I'm lucky to have her hatred."

Chumley becomes dutifully intrigued at that. "What history?"

Sighing, I prepare for whatever response Chumley will have to the mention of my dreams, and when I shut my eyes, I find that it is easier to confess my transgressions. "One of my visions, not long after I became King . . . condemned Venus's father for a crime I dare not speak of, and I . . . well, I think you know what that forced me to do."

"Oh."

I nod. "Touchy subject."

Chumley's eyes widen in both awe and unease. "Aren't you afraid that Venus might—"

"Kill me?" I suggest. "Afraid is not the right word. I suppose I'm just . . . hopeful she chooses not to. I am starting to think that even if she did betray me, I'd deserve it."

"Jericho . . ."

"No, it's true." I groan, becoming uncomfortable the more I dwell on the idea of Venus stabbing a knife through my heart or poisoning me somehow. "Venus could kill me. The longer I keep her around, truthfully, the smarter she'll get and the more intel she will uncover. Of course, I'm not just going to let her kill me. I still have some self-respect. But I know her skill sets, and as threatening as they are, they are also why I appointed her onto my Council in the first place. And I . . ."

Fuck, I don't want to say it.

I don't want to say, out loud, that I need her.

"What does she bring to the table," Chumley asks, "that's worth risking your life?"

For years, all I wanted was for one person to take my visions seriously, to never doubt them. After Mother, the closest confidant I had was Ardian, but even he plays along for the sake of sparing himself an argument.

However, I'm beginning to realize that maybe Venus intercepting my dreams is a good thing rather than an invasion of privacy. Maybe it is okay if it happens again—I almost even want it to happen again, if only to prove my newest working theory: that, like me, Venus might be Blessed.

"Being . . . understood again," I answer. It is the most honest one I manage to give him without delving too deep into the details, or showing too much of my hand.

"I understand you, Jericho," he explains, his tone settling over me like a reassuring hand. "I know I've lived on Mosacian soil almost as long as I have lived in Urovia, but I have yet to lose touch with my unyielding trust in the Saints. Ardian would send me postings of the U. Herald when you assumed the throne and . . . they never mentioned that your actions as King were prompted by Saintly encounters, but it makes sense, now."

That last addition to his response rubs me the wrong way. "What makes sense?"

"The violence. All those decisions that required so much bloodshed. I mean, the little prince I shared Broadcove with wouldn't hurt a fly—"

"I'm not that boy anymore," I bite out. "And even if I act on the will of what the Saints reveal to me, there are still times when death isn't necessary. Sometimes, I just need to make people hate me at the end. Other times, it's just fun."

I do not realize I'm heaving heavy breaths until I must take a moment to collect myself. Chumley graciously chooses not to comment on my disturbed state of being, and instead offers me a diverting sense of solace. "I understand that all we've spoken of may have you feeling cornered, but . . . you should at least know that, despite this momentary loss of control, you still have an ally in me. And if you cannot trust that fully yet, you can also rest in the notion that you still have the upper hand."

Chumley is right. Even as I stand in a donated bedroom in a foreign domain, speaking to a man that left his country to serve a new master, I could ruin, if not end, his life with only a few words to Harriet and Victor. I could sell him out about his wish to desert Mosacia altogether, or worse, his considerations regarding a Urovian army. Saints, I still don't get it. Why strike Sevensberg over familial matters we technically shouldn't even be meddling in?

And that's when a horrifying realization crawls over me like a thousand, tiny insects.

"It's not just Greer. That's just one of your reasons for proposing what you did." I narrow my eyes. "Do we have serious justification to make Mosacia our enemy?"

Despite his body language indicating that he wishes to see himself out, Chumley still manages to say, "We have a month to discuss additional logistics. Until then, see what the Saints have to say about everything in play. I trust that they'll provide you worthwhile input one way or another."

I want to force him to stay, give him no choice but to divulge every bleeding secret and spill his soul on the floor—but he makes a point. No need for Chumley to be suspiciously convening in private with me, especially not for too long. Yes, perhaps some time to think and meditate on what messages the Saints want me to hear is exactly what I need right now. And so, I lead Chumley back to the entryway of my suite, nodding in humble agreement. "I shall see you at dinner this evening?"

But Chumley shakes his head. "The dining table is maxed out now that you and Venus arrived. But not to worry, not all meals will be so formal."

I nod along, tracking his footsteps out into the hallway and towards some endless corridor or ornate patio. Unfortunately, the longer I watch him drift away from me, the more I begin to wonder if I overshared. Too late to amend any of that, of course. All I can do about it is try and find something to distract my mind—perhaps another shot of that horrid, green liquor.

But the moment I shut my door to the outside world, my vision blacks out.

Fearful that my body is powering down against my will or that I may pass out onto the tiled floors, I bend at the knee and find a comfortable, stable stance. My left hand reaches down into my pocket, drawing my emergency knife in case I need to blindly swipe it at an unseen attacker.

Then, as if prompted by my conversation with Chumley, a new vision starts.

Venus grins like a little girl as she bounds down a long hallway, the skirts of her blue gown billowing in her wake.

My mind focuses on her feet, her dress flats clip-clopping rapidly against the floor as she quickens her pace. Truth be told, her form is impressive, her speed more so—and I only hope it is because she would chase her sisters for leisure growing up, not because she needed to escape prior danger.

Gradually, the framing of this vision changes, sliding away as if to crop Venus out of view. It tracks the path ahead of her, the rooms she has yet to pass by in her pursuit of—

You've got to be kidding me.

Slater keeps up a decent pace, but in a matter of moments, Venus will surely catch up to him, and from the look on his face, that's exactly what he's hoping for. That he'll turn around at the precise time and catch her in a grappling embrace that—once their body deescalates from the running—will burn with new passion. That for as long as they'll allow themselves, Slater and Venus will savor the feeling of being joined together.

As predicted, it happens. Slater pivots just in time for the front side of her to crash against his chest, and his arms trap her from crumpling out of his hold on impact. They both laugh, but once their bodies deescalate and the sound of it dies out into frantic, united breaths, I can hardly bear to watch.

My brain and body and entire being practically begs Venus not to kiss him.

"I'd still like that tour sometime," she tells him breathlessly.

"Between you and me, there's only one place worth seeing, and it just so happens to be a place no one else knows about."

"Not even Jericho?"

Horror twists an imaginary knife in my gut, and suddenly, I'm well aware of how Venus plans to win Slater Seagrave over.

27
Venus

Halfway through my tenderloin and stew dinner, I apologetically excuse myself from Annabelle's conversation and exit the dining room. The sound of silverware distantly clattering once I'm down another hallway lets me know that Slater found a reasonable excuse to slip out not too far behind me. Tiptoeing through the vast passageways and trailing aimlessly towards a wrought-iron door that leads to the back gardens, I wait innocently for Slater to track me down.

A charmed sort of laugh carries itself across the pathway, echoing along the walls in a manner that almost sounds taunting. Still, it draws a smile out of me, and just as I pivot towards the sound, I feel a muscled chest press against my back. Heat floods me.

"You're getting warmer," Slater whispers, his words encouraging. Suddenly, I understand that this door might actually lead towards the direction of his secret hideout, probably a make out spot if I had to guess. Slater's hands run down the length of my arms, and despite my good girl, where-are-you-taking-me act, the chills that culminate along my spine are real.

Our steps proceed forward in a mirrored tandem, and each time I glance back just before we approach a fork in the garden pathways, Slater casually cocks his head one way or the other, and we conveniently continue forward. Blissful minutes pass on in peaceful heartbeats, my dress fabrics catching on the wind and Slater's dominant posture keeping guard as we stroll through bush lined pathways and spiraled, manicured evergreens. Too distracted by the endless maze of cobblestone roads and sweeping trees, I do not even realize we have drifted far away from the rest of the prying eyes still situated at the dining table until I turn around again, and the ground floor of Sevensberg Palace has become a faraway memory, only a fraction of its once towering size.

Slater signals me to stop, and as he closes the gap between us, his soft hands slide over mine. "Here we are."

Then, he spins me back around, and in front of me rests the most elegant spot I've seen so far on this trip—even the palace at a glance does not hold a candle to this place.

Marbled arches box in a clearwater pool that feels more like a private water lounge, and an equally pristine roof closes its guests off from the sky. And yet, I do not get the sense that I'm trapped. Rather, it feels cozy. Lily pads lay sprinkled along the water's brim, but with the sun lowered to the horizon enough to cast warmth and light onto the area, frogs and other creatures choose to seek solace elsewhere.

The sunlight shines differently here in Mosacia, I think. Most noticeably, with how pearly white Sevensberg Palace is, the sun seems to linger in the sky longer if only to provide the cold architecture some warmth in the evening hours. But here, there's a reimagined, technicolor glow, much like the luster I saw in Harriet's and Victor's throne room. Enchantments dance over each lily pad and floating, white lotus—like Slater and I stepped into a magical realm built just for us.

"I find it hard to believe that no one else knows this spot exists. It's gorgeous."

"Most of the younger siblings shoot for the other end of the gardens. There's a large playground on the east end. Diana knows, though," he mentions, rolling his eyes at the mention of his sister. "Although, she uses this place to mull over her thoughts and stare aimlessly out into the night whenever she's feeling despondent."

Funny, from what little I gathered about Diana—mainly how thrilled she seemed to have Delta back in her stomping grounds—I wouldn't have pegged her as one to become wrapped up in sadness. She's certainly beautiful, and rich. Personally, I do not understand what there would be for Diana to be up in arms about.

Diverting the attention from Diana, I try and see if Slater is as gullible as he is handsome. I force a blush to color my cheeks and twiddle my fingers over one another. "Does Jericho know about this spot?"

But Slater laughs in a way that sounds as though I knocked the wind out of him. "I escort you to my secret hideout, and all you wish to talk about is *Jericho*?"

"I didn't realize how deeply he got under your skin.

Have you two fought over a beautiful woman before?"

Slater lets my blatant ego go unchecked with a scoundrel's grin. "None as pretty as you."

"You flatter me," I tease.

"We have all month," he promises, dotting his index finger on the tip of my nose. "In the meantime, shouldn't you be asking me more advantageous questions that help you gain a better understanding for why your travels were summoned in the first place?"

I side-eye him. "Such as?"

He stews on the subject for a moment or two, remembering something from earlier on today. "The statues," he mutters, and up until now, I had already forgotten about them. "I noticed you staring at the people etched into the walls of the throne room. You don't recognize them?"

I shake my head.

"They're only the most revered gods and goddesses of our earth," he scoffs, as if not knowing about their existences constitutes a crime against nature. "Each possessing a mastery of different, individualized skills and domains. They're *legends*, Venus."

"Then how come I've never heard any of the stories?"

Slater laughs, my question humoring him as well as wounding him. "Because your country doesn't believe in mighty beings. In fact, your lot chalks all our history about the gods and goddesses up to *myth*."

I hear the offense in Slater's tone and play along as if I'd *never* scoff at anything he believes in. For good measure, I bat my lashes at him like some lovesick lunatic. "Why would anyone ever reduce such a vibrant history to fiction?"

"Because, much like bedtime stories or fables," Slater begins, though not before flashing a bashful, appreciative smile. "Our history seeks to explain the past and present happenings of our world. Sure, records may mention certain species and power capabilities that have long since expired throughout the age of our earth, but to us in Mosacia, it still holds true."

"Seems far-fetched, but interesting, nonetheless."

"More reasonable than basing your entire faith system on nationalistic propaganda," Slater cuts back through his teeth. *Noted.* I pretend not to have felt the weight of the disdainful remark, draping my legs across the lowering steps. "I'll prove it to you," he starts again. "What's something that you believe doesn't make sense about the world?"

In the silence, I struggle to find one, singular concept about life that particularly blows. The list is long. All I know to focus on is the problem that has haunted my sisters and I nearly our whole lives. "Why bad things happen to good people," I answer, trying to talk my thought process out. "You know, like . . . why diseases steal away our loved ones, why people feel the compulsion to kill, that sort of thing."

Slater seems to know the exact account I ought to hear, and he shifts in his spot to let his warmth shelter me against the evening wind.

"Long ago, there was once an extraordinary young woman that was a daughter of one of the gods. Her name was Pandora," he narrates, and something about the name strikes a chord in me. Both beautiful and foreboding. "She was bestowed several gifts that made her stand out from the other women of her day, but perhaps her greatest trait of all was her curiosity. She craved knowledge, which made the circumstances of her existence rather complicated. You see, one of the gods that gifted her wonderful qualities also gifted her an ancient box littered in heavenly runes and sealed tightly shut. It came with the strict instructions to never open it, as what lied within were not for mortal eyes.

"Years went by, and Pandora's curiosity began to eat away at her self-control. The more her mind drifted towards the box, the more maddening the idea of it became. Sometimes, when she'd draw near to it, Pandora even believed she heard voices speaking to her, as if someone had been trapped within the container and tried calling out for help or that the box had a heavenly voice of its own and wished for her to peer within. In time, Pandora's fascination transformed into an unbreakable obsession, and when she had a moment to herself, she cracked open the lid, just enough to get a single glance and then put it away forever."

Slater briefly stops, his eyes reading the anticipation in mine before continuing on. "Unfortunately, the moment the seal was broken, monsters and mythical beings and evil spirits escaped into the air, contaminating the world and erupting so violently out of the box, it knocked Pandora down and prevented her from trapping the darkness. Suddenly, the world felt as though a death cloud loomed overhead, and Pandora knew that it was of her own doing. She wept in anguish and in guilt, and just as she began to wonder if she could drown in those feelings, a new voice floated into her ears.

"It was the box again, but the sound that called out to Pandora now didn't possess that same eerie, demonic undertone she had fallen prey to before. Now, the voice was reassuring, soft—the sound of a mother's whisper. And so, Pandora peered into the box again, and this time, a glowing orb of pale, blue light rose into the air, illuminating her face, and sang a lovely song as it dissipated around her. Pandora knew that she could not reverse her original decision to release the contents of the box, but at least now, she knew there was hope to combat all the evil."

Hope, I think to myself. *Pandora brought endless pain, but she also brought about hope.*

"That's . . . kind of beautiful, actually," I muse aloud.

He cuts the mood, however, with a male laugh that proves to be rather condescending. "Of course you would be moved by the story of a woman who unleashed evil on the world."

"So is that your explanation, then?" I challenge. "That women are the reason evil exists?"

"You certainly seemed to stir up trouble the moment you arrived," Slater teases rather than answering my question outright. "I wonder what other bad things you'll wind up getting me into."

And before I ready myself fully, Slater's hands frame both sides of my face, cradling me, and he presses a tender yet suggestive kiss onto my lips. I feel his jaw already working, and I read his cues to know when to slide my tongue along his own. The responding moan tells me that he likes it rough—a note I take into account for future reference. "That pool would be a good start," I say into his mouth.

He dips his head downwards. "Care for a swim?" Slater proposes, his breath hot on my neck, dragging kisses on a sensitive spot that has longed for a lover's touch for quite some time.

Grinning, I slip out of my shoes and set my foot onto the first carved step beneath the water lily pond. Slater grips my wrist, however. "We cannot clue anyone in on where we were," he croons, crooking a finger beneath my chin.

Slater does not need to say another word for me to know what his previous statement specifies. This is the make-or-break moment—I know it—I've undergone it time and time again with men and women I'd lure into this position when I still worked in the Makers District. I defined it as such, not because moments like this were my last opportunity to bail out and spare myself any shred of dignity, but because if one wrong word slipped out of my mouth, the ploy would be lost altogether.

So, with careful calculation, I nervously turn to Slater with a virgin's confidence and say, "Help me out of my dress?"

I may as well have asked him to open a birthday present.

Slater unties the ribbons on the back of my dress, and when the waistband slackens, he runs his strong hands over the dotted, bishop sleeves along my arms. I savor what little morsels of our bare skin touch, letting my eyes flutter closed at the contact. Then, Slater's fingers move for the zipper.

Before I know it, his hands are spreading the split fabric at my back towards either side and down my arms. At the ease of how my garment glides off my body, I know with absolute certainty that I am not his first encounter, and it makes me feel slightly at ease knowing this may very well be as much of a game to him as it is to me. Although, there's a higher likelihood that Slater simply wants to play chase, and I'm here to play chess.

Reduced to my slip, Slater sweeps in from behind to press his mouth onto the dip of my shoulder. I wrap my arms around his neck, attempting to disappear into this moment fully—

I try not to search for the shifting object in the bushes. Try to ignore the rustling that somehow Slater doesn't seem to notice. I arch my back just a little more and shut my eyes, envisioning anything I can to keep my heart from pounding so forcefully in my chest.

Your eyes are deceiving you. You're used to evading people when you're most vulnerable. He's not here.

Slater guides us deeper into the water, not minding the way our clothes start to stick to our bodies. He kisses me again, deeper and claiming, and I prepare to meet him in equal intensity. But in a sudden slip of control, braving the idea of searching the greenery again, I open my eyes.

And find Jericho staring back at me.

He crouches between a thicket of leaves within a clover bush, nearly concealed. His blue eyes give him away, however, and he rests no more than thirty yards away. Pure fury ignites my blood knowing we've caught each other in rather compromising positions—yet, for some traitorous reason, the sight of Jericho makes my body melt into the feel of Slater's movement. It turns my core to liquid. It makes my head spin, and my mind plays an evil trick on me to where Jericho isn't just deliberately watching.

He's here. With me. As Jericho's eyes burn into my very soul, I dwell upon what the feel of him would be like. What kissing *Jericho* would do to me.

I don't allow myself to linger on the thought for long.

Instead, I deepen our kiss and tug Slater deeper into the water lily lounge, unbothered by how long Jericho stays around to watch.

28
Jericho

I swear to Saints, Slater Seagrave is on my fucking hit list.

It takes an unholy amount of self-restraint to make my way to my rooms without setting the gardens on fire and throwing loose pebbles through the glass windows. The rest of the valuables in my suite are likely too pricey for me to find justification in destroying, so I figure the longer route back should allow me some time and some well-deserved solitude to blow off some steam. Still, I cannot shake the notion of perusing through Sevensberg like I didn't just witness . . . son of a bitch, I cannot even *think* about it without wanting to get violent—

"Evening, Jericho," a perky voice greets me unexpectedly.

Delta's sparkly smile is likely amplified by her arm linked within Diana's. Despite the two looking nothing alike, their bond gives them an eerie twin sort of glamor upon first glance. "Say," she begins, her tone far too humorous as she asks, "did something squash Venus's appetite during supper? She barely picked at her food."

I refuse to take the bait outright.

Then, Diana grins up at me, and something about the way her bangs cast a shadow over her lightened eyes disturbs me. "Funny, Slater adores tenderloin, and yet, the moment Venus vacates the room, Slater suddenly itches for a reason to excuse himself—"

"What Venus does on her own time outside of mandated gatherings is none of my business," I try and tell them civilly—except when I attempt a smile, I think I pop a blood vessel.

"Pity," Diana sneers. "I expected a bigger reaction out of you. Maybe if I take her for a ride, too, it'll be a different story."

Delta blushes in a way that makes her seem uncertain Venus would consider having relations with a woman, but remembering those faint implications in my ever-haunting conversation with Calliope back in the marshes . . . Diana's threat holds weight. Worse, Venus might be insane enough to try her hand at two Seagrave heirs, if only to spite me for catching her in the act with Slater.

Curtly, I bid them goodnight even though remnants of the afternoon sun still stream through the hallways. Their petty laughter follows me down three long corridors, and the wrath that swarms my head makes me wonder if my ears are bleeding—or perhaps I'm breaking a sweat. Nothing a hot bath cannot fix, especially if I decide to drown myself beneath the scorching temperature.

On my way, I nearly crash into one of the twin boys, and despite nearly bulldozing the kid, he apologizes for not keeping his eye out for me. "Don't worry about it,"

I mutter without really looking him in the face. Even as I trudge down another endless, white-walled wing, no amount of time provides me any certainty on whether I collided with Kellan or Madden.

Finally at my door, free from the sounds of other passing Seagraves or Delta's incessant chatter, I turn the handle and step into—

"Hello, pervert. Nice to see you again."

Cross-legged beneath the overhead light, Venus smirks at me as if she has done no wrong. Innocent, yet sly. Her hair now lays unbound against the same dress I saw crumpled on the ground.

"What the hell are you doing in my room?"

"Oh, you don't like me intruding on your privacy?" she asks pointedly, tilting her head to the side like this is all so hysterically funny to her.

"What do you want?"

"I didn't know you were into voyeurism," Venus drawls, the nastiest grin spreading along her lips. "I'll send you an invitation next time Slater and I—"

"Venus," I snarl. I didn't stay for the whole thing, but I debated letting the sound of my retching ruin their moment. I'd never been filled with such disgust, such *loathing*.

Still, Venus looks like she's just getting started. "No, seriously. It's no problem, at least for me it's not. I mean, Slater probably wouldn't perform well under all that pressure, but—"

"You don't get to make this about me!" I shout, my body clenching hard enough to strain a muscle. "For starters, you're in my room. Second, you're on my Council, and

third, you letting Slater do what he did in broad daylight is only going to make things messier."

"Jealous?" she merely jabs back.

That's beside the point. "You don't know what you're doing."

"Sure, I do," she says calmly. "I'm gaining favor with the Seagraves. Sure, it's a little excessive in Slater's case, but I know it will pay off. Once I have him under my belt, the only ones I really have left to get on good terms with are Diana and Greer. Delta will likely have me accompany her and Diana on one of their future outings—perhaps a game of cricket in the courtyard. Greer . . . I don't know. She didn't say anything during dinner. I think she'll be the hardest to crack."

I dare not let my face give any indication of Greer's circumstances. Better to have Venus fail at something for once in her life than warn her about the young princess. "Why would you need to make the Seagraves like you? I thought you didn't care about anyone's opinion of you?"

That question, to my great satisfaction, seems to stump her. I see the debate for a believable answer take place behind her eyes. Unable to counter me quickly enough to her liking, Venus goes back on the offensive. "You don't trust me?"

"How can I?" I blurt out, my heart thundering as I raise my voice at her. "You don't know these people like I do. I've watched these children get bigger, stronger, more divisive. I've watched Harriet carry enough children to make me detest the idea of ever touching a woman in a way to have her end up in her condition. But most of all, I've seen the lack of empathy they are trained to exhibit when something in Urovia goes awry."

The intensity in Venus's face softens. "Your mother."

"Father, actually." I sneer.

An investigative curiosity begins to dawn on her. "But you despised King Ronan."

"What would make you assume that?"

Venus rejects the opportunity to speak up, staring back at me as if to say I do not assume. I know—and the decision is incredibly telling. I think I may very well be sick, both with mortification and with the unnerving understanding that my previous theory still holds up. "Which dream did you inherit this time?"

"The funeral," she whispers, like the words pain her to share.

Shit. Of all things, it just had to be when we buried Mother.

"Jericho," Venus quietly calls. "Why can I see into your mind?"

"I don't know," I insist, as if the response is pre-programmed.

"Don't lie," she says desperately. "This . . ." she gestures messily to the space between us, "strange, confusing connection is about to drive me mad. And the look on your face tells me that you at least have an idea of—"

"Even if I did, I cannot disclose anything," I interject, "if I do not, in good conscience, believe that what you're up to with the Seagrave family is innocent. And I *certainly* won't tell you if you are sharing a bed with Slater."

Venus cuts me a vicious glare. "Saints, Jericho. Do you even hear yourself right now? The double standard here is *unbelievable!*"

I meet her icy stare with as much intensity as I can muster. "I don't know what you're talking about."

"Oh, *please*. You can threaten people's lives to get your way or get to the bottom of some personal investigation you're conducting, but the second I want in on some information, too, I am not allowed to play to my own advantage?"

"I'd hardly call a set of breasts an advantage," I say under my breath, just loud enough for Venus to intercept the words.

"Just call it what is is, Jericho."

But I can't. "It ought to be better than that—than Slater," I snarl back.

Venus clicks her tongue at me. "Don't tell me you're turning soft, Jericho. You and I both know that manipulation is how we get what we want around here."

"Maybe so," I say, my words raspy in my throat. "But forgive me if I think you're better than that—than Slater. Better than needing to stoop to their level."

She goes quiet for an unsettling moment, looking me over with a gaze that promises violence—but suddenly wipes it clean, replacing it with an eerie, soft smile. "And what level is that?" I'm so caught up in how glitter dances her eyes somehow that I don't notice her close the gap between our bodies and press gently against my front. "Hmm?"

I wonder if Venus can feel my heart trying to break through my chest just to touch hers.

Her feigned curiosity may be the death of me. "Do I stoop this low?"

And down she goes, slowly sinking into the carpeted

rug on her knees. I watch the way her pupils drift higher into her eye sockets, staring up at me practically through her eyebrows in a manner that appears borderline psychotic. Foul, wonderful thoughts flood my brain as her fingers trail from my chest down to my thighs, her mouth now on the exact level as—

"You mean to tell me," Venus purrs, "that you wouldn't give up your deepest, darkest secrets just to know what this would feel like?"

If Venus is bluffing, she is committed. But in the rare case that Venus is serious, if she truly means to entertain me in my devious thoughts and disturbed wishes . . . *Saints above. How do I say no?*

But then, her cheeky grin vanishes entirely, her hazel eyes turning cold. "You want me to buy into all the things you've said and done? All the times you cut sidelong glances at me when Ardian swore up and down that we have nothing to worry about with these people, even if you thought I wouldn't notice you doing so? Then let me do some digging for myself. Let me get to know these people on *my* terms."

I don't know what possesses me to ask, but I find the words tumbling out anyways. "And if I cannot get on board with what you must do to attain their trust?"

She stares at me, unmoving. "You mean with Slater."

Not a question. I nod, only once.

Venus's responding smirk is utterly wicked. "Then even the score."

I temporarily blackout from the wrath that threatens to turn my blood poisonous.

Two can play at that game.

Mad as hell, I rip away from her and move to dig through my bags, and when I do not locate exactly what I'm searching for, I march across my suite and pick through the medicine cabinet in the bathroom. Finally, discovering a container of pills, I grab three or four and stalk back towards Venus, and with all my strength I chuck them at her. Two of them bounce across the hard floor. Venus chooses not to chase them down. "What the hell?"

"Ruin your reputation, but for the Saints' sakes, do not ruin your life, too," I scoff. "Those should make sure you don't wind up with any unwelcome reminders of tonight in a month or so. No need to have two Geneva's waltzing around Broadcove. Now *get out*."

And that's when Venus smacks me straight across the face.

I haven't been slapped this hard since Father was alive. Pure rage leaves a print on my skin, and I fight the urge to ease the sting there. Too late to stifle the gasp that comes out of me, all I know to do now is force myself not to strike back. Mother taught me not to hit women, even if they are the original agitator.

But . . . I pushed Venus too far. Sure, I've pushed her about her father before, but never about Geneva—and this appears to have crossed a line.

"I am on your Council," Venus growls, her temper rising. "In fact, you *begged* me to take up membership and come here with you. Which means I must be painstakingly convinced that none of these people are out to get you, no matter what Ardian assures me and no matter how diplomatic you choose to carry yourself all the while. I have skin in the game, and my sisters' lives depend on me helping you. That, and, believe it or not, I am working on forgiveness. I'm working every damned day and night to try and understand why you killed my father and why you refuse to tell me the reason for doing so. So if you want me to do so successfully, you will trust me. I will converse with whomever I deem necessary. If I befriend them, you will smile and play nice with them. If I avoid them, you, too, will stay away. And you better believe that I will sleep around as I please if it means getting what I want by the end of this trip. Either you turn your head or accept it"—Venus laughs darkly—"or you can watch. I won't deny a king of anything he feels entitled to."

Spit flies from her mouth as she throws that final statement in my face, and as she makes for the door in a fiery fashion, Venus stops suddenly. Her hand hovers over the handle, and in the same moment I watch her posture relax, half of her face turns back in my direction.

"Forgive me," Venus apologizes, her voice racked with guilt, "for my moment of weakness. I should've known better . . . than to touch you. It will never happen again."

But I cannot determine which touch Venus appears sorry for—the one across my face of the one trailing down my stomach.

29
Venus

Jericho has succeeded in giving me the silent treatment for almost a week, but I make a valiant effort to pay no mind to it.

Quite honestly, there are times when I prefer the company of the Seagrave children far more than Jericho's, and possibly even Delta's. I know Delta is happy here, but I didn't know her bliss came at the cost of her giggling at all hours of the night in her suite next door. Or her incessant, gleeful interruptions during mealtimes. Delta always finds something of minimal use to contribute, mainly a memory for us to relive alongside her when Mosacia was still her true home.

Since our initial rendezvous, Slater remains a worthwhile distraction from the business side of this trip. His bed also proves to be far more comfortable than the one in my suite ever was, and luckily, it comes with the blessed perk of being five halls down from Delta and her late-night tomfooleries with Diana. Meanwhile, I've let

Kellan and Madden conquer me in chess enough times to rot my brain, participated in Annabelle's private tea parties with her dolls nearly every day this week, and tried to strike up a conversation on Greer's hobbies multiple times with no avail. She barely even makes any noise when she chews her food.

However, today may prove successful in my attempt to cover some ground after all, as Slater walks a handwritten letter over to me and drops it on the wrinkled sheets between us.

It wouldn't kill you to share our guest with me for one afternoon, Dickhead. Please inform Lady Venus that I would love to take my lunch with her today if she is available. I'll even request that Delta busy herself elsewhere if she prefers.

— Diana

"Executive decision," Slater remarks plainly. "You're already booked with me."

"Relax." I sigh. "I think it would do me some good to get to know your sister. And it's only one afternoon."

Slater merely shrugs, trotting to the bathroom to hide his newest ego blow, his sister's scribbled letter in hand. "Your loss," he tells me, gesturing to his physique.

"Oh, please. I'll have you wrapped around my finger again by the end of the night."

No rebuttal. No denial. For all sakes and purposes, I'll take that as a win.

As I hold tight to my dressing robe and prepare to make the trek back to my suite and select an outfit for my lunch with Diana, I watch as Slater peers at the message one more time. Something draws a husky laugh from him. "At least she capitalized 'Dickhead.'"

Delta responds much better than I figured she would considering her two closest companions will be dining without her. She does not even skimp out on dressing me and fixing my makeup properly for it, either. "It's nice to see you two getting some alone time," she assures me. "But you're also not allowed to have fun without me, so I hope your time together is terrifically mundane."

Yep, that's more like it.

With a few more sarcastic remarks and the tightening of my corset, Delta sends me on my way and provides directions to Diana's rooms—one hall past Slater's living quarters. I make sure to take the route that cuts me through Slater's designated corridor, and I offer him a flirty smile through the cracked door.

Slater coughs out a laugh as he peeks his head out from his room. "Never thought I'd behold you in *pink*."

"Delta says it's Diana's favorite color."

The words are an outright guess, but they appear to land well. "Kiss ass," he still throws in my face. "And as lovely as you look, I cannot stand how Delta tends to make you look so . . ."

"Prim and proper?"

Slater disagrees. "Frilly is more like it."

"Well, what's your favorite color? Maybe I'll dress for your liking instead, next time."

That gets him to laughing again. "Isn't it obvious? Seagrave blue."

His answer makes me feel idiotic—and yet, something tells me that if I were to ask Jericho what his favorite color was, he wouldn't say Urovian red. Or black, for that matter. From the vision I intercepted of him attending Queen Merrie's burial, those two colors may very well be the bane of his existence.

"Yours?" Slater returns, yanking me back into reality.

Despite working amidst greenery every day of my life and finding a familiar sense of peace among it, my heart softens thinking of my true answer. "Violet." I do not feel particularly inclined to tell him why.

He nods in approval. "Yes, you ought to wear the hue sometime soon. For me."

He puckers his lips following his hopeful words, expecting a farewell kiss, but I'm already on the move, leaving him to look ridiculous in the open hallway. Fortunately, the moment I turn the corner, Diana already expects my arrival. "I figured you needed a jailbreak."

Slater's not too challenging to keep up with, but the change of scenery fairs me well. "I appreciate your thoughtfulness. And the invite."

"The pleasure's all mine," Diana insists, her tone indicating a well-kept secret of some type. "Shall we?"

My pastel skirts billow and my heeled shoes click as we proceed forward, taking a shortcut through one of the courtyards to descend into the southern wing of the grand estate. "Delta tells me that before you joined Jericho's Council, you worked as a topiary," Diana mentions casually, stepping lightly over a puddle before swinging open a door that leads back inside.

"Still do," I clarify, mirroring her careful steps as we

pass into a pale blue hallway with more of those god-like sculptures I first witnessed in the throne room. "I head up the design and upkeep of Broadcove's gardens."

"What's that like?" Diana asks, stopping to turn around and look me in the eye as she says it. Her genuine interest proves to be refreshing, yet . . . no one has ever bothered to ask me about my line or work. I'm not entirely sure how to describe it.

"Um . . . well, lots of weeds. And mulch. Saints, I hate mulch. Incredibly long hours, of course, and cruel temperatures," I rattle off, unsure about how Diana still acts enthralled by the concept of grueling labor. "But at the end of all the hustle and bustle, there's a technicolor masterpiece that stares you right in the face, and . . ."

I catch Diana laughing, tickled by something I said or maybe even the way I say it. We turn the final corner towards our unknown destination, and as she reveals a key she kept in her dress pocket, she murmurs softly, "Gods, you're just like her."

As she twists her swiped key within the knob, I mean to ask Diana what "her" she's implying—that, and why Sevensberg doesn't have guards posted outside of every room. But by the time the mechanism unlocks, and Diana swings open the door, I seem to receive at least one answer to my questions.

Diana and I drink in the spectacular art gallery, furnished with a few oak observation benches. Styled in the same manner as a museum—or from what Calliope had described a museum to be, as I've never beheld one myself—stunning paintings hang in a uniformed line. Consumed by color and composition within our first shared breath, a new air quality seems to dawn on Diana and me as we cross the threshold. A sweetened fragrance dances curiously beneath my nose, one that reminds me of North Star.

Without studying the brushstrokes and illustrations in depth, a sixth sense in me tells me all I need to know about these ingenious designs: they were made by Jericho's mother.

Each swirled signature in the paintings' various corners attest to the truth I cannot deny: Queen Merrie remains one of the most talented artists I've beheld in this lifetime.

There's an obvious beauty about each piece I marvel at the further I pace around the gallery, but beneath it, there also lies an unmatched discipline. Each stroke and flourish laid to rest on the canvases hold definitive purpose—not a single accident in sight.

Cemented on a dark accent wall at the back of the room, a massive portrait of Diana's entire family acts as the gallery's epicenter. In a single glance, I notice the younger glow each member has, but none more so than Greer—the jagged scars on her face, nowhere to be found. I want to know, so badly, what had happened, but out of fear of behaving insensitively, I cast my eyes elsewhere.

Every painting is unlike the one before. Bordered between an abstract interpretation of some jaded emotion and a vineyard in landscape orientation, a self-portrait of her younger self stares back at me. Sympathetic green eyes provide windows into what was likely a merciful soul. Rather than meeting beauty in its conventional standards, Merrie captures my attention because she exudes a life full of optimism. Her teeth glimmer like fine pearls in a curved, easy smile, temporarily unbothered by life's troublesome circumstances—and if I had to make a wager, I'd say she is no more than three years older than me here. So much promise in a single smile. So much sadness in the memory of a woman that no longer exists.

Queen Merrie was infinitely talented, but no one had ever mentioned her artistry to me before. Or . . . had someone? I forget—

Diana clears her throat.

I ground myself back to the present. "Yes?"

"I said, I hope you like halibut," Diana repeats. "I find the dish divine!"

Too caught up in the splendor of Merrie Morgan's cherished art, I didn't even observe the quaint foldaway tabled Diana had set up for us—a pale, gingham tablecloth draped over the top and tulle, pastel ribbons tied in bows against the backs of our chairs. "How kind," I say, knowing damn well I've never been able to afford a meal like this and fighting the sadness that pings in my chest at the reminder.

Before sitting, however, my vision becomes triggered by uneven stitching on the side of one of the canvases— the one with an experimental design that I immediately believe represents turmoil. Frayed edges splay out just enough for me to notice, as if the painting had been accidentally torn up during its delivery.

Still, I sink into my spot across from Diana and ignore it for the moment. Green herbs and sliced lemons coat the fish with a refreshing garnish, and beneath the cut of protein, a light-colored sauce pools at the base of my plate. In the upper corner of my place setting, a rosy beverage glimmers back at me from within a wine glass. "This looks magnificent." I sigh, my mouth watering.

Diana proudly cuts into her halibut, grinning as I pick up my fork and feel its unusual heaviness. "So tell me," she begins, her manicured nails clicking against her drink. "When did you know that he was the one?"

I nearly drop my silverware into my food. "Slater? Oh, no. I'm not interested in your brother like that—"

Diana gets to laughing so hard that her sides hurt. Grunting in pain and hilarity all at once, she shakes her head. Extending a hand as if to beg for mercy from what she assumed was a joke, she clarifies herself. "No, not my brother. I'm talking about Jericho."

Okay, *she* must be the one joking now.

"That's preposterous, Diana."

"Is it?" she challenges, setting down her glass and bracing her hands on the edge of the table expectantly. "The fact that you replaced Ardian's typical presence here set off the initial alarms, but the newest edition of the *U. Herald* Delta smuggled in her luggage confirmed our fearful suspicions."

"Well, I can assure you," I defend with no hesitation, "that Jericho and I are not romantically involved, nor will we ever be. I've only told Delta the same thing a hundred times over. You two would put your trust in a meddlesome tabloid rather than my own testimony?"

Diana takes another bite of her food while I squeeze the juice from the lemons on my plate over my fish, if only to clench my fist for a moment. "Hearts can deceive. Rumors tend to speak more truth than lies these days."

Frustration takes over me. "If I was enamored with Jericho, why would be I be sleeping with your brother, Diana?"

She doesn't balk from my audacious question. "Boredom, probably. Most couples nowadays need another outlet of entertainment and fulfillment to feel truly happy."

Then, despite never having been one for committed, monogamous relationships, I find myself defending the lifestyle. "I think it's awfully rash to assume that most romantic couples require an additional lover. It goes against the whole premise of marriage."

"That's because the marriages you witnessed growing up were likely forged for the sake of convenience," Diana lectures, and I feel my blood turn to steam within the shell of my body. "Given your particular upbringing, your own parents probably only stayed together to have a better chance of feeding you."

I feel the urge to stab my fork through Diana's eye, and I swear to myself not to consume another morsel of halibut.

Diana picks at her food again like she hadn't just said something so foul. "I don't say this to chastise you. Not at all. If anything, you're smart to have an affair. Better to control infidelity than to be blindsided by it like Mother will be one of these days."

My stomach knots up at the thought—Harriet happily going about her business, thinking her life is nothing but marital bliss and new babies. That she has not only secured an unbreakable dynasty, but she's also preserved a fruitful marriage all the while. But really, Harriet has only granted additional power to a man who remains unfaithful to her. Worse, her own children see through Victor's deception, which means they likely find her to be dimwitted as well as neglected. Devastation prickles my skin.

Then, a disturbed conviction courses through my veins as my mind recalls Octavian's strict instructions. I'm not here to deny the *U. Herald*, correct Diana, or screw Slater—I'm here to convince Jericho that he can trust me, that when he looks to me for support, he finds something deeper.

And so, swallowing my pride, I heave a sigh and say, "Promise you won't say anything?"

"You have my word."

Her word is likely as good as dust. Still, I tell her, "Jericho implied that I'm only on his Council long enough to prove if I'm intelligent enough to be considered for Queen Consort. And it made me so mad, to have him reduce me to one thing, that I just . . . wanted to hurt him back. But I regret it."

Diana doesn't understand. "Why take it back?"

"Because he caught us."

Diana's eyes widen, then, and humor threatens to make her spit out her drink. She barely manages to swallow before exclaiming, "Jericho *saw* you two down at the water lily lounge?"

"You *know* about the lounge?"

"Um, *yeah!*" She cackles. "I mean, no one else does, if it makes you feel better, but I am aware of Slater's tricks."

"It just drives me crazy, you know," I complain to Diana, "to not get a reaction out of Jericho. I know his talent for violence and vengeance. Why won't he fight for my attention?"

And it's then—*right* then—that I start to imagine things between Jericho and I that I hadn't noticed before. Like . . . the way he didn't blink when I knelt before him the other night. The way he tensed up but maintained his stare. How the air always seems to reach a boiling point when we stand too close. And how every time I uncover another one of Jericho's prophetic dreams, I begin to think that I may grow to empathize with the decisions he's made.

Or how, as I threw Slater in his face, Jericho told me that I deserved better.

"Touchy subject?" Diana finally acknowledges, sipping her drink once more. "Maybe we should move on, then. Delta tells me that your religious board, or whatever they're called, came up to Broadcove just before you all shipped out of Honeycomb Harbor. What was that all about?"

That isn't the most upbeat conversation topic, either, but no need for you to sink your claws too deep in my business, Diana.

"They wanted to inform me that if I truly wish to tie the knot with Jericho, I must undergo conversion assessments with the Church of Saints," I lie, praying it convinces her well enough. "Apparently, the Holymen get the final stamp of approval before royals can wed. They insist on proving that my faith is sound."

Diana's disgusted expression confirms my private

hopes. "Gods, if I had cranky old men trying to run my life and marriage, I'd obliterate them."

The laugh that comes out of me is pathetic at best. "That's what I figured upset me first: that they were so invasive and controlling. But the truth is, I think I expected a relationship with Jericho to be easy and was proved very wrong." Diana's eyes fill with superficial pity, and I try not to let my immediate annoyance give me away. "All Jericho had to do to appoint me to his Council was say the word, so I bet he could do the same in regard to tying our lives together, but no—he wants me to work for it."

Diana seems to understand my pain. "I get it. My father is far too invested in screening all my potential suitors. It's embarrassing."

I raise a brow at her. "You don't seem like the marrying type."

She takes it as a compliment. "Neither do you. Yet here we are, pining for attention."

This conversation becomes too insufferable to handle fully. I am not pining for anything. I'm here solely to investigate the Seagrave residence and intently search for any weaknesses Jericho's eyes might be missing— and that's when my mind wanders back to the paintings, specifically the tear I detected within one of them.

I turn to Diana, changing the subject. "How do you have all these?"

"The paintings?" Diana inquires, slicing through her fish. "Oh, Mother and Merrie were dear friends—pen pals, you could say. They wrote to one another often, but eventually, King Ronan grew cold to his wife's joy and intercepted all their correspondences. In time, though, they delivered their messages by hiding them within fine objects. Every painting you see in this room carried a letter to my mother, which she'd conveniently stitch into the sides of the canvases."

I chuckle at how oblivious Ronan must've been to not suspect so many paintings being produced at such a rapid pace and then sent off somewhere. Then, an afterthought occurs to me. "How did Harriet's messages reach Merrie, then?"

"Flower arrangements," Diana responds brightly. "Merrie had a fascination with peonies in particular."

North Star flickers in the depths of my memory, but I refuse to dwell on it long enough to recall the haunting voice that spoke to me within the green glass walls.

Diana throws back the last of her alcohol, her eyes casting down at my minimally touched plate of halibut.

"Venus, I need you to not shut down like this. Not over the likes of Jericho." It's only until the tone of her voice shifts into something soft that I realize Diana means to comfort me. "He can stomp his foot and tell himself that you're not the center of his universe, but . . . you're just like her. Come to think of it, how coincidental is it that your line of work produced the very things that made Queen Merrie the happiest? She would've loved you."

I excuse myself from my chair, pretending to find great interest in one of her many paintings on the left wall.

But really, I need a minute to hide my face from Diana. To take a deep breath and fight against the terror that floods my system when I piece it all together—that the voice that called to me in North Star and that now reaches out to me from every canvas in this room was Merrie Morgan.

30
Jericho

I’ve experienced this dream before, and the ending never turns out any brighter than the last time it plagued me—yet my mind tumbles onward, towards the source of so much misery until the image restores its clarity and I’m right back to where the vision took me the first time.

Springtime in the Makers District renders a unique sort of beauty. Flowers litter the yards and create wholesome pathways between different shops, pubs, and service centers. Cascading purples and blues bud faithfully from the greenery that . . . Saints, did Venus plant these? Am I just now realizing it?

I force myself to regroup and guide my attention on the real subjects of this vision: the two gentlemen conversing at a table within a dingy pub. One looks to have just arrived, and he carries a few sacks of concealed resources. The other is a common man, his body frail from an unknown injury that lies beneath bandages wrapped around his torso.

“I brought you what you asked, Tristan,” the first gentleman utters, his breathing uneven and strained from what was likely a *long walk to this meeting spot. "Medicine for your back, the lump sum you requested for your testimony, and my notebook." He flips open the final object, coursing through the pages until he finds an empty one, which isn't until the halfway point. "You better be confident in what you're about to tell me, because this is serious shit."*

"Oh, I am, Parson," the weaker man assures him. "I just hope you're brave enough to put the pen to paper when I tell you how messy this is going to get."

Parson only becomes more enticed by the mysteries Tristan will soon unravel, his eyes gleaming with his future glory and the imaginary prospects of where this story will bring him in his career. "I'm ready when you are." He exhales, his hands already becoming clammy with anticipation.

"One condition," Tristan drawls quietly. "My name will not be attached to the article."

"It doesn't work like that." Parson instantly laughs in his face. "There has to be a source, and when it's something this drastic, any anonymity won't cut it. Your name goes down in history, or you live to be ordinary, poor, and purposeless." Then, Parson snags the medication from Tristan. "And injured."

Backed against the wall, Tristan dwells on the concept for a long while, a tortured expression on his face.

This is where the dream usually stops—where I wake up, assume he unraveled what really happened to Mother, and I hunt him endlessly to silence him altogether. It's why I have never dared to tell Venus what Tristan died for. It would be bad enough to tell her that he did nothing wrong, that he uncovered the mystery behind my murderous deeds, and I simply didn't want to be outed by anyone. It would be another beast entirely to have Venus realize that I killed her father on the assumption of him figuring out the truth.

But the vision doesn't fade to black like all the times before.

Instead, Parson braces himself, hands white-knuckled on the lip of the table, and a dwindled smile crosses Tristan's lips. "Fine. Run the story, but I must first confess that all my intel is not truly my own," he concedes in a manner that demonstrates regret, but the Saints' discernment within me indicates that what he is about to say is a lie.

Why isn't the vision stopping?

Parson glares at him with growing exacerbation. "I need to cite a source if this has any shot in hell of making it into the U. Herald, Tristan. So, either you tell me how you acquired all this information, or I walk."

A long pause settles over the table before Tristan finally dares to speak again, taking back the items Parson brought him in submission. "How soon can you have this printed?"

Pride swells within me. Tristan is scared of me, of my visions. He should be.

"If the publishing staff can reach a majority vote to approve it—and with a provided source for any quotes—I'd say within a week's time," Parson answers.

The battle in his mind shows through his misty eyes. A week. That's seven days to lose sleep over the possibility of my dreams figuring out what he's up to—and ultimately, that's three more days than he truly had to evade me in the end. Still, he forces himself to agree to the terms. "Alright, then. Her name is Venus. Venus Deragon."

My stomach lurches hard enough to nearly wake me from my sleep.

Parson's lack of a reaction to the mention of her surname— the same that Tristan bears—tells me that the two men are not the companions I believed them to be. As he writes down Venus's name and requests that he provide the correct spelling of her name, Tristan counts the silver coins that Parson brought him as part of their agreed terms.

I scoff. Tristan is fatally selling out his daughter for enough money to pay a month's rent.

"Well, then." Parson sighs, ready to document every blasphemous detail Tristan has for him. "Where would you like to start?"

I know better than to stampede down every damned hallway in Sevensberg shouting for Chumley—especially at this unholy hour of the night—but with no understanding of where his living quarters are, I feel at a tremendous loss.

Mindlessly stumbling down tiled corridors, catching sight of their sculpted saviors I refuse to buy into, I turn a corner to get away from it all but unfortunately select the worst hallway to traipse through.

"You look like you could use a drink," a bitter voice calls out.

Victor Seagrave looks particularly unhinged at this early hour, and he proves to be the last person I'd like to see at this particular, given moment. The moonlight brings the silver out in his facial hair, and his hair is tousled hard enough to look like he's been dealing with factory explosives. His eyes are ringed in darkness, and in an all-around sense, Victor looks like hell.

The thought makes me smile.

"Or a sleeping pill," he adds snidely under his breath

at the look on my face. I'm tired, but not deaf. "You do know what time it is, don't you, Jericho?"

"Yes, Your Majesty," I say with proper salutations, already bothered by the way I play coy as I say to him in return, "I'm just a little restless tonight. Thought a walk might help straighten myself out."

"I'd be anxious, too, if this was my first concord as King," he bites back, his words obviously spoken in an insulting manner.

Truthfully, I forgot that tomorrow marks the halfway point of the trip, which always gets hallmarked with the annual concord between Urovian and Mosacian rulers. Not that it hadn't been high on my radar, but . . . I have been feeling a bit distracted as of late.

Since Venus's confrontation in my rooms a few days ago, I've been trying to offer her some space for several reasons; although mainly because if I catch her with Slater again, I may kick several holes into the Sevensberg drywall. But beyond that, Chumley's ominous desperation to escape Mosacia and the Seagraves makes me wonder if Venus might be onto something. That she may be closer to unraveling something I'm not seeing. I just need to find Chumley and talk this out.

I hear frantic movement from behind Victor, deeper into his shared rooms with Harriet, and he winces just before the sound of retching faintly echoes out into the hallway. "Gods, I hate the sound of it."

A memory pings into my thought pattern. "Someone once told me that if the woman experiences physical sickness like that, it means the baby is healthy—"

"I've already had six before this. You think I wouldn't

know that?"

Whatever. Victor proves to be far too hot-tempered when he's running on fumes, and the less time I must linger in his dreary presence, the better. "I'll leave, then," I respond curtly, already pivoting away from his door. But a twisted sting flares up along my wrist, and only when I'm yanked forward do I realize Victor has grabbed onto me.

"Let me make a few things very clear," he sneers through his teeth. "I do not know what mischief you're up to, but whatever it is, I will sniff it out."

I look at him with disgust and confusion. "I'm not sure what you mean."

Harriet throws up louder, now, and Victor shuts the door behind him, unable to tolerate it. *Saints, what a pathetic excuse of a husband.*

Both of our chests puffed, we size each other up with clenched fists at our sides. For whatever reason, Victor prefers to pass his lackluster rapport that he held with Ronan Morgan down to his son without seeing that I am nothing like my father—so I shall happily alter my outlook on him as well. I only hope that the recognition of us being equal in height irritates him just a little. Victor has known me all my life, has watched me grow into the king I am now since I was an infant. What could possibly make him flip a switch so fast?

"You know you are weak," Victor relishes. "It's why you haven't participated in a concord in years, why you stalled visiting Mosacia, and kept us from coming to Broadcove. Your father knew it back then, too—that the moment Merrie died, his reign was on borrowed time.

Ronan died before the wolves could descend on him, but your time is coming."

Victor slithers towards me, far too close for comfort, and with a devious grin, he tells me with an uncanny amount of audacity, "It doesn't matter why you brought Venus here, or what good she'll do, because the moment she replaced Ardian, I knew you were a fool. She may have my kids temporarily enamored, but Venus cannot distract your homeland from your trail of bloodshed. Your people will kill you and your pathetic excuse for a queen consort long before you get the chance to prove them otherwise—"

My fist collides with Victor's nose before I realize I swing at him.

Victor grunts in both surprise and pain, cupping a hand over the injury, and I don't give a damn if he's bleeding out or not. Straightening out before meeting his eyes again, I tell him, matching his rage, "I don't know what you have against me, Victor, but you better find it in your heart to move past it, or I'll tell your wife and everyone else at the concord tomorrow why Greer has those scars on her face."

Victor looks like he would burn Broadcove Castle down if given the chance.

"Say what you will about my people coming after me," I seethe. "I deserve it. But your crown becomes useless in the absence of the respect you'll lose. So, how about you wipe your nose, comfort your pregnant wife stooped over the toilet, and be really fucking smart about what you say, or do at concord tomorrow, because so help me," I snarl, "if you so much as *look* at Venus in the wrong way,

I will slit your throat."

I leave Victor's ass in the hallway, storming off loud enough to let the entire West Wing of the palace hear me if they're light sleepers. To my great fortune, however, five minutes of causing a scene through the different passages eventually brings me to a stairwell that spirals upwards with a sign screwed into the wall reading, *"Staff Quarters."*

Practically at the top of the stairs, a plaque bears Chumley's full name in a curled, obnoxious font in the center of a towering door. He must hear me coming, because just before I sound off two, brief knocks, he swings open his door and beckons me in without a sound.

"How did you—"

Chumley gestures for me to zip it—immediately. I obey, of course, still on edge from provoking Victor in his own home.

Unlike my room, Chumley's apartments are unkempt, littered with paperwork, and his furniture rests in crooked formations. This truly looks like the den of a mentally deranged individual. In the back corner, however, lies a single suitcase, likely already packed for his unmentioned departure.

"Chumley," I whisper once the door closes again.

He says nothing, simply waiting for me to spill.

"How familiar are you with the *U. Herald* these days?"

Sleep clouds in his eyes, but Chumley answers kindly. "Harriet and I read every published edition together whenever Ardian mails them to us."

"Any chance you would remember various staff writers whose names have been accredited to different articles?"

"Of course," he affirms. "After a while, I know how to associate a writer with their publications without even glancing at the citation. Each person possesses a signature, unmistakable style."

I shouldn't be making any more hasty decisions tonight, but against my better judgment, I've reached my limit on the amount of people who use Venus's name in association with something remotely threatening.

This ends now.

"Parson. Surname unknown. I am unable to recall any particular articles under his name, but I know for certain he was employed with the *U. Herald*. If you manage to get him here without any of the Seagraves finding out and arrange a private meeting between the two of us, offsite preferred . . ."—well, there's no turning back now—"I promise to help you escape to Urovia on Crystal Wrath at the end of this month."

No logistics on Chumley's covert escape have even been brainstormed—by me or with one another—but his hand grips my own before I can rebuke my offer.

"Thank you, Jericho." He breathes, as if his air supply had finally been restored.

31
Venus

After what Diana had implied about Slater's connection with me, I figured that coming up with an excuse for why I did not wish to sleep in his rooms anymore should've been easy. Instead, Slater nearly threw a tantrum about my decision. And just when I began to think his childlike frustration was merely an act to lure me back in, Slater chucked a paperweight at me. I dodged it, thank the Saints, but the sound of it turning to colored shards on the floor frightened me well enough.

From then on, I gladly learned to block out Delta's next-door chatter, though, it only lasted long enough to then face off against a new enemy: the nightmares.

Having unearthed an odd array of Jericho's previous visions—a skill I still do not have a proper explanation for, now that I think about it—I now know which dreams are his and which are my own. Within these last few days, back in my designated rooms, every dream has proven to be my own and has contained, in one aspect or another,

Merrie Morgan.

I never met the woman, never knew the sound of her voice while she still walked the earth, but every time I close my eyes, I see her. Hear her. *Feel* her in my unconscious presence. I do not understand why a woman, famed for her kindness, scares me so deeply, but my terror remains. In a mystifying manner, my fear holds deep reverence, which may likely be due to Merrie's previous authority and title—and yet, the same awed apprehension does not overcome me as I stare into the eyes of my gracious hosts, my newest unlikely friend, and the handsome man I scorned behind closed doors.

My original premonition about how this concord meeting would unfold proves to be a far cry from reality. For starters—and to my great relief—Jericho and I do not sit on wobbly, inferior chairs below the elevated dais in the throne room. In fact, neither Victor nor Harriet dons their royal crowns. However, the formalities still prove their value.

Situated in their version of our boardroom back home, although at least three times its size, Jericho and I stand side by side in Urovia's classic red and black. As Delta dressed me this morning for the event, she highlighted a notion of propriety I never knew for certain, but had briefly perceived when Jericho first arrived in the marshes—only the King wears crimson. That same, decorated uniform clatters every time he shifts his feet or turns his head, but it still proves to be crisp, polished, and dashing. His onyx hair has been gelled down, smooth-seeming, and tidy. Cleaned up to this degree, Jericho no longer looks like a madman. He looks almost benevolent, and something within me aches the longer I glance at him.

At his right, my body feels at home within a gown one of the seamstresses back in Broadcove commissioned for me, and it might just be my favorite thing I've ever worn in my life.

Midnight taffeta curves through my body like an inanimate snake. It winds around my neck, forming a makeshift choker—a detail sure to catch Slater's eye—as well as a plunged neckline for the captivation of anyone brave enough to look. The dress also comes with floor-length, draped sleeves that create a cape-like effect spilling down from my arms, and the rest of the fabric fits my body like a glove. This dress makes me feel like my namesake, at least in Mosacia's eyes: a goddess.

Meanwhile, the Seagrave representatives—Victor, Harriet, Slater, and Diana—stand dressed in their signature silver and blue. The ladies wear elegant, gossamer gowns that likely cost more than my house back in the marshes, while the two gentlemen bear their family's coat of arms. A sweeping, indigo cloak hangs from Victor's broad shoulders, and his facial hair twitches as he signals his wife to start talking.

She does not miss a beat. "Well, then," Harriet begins, "the Annual Mosacian-Urovian Concord is now in session. King Jericho, Lady Venus," she denotes to each of us, her gaze equally respectful, "we'd like to thank you, once again, for your presence here in Sevensberg. My husband and I understand the many hardships you have both endured prior to crossing the Damocles this time around, so we are additionally grateful for your cooperation. Hosting you these last two weeks has been an honor."

"The pleasure's ours," Jericho mutters briefly, his tone neutral. I merely nod my head, and we all sit, save for King Victor.

"Lady Venus," he begins amiably. "I know that this is your first agenda visit, and that you only recently gained status upon Jericho's Council—"

"Mr. Asticova already briefed me on the customs of these meetings. I am perfectly capable of keeping up without further instructions, Your Majesty."

He settles into his chair unhurriedly, as if annoyed by my prior knowledge, and without needing to look, I feel Jericho's mouth tug upward into a proud smile.

"Very well," King Victor says. "Since the two of you are our visitors, you may open the discussion. Please give us an up-to-date account of all economic resources, the state of your militia, and any detail on territory morale."

Neither Jericho nor I particularly have the desire to speak up, but given the authority he possesses, Jericho summons enough bravado to converse in a mild-mannered tone—even though we both know how bleak Urovia has become beyond the borders of Broadcove Castle.

"The Urovian militia has been retired since long before my parents went to be with the Saints," he answers, his eyes on Victor specifically as he pointedly comments on our religious system. With a better understanding of how deep the Mosacians' trust in the gods and goddesses run, I just know that Jericho aims every word to wound him. "And that includes the Hive."

Something about the latter mention forces Victor to

whisper something to his wife, and Jericho leans likewise towards me. I anticipate him to pantomime Victor's actions, but no, his lips brush my ear as he whispers, "The Hive was our congregation of battle ships once docked in Honeycomb Harbor. Mother dismantled their operations when I was only a child."

The Seagrave couple still whispers back and forth while Jericho and I readjust to our previous postures, and in the lingering quiet, I brave a glance in Slater's direction. He, apparently, feels empowered enough to give me the finger. Diana mouths an apology on his behalf. Unwilling to let Slater rattle me again, I wink back at him, leaning into the table just enough for him to look down the neckline of my dress—

Jericho clears his throat pointedly.

I immediately straighten out, but I discover that he's merely grown bored of Victor's hushed dialogue. "If you two have something you'd like to say, feel free to share with everyone."

Harriet takes this one, trying to help her husband unwind. Not even ten minutes in and I could cut the tension with a knife. "We just have a hard time believing, with absolute confidence, especially in Ardian Asticova's absence, that your word on this is honorable."

"Harriet, I can assure you—"

"Why not let us come to Broadcove and see your harbors for ourselves?" Slater challenges.

"Perhaps another time, Your Highness," I say, dismissing the subject like I have any sort of jurisdiction over him. He bristles at the remark.

"My apologies . . . for her," Jericho manages to say

courteously, but between the two halves of his sentence, a viciously delighted smile glimmers in his eyes. *"Thank you,"* he seems to say without words. "Might I go on? I believe you also wanted to know about Urovia's morale and economic—"

"No," Victor bellows suddenly. "I want to hear it from her."

Jericho's face scrunches in irritation, but Diana reads a hidden message in her father's eyes, announcing to all of us at the table, "Father wants you to do the honors, Venus."

"If you're not too busy riding Jericho all the time to know what your subjects are up to."

Diana smacks Slater on the arm, and Harriet may very well shave his head for his vulgarity. Victor nearly has to hold her down to her seat to keep her from erupting. "Disregard him, Lady Venus. But considering you are here to fill Mr. Asticova's shoes, I, at the very least, would like to know if you truly understand what's at stake for your home territory."

As discreetly as he means to phrase it, his words are a threat. I know it instinctively, and even if I didn't, Jericho's stiffened posture and stern frown would give it away. And so, I loosen a deep breath and let every word that spearheads its way into the world strike with absolute precision.

"First off," I say, eyes angled towards Slater, "I find it funny how you're quick to reduce me to my body, when you should really be worried about what really got me to my position at Jericho's side: my brain. Secondly, I am offended that you believe I do not understand the upkeep of my country when, quite frankly, all that my life ever consisted of before Jericho found me, was upkeep. I was as poor as you could get. I survived on scraps, spent my days in dirt fields, and came home to two sisters that were equally as hungry, and tired, and miserable as I was. And you know what? That was Jericho's fault. But that's why I'm here, now. Broadcove is thriving. The Royal Domain and the Noble District remain safeguarded from economic ruin, but only *I* have the inside perspective on how badly the Makers District and the marshes are suffering. The wealthy hire out people like me for minimal wages, and we take what work we can because if we don't, we starve. I bet none of you understand what that's like, not even remotely," I snap. "Not a single, spoiled one of you know what it feels like to spend years of your life picking weeds so that you and your family don't *die*."

I see my saliva spray from my lips as I speak, but it feels too good to dish out my anger on them, especially in their own home. I feel empowered.

"Yes, I hated Jericho for what he caused my life to become," I say through my teeth. "But . . ." I admit, drawing glares from Harriet and Victor, and maybe even Jericho, "when he took me to Broadcove, he saved my life—my sisters' lives, too. And I will do anything to help him be a better ruler because of it."

Harriet seems pleased, although still worried that my loyalty is a byproduct of Jericho's manipulation. "Such as?"

Silence falls upon the room, and I do not need to stall for time by gazing off into the curtains or pretending I didn't hear Harriet to begin with. I know damn well what the Seagraves want to hear: that I will tie myself to him in marriage to make things change. But something possesses me to think differently.

"Jericho is solely responsible for discontinuing the distribution of the *U. Herald* in poorer parts of the territory. I know so, because we haven't received an article since the day King Ronan died." Victor holds a great poker face, but his wife and two heirs bear facial expressions of shock. Jericho shifts uncomfortably in his seat, aghast that his own Council member ratted him out for something unjust.

"This is likely due to the fact that more citizens in that demographic are being convicted by Jericho's administration of crimes such as theft, corruption, and supposed treason," I continue. "I propose that not only do we provide public access to it again, but that we hire aspiring writers from the Makers District to help run the press association."

Jericho's jaw moves in smothered anger. "No, Venus."

Slater grins like a cat.

But I'm nowhere near finished. "What does the *U. Herald* help you hide from them?"

"Nothing."

"Then what's at risk by giving your subjects access to harmless information?"

I watch the lie form in Jericho's eyes before he speaks it into existence. "We do not have the budget for it. It would be a waste of funding."

"And where does that funding come from?"

My favorite part about this discussion is that I barely need to fix my attention on him or look him in the face to keep steering him where I want. That all my pain and heartache from the past prepared me to verbally spar with him in front of an audience like this. "Tell them," I snarl.

He does nothing of the sort.

And his denial sets my rage aflame.

"Tell them why you curried favor with the rich to try and create any alliances you could to protect yourself. Tell them why you taxed the poor in order to turn Broadcove into an impenetrable fortress. Tell them why you drove thousands and thousands of families into their graves and still managed to sleep well at night."

When I finally dare to face him fully, the ghost of tears lines the bottom of his blue eyes.

"You caused all these problems—influencing the *U. Herald*, increasing the taxes, renovating Broadcove— because you needed a distraction. Because you knew . . . when the world realized you were murdering people in the name of righteous obligation," I phrase intentionally, "they would burn you and Urovia to the ground."

Slater no longer bears his cheeky bastard grin, substituting it for a slightly open mouth. But while Harriet and Diana have enough decency to neutralize their expressions, Victor's curled, thrilled smile deeply unnerves me.

Then, just before Jericho takes my words too personally, he, too, notices Victor's lingering eyes on me, the devious shape of joy along his lips.

And despite having let my anger get the best of me— even going as far as to chastise him for being Blessed by the Saints, a near irreversible error—Jericho uncovers something deeper at hand. Studying the amusement on Victor's face, Jericho realizes that everything I just threw in his face, King Victor has likely been meditating on similar thoughts since the moment we arrived in Sevensberg. So to have Victor take pleasure in seeing Jericho dismantled in conversation and governing accountability . . .

Jericho's leg brushes against my own beneath the table, a rousing signal that he understands me now. He *trusts* me—trusts that all this time, I knew exactly what I was doing with Slater and Diana and the rest of them. That I was playing kind and coy until one of them could let down their guard and express how they really saw Jericho.

"Perhaps Lady Venus has a point," Harriet murmurs sweetly.

My soul may very well leap out of my body.

Whether Harriet shares her husband's vile intentions or not, she acts as an extension of support. Every polite agreement she's made and every child she's reared has only helped Victor get to this point, and the understanding of that notion seems to settle over Jericho. Yes, Jericho believes that the Seagraves are out to get him, and they very well may be.

He just doesn't realize that his true downfall is sitting next to him rather than across from him.

Feigning surrender, Jericho growls, "Have it your way, then," before standing from his seat and exiting the table in a dramatic, pissy fashion. The Seagraves buy it, four pairs of eyes tracking Jericho all the way out the door.

I expect to hear a snide comment from Slater next, but somehow, the room remains silent, offering me the floor once and for all to state my case, lay down whatever proposed policies I have in mind, and move on without Jericho. *I can do this . . . I think.*

"Is it true that you are revisiting the blueprints for a long-distance communication line?"

Victor nods, his previous, prickly nature seeming to have wafted out of the room with Jericho's departure. "Yes, although that information was *classified*," he says pointedly, his eyes looking towards Diana.

"She didn't spoil anything, Your Majesty," I try to defend her. True, though she played a role in getting the knowledge to me. Delta just happened to be the middleman, who happily blabbed all about it while getting me ready for bed last night. "And I only ask, because I was thinking. What if we created a . . . hotline."

"A *hotline*?" Harriet parrots back to me, making my suggestion feel weak.

"Yes, Your Majesty," I affirm. "What if your family created a line strictly for cross-territory use. From Sevensberg straight to Broadcove. No interruptions, no chance for espionage, and no more letters being passed back and forth. A secure communication line between the two governing powers."

I search for any sort of change in Diana's face— remembering what she had shared with me in the gallery about how Merrie and her mother were loving penpals— but no memories seem to contort their features with distant grief. In fact, I'm almost too busy looking at her to catch the gleam in Victor's eyes.

"That would certainly speed things along," Victor muses. "Less money down the drain in regard to delivery.

Yes . . . I quite like that idea."

"And the adaptations to the *U. Herald* operations?" I test my luck.

Harriet steps in on this one. "It proves to be a subject you're passionate about. Perhaps even your sisters might be able to lend a hand in the efforts."

Slater's been a little too quiet, so I merely cast my glance upon him and wait for him to say something smart, or cruel, or conniving. In the end, Slater resolves to be like Jericho and storm out of the meeting, his silver blue garments rustling as he pumps his arms in a runner's motion. Sweat coats his brow as he flies past me, and I know he's just dying to blow up on me. Knowing him, he'll likely wait for a bigger audience. Before he's fully out of the room, I recenter myself. "I believe it's your turn to share the state of your affairs."

Diana's smile curves with pride, thrilled to have outlasted both Jericho and her brother in a business meeting. It sends a chilled sensation through my body— the silent recognition that Ardian is immune to reality. Because the look of accomplishment in Diana's eyes proves my earlier suspicion.

Slater and Diana would spill blood for their parents' throne.

Harriet's words are buttery-soft as she starts with what must be the hardest battle they're facing, if only to prove themselves empathetic to Urovia's circumstances. "Economically, we're all good. We've only been met with minimal resistance about our most recent tax cycle, all complaints being filed from parties with terrible spending records. Territory morale remains steady since its previous spike two years ago, and that includes approval ratings for how we've kept the whole of Mosacia in good standing. As far as our armies are concerned, our main enlisted forces were disbanded nearly a decade ago when we established our neutrality policy."

"The Morgana-Grave Agreement," I recite. Another thing Delta had discussed with me before bed—suitably titled after parts of the two families' names as well as the darkness that would transpire if this policy came into effect.

If, or when, a civil war breaks out within either territory, the opposing nation cannot interfere negatively. Meaning if Jericho's people turn on him, bang down the doors of Broadcove, and demand his head on a spike, the Seagrave family will not intervene, and vice versa. The Seagrave family's confidence in their administration grew strong enough to disband their armies . . . but not enough to keep them from checking in on the state of forces any chance they could.

The Morgana-Grave Agreement, however, never included any specific procedures about what to do in the face of an attack, according to Delta's iteration—but having gathered what I know now about the Morgans and the Seagraves over the years, I see why. Merrie and Harriet loved one another like sisters. Hell, Harriet has practically memorialized the woman and her handiwork in the heart of her territory. Merrie retired the Hive, and considering how Jericho always becomes slightly on edge when referencing Mosacia's sustained glory, I truly believe Harriet when she tells me they do not have active military forces in place. They'd *never* go after each other.

Fiery Jericho, temperamental Slater, and unpredictable King Victor, however . . . that's a different story.

"Yes," Victor joins in again. "However, we have taken the liberty to establish a small, military-like force to protect each of our children. A squadron of sorts."

I do not miss a beat. "How many servicemen to each child?"

Victor smiles, as if noting my keen awareness. "Ten."

"And Urovia is supposed to turn the other cheek to your blatant confession of having hired sixty assassins?" I question.

"Yes, because these *employees*," he phrases skillfully, "are not designed to ransack your towns or torture your civilians. They are there to provide basic security detail for our children, or to assemble as a singular, lethal unit if one of them is in danger."

Sixty trained fighters against one idiot with the bright idea of laying a hand on the Seagrave children . . . Saints above, I can only imagine the carnage.

"And what about yourselves?"

"We have regularly stationed guards monitoring Harriet, given another heir rests in her womb," Victor tells me. "But they will assume allegiance only to the child following their birth."

Harriet smiles warmly. "I don't care if I go. So long as my children live."

Noble as her words may be, they sting some deep part of me, and I must fight the urge to back away from Harriet at the mention. "Is Jericho aware of these staff members?" I ask uncomfortably.

"He's never been smart enough to ask," Diana secretly

compliments. "Perhaps you should inform him."

I should . . . but will I?

"Of course," I lie for the time being.

Seemingly pleased with the results of this dialogue so far, King Victor stands to his feet. "Excellent. In that case, we shall reconvene with Slater and Jericho at a later hour. Let's allow them some time to climb down from their high, proud perches," he drawls, more so to his wife and daughter than to me. "It seems that Lady Venus knows how to weaken a man with only her tongue."

"Your son can attest to that," I comment instinctively, turning away from his face as fast as I can before the shock and disgust registers fully. I may have just uncovered the existence of sixty—about to be seventy—trained assassins lurking within Sevensberg palace, but I must always have the upper hand. Even if that can only come from having the last word, or in this case, tainting Victor's image of his Heir Apparent.

Diana's unrestrained laughter follows me out of the room and into the massive hallway.

My dress shoes click a metronome beat down the corridor, and halfway to Jericho's rooms, someone catches me by the wrist. I nearly jump out of my skin, fearing Slater is about to corner me without the presence of any witnesses—but when I tightly shut my eyes, preparing for the worst, the person's grip immediately slackens.

"It's just me," Diana's voice reassures me.

"Thank the Saints," I rasp, loosening a ragged breath. "You scared the shit out of me."

"Sorry." She laughs awkwardly, then shakes her head, likely understanding why I have not frequented Slater's rooms these last few days. "Anyways, I just wanted to find you and tell you . . ." she leans in closer. "You kicked ass at the meeting. You really held your own in there."

"Never doubted me for a second, did you?"

"Not one," she says almost sweetly, and I realize that Diana is telling the truth. "Delta was right about you. You have . . . a unique talent for making people feel close to you. To make them trust you."

Before I can let the remark sink in too deeply, she pushes me against the wall, and our bodies become concealed behind a sculpted pillar. Her green eyes pierce through my own, and enthralled by the sudden change of heart, my fingers begin to stroke her golden hair. "Which is why I feel oddly confident enough to tell you," she whispers seductively, her lips brushing my own as she talks, "that you're brilliant, Venus Deragon. And when that Dial Line goes into operation, I hope that I'm the first person you ring when you manage to kill that Urovian son of a bitch."

32
Jericho

"Venus is a *genius*."

After spending the better part of half an hour divulging my new understanding of Venus's, once reckless actions, Chumley's astounded features could be permanently carved at this point. The folds of his forehead remain etched across his skin, and they haven't dissipated since the moment he first raised his eyebrows. Chumley laughs in a manner that I confuse for a cough.

"Tell me again." He chuckles darkly, as if overcome with joy.

"The twin boys look at Venus like a shiny object," I start with, perhaps because despite my better judgment, I'm starting to do the same. "Annabelle basically insists that she sit by Venus at every meal when she's had a clear history of being standoffish with guests, and Diana clearly seems enthralled with the idea of Venus being close to her." I just conceitedly hope that attention is merely friendly—nothing more.

"Keep going," Chumley instructs gleefully, descending into hysterics as he props his legs on the ottoman and crosses them at the ankle.

Listing everything out that Venus has secretly accomplished in the last two weeks, I begin to realize that I underestimated her skill. Not just that, but also knowing my hypothesis stands firm: all these stubborn, spoiled royals are putty in her hands, and even Victor's once icy predisposition towards her seems to be thawing. How could Venus *not* be Blessed somehow?

"Victor never outright confessed, but when I confronted him in the halls last night, he did not deny my accusation about Greer's face. And at the meeting, I recognized that frenzied sort of look in Slater's face— the one that Victor bore when I charged him with his child's assault. Saints, Chumley." I laugh morbidly. "Just watching Slater lust after her despite trying to remain cold toward her . . . I could've sung her praises."

"Slater seemed cross with Venus? What happened?"

"Not sure. She probably cut the poor bastard loose right after she got what she wanted from him."

Chumley's smile dwindles. "Slater can have a pretty precarious temper these days. I just hope that, like his father, he hasn't . . . become violent behind closed doors."

I nearly snap the pen in my hand. "I'll kill him."

"Speaking of which." Chumley exhales, hoping that his attempt at a diversion from Slater will prove successful. "We got him."

I immediately understand whom he's referring to.

My eyes flare. "You found him?"

"He's unconscious—drugged, likely. I didn't give my

hired collectors any instructions on Parson's state of delivery other than to bring him alive and able to speak. But he's here, chained up in the lower levels of *Crystal Wrath*. You can—"

Chumley stills, and without needing to turn around, I comprehend his tension just before the door to his suite creaks in revelation. "She's behind me, isn't she?"

Venus's singular, dark laugh gives her away. "I'd like to speak with you."

Not bothering to bid Chumley a proper goodbye, I wink at him with a mouthed, *"After dinner,"* before turning fully to drink in Venus. She still wears her nightmare-black dress, which I affectionately dubbed after the internal chaos that came to haunt me when I first laid eyes on her in it. "I presume you mean alone."

"Indeed," she murmurs, her eyes alluring and narrowed in on me. Her tone implies that there's an unknown game afoot, and it stirs something within my chest.

I settle a hand along the slope of her back, leading her along as we depart down the staff corridors and down the grand, spiral staircase. "Then follow me. I think I know just the place."

Venus doesn't shy away from me when I lead her back to the water lily lounge Slater had brought her to the night we first arrived. In fact, she finds it hilarious to talk about private details in Slater's sacred sex oasis. At least this time I'm not observing from the bushes.

The immediate reminder of that moment, however— of seeing Venus at her most vulnerable and having her eyes burn back into mine as she unraveled—sets me on edge.

"So, now you know," she grins deviously.

"I think I do," I smile back, the action unguarded and true. "Except one thing."

She appears puzzled. "What's that?"

"What made you part ways with Slater? You had such a death grip on him, I figured you'd keep the ruse up the entire trip."

Venus takes a moment to find her answer, winces briefly. "He was arrogant."

"I can be arrogant, too," I counter.

"Perhaps, but your arrogance has grown on me, I'm afraid," she returns, and something inside me rejoices at the confession. "And anyways, we are partners in this— you and me. As painful as your presence may be, we stand together on the side opposite of Slater."

Partners.

You and me.

We stand together.

The words make my heart flutter unnaturally, make me want to lure Venus into the pool myself and have my way with her. To forever smear the one place Slater believed was sacred, and to make a show of it—

Jericho, what the fuck is wrong with you?

Venus's odd stare towards me makes me wonder if the words come from her rather than from my thoughts— that they hang aimlessly in the air around us. I shake out whatever filthy imaginings I can before clearing my throat and insisting, "I've been a bit remiss since I departed earlier. Forgive me."

I want to ask the real question bubbling up within me, want to know for certain if Slater did, in fact, harm her. But how would Venus read into that? Is that something that would pain her to relive? Would the question make her think I care more than I normally do about her wellbeing? Would Venus see too much of what I'm so desperately trying to hide?

So instead, I ask, "What did you want to tell me?"

In the following silence, I internally reprimand myself for allowing my headspace to reach such a forbidden place . . . again. Is the Mosacian air somehow an aphrodisiac? Is her temporary shift from overalls to flattering dresses swaying me somehow? Is it the sight of Venus stringing the Seagraves along that does me in? Whatever it is, I'm starting to worry that the damage will have a long-term effect, because even watching her gather weighty thoughts together in her mind makes my stomach twist up.

"I'm thinking . . . we need to reinstate the Hive—"

Instinctively, not realizing the heaviness of this conversation, my hand covers her mouth, but the force of which I touch her forces her back against one of the pillars. My full weight topples into her, and I pray to the Saints that as our bodies collide, she reads my frantic heartbeat as fear, not as sudden desire.

Her eyes widen, but she doesn't fight—and I do not entirely dismiss her suggestion.

"That sort of endeavor is a hard secret to keep," I tell her, my voice hushed. She nods, moving my arm in time with her head, and I consider my hand supremely lucky to know what her lips feel like. "But I'm curious to know why you suggest doing so despite the risks."

She says nothing, and her silence signals me to move my hand away. I mutter a brief apology that she doesn't hear, her response briefly cutting through my own words. "After you left, I learned about something they haven't shared with you. Something . . . I think they believe I won't tell you about."

I tick my head at that, almost tickled by the idea. "They believe that you will betray me."

"Yes," she says, her lashes casting a shadow over her murky eyes, even as humor shines a special light on them.

"Out with it, then."

Her smile vanishes entirely. "Each of the children have ten assassins hired on to protect them, an elite squadron of professional killers. Including the unborn baby."

The revelation hits me like a slap. "But how would the Hive make things better?"

"*Crystal Wrath* alone fits hundreds. Seventy people on land, against multiple ships from the Hive would be a glorified slaughter."

Watching her speak so passionately about battle strategies turns me on. I despise the feeling as much as I want to lean into it. Still, something in my gut clenches up when doing the math. "These squadrons are of no threat to us if we do not attack the Seagraves. We'd be stupid to deploy forces just to try and eradicate basic security detail. At any rate, assembling the Hive would be seen in their eyes as an act of war."

"Not if they don't find out," she challenges.

I force the frantic rhythm of my heart to slow as I step towards her, letting my height tower over her in hopes of quieting her concerns. "You have been brilliant, Venus.

Truly. But the Hive is not a covert operation."

She puts her hands on her hips, unwilling to back down. "They'd do it, you know."

Fear and uncertainty chill my skin, and I try to picture her idea in my mind. I'm instantly met with struggle. "No, Venus. I heard your words this morning, and if the rest of the Makers District feels anything akin to your pain, they would never agree to help a cause under my name."

"You promise them enough money and provide enough reparations for the collapse of their economic security," she insists, "and they'll do anything you ask. I'm one of the strongest-willed people to come out of that place, and I'm here, aren't I? Trusting you. Bending to your will."

I rest my head against her own, hoping the vulnerable gesture allows her to see the truth when I tell her, "I fear it may be working the other way."

I feel her body relax, as if my touch does not set her on edge anymore, and something about the notion makes me want to splinter into nothingness. "Yes," she murmurs suddenly, and I wonder if I imagine it. "I think so."

Something catches in my throat, and I wonder if it's the reminder of watching Venus writhe in the pool or the romantic, shaded canopy of the waterlily lounge that makes me feel the need to kiss her. To consume her like a man's first drink after days of deprivation. Against my better nature, I whisper the word, "Please."

Let me even the score.

Venus lets her eyes flutter shut. "Not here."

"Then where?" I ask her, voice dripping in need. "Say

the word and we'll go."

The fact that Venus isn't outright denying my request makes my blood rush through my veins. "I don't know yet," she replies.

I should be noble and say something like, *"Take all the time you need,"* but that would be a disservice to my wants. I want her to decide soon. Now. Saints, Venus could point to that tree down the cobblestone path and I'd tell her yes. My fantasies tend to involve us giving over to the darkness at a moment's notice, too riled up to make it to a bedroom in time.

But as much as I want to experience Venus, I worry I might . . . want to hold her. To let her surrender in a softer sense. To allow her emotional respite from having to keep everything under her control all the time. I want her to breathe.

To trust me enough to unwind.

My hands are wrapped around her wrists, not pinning her, but bringing her close to me—a hard grip meant to convey a gentle sentiment. "I want you to be my Right Hand."

It's a title I never throw around casually, perhaps even at all. Venus has likely never heard the term out of my mouth directly, but the look in her eyes tells me she understands its gravity. "You . . . but I would outrank Ardian. I certainly do not deserve that honor."

"I do not care about his opinion. Or anyone else's for that matter."

She stutters over an invisible thought. "I think you're speaking irrationally—"

"I think you are Blessed," I snap, squeezing onto her.

"It's the only way I can explain the way you understand me. Not only do you see my visions, but you seem to see me. And you don't run away from me. You're the *only* one," I choke out, realizing that the concept of it is so painfully funny. "The only one . . . that doesn't think I'm a lost cause. I've done nothing but ruin your life, and yet, the Saints have allowed me to keep you alive. For so long I believed it was because you were created to torture me; and considering how badly I want you to figure out your feelings on the pressing matter of you and I, I still partially believe in my original theory. But now, with so many enemies at my door, I wonder if you are meant to save me from destruction, not be the cause of it."

I feel as if I've shed thirty pounds. Having released all those words, I stand taller, now—I can summon enough strength to maintain eye contact with her. And Venus, as always, stares back. Unafraid.

"I do not know why you bother convincing yourself that you don't feel things for me when I can read it all over your face," I mutter, daring to brush a section of hair behind her ear. When she shivers at the intimate touch—more nervous than deeply frightened—my muscles tense in muted delight. "Every time you trespass into my visions, you begrudgingly discover that I am not the enemy you convinced yourself you've known."

Terror finally dawns on her. "How do we know for sure . . . that I'm Blessed like you?"

"It's a sacred ritual that I cannot speak about here," I reply. "But when we get home, I will show you. It will be the first thing on our agenda."

Venus breathes in deeply, as if worried she won't get

the chance to do so again. "But what if you're wrong about me?"

My smile is genuine. "I'm not."

Finally willing myself to let go of her, we both stumble back a little on the initial release. As she dusts herself off, if only to busy her trembling hands, I tell her, "Think on my offer. You'd be an excellent Right Hand . . . and reflect on my other request as well. I will see you at supper."

The Seagraves' chef made an overzealous attempt at a fish fry coupled with steamed, green vegetables and cheap wine. Truthfully, this meal is one of the worst of our trip so far, but if each bite means being closer to meeting Parson, I'll choke it down if I must.

Meanwhile, Venus has cleared her plate once already, opting for seconds. I suppose this cuisine suits her prior eating habits more so than the finer dining she's been subjected to lately. My pulse thrums so hard in my veins I fear it'll make the table tremble, because as much as I've deigned not to admit it aloud, killing carries to same addictive element drugs do—and with the way Broadcove gossiped about my recent dry spell, I begin to feel the withdrawals. Hell, just speaking of the Hive with Venus this afternoon nearly set my soul aflame with an aching desire to act out.

Venus curled her hair before dinner, dark ringlets spiraling in a way that makes me want to run my fingers through them, tangling them. She also changed garments since I last saw her, opting for a more relaxed, dark sage day gown. Just as it sinches in her waist, the crushed velvet pans out again, and the straight-cut neckline keeps my eyes from lingering too long. Delta must have loaned her a pair of glittering jewels to pierce through her ears, but the swirled design of them plays tricks on my mind. The way the fabric of her dress becomes reflected in the shine of them . . . they almost look like snakes.

A tribute to one of the Seagraves' stories, I realize. The Medusa.

Venus catches me staring, and I let her.

Then she's gone again, her attention poised on the younger boys who barrage her with questions about trivial things I don't care to listen in on. I do take keen notice, however, of Greer sitting next to Venus at the table. Not speaking, but . . . engaging. When Venus laughs at some unfunny joke Kellan and Madden share with her, Greer almost giggles, too.

Almost.

"Jericho," Harriet suddenly says to me, her words kind as she redirects my attention from Venus.

"Yes, Harriet."

She merely gestures to my right, and I catch sight of Chumley in the doorway. "I have a message from Ardian regarding a member of your King's Guard," he announces.

I rise from my seat, and Venus looks to me with a silent expression that asks, *"Do you need me?"* Chumley answers on my behalf, tipping his head politely at her to remain seated. Dutifully, she obeys, resuming her conversation with the twins, but as Annabelle places her hand sweetly over Venus's, her wariness doesn't fade entirely. I round the corner before I can assure her that all is well.

Chumley says nothing as we pace in the opposite direction of my rooms, towards the front of Sevensberg rather than the rear. "I thought that—"

"Change of plans. I had to get you out."

I narrow my eyes at him.

Chumley breathes a heavy sigh. "Parson is awake."

33
Jericho

Blindfolded and tied down to a chair in the lowest deck of *Crystal Wrath*—devoid of all light in the world—Parson Hartslew, a previous associate writer for the *U. Herald*, shivers like a wet animal as he begs for mercy. To his minimal credit, the man doesn't scream. Not yet, at least. Probably because Chumley stationed someone to stand guard with a sword—whom he now replaces—ready to silence his distress once and for all.

Beyond *Crystal Wrath*, the sun begins to set beneath the horizon, which means the younger kids in the palace are likely making their way to their rooms or taking their nightly baths. Venus may be putting forth one last effort to get Greer to open up, or perhaps sharing an after-dinner cocktail with Delta and Diana. I don't care—so long as she remains far away from the docks.

"Who are you?" Parson states in a normal tone of voice, a surge of courage coursing through him. "I think I would feel more comfortable looking at my interrogator."

His statement amuses me, and I let my voice drop down lower in an attempt to convey the nature of this discussion. "You don't get to be comfortable. You get to talk. So, start. *Now*."

Parson trembles. "O-okay . . . w-w-what do you want to know?"

A laugh rumbles through me. "For starters, what's a Urovian citizen doing in the Mosacian Empire of all places?"

"Traveling," he lies boldly.

"Work sabbatical?" I ask, and Parson's mouth thins into a flat line. "I would think that the other staff members of the *U. Herald* would be missing you, considering you've been gone since . . . hmm, what is it now?" I muse, glancing to Chumley for clarification. He holds up a finger, and I finish with, "About a year?"

Finally fighting the ropes tied around his wrists and ankles, receiving a vicious burn in his efforts, Parson panics. "I resigned."

"No," I correct playfully. "You disappeared. Our records say that you did not report to work the day you were set to submit an article for review, and that you never returned. None of the managers at the *U. Herald* ever formally fired you—"

"*Please*, sir," he begs, not knowing my name or having the pleasure of studying my face. "I do not understand why you want to know the details of my departure. I simply did not find fulfillment in it anymore. What do you want from me?"

Too exhilarated by how much fun I'm having, I tear off his blindfold with a forceful swipe and stare face to face with one of the slimiest weaklings I've ever met.

Even in the absence of my uniforms, Parson identifies me instantly.

"I want the truth," I merely state. "And if I do not get it in the next two minutes, I will sever you limb from limb."

I sense Chumley shift from his post in the corner, wracked with sudden apprehension at the way I speak with such indifference to cruelty. One look from me settles him, however, and I gear my attention back to Parson. "So . . . where were we?"

Parson begins to cry.

Knowing I do not have to force the act of uncovering who Tristan was—after all, I killed the spineless son of a bitch—I start off strong. "How did you first meet Tristan?"

Too caught up in his tears to answer, the familiar name obviously plaguing his conscience, I decide to take my knife out, twirling it in one hand. "I asked you a *question*. How did you first meet Tristan?"

His words follow in weepy fragments. "I was tasked to report on . . . a riot following . . . Merrie's death . . . m-m-may she rest in peace," he adds for, what he hopes, is good measure, but it only makes me want to spill his blood slower, more painfully. "Tristan had been injured, and I was only wanting . . . to ask him about how the fight started. But he offered me more. Offered insight on what really happened—"

"And you believed him?"

Parson shakes his head, but the Saints have shown me otherwise. "Don't lie," I sneer.

"I mean, I didn't. Not at first . . . but . . ." Parson drifts away into his sobs.

"But *what*?" I demand.

"Jericho," Chumley mumbles, his tone a warning that I do not wish to heed.

"You tell me, or you bleed!" I shout.

Parson thrashes in his chair, but wrathfully spits out, "But then Ronan died, you monster! Two monarchs died within a year of one another." Now, Parson feels empowered and confident enough to form complete, provocative sentences. "And the only one that didn't seem surprised by the concept of it was Tristan. So I heard him out."

My grin is wholly demeaning. "And that's when he had you convinced."

"No," Parson snarls, a surge of resilience flowing through his bloodstream, painting his face red. "I only hoped Tristan was telling the truth. The fact that you killed him yourself and have spent this long searching for me . . . I know now that it was the truth."

Just then, footsteps sound from above us, and although I expect Parson to put up a fight and call out for the attention of anyone who might be of help to him, we all fall silent at their arrival. They pad softly overhead, then veer for the stairs. "Chumley," I snarl, recognizing that he had tried to alert me a moment earlier, I revise my original, proposed outburst. "I thought you said no one would find us—"

But even with careful calculation, there's always the off chance that my private affairs will become fair game for one person in particular—and as she descends the stairs and opens the door, I realize I should've just killed Parson and left quietly.

Her nostrils flare at the scene before her, taking in the stranger strapped to the chair. "Jericho!"

I know what this looks like, and just as she's grown to trust me . . . still, I cannot have her stay. Even if it means forever tarnishing the reliability we finally managed to establish together.

"Venus," I implore her. "You need to get out of here—"

But the moment her name leaves my lips, regret overtakes me.

"*Venus*," Parson says, her name practically making him salivate. "Venus Deragon?"

Violence hovers within hazel eyes that have gone dangerously dark. "Who are you, and how the hell do you know my name?"

"Tristan told me about you," he immediately professes, forgoing the first question she addressed him with.

Saints, the moron thinks that divulging any information he has will save his soul.

I swear, a storm cloud forms above her head at her father's name. "Tristan?"

I begin to reach for my knife, hoping that his eyes stay on Venus long enough for me to gut him.

"Yes! Tristan," he acknowledges openly. "He told me that the two of you uncovered the truth behind the death of Queen Merrie."

I'm too late from stopping the emotional carnage, because something cracks within Venus at the words. "What are you talking about?" she croaks

"But—" Parson sits there, absolutely dumbfounded, stuttering like an idiot. "W-what do you mean? You two were co-conspirators in the biggest investigation in Urovia's history! Tristan gave me all the information on your shared findings but insisted that you were the one to be assigned the credit for the discovery."

She takes a careful step forward. "The discovery of *what*, exactly?"

"That Jericho killed his own mother!"

I figured that Parson's revelation, meant to demolish my character, would be the main nightmare for me to experience, but I am proven wrong tenfold. Because even though the statement hangs boldly in the air, Venus's body language informs me that she doesn't care if I murdered Mother or not. She only cares that her father conversed with a member of the public press about activities she was not involved in—ones that a mere accusation of would warrant a rightful execution for treason against my name.

I see a horrid transformation take place in her eyes, the way she mentally peels through her mind and through all of the memories she has about her father and about her time in Broadcove since leaving the marshes. Then, her eyes nearly stab through Parson's. "Tristan Deragon told you this?"

Parson begins to calculate his misstep, and the consciousness of it shows all over his face. "I mean, I . . . I never knew the man's surname, but—"

"My *father* was trying to make me take the fall for his traitorous babblings? And without any additional investigation, you were just going to print my name in the *U. Herald* and sentence me to *certain death*?"

Venus's temper could set this ship aflame. Worse, it could split *Crystal Wrath* down the middle—a mirrored reflection of how her heart must be feeling.

Parson starts blubbering, but Venus and I both are too far gone. Venus looks to the floor as I look to her, and watching Venus crumble shatters something in my soul. Destruction gnaws away at her, gobbling up all the beauty in her face as she comprehends too much at once. She doesn't know where to turn, her thoughts backing her into a corner. Even Chumley worries that Venus may pass out cold from stress.

My rock, my investigator, my ally—reduced to ashes.

And at that moment, I snap.

"Do you know who she is to me?"

Parson gulps.

Venus stills.

"Lady Venus is my **Right Hand**, and a member of my Council, which means that not only were your sources severely incorrect, but she now stands as the second most valuable individual in all of Urovia." And then, creeping towards him with an eased gait, I whisper, "How do you expect me to react to the attempt you had on her life?"

"King Jericho, please have mercy!" Parson screams, feeling his options for survival wearing thin. "I never published the article. I never spoke to anyone else about the conspiracy. Anyone! The m-m-moment I realized Tristan was arrested by the King's Guard . . . I burned all the notes I took. I came here—to Mosacia."

He's a sputtering fool, one I am far too fed up with to let continue.

I start to walk towards him, my blade braced within my closed fist.

Parson shrieks. "Oh, Saints spare me, *please*—"

And it all happens so fast.

A flash of golden light and a faint glimmer of dark red.

The sound of metal zinging through the air.

A wet cough.

A thick glob of blood dripping down onto the floor.

One minute, Parson Hartslew profusely asks for forgiveness from anywhere he can attain it—the next, Venus stands frozen in the exact position she last stood as a concealed dagger lodges deep into Parson's chest cavity. He dies before his body even begins to crumple inward.

My own knife remains clutched in my fist, the momentum towards the exact spot Venus's weapon struck, promptly cut off. I nearly drop it to the floor in surprise—but when I turn to meet Venus's eyes fully, I debate turning the knife on myself.

"Did you know?" Venus asks, silent tears flowing like rivers down her face.

Her name comes out desperate on my tongue.

Venus barely has any strength left in her voice. "When you killed my father, did you know my name? Did you know who I was?"

I swallow, gut-punched by the tragic look on her face. "No, Venus."

"When did you figure it out then, Jericho?" she asks so angrily that she could spontaneously combust. "How long would it be before I saw what you saw, too? How long was I supposed to go on living before I learned that my father had planned to betray me?"

I've never seen Venus cry this hard, let alone while forcing her voice to keep from breaking altogether. The sight of her all-consuming sadness makes me wish I'd never interfered with her life to begin with. Makes me wish I could be in a grave somewhere.

"I don't know," I force out.

It's the only truth I know to give her.

Refusing to wipe her tears or conceal her despair, Venus finally stalks over to Parson's body, retrieves her dagger with a violent yank, and turns to climb the wooden stairs again. Just before she disappears above us, however, she stops—as if she forgot something.

"Yes, Venus?" I ask gently, not wanting to trigger her.

Unable to crane her head at me fully, she angles her eyes in my direction.

"He was a coward," she tells me after many labored breaths.

And I know what she's forcing herself to do in these moments—Venus is mourning the image of the loving father she thought she knew. She's recognizing that all her efforts to uphold the legacy of his career were never meant to honor him, but to become him. To fit the description of the radical conspiracist Tristan had given the *U. Herald*—a poor, overworked woman who tended fields because every societal policy the Morgan Dynasty installed squashed any chances for her to do something different with her sorry life. And when he died, Venus had been given no choice but to assume that role forever.

"But I won't be," Venus finishes. "So, if you really meant it, I will resign from my position as a groundskeeper . . . and I would be honored to serve as your Right Hand."

34
Venus

Everything feels too heart-sickening to dwell on for longer than a few moments at a time. And yet, the hurt is all my insufferable thoughts know to focus on.

I killed a man.

Not injured. Not ridiculed or belittled or embarrassed like Slater. *Killed*. After promising Geneva and myself it would never reach this level, I surpassed it. And I do not feel remorse. I only fear how good it felt.

Then there's the new knowledge of my father, information that makes me regret so much of my life. Saints, I spent my time filling in for a man that ultimately would've been okay letting his daughter die for him. That's *fucked*. Having to comprehend that sort of treachery cuts to the bone, and it dents the strength I need to find my way back to my rooms.

Even deeper, there's the spine-chilling knowledge that my father died believing Jericho killed Queen Merrie, and now, Jericho has appointed me as his Right Hand. I exceed Ardian's rank.

I defy everyone's expectation of me.

But worst of all, buried beneath the rest of the mess, there lies the memory of Jericho all but saying the words, *"I want you,"* back at the water lily lounge, the realization that I might be attracted to Jericho, too, and that with my father's true intentions exposed . . . I'm running out of reasons to kill him.

And that ruins everything.

35
Venus

Twelve more days pass in a blur, and I've been very particular about who I spend my time outside of meals and required meetings with.

The idea of facing Jericho is . . . complicated.

Do I fear confrontation? No.

But I certainly haven't deigned to give him an answer as to where I want to be *alone* with him. I've only spoken with him sparingly, and only about the proceedings of my new role as Right Hand.

He shares more of his paperwork with me, the least joyous of all the new changes. But with that also comes the private records of hired staff, reports on organizations that have demonstrated long-term support to the Morgans, and even a detailed evaluation of Ardian Asticova through his years of service—which Jericho told me to keep private. Apparently, those documents are not known to exist by anyone else apart from the two of us. Jericho also vowed not to speak of the change in status to anyone, especially the Seagraves, and recommended I follow suit.

Apart from matters of business, however, it seems as though Jericho wants to offer me space, an uncharacteristically kind gesture.

I've put on a brave face around the others, primarily because I must. I know better than to believe I have the luxury of talking my pain out with any of the Seagraves, or even Delta for that matter, considering she's a direct line of communication with Diana. Only with Jericho . . . and I'm not ready to open up like that just yet.

I spend most of my hours sulking in my rooms, fortunate enough to have a sprawling window with a comfortable sitting bench. Aimlessly drifting my eyes out into the courtyards, imagining being back in the colorful comfort of the gardens back home, I think about my sisters. Out of the three of us, Calliope likely had the least amount of trouble acclimating to the riches of Broadcove Castle.

"Are you ready to go?" Jericho's voice cuts in.

I did not even hear him open my door. Not that he needed to knock, as I assured him that morning I'd be dressed and ready long before he had to drop by. Along with other careful conversation topics, I shared limited information about what had occurred with Slater—but he may as well have read me like an open book. Anytime I go anywhere, he offers to escort me.

"Ready as ever, I suppose." I sigh, rising from the sitting bench and fluffing out the skirt of my dress. Delta suggested I wear Seagrave blue in attempts to soothe the discord I sowed at the last meeting, but I opted against it.

Being loud and obnoxious felt more my style today, but donning red—even as Jericho's Right Hand—would not be wise.

After several minutes combing through our collective assortment of packed outfits, I selected a dress that Delta would call simple and unassuming—an autumnal, orange daygown with hints of rich brown in its undertones. Pleated at the front and tapering off into an elegant, neat flow that stops just before the floor, the gown is sure to compliment my skin and illuminate the lighter parts of my eyes. The neckline proves to be much more modest than the last garment I wore to one of these meetings— and damn me for succumbing to my secret delight for fashion, but . . . I treasure puffed sleeves.

The look on Jericho's face tells me that he approves as well, and he suddenly digs into his pockets. "I have something for you."

Jericho stands before me in long-sleeved white shirt that flows as he strolls towards me, a coffee-brown, buttoned vest tying the top half of him together in a sophisticated way. Paired with tan trousers and dark loafers, he stands as the portrait of handsomeness. "Words of wisdom, perhaps?" I ask in efforts to banish the girly nervous pooling in my stomach.

"Not quite," he responds, revealing a smooth, leather box.

Prying it open, a glittering emblem drawn in tiny red jewels sparkles back at me. The same symbol that Octavian and the other Holymen wore over their robes when I first met them nearly a month ago. "The Saint's emblem," I recall.

The swirls captivate me, as if the shimmering garnet is meant to create a flower I would find in North Star. My heart suddenly sinks at the thought.

Jericho nods, reading the sadness there. "It was my mother's . . . only she never really wore it. She never liked jewelry, yet Father gave them to her in droves." He laughs to himself, the sound both untangling something within me and making my nerves flicker to life, frightened. Then, he whispers, "I want you to wear it today. And after that . . . it's yours, if you'd like."

Already gathering my long hair into my hands and raising it up to expose my bare neck, I turn my face to watch his reflection in the grand window. I catch him studying my backside and fight the urge to comment on his lingering eye. "Thank you," I tell him instead.

Jericho's breath faintly kisses the skin along my neck and the beginnings of my shoulders as he wraps the thin chain around me, and Saints, I almost swear. I forget how to breathe altogether when his hands move to fasten the clasp, fingers brushing tender skin. "Right here?" he asks, the charm falling in line with my collarbone.

"Excellent," I say, but my voice reveals my sudden anxiousness. Jericho quickly removes his hands, and we back away from each other.

Jericho clears his throat, not sure what to say next. "You look . . ." he tries but cannot seem to finish his sentence.

I suppose his fragmented compliment is all I need to get rolling again, and a guilty smile tugs at the corner of my mouth. "Yeah, so do you," I mumble, already leading the way out of my rooms. "You coming, or what?"

This time around, the concord ran very differently.

For starters, Diana did not join us—probably because her presence was not permitted. I suppose Jericho may have had an inkling as to why, as he strongly recommended *he* do most of the talking as we perused the halls. *Less room for theatrics,* he phrased it. I resorted to believing that her coming to my defense set off her father, and that despite my best efforts with his children, Victor just wouldn't come around to me.

Smart bastard.

Then, there was the most evident issue: Slater's prolonged stare. Almost unblinking for the entire hour, he looked only at me. Not at Jericho, nor towards either of his parents. *Me*—and I had no way of deciphering whether it meant he wanted to crash his lips into mine and reconcile with me or crush me beneath his foot. I felt breathless, and as easily as Jericho noticed it, too, he did not dare mention it aloud or question Slater about it.

And yet, the fact that Harriet had as little to contribute to the discussion as I did—which was practically nothing at all—struck me the deepest. She looked ill, likely from the baby, but beneath it . . . there lay a deep sense of sadness. One that made me think back to the art gallery tucked neatly in the back of Sevensberg. All I remember being discussed was the installation of the Dial Line. That, and a covert suggestion that Jericho ought to speak privately with King Victor about something important following the discussion, which he's likely off to now.

Which offers me the perfect window of opportunity.

I snag some sharp hair pins from my cosmetics bag Delta packed for me on my way through the property, remembering that Diana carried a key to get in, and take the long path through the evergreen courtyards to get back to the gallery. Knowing the lingering effect that room had on me when I was with Diana, I desperately needed to visit the room alone—to intimately understand each piece of art, every frayed edge where a previous letter once stood, and perhaps even Merrie herself.

I've picked my fair share of locks in the past, so I greet the gallery door with unshaken confidence. It only takes me around two minutes in total to trigger the mechanism, and the moment I crack the door, the otherworldly atmosphere practically grabs me by the throat and yanks me inside.

Not having to show any courtesy to another person sharing the space with me, I start to notice things I did not catch the first time around. Firstly, the walls are not bare, but rather laden with wooden beams, jaggedly overlayed one on top of the other like a broken, abstract piano. A knee-high ledge spanning up from the floor provides a wash of cool-toned brown to break up the warmth of the high walls, most of which is covered in mounted artworks.

My prior observation of the variety of Merrie's paintings holds true. Assortments of abstract emotions, sweeping landscapes, and thought-provoking portraits consume the room in colorful splendor, and to the naked, unassuming eye, everything would seem at peace. This place would convince every passerby that nothing was out of the ordinary.

But a visceral part of me knows to keep digging. Gracious hosts and agreeable people the Seagraves may be—well, at least most of them—my curiosity cannot be disregarded. I either need to feed it, or it is bound to destroy me. And from the moment Diana revealed the previous existence of letters from the late Urovian Queen, I knew I had to learn more.

Immediately, I walk my way over to the tumultuous, thought-provoking piece that drew me in the first time I stumbled towards it. Unlike the other artworks, which look to have been intentionally crafted over an unrestricted span of time, this piece makes me as the perceiver feel incredibly frantic. It feels . . . rushed. Glancing down the evenly lined path of paintings and their canvases, I also note that the letter's prior stitching looks to have been pulled off with force rather than cut with caution.

"Hello again," a comforting, yet startling, voice says in greeting—distinctly feminine.

The same, eerie sensation that settled over me in North Star once again confronts me, and rather than run this time, I decide to stand my ground and keep my eyes open rather than shutting them and making room for more hysteria. "How the hell am I hearing your right now?"

The ghostly voice of Merrie Morgan laughs, the sound like an ancient lullaby. *"Because I want you to,"* she murmurs.

So many questions swirl around in my mind, so much to where I do not know where to start. But it seems Merrie's spirit finds my presence in her preservation gallery all too easy to understand. "Are you looking for something?"

I gulp, but seize my short window of opportunity. "Yes, actually. I'm . . . I'm curious about the letters you sent to Harriet while you were alive, and their whereabouts."

Her silence proves that she knows the answer, but it appears to be one she is not so inclined on giving me. Before I get the chance to grovel for her divine insight, she kindly replies, *"The past is dead, Miss Deragon. Why not look to the future for your answers?"*

"Is that what this painting was trying to convey?" I ask, pointing to the dark canvas with vague images reminiscent of anguish, disruption, and violence. "Your bleak view of the future?"

Silence falls, and several poisonous thoughts enter my mind. Should I have believed the imprisoned man on Crystal Wrath when he revealed what my father had predicted about Jericho? Was this fearsome future Merrie painted the depiction of Jericho turning on her? And if that was the case, was this painting a cry for help—a cry that ultimately went unheard by the Seagrave family?

Is this gallery an exhibition of posthumous guilt?

"You're so bright for your age," Merrie's spirit compliments me, as if reading my thoughts on the page of an open book. I long to believe they hint at an answer to any of those worrisome questions, but I already feel insane enough just talking to . . . a ghost? What even is this version of Merrie? *"So curious and explorative. I see why, now,"* she adds.

Her secrecy makes my skin crawl. "See what, exactly?"

Just before Merrie's essence departs from the room entirely—scared off by my persistent questions, or simply bored of having to converse with me in this unhinged state—I feel her mystical influence gear my attention towards one of the panes along the wall. The patterns of the beams resemble a wave, yet one panel in particular feels . . . off. Unaware of my feet beginning to move, my body carries my wandering eye towards the slab of wood.

When I lay a hand on it, I feel it loosen, like I'm accidentally about to knock the beam off the wall. In my panic, my hand taps it to the side as I jolt away.

And in only a split second, I see a brightened flash peak out at me before the plank resettles.

Unable to convince myself not to investigate, I pull the wood away with one hand and damn the risks before reaching my other hand into, what I now realize, is a secret compartment. My fingers immediately touch parchment, and without even needing to glance down, I know that I've uncovered an old copy of the *U. Herald*. A convicting nostalgia swells within me, and something about the paper's weathered scent makes me want to inhale its distinct smell. The closer I bring it to my face and the longer I breathe it in, the more my skin feels as though it is burning.

The title hits me like a slap.

Written by Parson Hartslew   21 AUGUST

THE TERRITORY MOURNS

The accredited author's name is one I've never heard aloud, but the miniscule picture of who wrote the article reveals the man I met on the *Crystal Wrath* that fateful night. The one I . . .

Unable to dwell on the memory for too long, I try to distract my mind with the picture attached to the story, but a dismal acceptance falls over me as my eyes drift over a photograph of Merrie's casket. Dark wood, without any blemishes or sharp ridges, forever tuck Jericho's mother away into sleep. Atop it, however, rests the fullest and likely most vibrant assortment of peonies I've ever seen, coupled with tulips, eucalyptus laurels, and scattered clusters of baby's breath—

The gallery door faintly creaks, and I catch sight of a singular eyeball peering into the room.

"*Shit*," I swear, and the person who discovers me takes off into a sprint.

Scrambling to convince myself I'm not going crazy and that maybe, just maybe, no one really saw me—that it's just my paranoia flaring up—I decide to stow away the article back in its hiding spot . . . only to discover a larger object packed away in the depths of the secret compartment. A splinter of gold catches the overhead light, glistening faintly, and upon further examination, thick detailing identical to the familiar sheen of all the other art frames in the gallery glimmers back at me in greeting.

One last painting.

The ornately bordered canvas weighs heavy against my strength, requiring me to use both hands and an athletic stance in order to slide it out of the rectangular cubby without breaking it. I nearly topple over in the process, and as I fight to steady it against the low ledged wall, I find that I've removed it with the backside facing towards me.

No loose threads draw my eye, but rather, an inscription.

Etched onto the back are four ominous words: ***The Fall of Jericho***

And when I turn it over, to my utmost horror, I find several illustrated versions of myself staring back at me.

Haunted by the madness of the day, I make it my mission to find any excuse to skip dinner, pack my things in advance, and promptly turn in for the night. However, just as I begin to drift off to sleep, after fighting the reminders of my visit to the gallery, and the possibilities of being found out by an unknown onlooker, a fervent pounding sounds off on the other side of my door.

Son of a bitch.

I'm barely even able to sit up straight in my bed before the door swings open, crashing into the wall.

"Delta, leave me alone."

My first friend in Broadcove doesn't let my bad attitude spoil her excitement. "Stop letting Jericho's killjoy personality rub off on you for one minute and read this!" Delta squeals, jumping onto my bed with a running start.

On landing, her body weight crunches a fancy, crème envelope she brought with her. Bearing a wax cerulean seal with the Seagrave family insignia, I realize I've forgotten about one of the most important notions of these kinds of visits—Harriet always hosts a party.

"Is this our invitation? I figured we were already invited—"

"Better!" Delta exclaims, grabbing me by the shoulders and shaking me further from my drowsy state. "It's the theme! Harriet always has the parties themed towards something extravagant and exciting. Uncle Ardian and my going away bash was a Creatures of the Sea theme, since we were crossing the Damocles."

When she says nothing else, we end up oddly staring at each other. Delta cocks her head towards the envelope. "Well . . . open it!"

She shoves the document into my hand, and only looking at it fully now do I read the inscription. "It's addressed to Jericho, too."

Delta scoffs, scooting closer to me the way a true gossip does when they get to the juicer parts of their intel. "Jericho *dreads* parties. I wouldn't be surprised if he found a way to skip the ordeal entirely."

I've never been to a party in my lifetime, themed or ordinary. The closest I've ever been to attending a celebration, let alone on such an enormous scale like this one, was tending the yards for a Noble family's wedding. Of course, once I finished shaping the hedges into something tacky like two swans forming a heart with their curved necks, I was paid and promptly dismissed.

But this—being a guest of honor, practically—is entirely uncharted territory.

Breaking the seal, I pry open the envelope and pull out a white, square piece of cardstock, with a fancy, crimson trim adorning the invitation.

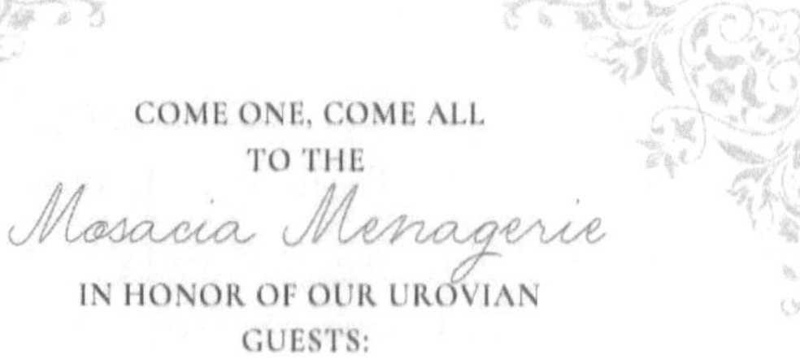

Delta giggles and kicks her feet like a little girl. "Can you believe it? Harriet has thrown together a *circus*! In *our* honor!"

I smile and clap alongside her, matching her bubbly excitement as convincingly as possible, but all I'm thinking to myself, unfortunately, is, *What the hell is a circus?*

36
Venus

I had fully planned on sleeping through breakfast and wasting the day away in bed until the circus, but at about a quarter past ten, a herd of ladies' maids came bustling in per Harriet's request.

Genuinely, it felt as though a small army laid claim to my rooms and began some kind of torture exercise on me. First order of business was to dunk my dark hair into the sink basin and wash it out thoroughly. One of the women felt particularly inclined to lecture me about my washing habits, which I gladly tuned out.

Yes, tell the poor girl from the marshes how to wash her hair. That's a brilliant idea.

While there, they scrub any grime off my face and apply a cleansing serum over any "problem spots," which ends up getting in my eyes and burning the hell out of them.

Two hours later, as if my eyeballs hadn't endured enough misery, they took five tries to glue on performative lashes. I eventually growled at them to simply let me use a mascara stick—a request they outright denied. And then, to make matters worse, they plucked my eyebrows *and* the hair along my upper lip. That shit *stung*.

Once that was over and done with, however, one of the ladies vacated the room while three others began curling my now dried hair, securing each heated cluster into a pinned updo for the time being. "Dress goes on first," one of them explained, their Mosacian accent thicker than any other resident I've met here. "Then we finish up the hair."

After another hour in the chair under the microscope of their commentary about how my hair is so thick or how my skin is darker than the range of most of their cosmetics, they finally leave me be. I just pray that Delta doesn't fill their spot, because I need at least five minutes to decompress alone.

In the stillness of nothing happening, I scan my room for any secret onlookers and shut my eyes once I feel comfortable enough. "Queen Merrie . . ." I sigh, feeling like an idiot as I do so. "I need you to give me some answers."

"About what, dear?" she answers me straight away.

"The painting of me, for Saints' sakes!" I bark, then cringe at my hostile tone. "I apologize, it's just, when you're drawn by a woman who has never laid eyes on you before, you tend to feel a little unsettled."

"Fair point," she recognizes, laughing to herself.

My vision starts to spot the longer I stay silent, trapped in my maddening thoughts. "When did you create it?"

Queen Merrie seems to understand my implications

fully. *"Around a week before."*

"A week?" I gasp.

"It was the last piece I ever made."

I definitely feel the need to sit down. An ominous inscription, several still-cast images of me on canvas, and within a week, Merrie was gone? My stomach roils.

"But wait . . . how did you . . . know me? My face?"

"Jericho wasn't the only one who had visions, Venus."

I feel selfish for being curious enough to ask, my mind revisiting the fateful caption on the back of the mind-puzzling painting of me. And yet, the words tumble out of me. "What did you mean by the title of the piece?"

She stops to evaluate her response before sharing it, a vague, lingering sadness weaving into her words. *"Visions are subjective to the person perceiving them. For instance, Jericho beholds something and reacts with rage. While I was alive, I found my visions . . . curious—thought-provoking. Everything I saw in that lens, I felt like painting. So despite my intentions for the piece and what it was meant to convey, those sentiments may not translate to you properly."*

Merrie draws near once more, her warm wind offering me an individual comfort. *"I always believed that falling was a freeing feeling, but to you, falling may mean peril—so who knows what emotions the concept of falling triggers for Jericho. I suppose that means you get to establish the true meaning for yourself. Do you understand?"*

Conviction simmers deep in my stomach. "Yes, I believe I do," I tell her regretfully.

But then, something disturbingly clicks—the realization that the first time I laid eyes on Harriet, and potentially her children, too, may not have been their first time laying eyes on me.

"What did you tell Harriet when you sent the painting of me to them?"

"I'm unsure what you mean by that," Merrie remarks.

Something about her reply makes me grow impatient, perhaps even angry. "You and Harriet wrote to each other often, at least that's what Diana told me when she first showed me this place. Every canvas you painted, you attached a secret message to evade Ronan's critical eye, correct?"

"Yes."

"And you're not going to tell me outright how you died, are you?"

That inquiry was more of a statement I hope she disagrees with. It'd make things a lot easier—but the imaginary presence of her sad smile makes my gut twist up. *"I'd rather not dwell on it, no."*

"Then, while I don't need to know every detail over the years between you and Harriet, I do need to know what you wrote to Harriet when you sent this final painting to her."

Because if this was the last painting Merrie ever made before she passed away, and I was the subject, that means Harriet has been hosting the muse of Merrie's death hallmark in her home for a month . . . and has played coy about it the whole time.

"Venus," she whispers carefully.

I close my eyes and brace for her answer, but my mental preparation attempts amount to nothing when she tells me, *"I never sent it."*

My body freezes. "What?"

"Every piece openly mounted in that gallery was one that I previously sent over to Harriet. That much is true. But as for that painting in particular, it made its own way to Mosacia somehow."

I think I'm going to be sick, my stomach and throat steadily filling with acid and dread—and as if Merrie hadn't just dropped a bomb on me, she hums to herself, the sing-songy sound drifting towards the ceiling in an evaporation pattern. *"Enjoy the party, Miss Deragon. Do tell my son I miss him if you get the chance."*

A foul word escapes my lips, and I try to beseech her to stay. "Merrie, please—"

"Lady Venus!" a cheery ladies' maid, who left my room earlier, calls out as she opens the door.

I feel Queen Merrie's otherworldly essence leave the room entirely, but despite my best intentions, Merrie's void is suddenly filled, replaced by the awestruck wonder that swallows me whole as I take in the spectacular gown the lady hauls into the room.

Calliope told me a long time ago that noblewomen would often wear white to their weddings or vow exchanges, mainly to display their wealth rather than their purity— but having spent the last ten minutes gawking at myself in the mirror, I'm starting to think that the idea of white is utterly foolish.

The gown that my maid, who introduced herself to me as Maia, helped fit me into may not even be made of fabric, but rather melted sapphires. A sheen sheet of dark blue hugs my frame, pouring down to the floor, and the bodice slopes in a soft dipped neckline. It takes all my strength to have faith in the thin, crystal-lined straps, which appear to be the only thing keeping me from flashing the other party guests. But the most flamboyant touch—and perhaps my favorite—comes from the massive, sparkling silver bow that rests on the lowest part of my back. The puffed ends look like low-drooping wings in the mirror, and the ribbon-like strands create a second, glorious train.

Maia had grinned from ear to ear, drawing a matching emotion out of me. Kindly offering me directions to the gardens through fits of laughter, she clasped her hands in accomplishment and joy just as I saw myself out of my rooms.

The five minutes I spend roaming through the back passageways and the final, descending stairwell help me navigate my shoes without an audience, but the moment I set foot on the ground level, I wonder if I've stepped into an alternate reality.

Beyond the stories-high windows, a red and yellow glow casts the outer corridors in artificial sunlight amidst the growing night. I haven't even entered the presence of other people, and yet, I feel hopeful, like the air promises good fortune and adventure. I begin to quicken my pace, my heeled shoes clicking against the smooth floors and the double train of my gown flowing like a river behind me. Right before breaking through the back doors, two men dressed in jester outfits pop out from the cover of large, potted plants that frame the doorway.

I jump back, startled not by their sudden appearance, but their matching, comical smiles. That, and their set of flexed biceps—guards, I realize. Never in my life have I seen a serviceman of any kind joke around like this, let alone crack a smile freely.

"Are you ready?" the guard on the left asks eagerly, jumping high off the ground and clicking his heels together.

I try not to look confused, laughing halfheartedly as I ask, "For what?"

They both look at each other like I may very well be the biggest lunatic in the entire Mosician territory. "For the greatest show on earth, of course!" the second guard exclaims, riling up the other one as they both begin to bop their heads to the music beyond the doors and rattling the jingling bells attached to their caps.

Part of me wonders if they sense my lack of understanding for whatever inside banter they're referring to, because once they settle down, they return to their quieted states of normalcy and swing the doors open in a swooshing motion.

Straight in front of me, bright red arches, shaped like towering hoops, run in a line down the grand steps and out into the palace yard, and a massive white tarp, that stands almost as high as the front doors of Sevensberg, hides the unknown wonders that lie beyond the tunnel. Picking up my gown by the sides and minding my steps, I watch as each hoop glimmers with warm-toned lights strung along each slope, as if magically coming to attention at my arrival. Stone pathways snake around the lawn to keep guests from sinking into the wet, muddy grass, and the deeper I look into the throng of people, the crazier my surroundings seem to get.

I start to believe I'm hallucinating as I see people

falling, in a revolving motion, over themselves down enormous spans of silks—the two strips tied to a beam mounted from one of the palace balconies. Down below, shirtless men with jagged tattoos consume fire only to roar it out of them like monsters. Crowds of people, dressed in their ballroom finery, applaud fervently for the performers, and some even reach for their eyebrows to make sure the flames didn't singe them off. Initially, when Leesa brought the sapphire gown to my rooms, I thought I'd stick out like a sore thumb, but I prove to be dressed far tamer than the lot before me. Women wear satin gloves, decadent earrings, and flamboyant hairpieces with interwoven braids or teased humps to make them stand taller. The general crowd tonight also seems to strongly favor floral prints, stripped patterns, and, for the men, silly detailing like monocles, obnoxious ties, and top hats.

"A kooky mix for sure," someone mutters loud enough for me to hear.

To my right, Thatcher Chumley snacks on a bag of nuts. How odd. Still, I haven't seen him since . . .

"Good evening," I greet him, eyes downcast as I try not to think too long about the night on *Crystal Wrath.* "Harriet sure knows how to host a party."

"Indeed." He sighs, musing at our surroundings with a conflicting sort of fondness. "Although, this may be her best one yet."

"And why do you think that is?"

Puzzled by my question, he crooks a brow at me. "As in do I think something motivated her to pull out all the stops this time around?" I nod, and he thinks about the possibility of it for himself. "Well, it's the first concord since the tragedies of Merrie and Ronan, not to mention your arrival. Perhaps she wanted to lighten the mood. After all, things between Jericho and Victor have been rather tense."

"I'm afraid so." I laugh uneasily. "From my limited experience, Jericho doesn't seem to be a people person."

Chumley concurs, cracking a mischievous grin. "You seem to be the exception to that rule, however."

Before I can catapult into further banter, a husky voice cuts in gruffly, "What rule?"

Jericho seems particularly smug this evening, and as I predicted, he still insists on donning Urovian colors—intense crimson paired with matte black accents. His midnight hair works in tandem with the onyx buttons that seem to hold his overall look, and perhaps even his composure, together—and his crystal blue eyes pop against his dark clothing. But even through all the regalia and unfortunate handsomeness, all I can focus on is his scowl.

"What the hell is your problem?" I ask, feeling my lips purse.

Jericho glances over me, flagrantly taking in my full attire, including how the palace beauticians enhanced my appearance. I feel rather beautiful tonight, but gut instinct tells me that Jericho will have something snarky to say that will repeal the self-confidence I still cling to.

"Your . . ." He contemplates his next words before answering with only one, "Dress."

Saints. He's peeved by the color of my gown. I only realize now that I'm in Seagrave colors, and I feel a little stupid for having been too wowed by the gown to notice its secret allegiance. "We don't look unified, Venus."

Still, I huff at his bitterness. "You can at least tell me I look pretty."

"But you don't—"

"Holy *hell*." A distant feminine voice gasps suddenly.

Although my eyes land on Delta first—dressed in a bright orange gown and a floral headdress—she only looks at me with a proud, closed-mouth smile, as if fighting back tears. It's Diana, however, standing next to Delta, that stares after me with her mouth hanging open. She even drops an assortment of finger foods on a small plate onto the grass in surprise. "You look magnificent!"

I flick a know-it-all glance to Jericho. "See?"

His face forms a frown, and as I mean to approach the two of them, Jericho grabs me by the bow of my dress when I'm too fast for him to catch onto my hand. He doesn't tug on it to where it comes untied, but he does so enough to muddy my steps. Delta's eyes flare at the sight of him reaching for me and guides her and Diana towards the tent's pinned up entry flap, not wanting to get involved. Even Chumley takes the hint and busies himself elsewhere.

When I turn to chew out Jericho for his lack of propriety, I end up almost mashing my nose into his own, his breath hot on my face.

"You think I do not find you absolutely mesmerizing right now?" Jericho hisses. "Pretty is too weak of a word for you. It's not even fair, even in enemy colors, your beauty cripples me."

His words knock the wind out of me, and I barely have

the ability to tell him in return, "You can't say things like that to me."

"Why not?"

I don't fight the forbidden truth we are trying hard to ignore. "I think you know why not."

Jericho laughs darkly, but only loud enough for me to hear. "You've been thinking about my offer."

Against my better judgment . . . yes.

"We've had our differences," I murmur, casting my eyes down his attire in an assertive manner if only to hide the bashfulness I'm smothering under the surface. A feline smile pulls at the corner of my mouth. "But I'm not blind either."

Jericho takes one, menacing step closer, our bodies nearly merged. "Smart girl," he whispers into my ear, and something inside my core turns to liquid. He means to say something else enticing and provocative, but I hear someone clear their throat behind Jericho's back, and when I glance over his shoulder, I back away instinctively.

Slater Seagrave stands with his feet shoulder-width apart and his arms crossed in front of his chest. I'm not surprised in the least to see him donning a blue velvet tuxedo with a snow white button-down beneath. His golden hair looks as if three or four lucky ladies have tussled it up prior to his arrival, and a clear love mark provides a patchy blotch on his neck. "I see you like the gown I had drawn up for you."

"You designed this?"

"Alongside the palace seamstress, yes," Slater says, far from modestly. "I knew you'd be a vision in blue."

Jericho stiffens at my side.

"But why?" I ask.

He shrugs. "I was hoping it would pair well with the apology I wanted to offer you."

Jericho scoffs, rolling his eyes. "What a joke."

"Jericho," I snap, even though we are on the same page on how insufferable the idea of Slater asking for forgiveness seems.

"Venus," he matches, not budging even for formalities' sake.

"There's one night left of your trip," Slater cuts in before Jericho can argue further with me, "and I'd like to spend it making amends."

Then, a guard inconspicuously walks behind Slater and secretly hands off an assortment of wondrous, blue flowers, which he then presents to me as a peace offering. Blueweed, I recognize instantly—and I wonder if he knows intimately of the plant like I do, or if he insists on having a uniformity for his heritage in everything he does.

"I reacted poorly when all you were asking for was some personal space," he finally admits. "And I never should have tried to pelt you with that paperweight."

I realize that Slater's apology is genuine just as the mention of him throwing the object at me slips past his defenses, and almost immediately, I feel a cold fury radiating from Jericho's body, his eyes turning to me in violent comprehension. "He did *what*?"

Truthfully, in a moment of temperamental weakness, if Slater is capable of throwing something at me that could've taken my eye out or cracked my skull, who knows what he could do when he has time to truly meditate on his anger. So, although all is not forgotten, I squawk out an, "All is forgiven," if only to keep Jericho from killing Slater in front of everyone, or vice versa. "Perhaps you two gentlemen can explain to me what the hell I'm getting myself into with this circus thing as you show me to our seats."

Slater is the first to offer his arm, a cheeky grin resurfacing. Jericho follows, his frustration palpable in a way that hints at jealousy—and I love the improvised competition. I'm all too thrilled that two formidable men would bare their teeth and destroy themselves over me for some odd reason. I loop myself into their hold, secretly grateful to alleviate the weight on my feet from my heavy gown.

We careen through the vendor carts with fine foods and beverages, then pass by the huddles of people in line to be photographed with their dates, and watch the scattered performers that ride by us on one-wheeled cycling devices, before we finally arrive at a towering white tent with vertical red stripes. What's new to me must be nostalgic to Slater, as I feel him sigh on my right. Jericho, still silently honoring the concept of my new position by standing to my left, looks at the makeshift building with disdain. In efforts to knock him out of his pissy mood, I clutch tighter to him, which I only receive a half smile for.

"Ditch the baggage on your right and I'll have some real fun with you."

"What's that?" Slater pipes up.

"He's excited to have some real fun for a change," I quickly improvise, knowing Slater likely heard part of his snide comment. "We never have parties like this in Urovia. In fact, I've yet to attend a single Urovian festivity," I remark pointedly.

"You haven't been on Council for very long," Jericho begins to counter.

But Slater seizes an opportunity that I'm not able to see coming. "Perhaps you should do something to celebrate her birthday, Jericho. After all," he says, smiling only at me, now, "it is fast approaching."

Jericho's face drops slightly. "I didn't know your birthday was coming up."

"June twentieth," Slater gloats. "You never even asked when her birthday is?"

"I never asked for his either," I offer up.

But Slater doesn't hear me, too happy to taunt Jericho some more to bother listening. "That's rather embarrassing, Jericho. That, and the fact that her Gemini and my Aquarius make for quite the astounding pair."

Jericho rolls his eyes at that. "I forgot you and the rest of your lot believe that the stars determine compatibility better than human emotions and true understanding do. My mistake."

"Then if it's no skin off your back, when's *your* birthday, Jericho?"

Sucked into Slater's trapping accusation, Jericho quietly mutters back, "July twenty-seventh."

Neither Jericho nor I understand the significance of the star signs, but we know by Slater's following silence that somehow, despite our cluelessness, he may have just been bested. Luckily, we cross the threshold between the outside domain and the entryway into the tent. The moment that we step forward together, I feel the tension between Jericho and Slater dissipate—if only because I am too wrapped up in the splendor of everything to give a damn about their bickering anymore.

The tent from the outside was certainly a sight to see, a miniature and comical version of Sevensberg Palace in a way. However, the cavernous interior feels far grander than I expected it to be. The red and white stripes have been substituted for darker tan fabrics that make me feel like we stand within the eye of a dust storm. There are observation bleachers with seating in several rows that gradually stretch towards the ceiling—with more strangely dressed service people helping guide guests up and down the aisles—and at the top rests a viewing box likely reserved for Victor and Harriet, given only two fancy seats rest within the glass-walled space.

There's a massive hoop hanging in midair, with a thick, horizontal rope of some kind cutting through the middle of it. Down below it, however, there are elevated stages, empty cages, seesaws, and ladders. And with a sudden horn-sounding from somewhere in the courtyard, the blocked letters along the black wall light up like a star that reads "MM."

"Come on," Slater urges. "I have two seats with our names on it."

"*Three* seats," Jericho corrects gruffly to himself, filing in after us as we secure a spot on the ground floor.

Not even ten seconds after we've claimed our spots, another staff member of the palace, dressed in a kooky costume, including big shoes with inflated tips, comes over and honks his red bubbled nose with his free hand.

The other carries a serving platter of what I assumed to be ice-cream cones, but the colored substance is far taller and wider than ice-cream—and dare I say it, looks powdery in a way. "Would the lady like to taste the clouds this evening?"

Each of the men have a different answer.

Jericho mutters a simple, "No."

Meanwhile, Slater grins from ear to ear. "*Absolutely* she does!"

"Splllllendid!" the man hams up, favoring the Mosacian in his home turf. "What'll it be, Miss? Blue Skies or Sunset?"

This time, Slater lets me choose, and given the two colors, I figure I should at least lay off the blue in one facet, if only to keep Jericho from cracking down the middle. "Sunset, please," I request.

The generous man hands off my odd-looking snack and wishes us a fun time. He vanishes in a blink, and Slater laughs at the confused expression on my face as I hold the item by its plastic cone, beneath the pink glob. He shows me how I can either bite into it or tear off a piece. I try it for myself, not too bothered by his instructions and the weird textures, but I vividly flinch when I put the contents on my tongue and feel the soft sizzle of it melting into nothingness.

Then, with enough time to get over the weirdness of it, I admit to myself the truth: this is delicious.

"Don't make yourself sick before we travel," Jericho gripes, seeing the joy materialize over my face.

Suddenly, screams of excitement and anticipation flood the room as the house lights shut off and an upbeat soundtrack begins to play. Consumed in darkness, my eye immediately catches a single spotlight as it falls down from the ceiling, scales the wall, and then casts a sunny exposure on a person Slater denotes as a *ringmaster* in centerstage. The clothing resemblance to my bitter seatmate is almost uncanny.

"Wait, Jericho," I comment, unable to stop myself, "I thought only the King was allowed to wear crimson?"

The only thing that keeps Jericho from punching Slater in the face for laughing along is the fact that I sit between them. But having already dipped my toes in the waters of this weird setting, I don't want to waste this night babysitting Jericho or buffering his bad behavior. No, I'm going to sit back, relax, eat this unusual food, and soak up this evening however the hell I want.

Starting with proudly offering myself up to ride the stunning show elephants when the menagerie's ringmaster asks for a volunteer.

Nothing about this evening has seemed to lift Jericho's spirits, and whatever developing emotion I have for him aside, I genuinely couldn't care less.

I'm utterly transfixed by the enchanting lights, the mastered performances, and the bizarre assortment of creatures that somehow mesh perfectly together—and it takes Slater practically having to carry me out of the big top tent for me to come to terms with the show being over.

The party is far from over, however, as people gallivant through the courtyards or gawk at the team of performers and circus staff as they help disassemble their equipment, or herd the animals into their transportable cages. Other members of the crowd stuff brightly colored foods into their mouths and rave about the staged magic they just witnessed. I mean to join them, my eyes expanding at the sight of a neon blue looking strudel at one of the vendor carts—but Victor and Harriet find us amidst the throng of guests. They rush over, Harriet more so dragging Victor behind her than the two of them running in tandem.

Jericho mutters something smart, along the lines of, *"Saints, really? Can we just call it a night already?"*

"Venus!" Harriet beams. "What did you think?"

"I loved it all!" I exclaim, not minding Jericho's opinion of me or my excitement about the circus. "Truly, I did. I feel so spoiled to have a party like this thrown partially in my honor," I confess, slowly forgetting about the illustrious foods down the outside pathways the longer I look to Harriet, who appears thrilled to have made at least one of us happy. How Jericho didn't find the show spectacular, I'll never understand. "It's perhaps the most magnificent thing I've witnessed in my whole life—especially the animals."

Harriet is pleased by my answer. "Yes, we wanted to make sure that you got to ride one of our finest elephants."

"*Your* elephants?" I ask, noticing her choice of words.

"Indeed," Victor finally chimes in, though nowhere near as chipper as Harriet and I. "We sponsor the traveling circus with some of our funds, and therefore, we sponsor the wildlife. The elephants just happen to be my wife's favorite animal."

"For me," I say, shutting my eyes to relive the memory

of them more fully, "I must say, my eyes gravitated to the tigers. Exquisite, fierce creatures."

"Much like yourself?" Harriet suggests, a blatant compliment.

Lethal and lovely, I think to myself.

I blush, and I catch Jericho's aggravated expression at the comment. I glance across the vast grounds that stretch far beyond view. "Does your sponsorship allow the animals to be raised here at the palace."

"Goodness no," Slater jumps in. "We are not nearly as skilled or dedicated to the animals as their trainers and the other performers. They have private, designated habitats for them to be raised in an open space like unaltered nature. But the tamers that have raised the different animals since their infancy have a tender spot in the creatures' hearts. The tigers seem to gravitate to the ones that care for them the most out of any other breed, however."

My brow furrows. "Why's that?"

"Because tigers are a severely endangered species," Jericho answers, to my surprise. "They've been hunted for sport for centuries, but by the mercy of people like the Seagraves," he continues, and the implied praise towards them does not go unnoticed by me, or even by Slater and his parents, "their numbers are slowly growing."

While Victor begins to form a companion point to Jericho's remarks, Harriet subtly summons one of the jester-dressed guards, whispering something undetectable to him before he darts off towards the circus tent. "The strong ones perform while the weak and young focus on their growth, but do trust that all of the tigers receive plenty of time on their lonesome with accessibility to the free-roaming, outside realm."

I turn to Jericho, then. "What was *your* favorite part?" I dare to ask.

Caught by surprise, Jericho adapts to everyone's full attention falling on him and uncrosses his arms from over his chest. "When Slater got up to use the bathroom," he says smugly.

Harriet laughs at that. Actually laughs. Slater, of course, purses his lips in annoyance at the response, while Victor seems totally zoned out of the conversation. But in the midst of it all, I think back on what did happen when Slater left to relieve himself—how Jericho's hand slid down the length of my thigh and gently squeezed. Reminding me that he was still wanting to be here for me beneath the misery of sharing the night with Slater.

That was my favorite part, too, I think.

And while I know the words are not spoken aloud, Jericho's expression shifts into something heavy. His head whips towards mine, and his gaze intensifies.

Just as I begin to raise my guard again, I hear a pointed yet faint sort of trilling sound I heard from one of the performing beasts, but smaller somehow. When I angle my eyes towards the source, I catch Harriet's blushed cheeks before seeing the guard she spoke with moments ago standing at her side.

Holding the most adorable tiger cub in the world.

I think I could collapse from how precious it is, its little whiskers poking out from its face and its eyes as glassy and blue as Jericho's. The cub's coloring makes it appear kissed by flame along its back and coated with snow along its belly, with bold black stripes cutting across both planes. Its thick tail swooshes upward and tickles the guard's neck, which draws a smile from him on contact.

And then, just as I see Harriet's eyes sparkle in my direction, the costumed guard extends his arms and offers the cub to me.

37
Jericho

Nearly fumbling the small creature in the process of taking it from the jester, Venus's gracelessness makes the rest of the gathered group laugh with the sort of adoration that usually is only reserved for children. But even Victor looks to Venus's joy with a touched expression. Slater likely hasn't seen Venus this happy, especially because this sort of happiness isn't fabricated.

Venus looks like she may burst into tears as its soft fur caresses the skin along her arms.

The tiny cub makes an almost chirping sound as it recognizes her nurturing embrace, and in delight, Venus mimics the noise before saying something mushy like, *"Oh, you're just a sweetie, aren't you? You're just a little guy. An itty-bitty little guy! Yes, you are!"* It's almost too much to bear.

Then Harriet kindly corrects her, saying, "It's actually a female."

Just then, Venus spins herself around, the young tiger

nuzzled against her chest, to show me how comfortable the tiny thing feels within her hold. She flashes me a smile so unrestrained and heartfelt that it hits me like a gut-punch.

I've never seen Venus like this, so uninhibited by the fact that people are watching her and formulating their own opinions on something she's so thrilled about—and she doesn't give a damn. In fact, just to rub it in, she takes the creature's tiny paw between two fingers and raises it towards me, bobbing it up and down to mimic a wave. "Look!" Venus says sweetly, her voice like candies. "She's saying hello."

Venus, to my unending horror, is most beautiful when she is truly happy.

I reach my wit's end. Not because I loathe the animal, but because the cub makes me realize that I've never seen her smile towards me in such a nonthreatening or defensive light.

And then, she shows Slater the little cub, as if wanting his approval, too.

Fuck that.

I know Venus still has her reasons for baiting Slater, but fuck them. Because even after implying that I want to be with her, sexually or otherwise, she still feels the need to throw it in my face. It's one thing to know that she's been with Slater behind closed doors, but it's another to see it smack in front of you—and somehow, this exchange stings more than watching Venus with him in the water lily lounge. This moment mixed with the sudden need to make him hurt, not to mention the recollection of his apology for attempting to mutilate her, and I'm fighting the urge to sock him in the mouth for just looking at her.

Suddenly, a quiet hissing noise triggers my attention downward, where a lime spotted creature slithers through the grass near my feet, its body curving around the edge of the stony pathway. And before I can contemplate reasoning or any consequences for doing so, I grab hold of the snake by its body and fling it outward, right in line with Slater's feet.

I must have aggravated the creature, startling it in my tough grip, because the moment it touches a new surface—which happens to be Slater's exposed ankle—its sharp fangs snag onto it in hopes of not crash landing to the ground so brutally.

Slater shrieks.

I have to turn my head away before he sees me laughing, my aim alarmingly perfect.

I mean, who the hell doesn't wear socks with their dress shoes? He was asking for it.

Harriet and Victor only see the snake after the bite has already begun to sink in, and Harriet mirrors her son's terror. Meanwhile, Victor darts off to get help without making too much of a scene, which leaves me and Venus with Slater.

He forces the tears to keep from spilling, but he certainly is letting the fearful thoughts of almost certain death take over him. In fact, the man starts praying, calling on Athena for wisdom and Hades for mercy and more time. It's laughable—but not to Venus. I actively watch as her eyes widen in . . . I cannot tell. Rage? Shock? Conflicting joy?

No—she's *thinking*.

She's thinking of how she can save the son of a bitch.

She certainly can't suck the venom out of his leg unless *she* wants to die for the no-good bastard, which I do not think she does. Venus may have Slater fooled, but I see through her expert portrayal of a naïve girl looking for his attention over mine. So why is she so desperately looking for a solution to this? Why not let the venom spread and save herself the trouble?

"My flowers . . ." she mutters to herself, her breathing short and jagged. "Slater, my flowers! *Where are my flowers?*"

He grits his teeth in agony as he grunts out, "In your seat. You . . . left them—"

Then, Venus violently kicks off her ridiculous heeled shoes and sprints back into the tent, regretfully shoving the tiger cub into Harriet's arms before collecting as much of her dress fabrics as she can in her hands, the weight of it stunting her typical speed. Hoping Slater takes my mirrored movement behind her as concern for him rather than an opportunity to speak rationally with her, I haul ass after her. My dress shoes clip the cobblestone, and I know she hears me, but she refuses to turn her head or halt her steps. The sparkling ribbons of her dress flow behind her like shimmering tails, and despite the heavy gown adding resistance, she forces her way through the menagerie tent and storms towards our previous seats.

"Venus, *stop*," I say, hunched over and panting for dear life by the time I catch up to her. Somehow, she doesn't even appear winded. "He's not worth it."

"You are an *idiot*, Jericho," she practically spits in my face, her tone vile. "You have no idea what your foolishness could cost us if this doesn't work."

"*My* foolishness? You're the one draping yourself over Slater like a lunatic!"

She wants to smack me again, I can see it vividly in her eyes. But Venus resists the urge, as if remembering how poorly she felt after doing so the first time. Instead, she grabs me by the shirt and yanks me forward. I almost expect a firm kiss, but am met, instead, with a death glare. "Have you kept count of how many guards are here, Jericho? The ones dressed as jesters or performers or members of the crowd. Well, I have, and the tally is astronomical. Which means all those guards the Seagraves have hired on to protect their heirs, they're *here*. Tonight."

My stomach lurches.

"And you just made a *direct attempt* on the Heir Apparent's life."

I do not wish to admit fault, but I'm forced to take ownership of the situation as I flatly ask, "So what are some pitiful flowers going to do to change that?" knowing she's the only one that can fix this near irreversible fuck up.

Venus yanks the blue blooms from their bouquet. They've begun to wilt from being laid on the floor, and good riddance. I wanted to set them on fire the moment Slater extended them to her. "I hope you know that these *pitiful flowers* aren't just going to save his life. They're saving yours, too."

She abandons me in the tent and thank the Saints her voice was hushed as she chewed me out, because we apparently weren't alone. Animal trainers still shuffle creatures back into their traveling cages and acrobats that we previously marveled at during the tightrope walk fold up their costumes and stretch out their tired muscles. One of them looks on after Venus as she rips back out into the night, then to me—likely thinking she just broke up with me or something. I roll my eyes, not wanting a stranger's pity.

When I dare to show my face again to the Seagraves, I return just in time to see Venus pick off the petals of her blue flowers and desperately shove them into Slater's mouth, instructing him to chew and swallow—an antidote.

I do not care to see their healing effect set in.

38
Venus

My head is swimming by the time I get back to my rooms for the night.

Grateful for the fact that there are no hooks or corsets to undo alone, my first order of business is to get out of this dress. As stunning as I felt and looked this evening, now that I am out of view of spectators or gathered crowds or even the Seagraves, all I feel is lousy and worn out. My body aches under the weight of the fabric and longs to let it pool on the floor and be a forgotten memory.

The jeweled straps fall down my arms as I loosen the back zipper, and, feeling the need to scratch at something on my shoulders, I realize the stones have left a reddened imprint stamped into my skin. My ladies' maids didn't bother with shapewear or nude undergarments, so the moment the dress is off, I'm completely naked, casually picking through my wardrobe for a silken robe when a knock raps on my door.

Distant noise, either out in the hall or out in the yards

nearby, make me think that the summons was accidental, but as I tie my sash around my waist and cover myself up, the sound beckons me again, more certain this time. "It's open," I call out, fixing the folded sleeves at my wrists when someone silently strolls in.

The air feels different the moment my guest closes the door behind them, and where I expect to hear Queen Merrie again, somehow in a physical form, an unknown voice whispers just loud enough for me to make it out. "I saw you. In the gallery."

Immediately, I whip around to face them head on, expecting the stranger to be wielding a knife or something dangerous to silence me forever.

But instead, the most harmless of all creatures stands before me with empty hands, sad eyes, and a scarred face.

Stunned by the fact that Greer Seagrave has approached me in private, her tone indicating that she's kept my whereabouts a secret, I marvel aloud, "I think that's the first thing I've ever heard you say to me."

Her voice is puny, but her words grab me by the throat. "Help me."

In the morning, *Crystal Wrath* faintly teeters within Mosacia's docks, and although my arrival here consumed me with grave fascination, the thought of us departing back for Broadcove sounds like a dream. I've missed my sisters, Ardian, and Tolcher. Meanwhile, Delta has to practically be dragged up the gangway, her eyes swelling with tears following one final embrace she and Diana have together.

It's not that I've envied their friendship, but rather that I've found it peculiar. Delta and I get along well despite our personality differences—but Delta clings to Diana like I would my sisters, like they expect never to see one another again. Not because of the distance across the Damocles, but because some outside force will forever sever their existences.

Once Delta boards the ship and cries her way down to the lower floors where her room lies, Jericho and I approach Victor and Harriet with pleasant smiles and neutral postures. "We couldn't have asked for a better trip," I share with them politely, my eyes lingering on Harriet to avoid reaching for my dagger and stabbing Victor. "Jericho and I offer you our deepest gratitude."

Harriet seems happier today, maybe even well-rested, but part of me isn't buying it. Her sunshine-toned hair starts to gray at the root, the byproduct of six, almost seven, children, and a husband I've recently discovered was abusive.

"It was our pleasure," Harriet responds, her tone as sweet as candies. "Right, Victor?"

He runs his hand along the scruff on his chin, too busy scowling at Jericho to listen to his wife. "Sure, dear."

I mean to escort myself up the gangway alone, but Harriet follows after me just as her husband makes a beeline for Jericho. We perch at the edge of the strip, my feet inches from fully settling aboard Crystal Wrath. "I hope everything was to your liking," she says kindly.

"It was, thank you," I reply briefly, not wanting to be rude, but just wanting to be left alone to ravage my brain about what happened last night—

"I also wanted to tell you, Venus," she cuts in, resting her hand over my own but not holding it. "That I think I've come up with a name for the baby. Well, at least if it's a girl. I was thinking . . . Emmaline."

I smile for her sake. "Pretty."

"If it's a boy, Victor may want to bestow his name on the child," she says, but then casts a prying eye towards the men speaking gruffly to one another below. Their body language doesn't look good, and Harriet's small talk is distracting me.

"My sister is with child, too," I share, trying not to focus on how two pairs of eyebrows angle downward in male aggravation. "I wonder if she has landed on any names yet."

Harriet watches as an unsettled emotion falls over me, the realization that in a matter of months, I'll be an aunt. I'll have a niece or nephew. There will be a baby in Broadcove Castle.

In an attempt to make me feel better, she suggests that, "Perhaps our children will be friends one day."

And while I hope it doesn't show on my face, the thought is revolting, especially when I'm once more reminded of the last time two friends, in two separate castles, dared to uphold a friendship and correspondence. Unsure of how to continue this conversation, I merely bid her farewell, thanking her once more for the party yesterday, and dismiss myself to my quarters.

Delta continues sobbing, and the sound remains so full that her door may as well not even be shut. It bleeds through the heavy wood divider, and even if I were to plug my ears, it wouldn't muffle the noise completely. I avoid the path to the room Jericho stored Parson in that night, veering towards my own designated bedchamber instead, and—

Someone's shoe sticks out from underneath my bed.

Unsheathing my dagger from where I fastened it against my thigh, I brace myself for a violent altercation, only to let it dip lower as the stowaway crawls out from below, their hands already up in surrender.

I feel my breath hitch in my throat. ". . . Chumley?"

"Jericho said you wouldn't send me back," he blurts.

"I . . . wouldn't? Wait, I don't even know what you're doing here."

"I cannot work for him—for Victor. I won't," he snaps, tensing up in every muscle. "I do not care if it means I risk every day back in Urovia waiting for Victor to find me and kill me. I will not serve a man who tortures his own children."

My head perks up. "You mean Greer?"

"So you know?" he cringes, as if he recalls the moment firsthand. I cannot imagine it. "Saints, I can never excuse that sort of behavior . . . but even so, I still do not know Victor's motivations behind it."

"I do," I croak, feeling like there are shards of glass in my throat. "It's because Greer uncovered Merrie's last letter to Harriet."

Chumley goes incredibly pale. "Dear Saints."

"Someone had opened it already, given she found it with the seal broken. But she doesn't know who opened it . . . and she only got to read part of it before Victor found her."

Chumley stares into my soul, eyes on fire with dread.

"She was begging the Seagraves not to murder Jericho," I finish.

I remember how the moment Greer shared that final detail with me, I felt so condemned that I nearly vomited—and Chumley appears to mimic the sentiment. Sure, I played it off to Greer as horror, as a protective nature for the man that helped my sisters and I out of poverty and gave me a new life. But at the same time, the dagger that I always kept beneath my clothes started to burn my bare skin. Convicting me, as it still does now.

Suddenly disrupted by the sound of loud arguing, Chumley and I glance out the port window to see Jericho and Victor becoming hostile with one another. I almost groan, though thankful for the distraction from our previous topic of conversation. "I should probably get him out of there."

"Or," Chumley says, hoping to make light of the situation, "we could eavesdrop."

And with the flick of a wrist, he undoes the lock on the window and pulls the protective glass inward so that we can clearly hear their sentences.

" . . . cannot possibly be serious right now," Jericho barks.

"Are you going to marry her?" Victor questions flatly.

Jericho cuts a curt laugh. "You have a lot of nerve to ask me something like that."

That's not a no, though, my mind panics frantically.

"Then what use is she to you?"

Jericho ticks his head to the side, displeased by Victor's sudden aggression. "I see where your son gets his prejudice from. Harriet must be ashamed to know you speak of women in this way."

"Not ashamed enough to stop riding my dick and giving me children," he retorts cockily. "M e a n w h i l e, I have it on good authority that your supposed Queen Consort spent the better part of this trip in my son's bed. So I'll ask you again, are you going to marry her?"

Jericho narrows his eyes. "Why do you care?"

A lengthy silence descends over the two of them, and from my port window, I almost fear that they can hear the thrumming of my anxious heart.

"My son . . . has found himself in love with the girl."

Without restraint, Jericho laughs more intensely than I've ever seen from him, almost needing to clear his throat after clutching his sides in hilarity. "Slater? In love with Venus? You cannot be serious, Victor!"

Yes, the idea is certainly odd, but . . . not impossible. I try not to take Jericho's words too personally.

"I am not bluffing," Victor states, not a morsel of humor within him. "What Slater wants, he gets. So, if you are not planning on marrying her, give me one good reason why I cannot rip her from your Council and betroth her to my son."

It's a threat, and one that sets both mine and Chumley's nerves on end. No, Victor will not go through protocol or ask for permission to bring me back to Sevensberg. He'll do it on his terms, and considering what happened when Greer resisted him . . .

Jericho, however, is not having any of it. Staring back at him with a look that promises infinite ruination.

"Venus is not just a member of my Council," he begins, his voice rough, "she is my Right Hand. She outranks Ardian and she rivals your wife in both status *and* intellect. Because of that, I take Venus's observations into account, and she suspects that there is a spy inside our lands reporting back to you." Victor huffs at the weighty accusation, but Jericho doesn't give him any room to interrupt. "Given her private research, Venus had every reason to be a nightmare to you and your wife, but I told her to play nice. And considering how lovesick poor Slater seems to be, I think she did a fantastic job, don't you think?"

Victor's silence is answer enough, especially paired with his deepening frown.

But now, Jericho looks like a volcano on the verge of eruption. "You say you are not one to bluff? Well, neither am I. So let's be clear about one thing: if you threaten Venus, you threaten me. And if you threaten *me* . . ." he says, rage lighting a fire within his eyes, even from far away. "May your useless gods spare you from the hell I will rain down on your territory."

39
Venus

The moment we step into Broadcove Castle again, a heavy anxiety is lifted from my shoulders. The May morning air casts both light and warmth onto the city I've grown rather fond of despite my original intentions, and before I can get two steps further into the grand foyer, Calliope squeals in relief to see me back in one piece, slamming into me with the tightest embrace I've likely ever received.

In a single breath, she catches Delta and I up-to-date on what she's been up to, which mainly consists of charting the growth of Geneva's baby. "Five months," she gleams. "The wet nurse and the midwife are already making preparations. Given her size and previous malnutrition, they think she'll deliver early."

Right on cue, my younger sister emerges from the dimly lit hallway, and something about the sight of her belly—now showing a slight curve along her previously hollowed torso—arouses Delta in a way that has her fleeing the room. When Genny's eyes cast upward, slightly behind me, I know that Jericho must be feeling the same as Delta, except he fights his urge to escape.

"How was your trip?" Geneva asks him, not me.

"Long," he replies briefly, his tone indicating uncharted territory. "I hope you've been feeling more like yourself these days, with less stomach disruption."

"Much better, actually," she murmurs, eyes dropping towards the small bump. "Thank you, Jericho."

I hear Jericho stifle a gulp at the sound of his name on her lips, and then, whether to steady himself or seek comfort at my side, his hand slowly brushes across my hip. A simple, almost imaginary tug pulls me closer to him, and he says to her, "I know we've been gone for some time, but might I borrow Venus until dinner? There's something important we need to take care of."

His tone with Geneva is gentle, and it sparks confusion and intrigue within my sister as she suddenly sees his hand on my body. Dare I say it, she even smiles faintly at the sight. "Sure," she grants him permission, and I find it heartwarming that he even bothered to ask for it in the first place. "But she's mine at dinner. No exceptions."

"You have my word." He smiles, turning both of our feet in the direction of what I think is the carriage we just took from Honeycomb Harbor up to the front entrance. Then, at the last minute, we veer down the curving paths that lead inland.

I know better than to ask where we're headed.

Zayanya Cathedral is sacred ground, but stepping into the

church building for myself, it feels like more than that. It feels holy—like I should've taken a scalding shower and cleansed every crevice of my body before approaching.

Unlike the coldness of Sevensberg, this cathedral is bathed in color. Golden floors set the bronze pews ablaze with the natural sunlight streaming through the windows, and the further the walls stretch towards the sky, the cooler toned the hues become. Limes bleed into periwinkles, indigos pour into purples, and along the blackened ceiling, silver speckled stars glitter around a bold inscription layered across the entire surface reading: *Forever and Always.*

"That's the literal translation," Jericho says, noticing my raised head, "for Zayanya. It's a reaffirmation for our faith in the Saints and an acknowledgement for the beloved dead buried here."

"In what language?"

Jericho chuckles softly. "A dead one. I couldn't tell you. One of the Saints blessed an ordinary scribe from the Noble District three generations back with the power of Tongues. He could write entire manuscripts in languages long since passed. But the Holymen liked the phrase and trademarked this place accordingly."

Something about his response stings, likely the mention of the Holymen and my mental rabbit trail towards Octavian. "How'd they end up in authority anyways?"

Jericho flashes me a wary look. "You don't know?"

I shake my head.

"It's a rather long, sticky history lesson, and one I didn't want to bother you with before traveling to Mosacia, nor while we were in their company." He instantly reads the frown beginning to develop on my face, and he holds out a softly dismissive hand. "Which I initially questioned, to be fair. But . . . the moment I realized you were playing spy—I was glad I kept you in the dark.

"Urovia used to be a larger sector of Mosacia," he begins before I can properly ready myself for the onslaught of details. "A massive continent forged from surrounding nations whose government establishments ultimately fell at the hands of their own disuse or the temper of their citizens. Politics became such a polarizing, demanding, and volatile concept, and after enough unrest, Mosacia was the only territory strong enough to stand on its own. And so, the Seagrave Dynasty single-handedly adopted the other nations into their umbrella domain."

I try not to let my eyes flare at the thought, at how monstrous Mosacia must have been back then. Having seen the territory on a map a few times before in present times, I can only imagine how indomitable they must have seemed to all those other fracturing territories.

"Mosacia survived because rather than depending on flawed human politics, their infrastructure survived because of religion—in their beliefs in the olden gods and goddesses recorded in ancient history," he notes pointedly. I remember the emphatic look on Slater's face as he explained the "myth" of the woman Pandora and her cursed box—and knowing that thousands of souls believed perhaps more fervently than Slater in those stories, I shiver.

"But on the western front, several thousands of people began to feel constricted by the faith they were forced to observe. As the dynasty collected new territories like gemstones in a crown, freedom of religious expression became virtually extinct, and a group of eight men—patriarchs of their respective families—eventually formed up to pray for deliverance. They secretly convened in their homes and wept for mercy to a nameless force they hoped would bring them guidance about what was true and what they could do to regain freedom on all grounds."

I cannot help but comment, "That sounds intense."

"It must have been." Jericho chuckles. "Because within an hour, all eight of them experienced the supernatural, and were blessed with diverse gifts that couldn't be explained other than to say they were miracles—otherworldly talents meant to reward them for their faith and bravery for going against the societal grain. That was several centuries ago, so there aren't many records on what all the gifts were, but what I do know is that one of them is what I possess. The patriarch who received visions prophesized a new and prosperous nation across the Damocles, which everyone had believed was an uncharted, violent ocean.

"Eventually, the patriarchs made a big enough stink to not only rile up thousands of people in Mosacia, but to also garner the attention of the founding Seagrave family. However, they were so amused by the idea of protestors willfully sailing towards what they figured was certain death at sea that they instantly granted them permanent leave. Unfortunately, for the Seagraves, in about ten years' time, they had people defecting their country for a new land called Urovia, and it became so concerning, that they relocated their capitol."

I furrow my brows. "That's why Sevensberg is right along the coast."

"To keep people from leaving," he affirms. "Yes."

"Is that why Chumley snuck onto *Crystal Wrath*?" I ask—a trick question.

Jericho smiles down at me, knowing I'm far too smart for my own good . . . but so is he. "One of them, likely," he answers shrewdly. "All that to say, I'm curious to learn what your blessing is."

He's not rushing me towards whatever fate lies within this cathedral, but he's certainly wanting me to get there faster. Still, I try to buy myself some extra time to steady my breathing by asking, "So, were the Saints the nameless force they cried out to?"

"No, actually," Jericho acknowledges. "To this day, no one knows what that raw force is. But when each of the patriarchs were nearing the end of their lives, they installed a replacement to resume their patriarchal duties, thus establishing the revolving door of Holymen. However, when the patriarchs died, they chose others to receive their posthumous blessings. Sometimes strangers, friends, family members, appointed Holymen—anyone of their choosing.

"When the pattern repeated through the generations, we revered the patriarchs as Saints abiding together in the afterlife—now almighty beings that could bestow their Blessings onto ordinary, living people in Urovia. And *only* Urovians. That is what has kept our growing nation strong amidst the impressive size of Mosacia all this time. We believe in an organized religion, but it is one that is so evidently rooted in Urovian nationalism that it has yet to be resisted." Then, suddenly, Jericho's features sink. "Well, at least not until my visions started to flow so aggressively."

At least he's self-aware, understanding of the mess he's caused—and yet, it stings like a slap across the face. For all I know, Jericho could anticipate my real reasons for being here in Broadcove. He might see my eventual betrayal from a mile away.

"So, does this place hold weekly services?" I find myself asking if only to add noise into the deafeningly silent room. "I know that there were a few churches by my old house, but they were nothing compared to this place."

"There are smaller venues scattered throughout the territory, although our faith is nowhere as strict as the Mosacian's. Those church buildings are open for citizens to frequent as they see fit. Zayanya, however, is reserved for high profile funerals, Holymen gatherings, and, in our case," he adds quietly, a glimmer of intrigue dancing in his blue eyes, "rituals."

We arrive at the altar after a few steps up to the stony dais, and laid out on the flat, oak surface is a small porcelain bowl of water the size of a teacup, and a dagger not too different from the one that sizzles to life beneath my skirts in remembrance. Jericho picks up the latter item with a discreet sort of confidence, twirling the hilt in his hand. "I'll show you first," he tells me. "So you know what to expect."

Quiet relief slowly floods my system. "Thank you."

"Sure." Jericho smiles back, then the expression dims. "You're not squeamish, are you?"

And before I can answer him either way, he slashes the blade through his entire palm in a single motion.

I jump at the hiss that passes through his teeth more so than the actual sight of blood, tensing just as he does. Jericho quickly wraps the blade in a spare handkerchief he kept tucked within his pockets. "You can pick which hand to cut," he shares with me, and I take note of how he cut into his right palm rather than his left. "But with the other, do this."

Jericho takes his left thumb, carefully running it over the bloody slice and bringing it back up to reveal a crimson, wet sheen. Then, with his eyes plastered onto my own, he takes his blood-coated thumb and paints his lips red. Part of me finds amusement in how akin the gesture is to putting on lip cosmetics for a fancy outing, but when Jericho finishes up, nothing feels funny anymore.

I've always known Jericho was a violent person, that he has innocent blood on his hands. But seeing fresh blood slowly dripping from his lips, he finally looks the part of a killer. He's unmoving, save for the rise and fall of breath in his chest as he stares back at me, his muscles tense. As a streak of scarlet slowly glides down to his chin, Jericho looks as though he just ripped out someone's throat with his own teeth. It forces me to see him as I first perceived him, how Octavian needs me to observe him despite my gradual indecision on the matter—a monster.

"And now, I call out to my Patron Saint, just as you'll do," he tells me.

"But I don't . . . how do I know who mine is?"

"You won't at first. For now, just send some sort of signal for them to find you. All that matters is your intention of speaking with them, and since their bestowed power runs in your blood," he indicates to his coated lips, "any words you call out will not go unheard."

His eyes fall shut, then—softly and unhurriedly. It's the first moment I think I've ever seen him with his eyes closed, or at least undeterred by his surroundings. It makes my heart warm within my body—and then, he begins to whisper, or perhaps I imagine him whispering.

Forever and always and forever and always and forever and always and forever and always—

Over and over with not a moment of air between each word, mirroring the clustered phrase above our heads.

Slowly, I hear the faint movement of water from within the cup, and while my memory tells me that there are no more than a few swigs worth inside, I watch in awe as enough water to fill a feeding trough rises into the air and forms something amidst Jericho's murmurs. The water, carrying a life of its own, tussles back and forth within a disjointed sphere as it concentrates on its task. Yet, not a single drop sprinkles onto the floor. In a final, upward swoosh, the waves stretch vertically, sprout limbs, and create the apparition of a man I've never seen before.

"Jericho," the man bellows.

"Gabriel," he returns reverently, his eyes still shut, as if only allowing his other senses to bask in the presence of a Saint.

"I never thought I'd see the day when you would share our private interactions with another."

I stiffen at that. *Is Gabriel offended by my presence? Should I kneel? Curtsey? Introduce myself?*

"Venus is like me." Jericho finally opens his eyes, hoping to calm that calamity of questions beginning to take my brain hostage. "I'm just showing her the ropes on what she ought to anticipate with her own Patron Saint."

Saint Gabriel smiles at that, like he knows *exactly* who my Patron Saint is. "Oh, yes. Venus Deragon. Well, I'm pleased to know that Jericho is in good company."

A bitter laugh forms in my throat. *Good company.* Perhaps he doesn't know *everything* about me . . .

"Would you mind," Jericho resumes, "telling Venus what you told me the first time we ever spoke?"

He doesn't answer with words. Instead, the enchanted bowl teeters slightly as the water-formed Saint Gabriel starts to pace about the open air—getting into character. "Do not be afraid. My name is Gabriel. I am a benign messenger—your Patron Saint—that has blessed you with a supernatural gift. I only wish to provide you clarity, conversation, and comfort regarding your special ability. You possess clairvoyance, just as your mother before you did."

I remember when Merrie's voice had informed me of that final piece of knowledge—a shock, but one that made sense the longer it sunk in—but I wonder how Jericho reacted to it when it was first announced. Had he already known? Had his mother shared the notion with her son before she died, or had he been blindsided by the revelation the moment Saint Gabriel spoke of it?

"If at any moment you have questions regarding me, your gifts, or anything else within the realm of our shared jurisdiction," the Saint finishes, "simply perform this ritual and I will reunite with you."

Jericho nods. "Thank you, Gabriel. You may leave us, now."

"Always a pleasure," he says as a goodbye, and the water zooms back into the bowl, once more without spilling.

When the water settles, Jericho offers me a look that questions whether I'm ready or not to proceed on my own, but instead, I find myself asking, "How did you know to perform the ritual the first time?"

The light in his eyes turns the bluish hue slightly gray, and it's all I need to know about my question, about a lot of things, actually—and I approach the knife knowing exactly what's about to go down.

Jericho slowly steps behind me, his body forming a protective frame around me as I grab the blade and angle it along my palm. I feel his studious gaze falling over my hands, watching in wonder as I decide how to cut myself open, opting for a smaller, and less aggressive slash than he had done. As the blood pools in the jaggedly drawn line, I feel Jericho tense behind me, nearly sending the knife clattering onto the podium the moment his body bumps into the back of me. Hoping Jericho cannot see how badly my hands tremble, I draw my thumb across the cut, smearing it over my lips, and finally turn to face him.

A single scarlet teardrop drips from my bottom lip.

"Venus," he whispers dryly, hunger in the sound of my name.

Knowing I'd be a fool to fold into him now, I shut my eyes and mimic his call to Gabriel.

"Forever and always and forever and always and—"

I hear the water stirring from within the cup again, the presence of my Patron Saint taking its form faster than Gabriel had. Still, I keep my eyes shut, too fearful of being right about who my Patron Saint is, even as Jericho urges me to look.

Then, his grip on me slackens. I feel his hand drop like a dead weight at his side.

The first thing I see when I dare to take in my surroundings are tears brimming at the edge of Jericho's eyes.

"Mother?" he croaks.

The water paints a near perfect image of Merrie Morgan, and the droplets move to curve into a makeshift smile. "My wonderful boy. How I've missed you."

Jericho has gone into shock.

The levitating, liquid form of my Patron Saint—of his deceased mother, for Saints' sakes—stands with her hands clasped in quiet serenity. She's confirmed my lingering suspicions since the moment I first felt her invisible presence in North Star and in the Mosacian gallery, and now, she witnesses the supernatural alliance of her two most significant earthly subjects. Her son and her Blessed.

My heart wants to burst in both sadness and in joy as I watch Jericho fight off the intense, tidal wave of emotions going to war within his soul. He hasn't seen his mother in two years, and was fully prepared to never see her again. But through this ritual—through me—he achieves the impossible.

And to keep from sobbing uncontrollably, he looks at me like I'm his single source of restored hope.

It kills me.

"Hello again, Merrie." I sigh.

From what I can make out of her face, she greets me with a congenial smile. The water even forms her signature side dimple that deepens when her eyes flick over towards her son.

"Oh, Jericho," Merrie croons in an otherworldly voice that makes my heart rate slow. "I'm so lucky that you've finally found Venus."

Found me.

I remember the dream I inherited from Jericho that made him track me down in the first place. How I beckoned him to find me. And I begin to wonder if the words that lured King Jericho into the marshes weren't even mine to begin with.

I begin to wonder if Merrie orchestrated our fates herself . . . and I even wonder, perhaps, if I should thank her for it.

You possess clairvoyance, just as your mother before you did.

"How is this—" Jericho finally manages to sputter, though he cannot seem to finish.

"Your mother is my Patron Saint," I tell him, knowing better than to play coy. "And I think I've known for a while . . . I've just been unwilling to admit it to myself. Or to you."

Suddenly, he seems out of breath, as if he just ran the perimeter of Broadcove Castle. "What is a while?" he stammers.

But Merrie cuts in before I get the chance to defend

myself firsthand. "That doesn't matter anymore, Jericho. What matters is that you two have found each other. Two Blessed individuals from opposite walks of life—"

"If you're her Patron Saint," Jericho realizes, "then does Venus have clairvoyance as well? Is that how she's able to inherit my visions?"

It would certainly make sense, except I have yet to have a vision of my own—one completely separate from Jericho's mind. So I'm not entirely taken aback when Merrie answers, "Not quite."

It's what she says next that really throws me.

"Venus possesses a new gift. One that I granted her myself." She sighs, looking at me with adoration and love. "Divine connection."

40
Venus

Jericho won't stop staring at me, and as invasive as it feels, it also strikes me in a magnetic way. Like I may break out into a cold sweat, or like he's about to lunge for me. And yet, "Connection?" is all he can manage to blurt out in response.

"*Divine* connection," Merrie repeats pleasantly. "For starters, Venus can inherit your visions because of it, because the two of you are connected through the Saints—through me. The longer she spends time with you, and the deeper your connection grows, the more she'll be able to pick up on them and at a faster, more detailed rate."

It would explain why I didn't see much into Jericho's mind when we stayed in Mosacia, as I was busy entertaining Slater and the other heirs. I hadn't been focusing on him hard enough to get a decent glimpse of his subconscious. "What else does that mean I can do?" I ask.

Merrie grins at that. "You have a distinct energy that

makes you more approachable and inviting to others. It's why people feel comfortable around you, perhaps even attracted to you, and it's likely why you eventually became the subject of Jericho's visions."

No wonder so many people mentioned that my name shared a likeness with the goddess of love, I think. That, and the fact that every Seagrave child eventually turned to putty in my hands. The twins, Slater, Annabelle, even Diana. Greer was the final one to fold, but unlike her siblings, she approached me with trust, not fascination.

Then a second wave of understanding washes over me, and I slowly realize that the first person to mention my namesake in reference to the goddess of love was none other than Jericho himself.

That's when, his open mouth having gone dry, Jericho suddenly barks out a laugh. "Mother," he says insistently, shaking his head in dispute. "No. You cannot possibly tell me that—"

"Would it be so wrong, son?" she counters. "Would my own gifts, would I, be wrong?"

The words are a challenge, and although I am left to piece together the implied contexts, I know from the crazed look in Jericho's eyes that her response is an affirmative one. Instantly, just staring into the depths of his eyes, complete understanding falls over me.

I possess connection—a love connection.

Merrie knew she was living on borrowed time when she painted me, and while I have yet to nail down the exact manner of her death, I know that she painted my portrait with her son in mind. Jericho looks to his mother with sadness, and such . . . guilt? I don't know for certain.

Whether Jericho did kill his mother, or she committed suicide like he implied the morning I threatened to hop the terrace ledge, it lends the same answer. Merrie made sure the last days of her earthly life went into orchestrating the right means for a partner to come along for Jericho. To change him. To understand him fully. She'd seen me coming—and though I may never know the context of what she saw me doing in those visions, Merrie still chose to Bless me the moment she entered the Beyond.

I wonder if Merrie envisioned me betraying her son—stabbing my dagger through his heart—when she painted me.

"Does that mean," I try to comprehend, if only to put off the convicting, awful thoughts that swarm my headspace, "that when Jericho and I die . . . we will become Saints?"

Oddly enough, the thought hadn't registered with Jericho either until I mentioned it, and my stomach sinks as she replies, "Yes. Anyone blessed on earth becomes a Saint in the Beyond."

That makes Jericho stand a little straighter, like it's a high honor to know that no matter what destruction he's caused, he'll enter the afterlife with high accolades. The *highest*. It seems to elevate his mood, meanwhile I fear I may begin to wilt under Merrie's convicting gaze. Because if I do kill Jericho at the end of this, I'll still be honored. And I'll have to face Jericho in the Beyond for it.

"So going forward," Jericho returns, "what does that mean for Venus and I?"

"It means whatever you'd like it to mean," Merrie says

soothingly. "Yes, I Blessed Venus, but that doesn't require the two of you to comply with any set rules. You can remain allied to one another, or you may sever your ties," she states, but a mischievous look glimmers in the crystal blue water composing her eyes. "Although I imagine you two will never truly be able to stay away from each other after today."

Fuck. I really didn't need Merrie to say that, because now, Jericho and I are staring so deeply into one another's eyes, we may very well melt our souls. We stay like this for minutes—which feels like endless hours, maybe even years—and in the split second we both look to Merrie in recognition of that statement, the enchanted water returns with a grand splash back into the bowl.

I have no idea what to say to him, too awestruck and terrified and delighted and confused by what just transpired. All I can manage to do is keep looking at him, studying the way his blood has begun to dry along his lips. But the longer I set my focus there, the longer I fear I may fall into them. And I want to . . . I want to—

"My mother saw you," he breathes, as if recapping the conversation to convince himself Merrie's words were real. "She picked you. Picked you . . . for me."

"Jericho, I—"

"When did you know it was her?" he mutters quietly, his voice grave. "Tell me."

I shut my eyes, too consumed with embarrassment to meet his stare any longer. "I first felt her in North Star. But when we were in Mosacia, Diana took me into an art gallery of some of the work your mother sent to Harriet and . . . I knew then. I didn't want to admit it, but I knew.

And I'm sorry."

He drags a hand over his mouth, smearing blood across his face as he comes to terms with the timeline of my knowledge.

Then, his expression turning dark, he whispers, "And what we talked about . . . about going somewhere. Just you and I—"

Shivers start to prickle at my skin. "Jericho we can't."

"I don't feel that this changes anything."

"This changes *everything*," I resist.

"How?" he asks, stepping closer, making his intentions for him and I well known. His body heat permeates the air, seeps through my clothes and touches my bare skin beneath.

"How do you know that you're not just drawn to me because of what we just learned?" I challenge, hoping to give him a reason not to cross a line that will change our lives forever. "What if, apart from your mother's Blessing, I don't really matter to you?"

Jericho looks at me with anger. True anger. "How could you say that about yourself?"

"Because it was so easy to keep the Seagraves entertained. Slater, Diana, the rest of the children. Even here in Broadcove, I feel like Delta and Ardian treat me differently. They may not even like me, but my Blessing forces them to draw near."

"But I'm not them. *Any* of them," he seethes, and I realize that in my efforts to backtrack away from the conversation, I've ended up trapping myself between a tall pillar and Jericho's rumbling chest. "They are ordinary," he grumbles. "Not like you and I. Our Blessings unite us.

Don't you get that? You see my dreams, Venus. You see *all* of me, and yet you don't desert me. You'd never sell me out to the people who hold hatred towards me. You choose to stay—you choose to fight for me. For *us*."

My heart thunders against my bones. "Jericho, don't—"

"Even now that we know what you're blessed with, it doesn't change the fact that I can't quit you. Because even as you loathed me and I you, I felt I could trust you with everything. My life, my secrets, my visions. The only thing altered by what just happened here," he pants, "is how I'm going to conduct myself around you, now. Because unless you tell me to stop . . ." his hand gently trails along my jawline. "There's no point in denying the way I feel about you. That I want to be around you. That I want you to fill my days with conflict and fire and friendship and passion—"

"Jericho, I beg of you," I say breathlessly, but the will to form the word stop doesn't pull through.

"I suppose I don't have to say it," he smiles shrewdly. "You know it in your heart to be true—my feelings for you, and your feelings for me." He draws his face against my own, his nose nudging along the side of my own.

The pulsing in my chest is almost excruciating. "We can't," I say again.

"Sure we can," Jericho whispers dangerously, his lips briefly brushing my own as the words tumble out.

The touch shreds the last of my restraint, and he knows it.

"Shit," I say through a jagged breath and close the distance.

We collide into each other hard enough to bruise, and the moment I give myself over to him, I taste the blood on his lips. *His* blood. The irony tang sends a shock to my system, one that makes me want to set this cathedral on fire just to lay with him in the flames.

I pull him down to me by the back of his head, my nails digging through his soft head of midnight hair, and he hums darkly in approval. Shamelessly, he lets his hands slink down my spine. *Further.* My breath hitches.

"If you'd have spent enough time around me during the back half of our trip," he tells me as a soft groan escapes my lips, "you'd have discovered that this is what I dream about. I dream about you."

The words are scarier than any threat he's made on my life, because the danger that comes with looking at him isn't a cruel death, but mercy. Perhaps even love.

And I don't know if I can give him that.

When I do not speak nor move, Jericho releases me, even helps me straighten out the skirts of my daygown. But I still avoid his gaze—that is, until his hands turn my chin towards him. "Venus—"

I find the will to peel myself away from him and run down the aisle of the massive cathedral. I keep running until I'm past the doors, up the steep hills we once descended, and all the way through Broadcove. It's all a blur, but I think I pass Calliope blindly down the halls. Relentlessly pumping my arms and forcing my feet into motion, I don't stop running until I burst through the only room I feel truly safe enough to express my frenzied feelings in.

Genny sits up sharply in her bed, obviously roused

from sleep at my arrival.

A sloppy apology is already spilling out of me, but Genny shakes her head, not bothered in the least by my reasons for waking her. Instead, she motions me over, shushing my immediate blubbering as I climb onto the bed beside her. It's only as I get closer that she sees the dried blood smeared across my mouth, beneath my nose, and along my chin.

"Are you hurt?" she asks.

Unsure how to answer her, I begin crying into her satin sheets, flustered and frustrated and unable to dwell on anything else but the way my body felt—how it still feels—at Jericho's touch.

I was right, I did stampede past Calliope, because I only have a few short moments to hear her own pounding footsteps before she, too, bursts into the room.

"Venus! I tried to call out to you, but you—" Calliope pants, and in the single instance she stops to catch her breath, she listens to the beginning of another heavy sob. "Saints, Venus, are you okay?"

But the truth is, nothing about this, or me, will ever be okay again. Because the way I see it, I only have two options left for my life.

I could follow my head—follow Octavian's threatened guidance—and kill the man I've grown to form an unbreakable attachment with, and set Urovia back on track towards supposed tranquility.

Or I follow my heart, forsaking my original intentions to follow the part of me that is starting to tell me, against my better judgment, to protect Jericho with my life. To save his life even if he's guilty. To love him without any ulterior motives or reservations.

And with no questions asked, my sisters let me cry until my eyes dry out.

41
Jericho

I've never had anyone run from me like that.

I've had people run from me, sure, or at least try to—criminals, subjects of visions, opponents of mine. But even with death in their prospects, they've never taken off at the kind of speed that Venus just did.

My lips still carry the heat of her skin, the smell of her body now cemented into the fiber of my clothes. I'm still hard for her—my hands immediately trying to straighten out my fumbled clothing and my tousled hair.

Never—never in my life has something ever felt so magnetic. So sacred. I feel so alive . . . yet, so defeated.

I'm grateful for the progression we've made so far. From hating one another to tolerating each other, then to becoming partners. Dare I say it, I think Venus became the closest thing to a friend I've had in years. I feel . . . well, I don't feel alone anymore. And she did that. Venus did that. The way that Venus made my life complicated made me the happiest I've been in a long time.

But perhaps the things about me that made her life complicated finally caught up to her. Maybe the idea of all her new obligations to me drained the joy of being with me out of her, right in the moment when I thought I had closed the deal—when I thought I was about to make all my wrongdoings up to her. To change the game forever for both of us.

In a blinding rage, I kick my foot through the wooden podium, and the porcelain bowl full of water shatters on the floor.

Silently—apart from the uneven breathing in my chest, the kind that overtakes me just before tears do—I sit myself down on the ledge of the steps just beneath the broken altar. My mind drifts off a thousand miles elsewhere. Not knowing where Venus is hiding out, or how long she'll stay huddled up there, I know not to go after her.

Not this time.

I suppose I should be thankful that it took this long for her to finally run away from me, that I got any semblance of time with her to begin with.

"Shit," I grumble aloud. Aimlessly looking through the stained glass windows, I try not to let the words wound me as I say, "I was so close."

I do not send for Venus for another three days, mainly to save myself from my private embarrassment. When she doesn't make any efforts of her own to track me down, I know it was the right call.

However, today is different. The events of Zayanya

aside, Thatcher Chumley needs a place to go, because it's a damned *miracle* that not a single busybody in Broadcove hasn't spotted him squatting here yet. That, and I'm quite tired of sharing my living quarters with the man. He snores in his sleep.

So late in the evening yesterday, I sent an urgent inquiry to Venus's rooms, beseeching her to meet me after her breakfast with Delta. Because, given my lack of familiarity with my own territory, the best scouts person I could call in for the job of helping Chumley relocate was her.

"You summoned me?" she says, already standing in the boardroom doorway. I hadn't even heard the door open, and it takes effort not to let a tremor overtake me when I drink her in.

Venus's dark skin pairs well with this light-toned outfit. A casual, beige dress with a corset sort of lacing across the bodice. Beneath the sleeveless day gown, she wears a white, billowy layering piece, the sleeves tightening at her delicate wrists and then rounding up along her forearms. The high neck hides my lingering gaze over the top half of her body—likely a purposeful move on her part—and pairs well with mother of pearl earrings that droop from lobes I'd had between my teeth only a few days ago.

To my eternal amusement, she also dons white stockings. It's May, which means the Broadcove sun may very well pack a serious punch if she braves a walk through the gardens.

I watch her watching me, studying me and my outright, silent evaluation of her. She scoffs, her playful nature peeking through once more. *Thank the Saints.* "What are you ogling at?" she chides, offering me a sly smile.

"It's nice to see you've opted for something other than your overalls," I remark.

"Well, I'm not your groundskeeper anymore," she notes. "I don't need to wear them."

Something warms my soul at that. That she feels less restricted, now, even if the pertaining category is something as simple as clothing.

Still playing along—pretending like we both aren't secretly thinking about my hands on her body or the sound she made when I took her over the edge—I tell her, "Well, let's see the rest of it." For good measure, I make a twirling gesture with my finger.

Venus rolls her eyes, but obeys, nonetheless. Only when she spins around for me, the skirts of her dress flaring like an enchanted bell, all I can set my sights on is the girly ribbon tied through her hair, pinning half of it up in a neat little bow. She is borderline precious, looking like she just came back from wistfully exploring a massive library, or picking berries in the gardens.

"It's a shame you're so nice to look at," I begin to say.

But down the hall, Chumley's footsteps give him away, and Venus immediately snaps to attention, her smile disappearing. When he resurfaces, he smiles gregariously at her, tipping his head in acknowledgement of her new rank. "Morning, Madam Right Hand."

She flinches at the title. "Venus is just fine."

"Venus," he amends kindly.

"I've gathered us here," I begin, "to discuss your discreet removal from Broadcove." I flick my gaze towards Chumley specifically. "You obviously cannot remain here forever, and with Venus's previous fears of information being leaked back to Mosacia, your safety is at risk the longer you stay here."

A sad look falls over his features. "Where have you decided to station me?"

"You're to stay in my old house," Venus answers, and I try not to let an expression that tells him *"Good luck, that place is a fate worse than death"* seep through my defenses. "It's on the edge of the marshes, extremely unsuspecting. If anyone asks, you tell them that you are only there to eventually sell the property. Do not mention your affiliations to Mosacia, Broadcove Castle, or either of us."

Her eyes gear back towards Chumley. "Shortly after you settle in, prewritten messages I've drawn up under a code name will arrive at your new dwelling. It will recommend places to eat, banks to trust your outstanding funds with, and recreational sites you can visit to make use of your time there, at least until you can find a kind gentleman to share your remaining days with."

My head ticks towards him, not having known this personal detail about him before. Although, I suppose it was never any of my business to know. I've also never been entirely aware of how that way of life is received by the broader whole of Mosacia.

"Thank you, Venus," he breathes. "You've been too kind." And then, filtering in from out of nowhere, Chumley starts laughing to himself. When Venus offers him a puzzled expression, he professes that, "I cannot explain it. How come this assignment seems like it will surely be miserable, but I feel as though I can trust you?"

Venus and I share a passing, targeted glance, and a faint smile blooms along her lips. "Because even though so much loss came out of that place, it will provide you shelter. Privacy. And perhaps," she adds solemnly, "if you try hard enough, you'll feel the love that I once felt while growing up there."

Chumley smiles dimly towards her, though not directly at her. "Then I shall forever be in your debt, Lady Venus."

Venus clasps her hands behind her back. "One of the King's Guard will be able to escort you covertly to a carriage at high noon, when the rest of the staff will be frequenting the dining quarters for lunch. You can trust him," she assures Chumley, although I know that the sentiment is privately directed towards me. "Tolcher will knock thrice at the door to signal his presence. He'll take care of everything after that."

I must hand it to Venus. Considering I delivered the letter about this current predicament a matter of hours ago, likely right before she prepared to go to sleep, she's handled . . . well, everything. I feel like I only had to lift a finger to write the initial beckoning.

And then I hear something. Something in Venus's voice, though her mouth doesn't move.

"I never cease to amaze you, do I?"

"What was that?" I say aloud.

Chumley stares, perplexed.

Venus blushes.

"Did you just talk to me . . . with your mind?" I think hard enough to crease my forehead, unsure if it does anything or if I am only making myself look idiotic in front of an audience.

"Just a little something I've been practicing these last few days," she silently taunts in return. *"Your mother talks to me this way."*

My heart skips a beat or two, suddenly struck with a quiet kind of sadness. Venus senses it, too, and straightens out her posture before saying to the open air. "Is that all?"

Too spaced out to try and argue with her or keep the conversation going if only to keep her in the room with me, I say, "Nothing more. Thank you again."

"Of course," she nods minimally. "Well, then, it was an honor to know you, Thatcher Chumley," she tells him with the utmost respect. Gentleness exudes from her every pore, and it softens a hardened knot that has invisibly formed within my chest. "If we ever meet again, I apologize for pretending to never have known you. But I only wish to keep you safe."

"The same to you," Chumley returns.

Venus turns to leave, her footsteps feather-light—but she pauses at the door, as if recalling something. "Ardian requests a Council meeting soon. On your terms, of course." She doesn't wait for my response before sauntering out.

Once the door shuts again, I turn to tell Chumley not to leave this room until Tolcher comes for him, but I'm met with a childlike, giddy look on his face. "What the hell is so funny?" I ask.

He outright giggles like a little boy, then says, "You two like each other."

"Shut up." I sneer.

But he presses further, taking an audacious step

towards me. "Want to tell me what happened?"

"Not exactly."

And that's that. Still, Chumley is certainly pleased with himself for having picked up on our mental cues. "You love her?"

"I don't have enough of her to love," I tell him instinctively, a bitter taste in my mouth as I do. "She always has one foot out the door."

Chumley sighs sympathetically to himself, as if knowing that this moment is the last time he and I will ever speak to one another. "Then find the means to ease her back in. Even if Venus has reservations, the energy of the room still shifts when the two of you look at each other. You clear that obstacle, and who knows? Maybe you and Venus will come to . . . an understanding," he finishes, a crafty look on his face.

I thank him for his time, his service, and his advice, before confidently striding out of my rooms and onward. I stumble through the gilded halls and head for my private office, noting the absence of guards and other prying eyes as I shut myself inside.

Unlike the other rooms I take my paperwork in, this space has never had another person cross its threshold other than myself. Even when administrators call on me or bring a delivery to my door, they always stay beyond the room's frame—a sacred gesture that has been practiced since I became King.

My window looks out onto a massive tree sprouting countless limbs with green-lined leaves. On the tips of most of them, if not all, bud several, scattered violet blooms. I don't know their names, but my heart knows that Venus would. If I brought her in here and simply asked, she'd likely tell me as if the notion were second nature. And she'd smile at them while I'd smile at her, and—

I know better than to tell myself I haven't gone off the deep end for her. Really, I do. But Saints . . . is this what love feels like? Relating everything back to her, to the one person I cannot seem to banish from my mind? To simultaneously find her within the fire of my hatred, but also within the deep, hidden realm of my adoration?

It's out of character to say the least, but for the first time in a long time, I stare out the window and pray with all my might.

For as long as I've been stubborn, I've also been so alone. So if you can hear me, please let her be what's right for me. Impart the divine knowledge I need to fix things, to tear down whatever remaining barriers separate me from Venus. I'll do anything you ask of me . . . just please let me keep her.

42
Jericho

Despite Venus having relinquished her role of groundskeeper to become my Right Hand, I've come to the realization that when you do something for long enough, it becomes a part of you. The habitual need to repeat one's daily pattern—especially one that previously determined a person's survival—shined through clear as day when it came to Venus. The moment our first Council meeting ended, which mainly discussed the timeline for the Dial Line installation, she was back to her tools, and her mulch, and her sunshine.

She became so immersed in her personal work, in fact, that I ended up creating weekly meetings for just her and I—secretly, of course, given I hadn't found the heart to tell Ardian about her promotion yet. But even then, Venus still chose to spend six out of seven days a week in her overalls and boots again, her hair always braided either down the back of her head or on either side. Delta had commissioned embroidered gardening gloves from one of the seamstresses on staff, and while I figured Venus accepted them out of courtesy, I've yet to see her go without them these last several weeks.

Truth be told, the grounds are flourishing. I've been so invested in keeping tabs on her and on the gardens that I haven't realized—at least until today—what Venus has really been up to. I've been too busy watching her cultivate new artwork in the hedges and repave the stone pathways to understand that she never really wanted to subject herself to this again. She was just trying to avoid me.

Still, as I instructed initially, Venus has yet to lay a hand on North Star. Although, in the evenings, I've sporadically caught her pacing the greenhouse alone, talking aloud to herself—to Mother. Tonight appears to be one of those nights.

"She never stops, does she?" a male voice asks from behind me.

I turn—expecting Ardian to lecture me about cutting her hours or insisting she take lunch inside to avoid sun poisoning or some shit like that—but instead find Tolcher leaning against the column of the balcony. He bows deeply. "I didn't mean to startle you."

"What's she to you?" I find myself asking stiffly. "She commissioned you to help Chumley escape, so she obviously trusts you. So what is it? Are you trying to—"

"I have a wife," he interjects. "If that's what you're trying to insinuate, and I am an honest man. But I suppose I'd consider Venus a friend. She's generous to my mother-in-law, given that most of her inventory is what currently makes these gardens so colorful and bright," he notes.

"And considering she shares my upbringing, she helps me feel understood. That's it."

No clear indication of nervousness. Perhaps Tolcher speaks the truth. "Well, then, if you're her friend, enlighten me. What's something that she's told you that I wouldn't know about?"

Tolcher narrows his eyes at me, even as he flashes me a smile. "That's a loaded question, Your Majesty."

"One that you would answer if you were smart."

But then, as Tolcher formulates something to share with me, I recall a facet of knowledge I didn't know before, until Slater of all people shared it with me. The realization makes my skin crawl. "Wait," I blurt. "How many days are there until the twentieth?"

Tolcher smiles, completely understanding the look in my eyes. He silently does the math before stating, "Eleven."

"Then tell me this," I revise my original demand. "As her friend, would you say that Venus would . . . want a party thrown in her honor?"

Despite worrying that Tolcher will use this conversation to poke fun at me later down the line, I watch him toy with the idea, formulating different options in his head. "It's a tough call," he eventually answers, his tone mellow.

"Why's that?"

He sighs. "Well, as much as she's raved about the menagerie the Seagraves put on during your trip, I have it on good authority that Venus hasn't celebrated her birthday for about a decade. She loves parties, really, so I bet she'd be ecstatic about it. But . . . perhaps not on the actual day."

My brow furrows. "How come?"

"Because Venus's mother died the day Venus turned thirteen."

My heart sinks as if an anchor were dragging it to the bottom of the ocean. I remember Venus briefly mentioning that her mother died before her father, likely from a sickness or malnourishment from living in the marshes. Three kids, two parents, not enough food—I suppose in a situation like that, a parent, at least a good parent, would always opt to feed their children first. But to lose her mother at such a pivotal age, to grow up knowing she could've had several more years with her . . .

Still, what a shame to spend the very day others are meant to recognize your presence in their lives by mourning the dead.

"Don't tell her I asked anything of you, alright?"

"Of course, my King," Tolcher addresses. "Is there any way I can be of additional service before I return to my post?"

I cast a passing glance back to North Star, where Venus is now making violent gestures, arguing with the ceiling. She and Mother must be going at it again. I try not to dwell on the possibilities of what their conversations pertain to, and why it has Venus appearing unhinged as of late. "Yeah," I say, though I'm no longer meeting his eye. "Two things actually."

Tolcher simply waits for my word.

"Do you know . . ." I ask, turning to face him once more, forcing my face to not fall in melancholy. "Does Venus still leave her rooms at night to sleep on the office floor?"

I'm almost too scared to hear his reply, but before I can call him off, Tolcher tells me, "No, Your Majesty. It seems that those sleeping patterns fell out of practice once she knew for certain her sisters were comfortable here in Broadcove."

I think I could leap for joy right into Tolcher's arms if I were insane enough. For now, I let my satisfaction take the form of a sidelong grin. "And second?" he inquires.

Right.

I brace myself for the worst. "I'd like to meet privately with both of Venus's sisters, one at a time. If you will, please instruct Calliope to meet with me tomorrow at noon in the boardroom."

"And Genny?"

I privately note the way he defaults to the same nickname Venus gives her sister rather than her full name—the name I've felt strictly confined to calling her. "The day after. Four o'clock. In the kitchens."

Despite getting more than enough hours of sleep, the previous, persistent thoughts of this conversation killed any chance of those hours being truly restful. I'm such a nervous wreck, I may as well have stayed up all night and drank myself sick by the looks of me. But I hear Calliope's dress skirts dragging down the hallway towards me, and I have all of eight seconds to mentally prepare myself for part one of the most awkward, dignity-crushing meetings of my entire life before it begins.

"What do you want?" she says, crossing her arms over top of an apricot bodice.

"Good morning to you, too, Calliope," I mutter flatly.

I'm not scared of Calliope. It is more so that she exudes a sort of haughtiness, at least in my particular presence. It's a change I've noticed in her ever since Venus ran out of the cathedral, and while my gut instinct tells me that Venus never fessed up about what happened between us, Calliope now embraces the protective, eldest sibling role I first saw in her back in the marshes. If it's her way to stand up to me—to feel, in some way, that she might be an equal match for me—she's sorely mistaken. In fact, out of respect for Venus, I tolerate her presence rather than fully detest it. "Shall I call for some tea?"

Her nose twitches at that. "You're not the type to *call for tea*," she jabs, poorly mimicking the timbre of my voice. "That's too nice of a gesture for you."

"Would you prefer a shot?" I seethe through a flimsy smile. "Maybe that will loosen you up a bit."

Calliope eyes at me in a way somewhat akin to Venus's typical glare, but with less violence beneath. No fun at all. "Tell me why I'm here or I'll go back to my rooms. Or better yet, I'll tell Venus—"

"That won't be necessary," I insist as best as I can manage without sounding too desperate for her secrecy and compliance. "I only require your cooperation for a few moments. Have a seat."

Thankfully, she doesn't fuss. Finally deciding to step into the room fully, Calliope closes the door gently behind her, selecting the seat across from me. "I suppose," she drawls slowly, "that I should thank you for the generous lodgings you've provided for Genny and I."

I shake my head. "Thank Venus. Her work is what

keeps you here, not me," I respond, although the words are not entirely truthful. I just need to knock her ego down a peg.

"Understood," she notes.

"Although, if you don't mind me asking," I decide upon, hearing a slight insecurity pricking the edge of her voice. "Has Venus mentioned her job to you or your sister at all?"

Puzzled by the question, she tells me, "Of course. I mean, hell, she's covered in soil by the time she washes up before dinner. It's pretty obvious what you've hired her to do, and she's damn good at it, too."

Translation: Venus hasn't said a word about becoming my Right Hand. At least not to Calliope.

And then, something hits me. "Did Venus often ask you about your job?"

"Pardon me?"

"When you'd get home from an event you were hired to perform at," I rephrase. "Would Venus ask you for a rundown of how things went, or did you tell Venus about your day unprompted?"

Calliope rolls her eyes. "Why does that matter?"

Message received. "Fine, if you won't tell me that, then at least tell me how Venus would react to your stories, if Venus ever seemed entertained or mesmerized or disgusted."

She mulls over her thoughts for a moment or so before eventually returning with, "Venus only truly listens for about two minutes before she mentally checks out. It helps me prioritize what parts of the job I share with her. I will note, she's always been curious about the dancing aspect, though. I'd keep telling her that the music was far more beautiful than any of the befuddled attempts men would make at waltzing with the female nobility, but she would never listen!" Calliope ridicules.

The list begins to rack up: dancing is a must, waltzing in particular, and while the music may not require specific arrangement, a decently skilled ensemble ought to be hired for the night. I can certainly work with this.

The conversation flow stills, and it's almost painful— Calliope and I staring wordlessly at each other like this. She waits for my dismissal while I wait for something bright to say, hopefully something that doesn't make me look like a dimwit. And in my sudden, internal panic, the question falls out of my mouth before I can trap the words within.

"What was your mother like?"

While my dreams helped discover Venus and her father, the only member of the Deragon family I have yet to learn anything about is their late matriarch. No name, no mentions of her aside from her manner of death. Even when Venus took me back to their house in the marshes, there were no pictures of her in sight.

"Wonderful," she muses aloud, and I watch her eyes glaze over with the memory of her mother's face. I at least didn't fumble hard enough over my initial question to make her refuse an answer. "The kindest person you could ever meet. She could cure any sickness with a single embrace." I try not to instantly picture the woman as a total marshmallow, all soft arms and cozy build. "And she had the voice of an angel."

It takes strength to keep from rolling my eyes. "I see.

So that's where you got it from."

"Yes. I always wanted to be just like her—endearing, talented, charming," she says, batting her lashes at me before dropping her smile entirely. "I suppose that's why Venus chose to take up father's path in life, because I had already adopted mother's."

And for as much as Calliope irritates me, I do not have the stomach to tell her what Venus and I have come to know about Tristan Deragon. About his treachery, and how he jumped at the chance to betray the daughter that went to such length to preserve his legacy.

"Were your mother and father happy together?" I ask, knowing it likely comes across to Calliope as contemplative thought, like I am jaded by my own parents' relationship to where I believe love cannot exist for everyone else.

"As much as they could be," she remarks, "given the circumstances."

Yes, I suppose watching each other waste away into starvation and sickness kills the mood for romance and everlasting love. "Was Venus happy?" I find myself saying. "When your mother was still around?"

Calliope's eyes fall shut. "The happiest. In fact . . ." she begins to drift away.

"In fact, *what*, Calliope?" I ask so seriously my voice nearly breaks in half.

She looks me dead in the eyes, her gaze cold and incriminating. "What have you done to her?" she seethes.

The question comes to me by sheer surprise. "Nothing."

I watch as Calliope mentally amends her question. "What do you want to do with her?"

"That's none of your business."

"I'm afraid it is," she says, bracing her hands onto the boardroom table in order to rise to her feet. "Because if you fuck this up"—she points at me—"if you fuck her up, I will gut you like a fish."

Like you'd ever get close. "You think I am playing a game with Venus?"

"All I really know about you," Calliope counters, "is that your reputation precedes you. But even if that's all I really know about you, I know Venus."

A gleaming smile parts my lips. "Do not be so headstrong, Calliope."

"I know that she is good. That she is hard-working and kind and everything that mother wanted us Deragon girls to be."

"No, Calliope," I challenge, now coming out of my chair as well. "Your sister is not good nor is she kind. Your sister is manipulative, bitter, and racked with guilt about more things than you could possibly ever understand. Do you think she liked hearing you yap about your luxurious parties and your singing while you sign her up for extra field work? Do you think she was courteous and well-behaved and feminine to our hosts in Mosacia? Do you think your mother would be proud of the woman Venus has become?"

Calliope says nothing, eyes wild and nostrils flared.

"Your mother would be *terrified* of the Venus I've come to know, and you'd be, too." And in the heat of the moment, as my body craves the feeling of proving Calliope wrong, I inch so close to her I can hear the frantic pounding beneath her chest. The horror of sharing my air. "Venus spends her days pulling weeds because she's afraid to be close to me. Not because I pose a threat to her life, but rather because if she stands too close, she allows me to have a grip on her heart."

The concept settles over her, and then, Calliope grins in a way that promises an agonizing death. "You think she loves you?" she mocks. "You think that your sick, twisted version of adoration has been enough to woo her? To win her over?" She chuckles darkly. "You're a fool."

"I am *her* fool," I snap. "Hers and hers alone. And you would be incredibly wise not to assume that your sister is aimlessly falling for my whims. No, Venus is avoiding me. Keeping me at arm's length so that she maintains control. Her real job does not lie in the southern gardens like she makes you think, but in this boardroom . . . with me," I nearly spit.

Calliope takes a single step back from me, surprise lifting her eyebrows. "Do you know my sister's favorite color?"

"Like that's even relevant right now," I bite back, but still attempt a guess. "Orange?"

"It's violet," Calliope corrects, though not in a manner that is arrogant or wiseacre. "After our mother."

Violet Deragon.

"When she was twelve, Venus contracted a horrible virus. It was a come-and-go sort of disease that we expected to pass after a matter of days, but it stayed for weeks. We were all told by physicians to abandon the house and leave Venus behind—to evacuate and let the disease . . ."

Calliope cannot find the words to finish, but I can paint the picture. Venus curled up in a heap on that cold floor, shivering to death with nothing left in her stomach to warm her, to keep her fighting for the air in her lungs or for life at all.

"But Mother couldn't bear the idea, so she sent Genny and I away with Father, promising to care for Venus properly until she passed on," she says, her voice strained. "We said our goodbyes to Venus and everything. She knew that . . . that this was the end for her."

To think that I could've lost Venus so long ago, having never touched her, never met her icy stare, never bickered with her. To contemplate a world where she never came in and disrupted my way of living for the better . . . I feel sick.

"But one day, about a month later, after we celebrated Venus's thirteenth birthday just Genny and Father and I, Venus stumbled to our safe house—alone." She hangs her head. "Mother had nursed Venus back to health but had contracted the disease for herself soon after."

My stomach roils.

So Venus blames herself. For everything.

An untimely illness killed her mother, but Venus believes that she is directly to blame. And she hates herself for it. That's why she swore to be there for her father. But then that went to shit. Saints, she likely tells herself that had she been a better daughter and a better carrier of his legacy, Tristan would never have thought to sell her out to the *U. Herald*. Now, she fears—with the explicit understanding of our divine connection—that if she does not give in to what I want from her, Calliope's and Geneva's lives are on the line, too.

And there it is: the final obstacle.

Venus is tiptoeing through her own life, scared to death that she'll outlive everyone she's ever loved, and that she will forever be the reason for the loss she has endured. And she refuses to share that fear with anyone.

My, how alike we truly are.

Calliope, unable to bear the weight of the subject any longer, turns to leave, her peach skirts sifting in her wake. She pauses just before the doorframe. "I know my sister more than you care to admit to yourself. Which means, if she does share in your feelings, I know that she'll tell you all this herself, even if I think you're full of shit."

Hope thrums within my blood.

"But if it is too much for her to face," Calliope continues, "which it very well may be, you should know now that she will never love you in the way it seems you're looking for. Can you live with that?"

43
Jericho

The next day, I enter the kitchens thinking that the staff has vacated the area in preparation for this meeting. Instead, I walk in—assuming I've arrived early— to a crowded huddle of servants laughing at something Geneva had said just before I came within earshot of them.

The laughter dies, however, when I'm not even three steps beyond the threshold.

"I'll catch up with you all later?" Geneva kindly inquires to the people around her. Everyone nods silently as they scatter in every which way, happily willing to leave my presence. Geneva, however, seems pleased to see me. "Good afternoon, Jericho," she bids me sweetly.

I try and offer her a warm smile. "Geneva."

"I won't be upset if you call me Genny like the others, you know," she says. "It's okay."

I dip my head down as I take a seat in one of the elevated countertop chairs beside her. "You've noticed that, huh?"

I look around the room and see several glass bowls full of apportioned ingredients: flour, softened butter, cracked eggs. And there, in the center of the island, rests a massive container of melted dark chocolate.

"Back in the Makers District, I was a chocolatier for one of the local shoppes," she explains. "I didn't know what you had in mind for our conversation today," she additionally mentions, a blush staining her cheeks, "but I thought I'd get started on Venus' birthday cake. She prefers celebrating before the actual day."

Geneva says it so casually that, had I not been supplied Tolcher's and Calliope's knowledge already, I wouldn't have thought twice about it. "No wonder you like spending your time down here," I say instead. "I should only hope the company down here is to your liking."

"The best," she declares, then feels the need to add, "Don't mind their jitters. They respect you very much. They just do not see you often."

Understandable. The only times I've ever deigned to visit the kitchens were to assert that someone was fired because the food was unsatisfactory. Perhaps I should work on that.

Genny circles the counter to start combining raw ingredients together in a metal bowl. She draws water from the golden faucet in the center of the sink, then goes from largest ingredient to smallest to ensure minimal spillage. A few specks of flour snowflake onto her teal blouse, and she giggles at her happy little accident. The sound is so childlike and undiluted that it pains me. "She'll be twenty-four, yes?" I say as a means of filling the silence.

"Correct." Geneva smiles. "Although these days, Venus acts older than Calliope. I wouldn't be surprised if she were blowing out thirty lit candles instead—"

"Genny?" I blurt out.

She meets my eyes with such gentleness, the last thing I deserve. "Yes, Jericho?"

Bloody Saints this is going to be awful.

"I am so unbelievably sorry."

It takes her a minute, but she eventually returns with, "What for?" Voicing the words in a way that shows she truly does not understand why I feel the need to apologize.

"For Kurt."

That's when it hits her, like a thrashing wave dousing her in freezing water. "Oh," she merely says, glancing down at her belly in recognition. In remembrance.

"You were right, that day in your old home. When you told me how your child would be fatherless because of me. It's true, and while I may have an explanation for my actions, it will never undo the past and it likely will never bring you peace, so there's no use in voicing it. But I just want you to know that—"

"I forgive you," she whispers.

She may as well have slapped me. "What?"

"You heard me," she insists without repeating the words.

I look for the tell on her face to know whether she's pulling my leg, playing some sick trick on me. "You cannot be serious."

"Oh, but I am." Geneva sighs. "You see, life's too short to hold onto your hurt. Kurt taught me that. But for as long as I hold onto him, I willingly cling to the hurt his absence leaves me with. So instead, I'm choosing to focus on the present—my child and me. Calliope and Venus becoming aunts soon. And you . . ." she adds, her soft eyes floating across to meet my own.

"But I took that life from you," I find myself sputtering in disbelief. Geneva isn't even shedding a tear over this. "I robbed you of a family. I ruined your life."

Geneva only shakes her head. "You do not dictate what ruins or rescues my life, Jericho, just as I cannot dictate how I impact yours. And you didn't rob me, or my baby, of a family," she says softly. "You just . . . changed the way it looks. Drastically, sure, but what I have here in Broadcove remains a family, nonetheless."

"What makes you so sure?" I ask, my chest constricting in palpable remorse.

Geneva dips her finger in the chocolate batter before popping her finger into her mouth. She hums in delight at the taste. "Try some," she encourages, and though the movement is hesitant, I repeat her actions and taste it for myself.

Not only did Geneva love her job, but she was damn good at it, too.

I immediately reach a different finger into the bowl for seconds, and as I do, I hear her say with a wandering eye, "I'll admit, I was furious when Venus first brought you to our house. But the longer I've stayed here, receiving ample help throughout my pregnancy, and now, how I've watched Venus regain a sense of passion in life . . ." Geneva marvels. Then, she clasps her hands together, her sticky finger rubbing across the side of her thumb.

"The more I've come to learn about who you are. Truly."

At this moment, Genny proves to be more frightening than Venus.

"I don't know how your visions work," she says solemnly, "but I know in my gut that they're real. And in a way, that belief allows me to forgive you for what happened to Kurt, it also fills me with solace knowing that they are what ultimately led you to my sister."

Fighting the stinging sensation in my eyes, I say to her, "So you're . . . okay?"

"You asked me what makes me so sure that this depiction of life still qualifies as a family, so I'll tell you. It's because I know what follows your apology, Jericho," Geneva murmurs, and that same, childlike grin greets me like an old friend. "You're here to ask for my blessing to propose to Venus."

I can't compose a coherent thought—it's amazing enough that I maintain eye contact with her—but Geneva knows better than to ask for clarification or insist I verbally respond on whether her claim is correct.

Still, knowing the significance of her possible answer, I nod. Just once.

"I remember how helpless I felt when your guards rode into town. Calliope is wonderful and all, but sharing a room with Venus over the years really bonded us. She was more than a sister. She was my greatest friend, and when I thought I lost her . . . right after I lost *him* . . . I couldn't imagine enduring another day of life.

"The baby changed that perception, of course, but not nearly as much as when Venus returned that night, and when she brought you with her. I hated you at first, and in the privacy of my own thoughts, I wondered if hurting you could help avenge what I'd lost. But in time, and in trusting you with my sister," she explains, "I discovered that you two share more in common than I thought."

Geneva spares me the details of listing off our mutual transgressions and stirs the bowl of mixed ingredients with a wooden spoon. "Calliope mentioned that you are now aware of what happened to our mother," she says, her voice mousy.

"I cannot even imagine Venus's grief," I tell her earnestly.

"I think you could, actually," Geneva counters concisely. "In fact, I think you're the only other person that could truly, intimately understand the weight of feeling responsible for a loss that precious. Wouldn't you say so?"

Too stunned to respond in any outright manner, I merely watch as Geneva fetches a silver, rectangular pan and begins pouring the chocolate concoction from one container to the other, using the spoon to drive out the difficult remnants along the sides. "Calliope thinks that Venus will never change, and that Venus will ultimately not commit to a relationship with you because the only person she knows how to trust is herself. But I tend to think Calliope is rather close-minded," Geneva states as she turns the temperature dial on the oven. "Personally, I think that all Venus needs is a little . . . nudge," she concludes.

As Geneva washes the goop off her hands, slathering warm water and soap practically up to her elbows, I take the hint and decide that, despite Tolcher's initial warning, perhaps a party will serve her well. Maybe it will allow Venus the opportunity to finally feel the weight of how much she means to me—how much I may very well mean to her.

"I swear, Genny." I breathe. "I swear that if Venus can look past my unforgivable faults and find the confidence to be with me someday, I will—"

"There's no need to rattle off promises I already know you'll keep." Geneva smiles gracefully, reaching a hand across the countertop to squeeze my own—a gesture so motherly and familiar that I feel like weeping. "And do not tell yourself that your offenses cannot be forgiven. Something tells me Venus has already moved past them."

"Just us two today?" Ardian says by way of greeting as he enters the boardroom. Five minutes late, but still.

His tardiness only sets my current disposition further on edge. My unbearable, restless foot thumps repeatedly against the paneled flooring and I cannot seem to find a comfortable enough seating posture. Ardian notes my agitation to himself, even considers inquiring about it, but the sound of the door reopening behind him halts his train of thought.

Peering into the room with a puzzled expression on her face, Delta looks at her uncle with faint concern. "You wished to see me, Your Majesty?"

"This will not take long," I assure them both, although the sentiment may only turn out to be wishful thinking. "Have a seat."

Ardian pulls out his niece's chair without hesitation,

tucking her in towards the lip of the table like a true gentleman. Then, he seats himself across from her. Looking over them both, it appears that Delta's presence now alarms Ardian—which I do not understand entirely. I've never given Ardian any reason to suspect I'd embarrass or endanger her.

"Does this pertain to the Dial Line?" Delta suddenly asks sheepishly. "Because if so, I didn't mean to hog it for so long. I know it is designed for vital communication, but Diana and I just got to talking again, and she—"

Truth be told, I had forgotten about the device, given it was installed the afternoon I paid a visit to Geneva, three days ago. By the time I left the kitchens, my heart was so full of reassurance that my head had been significantly clouded by it. I'm not even sure if I took an evening meal that day. But as I glance over to the corner just before the windows, I see the red lacquer mechanism clear as day. Situated in its holster, I also notice a small switch, which I presume triggers the alert ringer over in Sevensberg Palace.

Delta still appears to be rattling off a reluctant apology by the time I have the sense to interrupt. "Water under the bridge," I insist with the illusion of understanding. "No, this is about an event I need help organizing here in Broadcove Castle. It's rather urgent."

"Oh," Delta says flatly.

"And it needs to be planned discreetly," I add.

"Of course, sir," Ardian amends on her behalf. "What did you have in mind?"

44
Venus

All I've learned from avoiding Jericho these last few weeks is that now that I've known life beside him, time apart from him truly dulls my days. I knew it—the moment I let the tears flow in front of Genny and Calliope, it was over. Any sense of salvaging my composure or hiding my want for Jericho went out the door without needing to speak it aloud.

But even as I wept with indecision, I still felt the phantom, lingering touch of his hands on my body. I felt the softness of his lips burning through my own, the thundering of his heart teaching mine how to properly pulse within my chest. And deeper, beneath the wildfire desire and electricity, a part of me awakened to a heartbreaking realization:

I cannot kill Jericho.

No longer is it that I don't want to. I simply can't. Not for my own reasons. Not even for Octavian. A mountain of indignations against him could pile up in print, could cover the surface area of my rooms, and I'd still find myself dismissing them somehow. Because consequences be damned, as Jericho kissed me with everything he had, I wanted to take out my concealed dagger, lay it on the altar, and forsake it forever. I wanted to plunge it within me and remove it as penance for my secrecy.

So here I am again—covered in pollen, dirt, and scattered orchid petals just to keep away from the one person I want to be around the most—talking to a dead woman in efforts to purge my guilty conscience.

Today's conversation topics range from confrontation styles, self-sabotage, and fear of the unknown. Unsurprisingly, this is not the first time they have been up for discussion. Still, Merrie, as always, remains gracious as I angrily expel those aforementioned insecurities, vowing not to allow our dialogue to conveniently appear in one of Jericho's future visions. However, when there's an open moment, she certainly doesn't take it easy on me, either. Having discovered that I can perform the apparition ritual in the presence of any water source, Merrie now levitates above the carved sitting fountain within North Star. I'll admit, I do not feel half as insane finally being able to make eye contact with her in conversation. But it comes with the caveat of seeing her smile at me just before I watch an assortment of flowers magically bloom before me, be cut at the base of each stem, and fall before me in a perfect pile. Too bouquet-like.

Then, she warmly wishes me, "Happy birthday, Venus."

I cringe at the flowers, honored yet embarrassed by the gesture somehow, but still note which kinds she hand-selected for me. Peonies, of course. Her favorite. Then white roses, huckleberry, and—

Providing a darker accent to the otherwise rosy set of blooms, lies a cluster of violets.

"Merrie, I can't—"

"She loved you, Venus," she insists. "She adored you and believed in you. She knew the risks in staying behind, to take care of you, and that didn't matter. She was never going to abandon you."

"Well, she *should've*," I seethe, hurling only the violets into the fountain until the water drags them under the surface. "Because the daughter she loved so much died in that house with her."

"Perhaps," Merrie returns calmly, and it's the first time that I feel validated in that notion. She doesn't argue with my emotions and insists that I am just as wonderful and innocent as I was ten years ago. "But what if this new you is a better you? What if you endured that loss to help discover who you were meant to become?"

My knee-jerk reaction is vile and instant. "Like you'd be confident enough to say the same about Jericho."

Merrie pauses at that, the rushing water stilling for a moment. "Yes, I am," she gathers. "Not at first. Watching my son grieve me was . . ." she shudders, and it is the most human sentiment I've ever seen from her. "It was horrible. And it came with the additional gut-punch of seeing him spiral downward. But when you came along," she says, her tone lifting in hopefulness, "I started to see a newer version of my son, and that's all I could've ever wanted for my boy after seeing him suffer for so long."

Then, slowly, I watch as Merrie's apparition draws

up all the still water from the fountain to dry out the discarded violets. Her almighty air lifts them only to set them back on the lip of the stone again. "So tell me, Venus. Why dishonor your mother by spending your birthday neglecting the very thing she *died* to save?"

My eyes linger over the violets until my vision blurs with hot tears.

"Because I wasn't worth dying for," I whisper. "Because if she saw my futile attempts at keeping my sisters fed after father died, how I traded out my body to people when I got desperate enough, or worse, if she knew how hard I am struggling between choosing to love your son," I clench my teeth, "or to kill him . . . she'd be ashamed."

I bow my head and let the weeping overtake me for a time. I do not know how long, nor do I care—and neither does Merrie. She lets me sit there and sob until my heart is content. No arguments, no lecture on negative self-talk, just silent understanding.

Eventually, I find the will to stop, though only to keep my body from dry heaving, worn out from the exertion of my renewed sadness from speaking my truths aloud. It takes great effort to form a sentence without the words bobbling in my throat. "I . . . just . . . miss her."

"I know, dear," Merrie croons, and though she does not reach for me, something about the words touches me somehow. Warmth fills the skin along my shoulder, spanning slightly down my back in a rubbing motion. "And while it's okay to miss her, your pain does not honor her memory. It taints it."

I've never thought of it that way.

"The people who survived her loss alongside you, your sisters," she continues, "they do not condemn you to a lifetime of guilt. You were just a girl who happened to fall ill, and rather than leave you to die, your mother took care of you. She did the right thing."

She did the right thing.

She did the right thing.

"That's what mothers do, Venus," Merrie resumes, "they sacrifice. They lay down their pride, and their rest, and even their lives for their kids—for their spouses. No matter how loving or wretched or wonderful they each may be to them—they make the daily decision to put themselves last for the ones they love."

"Then I don't think I could ever be a mother, Merrie," I confess through broken sobs. "I do not have the necessary qualities for the role, and certainly not enough to even be half the mother Violet Deragon was."

"And that's okay," Merrie soothes. "Not everyone is meant, or required, to be a mother. I think, with enough time, you may come to change your mind—but even if you do not, even if you were to turn into someone you believe your mother would scorn, Violet still knew in her heart that you were worth it." Merrie's voice begins to break, but she still manages to get out the words, "Graveyards are not meant for the young. They're meant for those who have enjoyed a long, happy life—and your mother died to ensure that you got that life. Do not waste her sacrifice."

Merrie's words are final, and as she devolves into the water she gathered up—sloshing back into the holding pen of the fountain with undeniable ease—I no longer feel the need to prove her or myself differently.

I exit North Star feeling drained . . . but beneath the heartache, I think I discover a morsel of something I hadn't dared to look for in years and as I carefully pick up the soaked violets and begin the journey back to my rooms, I realize what it is.

Hope.

45
Venus

For the last decade, I've started every birthday with a massive cry—but with all things considered, I figure year twenty-four ought to be different.

Genny and Calliope will likely leave me to my own devices today, suspecting I'd prefer my space, but I am tempted to call on them and request they take breakfast with me. Even better, as I already feel the sun's rays battle against the glass window barrier, we could dine outdoors, perhaps among the gardens I think are finally adorned in the way I was intending all this time.

And as for Jericho . . .

Saints, the thought of him makes the devil on my shoulder do cartwheels in my stomach.

I think back on that final evening in Sevensberg, when Slater nitpicked the way stars impact compatibility—particularly how he'd fallen silent at the mention of Jericho's astrological makeup. Any truth in that aside, I just hope Jericho remembered the date I gave, hope that my sisters, or anyone else, didn't get to him first and discourage him from saying anything to me today.

A knock sounds at the door, and before being prompted otherwise, Delta peeks her head inside. "You have messages on the Dial Line!" she says, far cheerier than her already boisterous self. "Up! *Now!*"

Before I know it, Delta drags me hand in hand down the golden hallways of Broadcove all the way until we reach the West Wing. Still in my nightgown and socks, it is a true miracle that I do not slip and bust open my lip in the process, let alone frighten those we pass with my state of dress. After a series of minutes sprinting past other staff, Delta stampedes through the boardroom, nearly kicking the door down, and—

"Jerichooooo," Delta groans instantly. "Off! The calls are for *her*, not you!"

Slouched against the back wall, the red Dial Line in his hand and his mouth hovering over the receiver, Jericho means to flash Delta a sour look, but the moment his eyes land on me, the intended expression instantly shifts.

The Dial Line sinks as his hand drops at his side and his mouth parts. The ghost of a smile lingers along the corners but doesn't fully bend. I study the circles under his eyes only because this early in the morning, the piercing blue would likely drag me under, and I realize that he hasn't been sleeping well. "Good morning," I bid simply.

Delta clears her throat before he can reply.

He nods shortly before extending the mechanism towards me, and Delta shoves me in his direction. My breathing hitches, but I manage to grab onto the receiver just as Jericho lets go. He strolls out without another sound, and suddenly, I regret those weeks of keeping my distance. Where I first considered his expression sad, Jericho truthfully appears . . . indifferent.

After a shaky hello, the first voice I hear through the Dial Line is unmistakable.

"I'd bet money you'd have more fun celebrating your birthday here than with cranky old Jericho," Slater remarks casually.

"You might be right," I joke halfheartedly. "Still, I'm surprised you remembered that today was the day."

"I remember everything, Venus," he says pointedly, and I can hear his playful malice in his voice. "And that includes the approximate shipping time it would take me to ship something from Sevensberg to Broadcove."

Delta giggles from behind me, no doubt eavesdropping our conversation—but it is only upon further examination that I realize she's holding something. A sleek, velvet case, likely containing something too expensive for me to immediately and instinctively identify it. But Delta's eyes gleam like I've just struck gold.

"What kind of strings did you pull, Slater?"

"Just open the damn box," he instructs humorously.

A part of me sinks at the prospects of Jericho lingering just around the corner, standing idly by in the hall as I give Slater another measure of attention. For my sake, at least, I hope he now stands somewhere far away, mainly because the idea of burning him burns me. But then I remember that Jericho had been using the line before passing it over to me—and I feel like shutting myself in my room for the rest of the day.

Unable to resist Delta's slightly aggressive prompting, however, I finally take the object and pry open the lid just to nearly go and drop it on the floor.

Glittering stones shimmer in the place of a cheap silver chain and situated in the center rests a magnificent sapphire in the shape of a heart. "What do you think?" he inquires happily.

The cut of the gem alone tells me all I need to know about the motivations behind such a gift, and with as much propriety as I can muster, I answer him with, "I'm not sure what to say. It's . . . captivating."

"Much like you are," he whispers slyly. "Wear it tonight for me, will you? It's only fair, considering I cannot see you don it firsthand—"

"Of course," I murmur.

Then, there's a fussy sort of sound before I hear him bark out a slur of profanities into his end of the Dial Line. A feminine voice equally bites back at him in return. Diana, no doubt. I briefly make out the words, "—Miss you! Happy birth—" before she's shoved out of range.

I expect to hear Slater's voice rattle off one last one-liner, but the line goes quiet. I stand there, waiting for a series of moments before deciding to give up on speaking to anyone else. But just as I remove the device from my ear, the other line scratches. Someone new breathes my name.

Greer.

"You're too much," I say through a false swoon, pretending to still be speaking with Slater and then promptly shooing Delta away from the speaker. She scuttles out of the boardroom, not entirely embarrassed to have intruded on my space. When Delta closes the door behind her, I whisper, "It's just me, now. How'd you get away with the line?"

"Ours isn't mounted," she mutters rapidly, as if checking over her shoulder.

"Is everything okay?" I ask, then quickly amend the phrasing to, "I mean, is something else wrong that I should know about? Anything I can help with?"

Her side of the line stills for a moment before Greer answers, "I am safe, for now." And then, before I can truly absorb any sense of relief in her words, she bleakly adds, "Father is gathering a search party to find Chumley. He suspects . . . abandonment."

Unfortunately, your father would be right, my gut longs to say. Still, fearing that this conversation is being monitored somehow, I opt to reply coyly with, "I do not see why that is a matter of concern—"

"You and I both know he's not in Mosacia," she whispers in haste. "And my father doesn't think so either. Still, a witch-hunt in your territory requires Jericho's consent, and not only has he not given it, but Father likely will not ask for it," Greer says, her tone hinting at the fact that I already am aware of the severity of the circumstances. Because the Seagraves sending armed forces into our land without prior knowledge is considered an act of war.

Meaning we can reassemble the Hive.

"When are they coming?"

"Soon, but no formal preparations have been made yet."

I want to ask her the selfish question of why she broke her streak of silence on me. What about me earned her trust fully to where she felt safe enough to speak up after so long, let alone about this? But before I can determine the proper phrasing that wouldn't make me sound so narcissistic, I hear her tell me briefly, "Don't trust them."

"Who, Greer?"

"Any of them," she hisses. "They may like you, but they don't like him. So if you have any care in the world for Jericho at all—"

She gasps, then promptly terminates the call.

I do not have time to try and rationalize what the back half of her heeded warning could be before I cup my hands over my mouth and scream his name, suddenly hoping he lingered along the other side of the door all along.

And sure enough, at only a moment's notice, he returns—although his heavy breathing suggests he chased my frantic voice down a long hallway or two.

"Shut the door," I order, unsure if the words come out flustered or firm. He obeys, nonetheless, and I find enough control over my faculties to finally return the crimson receiver to its holster.

Jericho's eyes are wide with worrisome anticipation. "What's wrong?"

"I have news. News that can only stay between the two of us."

The Seagrave children's assassins are set to leave their posts to hunt down Thatcher Chumley, and were it not for Greer's warning, we wouldn't even know about it until they docked in Honeycomb Harbor.

They are not looking for an invitation, and they are not asking for permission. They are storming in with a squadron of trained soldiers and eliminating any suspects that could have to do with Chumley's disappearance—which means they're after me. After Jericho, too.

And I cannot have that.

"What do you recommend we do?" are the first words out of his mouth.

"Someone needs to convince the people to enlist. Nobility, Makers, members of your King's Guard. It doesn't matter. We need willing participants," I explain. "But how we do that, I am still contemplating—"

"Okay," he cuts in with a soft, cautionary hand held out towards me.

I flinch. "Okay, what?"

"Just . . . okay. Thank you for updating me."

I bark out a curt laugh. "Jericho, we need to do something. Right now."

"And we will," he responds calmly before extending his other hand, a sleek envelope with his royal signet stamped over the lip. Where I first suspect a handwritten letter, I suddenly dread the prospects of it being an invitation to something.

"I meant we need to do something about the Hive, Jericho," I complain, all the while my fingers remain focused on opening the envelope. The waxy seal feels funny on my fingertips, and I try not to laugh in anger at the ridiculousness of how relaxed he is about all of this. "We could go to war and you're more concerned about—"

The mysterious cardstock within the envelope is the most beautiful shade of violet.

My chest tightens strong enough to withhold breath from my lungs, but I must convince myself that the choice of stationary is merely an ironic coincidence on Jericho's part. It is the only way I garner enough strength to read the embossed cursive:

IN HONOR OF LADY VENUS DERAGON'S 24TH BIRTHDAY

"Jericho," I exhale achingly.

"Keep reading." He chuckles. I concede, if only to curb my growing curiosity.

JOIN US FOR A SPECTACULAR EVENING OF

MUSIC, DANCING, AND DINING.

HOSTED AT BROADCOVE CASTLE

JUNE TWENTIETH

SEVEN THIRTY IN THE EVENING

"We can have war tomorrow," Jericho murmurs gently, his hands gliding along my bare arms, the sensation scorching my soul. "But today, we're celebrating."

My lip quivers, trying to form a grateful smile.

So overcome with emotions I cannot form into coherent words, I simply throw myself into him, and Jericho catches me both tenderly and tightly at the same time. His broad chest vibrates against my body as he chuckles in confused enjoyment. "I'm thrilled to see what kinds of torture you have lined up for me this year, Venom."

I raise my head only meaning to meet his eyes, but by accident, our lips touch. The moment is brief, but I'd burn down Broadcove Castle itself to savor the feel of it forever. "You're in for a world of hurt so long as you're with me," I tell him, aiming to be lighthearted but not catching its double meaning until the words already hang overhead.

But I must hide my inner defeat well enough, because Jericho only responds with a wicked grin. "I think I can handle that."

46
Jericho

Delta assured me two hours ago that Venus was set to take her first two meals of the day with her sisters out of sight from the grand ballroom, and afterwards, she'd begin dressing for the party. Too panicky that Venus would somehow wander towards the battlefield that is the ballroom's current state of setup, however, I commissioned both Ardian and Tolcher to ensure Venus stayed out of range. With all three of them running around micromanaging Venus, I'm now left to fight tooth and nail not to lose my insanity over how slow it is taking so many people to assemble decorations. I'm nearly about to bark at the team stringing up lights when a gentle hand briefly glides over my arm.

I turn to lock eyes with Geneva, then her belly—now clearly showing the evidence of impending motherhood—and it takes strength not to grit my teeth as I say, "Hello."

"How about we take a turn about the wing?" she suggests, instantly understanding the unsightly look on my face.

"I can't go now," I grunt, side-eyeing one of the buffoons at the top of the steep ladder overhead. "The moment I leave, something will break, or the fireworks will accidentally fire off in the yard, or—"

But Geneva does not listen, deciding to pull me out of the room behind her without my permission. I choose not to resist, though, secretly thankful for her insistence as we cross through a few hallways before stopping outside of Ardian's rooms. "Feel better?" she asks.

Unable to hear the hullaballoo of the congregation, I let out a breath. "Yes, actually."

"Everything will turn out wonderfully, Jericho," she replies reassuringly, but as she goes to fish something out from within her skirt pockets, I try not to let the opposite show on my face. Truth be told, I think drowning myself in decorations helped distract me from all the things I do not want to think about.

Reassembling the Hive.

Assassins on Urovia's doorstep.

The idea of Chumley's potential discovery.

But even so, even alongside any other dreadful possibilities, the prospect of any danger coming back to Venus fuels my fury more so than anything else. The people of Urovia could peel me off my throne and throw me to the Mosacian wolves and kill me if they wanted— but if any of them so much as lay a hand on her—

"Tell me," Geneva whispers. I shake my head, but she merely looks up at me with her doe-like dark eyes. "It's okay."

I shut my eyes, not willing to look her in the face when

I admit to her, "I want to keep your sister safe, I really do. But for reasons I'm not willing to disclose, I fear that I'm the biggest threat to her."

Genny only chuckles. Just once. "Venus never plays things safe. You of all people should know that, and you shouldn't be scared for her." That's when she finally finds what she went digging through her fabrics for.

In her hands rests a single pearl.

"It fell off a nobility woman's earring one night when Calliope was performing at a gala, and she grabbed it before she came home. It was the nicest thing she possessed before moving to Broadcove, given she never sold it. She told me that she wanted you to have it," Geneva shares softly.

I know better than to ask why Calliope of all people would grant me this—it is a peace offering. A silent acknowledgement of trust despite all the things she said the last time we spoke. As to what thawed her icy disapproval, I say, "Let me guess. It's because I let you two design your gowns for tonight's ball."

Genny shakes her head, her cheeks pinking with humor and subdued delight. "She went to wake up Venus this morning and heard her mumbling your name in her sleep. That pretty much turned her."

My skin heats and my nerves run haywire. Mumbling my name? How so? Desperately? Fondly? Longingly?

"Calliope approves?" I say, something balling up in my throat.

"She . . . understands," Geneva amends carefully. "Calliope has her reservations, of course, but none of them are strong enough to sabotage any plans you might have up your sleeve for the day." A clever little wink flashes over her kind face.

The gesture is almost enough to soothe the hot rage that boils at the sound of distant glass shattering. Almost. My body instantly tenses and my jaw trembles with whatever incoming profanity my mouth prepares to shout first, but Genny steps in front of me. "Let me handle it," she offers. "You go eat or something."

Before I can argue, she pivots on a heel and hurriedly returns the way we came. I expect for her to try and peacefully instruct them to resolve whatever issues they just created, but instead, moments later, I hear the distant sound of her voice scolding the staff. The responding sound of mumbles and shuffling make me smile devilishly to myself.

Unable to stomach much of lunch, I retreat to my rooms until showtime—and the moment I step through the doorway and shut myself in, my inner peace returns like a rush of blood to the head.

Despite most of Broadcove's walls being a splendid gold, I've always found secret solace within the dark cave that my bedchambers provide me. When Father died, I had the walls reconstructed, glazed over with near-opaque stained glass. The previous builders of Broadcove insisted that a prince shouldn't dwell in a room without windows, but the moment Father went to the Beyond and I took the throne, I fired them, replaced the windows with frosty, translucent glass, and removed the chandeliers. Sure, I resent the fact that, to attain this private darkness, sunlight has been substituted for a bluish glow akin to the Seagrave's signature hue—but even so, the transformative feeling of finding rest in the shadows outweighs the unfortunate likeness.

The bed is massive, an amendment to my rooms I made as my visions became more frequent. Some nights, I'd go to sleep on my back in a normal section of the mattress and wake up sprawled in the center atop the covers— much like the night I first dreamt of Venus. Neglected, waxy candles litter my various nightstands along with the powdered substances I've been slowly trying to wean myself off of, and as the persistent daylight tries to peek through the murky glass along the walls, a surge of warmth mimics the same movement as one would see from beneath the waves of the Damocles.

With nothing remaining on the agenda until I need to begin dressing for the party, I clamber atop the comforter and sigh at the familiar embrace of cushy fabric. I instantly sink lower, as if the bed itself wishes to wrap itself around me and tell me that everything will be okay in the end. That tonight will go well. That Venus will be happy.

Happy with *me*.

These days I have a hard time remembering whether or not a vision has come over me in sleep or if they are beginning to descend in the midst of my waking hours. And while I would consider investigating the notion further, the recognition of this new setting has me second guessing that decision.

Bushes rustle in a familiar, abandoned marsh. It is evening, but unlike a dream I once had about this place, the greenery gives way to small blossoms and revived color. Nature has healed, and it appears that the same girl who once studied me through these shrubs, and lured me across the territory to her has changed for the better as well.

Venus stands up, revealing herself fully from her hiding spot, and instantly I realize that my original vision of her has changed. Her dark hair lays unbound against her back, and completely barefoot, she steps across the dirt-lined path towards me with a soft smile. Her chestnut skin gleams against the white satin slip she wears, my eyes lingering over each indentation of her naked body the slim fabric gives away. It's almost unfair to see her so ethereal in this liminal space—free to have my way with her but doomed to wake up to the absence of her touch, her taste, her warmth. To have my body return me to a room I do not share with her.

Still, I cannot deny that the Venus that stands before me now looks as though she's lived in Broadcove all her life—perhaps a portrait of the woman she could become with enough time together. Raised to uphold the utmost confidence, fed the finest foods to sustain her healthy physique, and taught how to make a man go mad for her with a simple look—the exact look she flashes me, now.

"You're a vision," I say softly enough that my lungs burn.

She does not hesitate.

"You're a monster," she seethes.

Only it's not Venus's voice coming out of her mouth.

47
Venus

Earlier this morning, Calliope insisted that the three of us all get dressed for the party together, and although I initially resisted, the several midday mimosas, and the meals we've shared today have loosened me up to the idea. Calliope gushed about commissioning her own gown over breakfast while Genny uncharacteristically had little to say over lunch. Her behavior only partially added up when she slipped into the hall for a half-hour or so and eventually returned with a handmade cake with my name frosted on it. We each happily picked it apart with our shiny forks, but I could see there was more. She saw something in the halls—maybe she saw him.

Hoping to crack her, I passively ask them both, "Should I be worried?"

"About what?" Calliope returns on Genny's behalf.

"Whatever Jericho's brewing up that's had the two of you caging me in here all day."

Genny rolls her eyes just as the seamstresses and ladies

maids file in, kits and boxes full of goodies meant to doll us up for the evening. "There's nothing that I can share with you," Genny replies slyly, and as the last three maids enter the room, I notice their bodies hunched over as they carry in our gowns, all of them hidden in concealed bags draped over their backs.

Calliope instantly strips off her beige day gown, too thrilled to keep any composure, and the ladies designated to her preparation giggle amongst themselves. Unzipping the garment bag herself, Calliope yanks out a dress that reminds me so much of the gardens I worked so hard to cultivate here. A deep teal dress with scattered, colored flowers and cascading petals glitters faintly in the setting sunlight. As the fabric curls at the bottom, I almost imagine that the flowers bloom with a life of their own—more so, I believe I even smell the design, as if the embellishments were picked straight from the earth and sewn in. Already listing out her desires for her hair and makeup to the reluctant maids, even as she's being stuffed into the rather fussy gown, I turn to make a comment to Genny and fall silent as I discover she has undressed as well.

In nothing but her undergarments, my little sister sits on the chaise before the mirror, watching as one of her maids dutifully rubs a cream of some kind over her belly, where darkened, jagged lines have begun to appear.

I'm normally not one to so blatantly stare at another woman, let alone in a vulnerable state of dress, but my eyes wander over Genny nonetheless, studying her developing body. Her beautiful bump swells with life— and while I always wonder if the proof of her and Kurt's intertwined existence brings her anguish, I realize as she catches my gaze that it has the opposite effect.

His love for her spurs her onward, drives her to keep going. Just as my love for—

But even as I stop myself mid-thought, Genny flashes me a knowing look as another one of the mild-mannered maids helps pull her gown's neckline above her full breasts.

Genny decided on a gown of the most stunning, sunflower yellow. She glows like the sun at this stage in her pregnancy, and the longer I look at her, the more I feel like weeping. She's the portrait of sunshine, resilience, and mercy. Each additional second I stare lovingly at her, the more I feel the need to grovel at her feet and beg for forgiveness, for having these stirring feelings for the man who killed the great love of her life. For breaking my promise to her.

"Stop," Genny whispers. "Don't do this to yourself. Not today."

"You're the most beautiful thing I've ever laid eyes on," I tell her as something knots up in my throat.

"Love you, too, I guess," Calliope snorts, feigning the feeling of being disregarded.

We all get to laughing, then. Even the maids join in— and the chatter proves to be just enough to help me find my way back to normalcy before the woman carrying my garment bag reveals what I'll be donning this evening.

Ethereal and flowing and undeniably magnificent, the lilac gown comes spilling downward like water. A high slit reveals itself along what will be my right leg, the waist swerves inward to accentuate my healthier frame, and the bodice gathers over to one shoulder. However, where fabric should sweep over and drape along my back, a cutout along the shoulder is framed delicately by fresh violets, creating a small wreath, allowing the long sleeve to fall gracefully along that arm. A gown like this belongs on a woman much like those I witnessed in stone along the walls of Sevensberg Palace—on a goddess.

A fond sense of recognition flickers behind my eyes at one of my first memories of Jericho—and the twisted smile that blooms in response quells the ache in my bones that the violets mean to leave me with. "I have never stopped missing her," I say to no one at all, untying the sash along my dressing robe to try and distract myself from any sadness that may seek to overcome me.

And while Genny is normally the one to soothe the soreness inside of me in moments like this, it is Calliope who waltzes over, her dark dress flourishing in the light from the window, and tells me, "I see her in you, Venus. Every day. Having you in our lives," she whispers, her eyes welling up with tears, "it's like she never left."

Before my own tears come, both of my sisters wrap their arms around me, sheltering me. Safe in their embrace, I let my eyes leak out all my remaining grief, undeterred by our audience or by the time. No one rushes me, no one interrupts, and it's that small mercy that allows me, after a few minutes, to stand up again. To approach the soft, purple gown and my mother's flowers and speak into existence, "I can do this."

The last thing I was informed of before both of my

sisters headed towards the epicenter of the action was that guests had been arriving in troves. I think I even heard a gleeful exclamation from one of the attendees as they neared the ballroom fluttering down the hall as both Calliope and Geneva slipped out, assuring me they'd find me for a dance sometime during the night.

Now, as my stomach toils in both excitement and apprehension, a knock comes upon the door, and I stiffly rise from my chair. Heart thundering in my chest, I find my feet skipping towards the sound, and where I expect to see Jericho, I open the door and lock eyes with Tolcher.

"In the mood to attend a ball?" he muses, a boyish grin across his lips.

His presence is a relief, yet knowing it comes with an escort into the madness beyond, my hands feel clammy. "Not if I'm meant to be fawned over the whole evening," I return as coolly as I can manage.

"And yet you got dressed for an event held in your honor."

"Vanity becomes me," I drawl.

Tolcher chuckles at that. "I will say, though, you do look . . . regal."

"You can blame that on my sisters. They certainly got carried away in the fun of designing this dress for—"

Stopping mid-sentence at the sight of Tolcher's puzzled expression, I reroute my words and ask him what's wrong. To which Tolcher replies, "You think Geneva and Calliope helped make this dress? No, Venus. He orchestrated everything. He did this."

He did.

"Oh, that reminds me," Tolcher adds. "We cannot

have you going in there without one last finishing touch."

From behind his back, he reveals a set of decadent earrings he must've carried in his gloved hand all the way here. As he lifts them up by the needle, I watch as pearls arranged in three stacked crosses cascade downward, and branching towards each stone is a near iridescent cord of sorts. In a way, it reminds me of an elegant duplication of the Saint's Symbol, and for a moment, my heart sinks, wondering if Octavian had something to do with this.

But then, I notice a peculiarity. One of the pearls—the bottom one on the left side—appears uneven. Bigger than the others, with a miniscule dent along its side, but just barely. A familiar sheen glimmers back at me, as if understanding the confusion of my thoughts, and just as I mean to tell Tolcher that they are too grand for my desired taste, the breath leaves my lungs as I finally place its source.

Calliope.

Yes, now I remember the night she came home with this, how she swore up and down that she would barter this for a splendid holiday meal two winters ago. How Genny and I eventually talked her out of it, explained that more money and more performances would come along, that she deserved to have something beautiful all to herself.

"Everything?" I ask Tolcher.

"Yes," he sighs kindly. "Jericho had his hand in everything."

Slowly, I choose to take the wondrous earrings from his hands and approach the vanity. Sitting briefly before the mirror, I remove the several rusted hoops from my ears and weave the needle through the primary slot. Looking over my reflection, I take one final glance at the maids' work—likely all instructions from Jericho. Hair twisted upwards and pinned atop my head, with delicate pieces framing a face minimally painted over with cosmetics. My lips caressed with a neutral gloss. But the color in my cheeks . . . that's real. The sparkle of excitement in my eyes, that's real, too.

Just then, Ardian approaches the doorway, speaking directly to Tolcher. I briefly make out the words, "—says he's ready for her," before he glances into my rooms and stops abruptly at the sight of me. Instantly, he smiles with a sense of pride that feels almost fatherly. "Oh, my dear, you are a vision."

I rise from my chair, meaning to extend a similar sentiment towards him in return, but he darts back off the way he came as someone distantly calls for him again. His frantic steps rhythmically pad down the hallway until he turns the corner, and Tolcher merely says, "That's our cue."

And suddenly, I am more nervous than I have ever been in my entire life.

Blindly walking towards an unknown fate, I follow behind Tolcher with the growing suspicion that I may pass out right here on the floor. My feet are working just fine, but damn, my head is *swimming*—

"Venus," Tolcher calls out, not having noticed him turn around to assess the space between his strides and mine.

"Why am I panicking?" I ask in fragmented breaths.

He merely takes my hand in his own, walking alongside me rather than in front of me, and leads me towards a distant glow of cold light at the edge of the hall. "You'll feel better when you see him," he remarks with no judgment in his voice, and we both know it's the truth. That after all the fights, the hatred, the compromising, and the alliances, something new has formed between us. For both of us. An understanding. An appreciation. An emotion that I fear goes deeper than any words I could conjure up right now.

And then, as we turn the final corner, Tolcher wishes me well before scurrying forward and alerting the guards at the checkpoint of the room that I have arrived.

Where a hallway once led into a ballroom of golden splendor, the pathway now sparkles with near-magical, purple light. A mystical lavender haze envelops me in mist, and twinkling stars flicker with recognition as I pass through its makeshift tunnel. I hear someone in the ballroom strike up the orchestra, and in a bellowing voice from somewhere within, I hear Ardian announce to the world, "Ladies and gentlemen, please raise your glasses to the lady of the hour, King Jericho's Right Hand, Lady Venus Deragon."

It only hits me once I resurface from the purple smoke and arrive in the cavernous ballroom that Ardian used my title—the very title I thought Jericho wanted to keep a secret.

I've never seen so much finery and friendly faces in one, shared spot. Hundreds of people applaud or gawk over my dress or crook their heads in my direction. Glasses raised and voices laden with praise and acknowledgement, the world around me erupts with the sounds of celebration and honor—and none of it matters.

And how could it? How could any of this compare to the moment I catch sight of Jericho standing at the base of the stairs, smiling at me in a way that promises my destruction?

48
Jericho

Looking at Venus, I know that I could relish this night without a single drink. I could die from this joy—because out of the hundreds of people here to shower her with love, the first thing she chooses to do is search for *me*.

In the brief moment she takes to curtsey in the direction of the guests, I straighten out my tie and try to banish the dream that haunted my rest earlier in the day from my memory, knowing Venus could easily pick up on it the closer she gets to me. *Think, Jericho. Think of something else. Anything else—*

"I see you've chosen to forgo your colors this evening, Your Majesty," Venus says to me. I must have retreated into my mind for too long. *Can she see it on my face?* I guess not, given she waits for my reply, her mouth curved in a wicked grin.

"Don't get used to it," I say flatly, knowing I cannot resist a battle of wits.

"Shame," she replies. "You look good in violet."

"None more so than you, however."

Pink proof of flattery and nervousness blooms along her cheeks, and part of me longs for the day I get to watch them burn red for me. One step at a time, I suppose.

I witness a silent conflict take place within her shadowy eyes, quietly realizing she plans to resist my subtle advances. "Do we have an order for this evening's events?"

Yes, I think to myself. *The order is whatever you want so long as it ends with you and me away from these preening eyes and together some place where they can't hear you scream my name, scream for more—*

"Jericho?" Venus laughs gently, reaching for me without knowing exactly where to touch me. "Are you quite alright?"

"Yes," I clear my throat, shaking out the cobwebs in my mind. "Just unable to relax, that's all."

"I can see why," she says, drinking in the tinted room. "I must say, though, you throw quite the party. It almost makes up for the fact that you're such a pain in the neck to be around."

The orchestra resumes, right in time to snuff out the sound of my feigned offense. Still, the look on my face seems to draw laughter from her. The tiny violets knitted along the shoulder of her dress fabric rustle with the movement, and our mutual attention to that small detail brings us both back to the present. "Can I get you anything?" I ask. "Wine? Plate of food?"

She doesn't need to think longer than three seconds. "A slice of cake."

Of course. "We're actually set to cut it in about an hour or so."

"Cut it now," Venus insists, her eyes enlarging as she looks at the spectacular, triple-tiered masterpiece the pastry chefs whipped up over the last few days. Chocolate base, almond-vanilla center, and strawberry top. When I don't respond with anything other than a pointed look, she merely rolls her eyes at me. "You're going to make me say it, aren't you?"

"Of course, I am."

Venus's stare barrels through my own as she kindly whispers, "Please."

To which I fold and answer with a sigh, "What kind would you prefer?"

"Whatever your favorite is," she answers to my surprise, knowing damn well that Venus prefers chocolate—had never touched the other flavors.

Wondering if this is another one of her games, I stride past the stairs and beeline straight for the cake. Every time I turn around to see if she'll wander off and leave me stranded with a slice of cake, she daintily waves at me from the same spot I left her at, the gesture saying, still here. At last, I turn my back, grab two small dessert plates, and raise my selected knife towards the top layer. Gently cutting two pieces of the pink layer for us and miraculously avoiding dropping them on the white-clothed table, I apportion them to their dishes and top them off with tiny forks before returning to her. I watch as Venus studies her own slice, then the look on my face. "You've never seen a strawberry cake before?" I ask, handing her the bigger piece.

"Of course, I have," she gripes, good-humoredly narrowing her brows at my assumption. "I just wouldn't expect strawberry to be your favorite, that's all."

"What did you expect?"

Venus smiles shrewdly at that. "For you to tell me that eating sweets is beneath you. Which would check out, given you're not the sweetest man I've come to know."

"But you like me that way," I return a little too loudly, then hastily proceed to start eating.

Whether she heard me or not, her face remains a blank slate. Venus takes a seat on the third step, settling her dessert plate in her lap before poking at it with her silverware. Her eyes flare with delight at her first bite, and as she begins to shovel more of it in her mouth, I test my luck and sit down next to her. "Have you had any new discoveries," I dare to ask her, "in regard to your gifts?"

She stops mid-bite at the question. "Not entirely," Venus answers. "I'm more so trying to master the things I know I can do already, mainly the nonverbal communication I tested out on you when we sent Chumley off to the marshes."

I nod at the memory. "Tell me something, then."

"Like what?" she says with the beginnings of her infamous, seductive smile.

I take advantage of my opportunity and return to her, "Tell me why you ran from me in the cathedral. Tell me what happened in that head of yours that scared you away from what was about to happen."

Venus blanches for a moment, but only up until she chooses to fight the urge to run from the discussion and mull over her thoughts. She stares aimlessly at her cake, though not unable to take one more bite before settling upon a response. Without meeting my eyes, her gifts answer in turn, *I don't know.*

"You little liar."

It has nothing to do with you, Venus amends.

"Stop lying to me, because it absolutely does," I sneer, glancing around to make sure no unwanted, lingering eyes are trying to uncover this conversation. My fists ball up at my sides and I set my plate on the steps. "Look at me, Venus," I almost growl.

Instantly she looks up, always unafraid of my intensity.

"What are you so scared of?" I want to scream.

She ponders for a moment, wondering what is too personal to share or too dangerous to voice aloud, but after a moment, she shocks me with the truth I've been waiting for her to tell me. "Loss," she murmurs painfully. "After what happened to Mother, and rehashing everything I thought I knew about Father, I just . . ."

"I understand," I tell her truthfully, a familiar agony creeping up within me. I lay my hand over her exposed thigh in attempts to ease the ache there, to ease my own discomfort. "Who can you not afford to lose?" I find myself asking next, and before I can assess how intense the question might have been, a selfish thought lingers beneath.

Please, Venus, say my name.

Saints, let her say my name.

But she stands before me utterly silent. "I can't—"

"Because nothing scares me more than losing you forever."

I didn't mean to say the words, but the freedom of

sharing them with her in this moment—no matter their repercussions—feels right. I hear the beginnings of Venus stumbling over her words to ask if she misheard me.

"I know you're afraid that putting your fears out in the universe increases your odds of enduring more pain, but damn it if I don't tell you once how terrified I am of never letting you know the truth, that I can no longer talk myself out of how I feel for you. Not for your sake or even my own. My heart cannot help but beat for you, my body cannot help but long for you, and since the very beginning, my dreams cannot help but seek you out. The habit of wanting to be in your presence, or to make you happy, has only gotten worse with time." I breathe raggedly, laughing at the sick reality of what I'm saying. "I need to know why you ran from me . . . and if you want to keep running from me for the rest of time. If you want to leave Broadcove. If this . . . if *I* am too much for you to endure."

Venus stares at me as if I've just struck her.

"Well?"

Suddenly, Venus stands to her feet, forsaking her cake on the floor. With the mere turn of her head, she extends a hand towards the orchestra and summons a song out of their instruments. With how promptly the music begins, I can only assume her gifts have something to do with their urgency. Then, Venus angles her icy stare towards me again. "Convince me to tell you everything."

And she holds out her hand, silently asking me to dance with her.

49
Venus

I always wanted to be a dancer, though only in secret. Vocal talent, like Calliope's, is often obtained naturally and then further enhanced by skill and time commitment. Dancing, however, always felt like an even playing field art form. Everyone needs practice. Everyone needs to understand rhythm. Everyone has to master technique and form and then embellish those skills with their own personal style. But my strength has never been more exerted than in this moment, as I try to remain calm as Jericho instantly takes my offered hand and escorts me onto the dance floor—as the eyes of a hundred hawks careen towards us.

Alas, a sound unlike anything I've ever experienced begins from the gathered herd of musicians. The rhythm of this song is a waltz, but one that holds a bizarre, contorted sound. Almost distorted compared to the classical tuning of the string instruments. And yet, it provokes an emotion of great delight deep from within my chest, quickening my pace as we find the ballroom's center.

When Jericho bends at the waist to begin our dance, a neutral slate over his viciously handsome face, I realize that he has never bowed to me—to anyone. He's never had to.

I dip lower to the ground, matching his level. "If you step on my toes, I'm not telling you shit."

Jericho coughs out a laugh at that, but nods, nonetheless. He decides to play it safe for starters, sliding his free arm securely along my back and swaying us to the odd, electric tone of the pianoforte as it plinks out dynamic chords and the strings introduce a captivating interlude that helps drive more of the guests onto the dancefloor. I try not to let it show on my face how badly I wish to remain in his hold forever. "I bet you dread dancing far worse than you dread parties."

"I dread your present diversions," Jericho says all too seriously, starting us on our first rotation about the room. Our feet pitter-patter across the floor as hints of percussion mark time for us. Calliope's wistful voice lilts through the cavernous space, and the purple lights within the cloud-like fixtures overhead glimmer with hopeful anticipation. When my vision makes out Geneva smiling towards me, a closer examination traces her focus not on me, but rather on Jericho.

"My sisters . . ." I feel brave enough to mention aloud. "They suddenly seem particularly fond of you."

"Had to share my time with *someone* when you stopped spending your days with me," he criticizes, though with a scheming smile on his lips.

"Which reminds me, I wanted to tell you that I love my earrings."

Jericho smirks, realization heating our shared embrace. "Must you be so damned observant?"

Suddenly, I'm thrown outward, one hand still clinging to Jericho's, spiraling away from him with my eyes shut. Praying to the Saints I don't fall on my ass or trip over my own feet, I hear the hushed voices of stunned attendees marveling at our movements. The feel of the air on the back of my neck as I spin back into him soothes me, and I open my eyes in time to see the most radiant smile I've ever seen on Jericho's face.

I could splinter apart just looking at him—seeing him in that deep purple shirt beneath his onyx suit, smiling at me like I may very well be the center of his universe.

We continue on, following the pattern of the other couples without really needing to look at them. Glued in on one another, we weave our arms in complex patterns and I let him lead me across the floor. I envision our steps drawing an intricate shape across the room, a flower, perhaps. The fabricated clouds don't appear to bring incoming storms, but they do fill me with enough courage to whisper, "Show me what I'm trying to resist, Jericho."

His smile turns wicked, and I feel the atmosphere shift entirely before his hands rake down the sides of my body and perch along my hips before hoisting me in the air. The swelling crowd swoons at the sight, cooing as Jericho sets me on his shoulder. My arms rise to fifth position, I point my toes within my translucent heels, and I raise my chin with poise as people below me applaud at our spectacle.

Nothing could prepare me for this moment, for the insurmountable bliss of being held within Jericho's hands and showered with praise. I feel like I've ascended to the Beyond. Like Merrie Morgan will appear from the haze engulfing me and inform me I died moments ago from a lethal dose of delight.

Just then, I feel myself being pulled back down to earth from the heavens, my backside dragging along his front. I nearly shiver at the feel of him, at the satisfied rumbling in his chest as Jericho feels me, too. In a single swoop, one of his arms wraps around my back, whisking me off my feet entirely, and we spiral through the room once more. Jericho carries me through our previous dance pattern, the wind coursing over my shoes, and the skirt of my dress billows in our wake. Jericho bristles as the brim of the lilac fabric grazes his ankles, like the touch provokes him somehow. He sets me down, and while I presume we've reached the end, he gives me one last yank, spinning me inward, and catches me right on his desired cue. With a slow, suspended strength, Jericho dips me towards the floor as the music diminishes. Just before the throng of onlookers erupt with applause, I hear him intently whisper to me, "Let your head fall back."

My eyes fall shut and I obey my king.

I catch fire the moment his mouth presses a single kiss along the column of my throat—and when Jericho feels the shift in me at the touch, it triggers a landslide of pent-up desire. His kiss turns harsh, desperate. His teeth close around my earlobe, and his hot breath on my neck covers the skin there in goosebumps. Jericho's hands tense up around my back, one of them drifting lower, and a needy whimper escapes my body.

"We should go," he murmurs huskily against my collarbone, my body still lowered and at the mercy of his whim. I hear him swallow. "I need you. Right now."

Is this real? Am I about to say yes to him? Are we—

But the moment I open my eyes, reality comes crashing in and I realize I've lost him.

Because standing among the admiring crowd, conveniently positioned between Delta and Ardian, is Octavian. He bears the hideous smile of a snake, and as I use my connection to read his mind, I am disgusted by the thoughts I uncover.

She's done it. Venus has actually done it. He is hers entirely, and by the looks of it, she's convinced herself that this illusion of love is real, too. Now let's see if she's ready to get her hands dirty.

Something vile settles within me, sickening and cruel, and almost instantly, Jericho can sense that something is wrong. He sets me on my feet again before the guests finish their reverie. "Did I do something wrong?" he asks frantically. "Was it something I said?"

"I'm sorry," I merely say, knowing that I'm about to head down an irreversible road of self-destruction.

But Jericho still doesn't understand. "For what?"

If you have any care in the world for Jericho at all, you'll get him as far away from you as possible.

"For convincing you that I can be trusted," I finally tell him, my words coated in venom.

Jericho stops moving just as the crowd begins to still. "What did you just say?"

"You have ears and a brain—use them. Or you know

what? Let me just spell it out for you. You're violent, you're selfish, and you're the reason that my sisters and I almost died. All the things that are wrong with me, you brought them about, Jericho. No position in your Council or cushy suite here in Broadcove Castle can erase that fact. And certainly, no party can convince me to love you on top off all your treachery."

The lies fly out of my mouth before I can lock them back in—before my brain realizes how vicious they truly are in front of such a massive audience. But it's all I know to do—all I can do to evade the fate Octavian forces me towards the longer I keep up this charade, even if the act has become real.

Jericho looks at me with the most appalling expression—not one of rage and offense, but one of overwhelming hurt. "I thought . . . but everything that happened back in Zayanya—"

"Is dead to me," I stammer.

The many different looks on the faces of those gathered in the room will likely haunt me for years, but the unraveling feeling I can sense deep within Octavian is the only thing that drives me forward. "What was the point of it all, Jericho? You finding me in the marshes, you bringing me here? You knew that this would never work," I say, speaking through my internal anguish. "So, why don't you just go on and do to me what you did to my father when you dreamt of him."

Jericho's eyes glimmer with tears.

"Why don't you just kill me already?" I seethe.

Jericho's sadness transforms into the portrait of fury, the depiction of a madman who could easily seize the opportunity to gut me right here in front of everyone. "Don't be a fool, Venus." He grins before reaching into his suit coat and holding cold, sharpened steel against my exposed throat.

The crowd runs for any escape route they can find, and the only people left gawking at the scene before us are Delta and Ardian along with my sisters. The color has leached out of Calliope's skin, and Geneva grips onto her for dear life. Meanwhile, Octavian lurks behind a pillar, waiting for what's next.

Good, I murmur into his mind, even as my eyes bulge with terror.

What . . . what are you doing to me? Jericho's mind reaches out to me.

My response is cold and unrelenting, *You'll do as I say.*

I shut my eyes, simulating the act accepting my bitter defeat. "Delta," I gasp out, not turning my head all the way to her in an effort to keep from slitting my own throat. "Get my sisters out of here and . . . somewhere safe. Now."

They try to resist, begging Jericho for mercy on my life as Delta, rather roughly, hooks her arms through Calliope's and Geneva's. Her feat of strength is no simple task, and as impressive as her resilience against their efforts to remain with me is, I refuse to look their way. Ardian's sudden babbling helps distract from the sounds of their screaming. "Jericho! Stop this at once! You're better than this!"

Tell them that you're not better than this, I instruct him. *Tell them how much of a monster you are.*

So Jericho does. Through gritted teeth and a heart I

know to be shattered, he says, "You're wrong about me, Ardian." He presses the blade closer to my throat. "You think that I've changed, that Venus has been the one to inspire it. And maybe she did, for a short time—but she's made her choice, now. She doesn't want me. And if that's the case, I don't want to be a changed person. I don't want to be good. I only want to make the world bleed on her behalf."

And as his haunting words loom over us, my connection reads deep into the shift in the atmosphere and discovers the worst—Jericho believes my words are an exercise of control over him, not a plan to save him. He thinks that this moment is my last, glorious act of revenge. That I've rejected him in front of his own kingdom and solidified his reputation as nothing more than a murderer with a hot temper and violent dreams. That rather than understanding his pain, I chose to capitalize on it.

"I forced her into one dream of mine," he finishes. "I won't force her into another."

Octavian hasn't moved from his hiding spot, and I catch him licking his lips in thrilled anticipation as he peaks his way into the action.

Ardian tries to steady his breath, but his shaky hands betray him. "You . . . you wouldn't kill your Right Hand!

Octavian fully steps into view, now, mouth agape. "Venus is your *Right Hand*?"

But Ardian is not finished begging for mercy. "This isn't you, Jericho! You wouldn't kill the love of your life! Don't do this!"

The love of your life.

Without letting it show, I mourn the life I could've

had with Jericho. One filled with endless laughter and annoyance, petty fights and makeup sex. I put my dreams of getting to watch Genny raise her child together in the grave, knowing I'll soon follow, and I silently send up a prayer to Merrie. One of forgiveness.

Jericho looks at me as though he could hear my thoughts.

"My King," Octavian murmurs gently, stepping towards us with his hands outstretched. "You are not thinking clearly. The girl, she is an asset to you—"

"No," I tell him aloud, drawing Jericho's sharp gaze back to mine. "Kill me. I deserve death."

Though he hasn't been one to question my words as of late, a battle of wills takes place behind his searing blue eyes as Octavian and Ardian both try and rationalize with Jericho, but it appears that his fury has surpassed their efforts to reason with him. Jericho's grip tightens on the blade at my throat, and as I go to swallow, I feel its sharpness cut the surface of my skin. Squeezing my eyes shut, he tells me in a harsh, hushed tone, "And why's that?"

"Because all the good I see in you has surpassed my hatred. And it sickens me."

Wrath overcomes him and Jericho slashes the knife.

Only not across my throat.

No, Jericho pulls it away from me, gearing it behind his ear before launching it with all his strength. I hear the steel whistle through the air, never veering from its lethal path.

The squish of its impact on Octavian's vital organs nearly sends me to my knees. The light leaves his eyes instantly, but just before he completely folds in on himself, the golden glimmer of Jericho's knife catches my attention, specifically the ruby jewel encrusted in its center.

It's the dagger I intended to kill Jericho with.

50
Venus

"Take your niece, Venus's sisters, and the rest of the staff to the tunnels until I return for you," Jericho bellows towards his Head Council. "Half of the Holymen have turned against us and have fatal intentions for Venus and me, and I do not want anyone caught in the crossfire if they are nearby. Do not use the Dial Line to alert the Seagraves. *Go.*"

Ardian dashes out of the room without another word, faster than I've ever seen another human move. Heartbeats later, chimes and other alarms begin to ring, forcefully ushering out any lingering attendees and alerting the staff where to head for. Meanwhile, Jericho grabs hold of my wrist and tugs me along in a different direction.

So if everyone is rushing towards shelter . . . where are *we* going?

Jericho's wry smile returns, and he slides an arm around my back and cups his hand around my waistline.

My body swelters within his hold as he casually leads me down hallways I've never wandered through.

Wicked joy radiates from his entire being as he tells me, "Time to fess up. How long have you been planning to murder me?"

Oh fuck.

Considering where lying landed me before this moment, I figure honesty may be the proper response after all—but that doesn't make it any easier to confess. My mouth flattens. "Since the moment you came for me in the marshes. Since you killed Kurt and left Genny to mother a child without the man she loved, and when your arrogance outshined any of the merits I see in you now."

Jericho's eyes narrow at the same time his smile turns crooked. "What made you change your mind?"

I shut my eyes, unable to look at him as I finally admit, "A lot of things, really. Killing Parson was a turning point, though, not to mention realizing what you did to Father was . . . justified. But if I had to nail down a precise moment, I'd say it was that day in Zayanya, after you discovered who gave me the connection I have over people. And then, when we almost—" I try and force myself to remain in reality with him rather than drift back into the heated moment, but Jericho draws nearer, his gaze crazed and foreboding. "How did you find out, anyway?"

He merely cocks a brow at me. "That you were planning to kill me? I had a vision this afternoon. You told me I was a monster, but it was Octavian's voice coming out of your body."

Tell them that you're not better than this, I had ordered

back in the ballroom. *Tell them how much of a monster you are.* I feel sick at the thought.

"I knew then that you were being puppeteered somehow," Jericho continues, providing a small semblance of reassurance. "So, I had the other Holymen arrested this afternoon and brought in for questioning. The first one broke under my interrogation like a twig. Pathetic. Confessed everything. All eight of them believed you were the solution to the problems they believed I created," he tells me quietly. "Half of them, however, believed the proper solution would be to have you put the last surviving member of the Morgan Dynasty in his grave."

Spite and disdain coat his words, to the point where I can hardly stand to think about it much longer. "The traitors?"

"Dead," he answers with a disturbed smile.

"The innocents among them?"

"Personally escorted back to their homes and compensated for their time and service."

"Then . . . if there is no danger present . . ." I remember, my brows scrunching up in confusion as we halt before an unfamiliar door. "Why is everyone taking shelter in the tunnels?"

That devious little smile I've grown to adore reappears as he turns the knob, and Jericho leans in, whispering, "Because I want to be undisturbed while I finally get to have my way with you."

I put the pieces together all too soon, but before I make the first move, Jericho sneaks into the room and yanks me inside, deftly shutting the door behind us. The soothing scent in the air instantly tells me that this space belongs to him.

Shrouded in darkness save for the scattered, colorful blurs of glassy light, I feel as though I've been pulled into a mystical cave. Instantly, Jericho corners me, my back gently resting against the other side of the door. "I think there's still one last thing you want to tell me, Venom."

"I don't know what you're talking about," I taunt, knowing damn well what he wants to hear. Unfortunately, I'm too enamored to bother telling him he's full of himself, and as I fall into him, he meets me halfway.

This kiss. I'm unable to form the words for it in my head. All I know is, no one has ever kissed me like this. I've always known Jericho to take what he wants and do as he wishes, but with me, in this moment, he is so unbearably delicate. Jericho seems scared to unleash himself on me in fear that I'll shatter. It's . . . beautiful. Romantic. Reverent. "You're so gentle."

"Don't tell anyone," he murmurs sweetly.

I laugh against his lips at that, and Jericho finally allows his hands to roam elsewhere. The first touch along the bodice of my dress makes my knees go weak, and I lean against the door fully. "You really won't say it first?" he asks in a rasp.

Not a chance, I sneer into his mind, even as my mouth curves into a smile.

Jericho doesn't seem too hurt by my response. In fact, his smirk only deepens. A short laugh escapes him, and then, his eyes drift towards his desk.

I track his gaze to the source. It's then, however, that I notice a peculiar accessory along the back corner, nearly covered by stacks of paperwork and old books. A pot, and within it . . .

Venus fly traps.

I look back at Jericho, my heart melting within my chest and my eyes burning.

"My visions never foresaw kind things for me. Only torture. So when you came into my life, my dreams, I *knew* that you were trouble, and yet...I felt that tug. That supernatural sense of *trust* in you."

"Jericho—"

"I love you," he rasps, unbridled joy and the absence of all fear radiating in his bright eyes. "With no ulterior motives," he answers, the words guttural and real. "None of my dreams felt as holy and divine as spending my days by your side."

There's nothing more he needs to say—not for my sake or his. Instead, we touch and kiss and converge. His only words are the murmurings of my beauty, how he cannot fully fathom it, both now and all this time.

And only once my soul and body is bared before him do I say with my whole heart. "It's you and me against everyone, my love."

51
Jericho

In all my life, I never experienced intimacy that raw and uninhibited. My sexual history has never been a subject I cared to discuss with anyone—and considering how I reacted just being in the same ramshackle town as her pathetic playmate Drue, I would never dare to inquire on Venus's perspective of the matter. But she may as well have wiped the other women off the map. A gross, sentimental part of me almost wishes that there were never any others, that it had always and only ever been Venus, but all that really matters now is that we've found each other through the smoke and mirrors of our own malice, and that I'll be in my deep grave before I come to know a life without her again.

Venus fights for control over her sinking eyelids and sore muscles, and I choose to offer her mercy, just this once. She certainly deserves a break, given she spent the entire night *making up for lost time*, as she worded it. I'd watched her do things to me that no sane woman had ever even contemplated, all with the most shit-eating grin on her face. The mental image makes my hair stand on end and draws a smile along my lips. "I'll get everyone out of the tunnels," I tell her softly after putting on last night's clothes and heading for the hall. "I'll let you rest."

"I'm not . . . even tired."

I mean to argue with her about how her knees had buckled as I bent her over my desk, or that there was no way that we'd show face when it was clear she'd need me to support her standing weight—but Venus begins snoring before my hand reaches the handle of the door.

Down in the lower level of the castle, past the trick door in the kitchens, I find Ardian holding onto a sword before the massive herd of anxious tunnel-dwellers. Delta sits huddled up in terror against a rather irritated Calliope, and beyond them, scullery maids, seamstresses, cooks, event assistants, and—

Geneva.

It occurs to me, then, that the last time I saw her, Delta was dragging her and Calliope out of the ballroom against her will. Hell, Genny was reliving the same nightmare I had put her through once before—watching Venus wind up in a position that most people before her have died in. It makes me feel the need to assure her that, "She's safe."

And thank Saints that she's in the back of the group, because her wicked, all-too understanding smile would prompt intense questioning from the rest of the busybodies present.

"Dear *Saints*, Jericho," Ardian bristles, wasting no time as he hops to his feet despite his age. Apparently, the disarray of my clothes happens to make for the perfect cover, convincing everyone excluding Genny that I have fended off attackers. "Had you not come down in another hour . . . I mean, I was beginning to worry that you were—"

"Well, I'm not," I say stiffly. "The castle is clear now. You're all safe to report to your stations at noon if you haven't slept yet."

Murmured words I cannot make out fill the room with dull echoes, hopefully a few *thank you's* among them, and as everyone skirts past me with little to no eye contact, I watch as Calliope shoves Delta away from her and looks up at me with pure, molten vengeance. "Where the hell is she?"

"Like I said, she's safe."

"Then what the hell was a knife doing at her throat last night? In your hand?"

"Your sister got involved with the wrong people," I inform her, my skin beginning to heat from my short temper. "It required a convincing act to get them off her scent."

"I want to see her."

Yes, do come and see your sister sprawled out naked in my bed to know she's alive. I bet that will make you feel a million times better.

"Later," I answer, not bothering to engage with any of her babbling.

Mercifully, Geneva tells her sister that no one should see them like this, hair rumpled from uncomfortable sleep and dresses wrinkled from sitting on the rocky floors. Yes, vanity easily convinces her, but Genny's eyes catch something I hadn't noticed as she crosses past me. She briefly mouths, *"Your zipper is down."*

"Dammit," I snap, reaching for the zipper just as Delta and Ardian both turn my way. Delta's widening glance unsettles me more than I should allow it to, but she scurries off soon after.

Then Ardian approaches me cautiously. "Your Majesty, you gave us quite a scare."

"Unlearn your fear, Head Councilman. All is well, now."

But the sentiment seems to turn something in his stomach—something I know to be guilt.

"What did you do?"

To his credit, Ardian stands tall as he tells me, "I used the Dial Line."

"You *what*?"

"Sir, you had a knife to your Right Hand's throat. For all I knew, you were going to retrieve it from Octavian's body and kill Venus once I left—"

"I don't care what you thought!" I roar, pounding my fist into the counter. It also doesn't pass me by that Ardian no longer addresses me by name, only by status. I try to shut out the thought. Focus on the more pressing matter. "Who picked up the call?"

The tone in my voice makes Ardian regret his very existence.

"Who the fuck took your call?"

"Harriet did," my Head Councilman croaks, every muscle in his body tensing, bracing for the impact of my anticipated abuse. "But with her being so far along with the baby, she told me that she'd dispatch someone else to help."

My heart falls into my stomach, and I don't realize I'm holding onto Ardian by the throat until I feel him begin to choke in my grasp.

"*Who. Did. She. Send.*"

Venus is dressed and awake when I barge back into my bedroom, my blood thrumming with adrenaline and anger, and not even the sight of Venus's playful, expectant smile smooths things over.

"What could possibly have gone wrong in the one hour I spent asleep?" she says, easily picking up on the change in my temper.

"Everything," I snarl.

Venus's eyes drift inward, as if she ruined the moment, or that I lied about my portion of the feelings I confessed last night. "Saints, no, Venus," I immediately cut in. "Not about us. *Never—*"

"Then tell me about it."

A sour look crosses my face, and I'm too enraged to break the news just yet. I just want to keep staring at her beautiful, concerned face. To savor the sight of it as long as I'm allowed to before things go to complete and utter shit. "Tell me, Jericho," she prods again.

"Ardian used the Dial Line."

Her face turns cold, frozen with righteous fury, but she lets me proceed.

"After I told him not to call the Seagraves, he fucking called them anyway. He thought I was going on a damned killing spree! And it'd be bad enough if he had to leave a message for them, but no. Harriet picked up on the second ring."

Her knuckles turn white as her hands ball up into fists at her side. She knows better than to ask if Ardian called them back, because this conversation wouldn't have occurred if they decided to stand down. "Give it to me straight."

So I do. "Ardian believes that they boarded a ship this morning."

I feel the air constrict around me, and I no longer hear Venus's breathing. "Who boarded a ship this morning, Jericho?"

I barely find the will to say their names. "Slater and Diana."

Venus realizes the magnitude of our impending ruination before I do and sits on the edge of my bed in a manner that looks like her legs gave way in defeat. "Oh, *fuck*."

My heart pounds loud enough for the both of us to hear.

"Ardian doesn't know," she exhales, her voice lighter than a whisper. Devastating and brittle. "He doesn't know about the assassins. That ten are appointed to each heir, meaning there's..."

Bloody Saints.

Twenty of them.

I fight the urge to be sick with dread. "We have guards."

"They'll pick them off," Venus argues, completely faithless in our staff.

"Our men are stronger than you think—"

"It's not about what I think, it's about what I know. And what I know is that Slater and Diana aren't coming to play allies. They're coming to kill you." Her eyes swell with a sadness I never wish to see overtake her again—and though she doesn't say the word aloud, her mind shouts it, over and over. A cacophony of despair.

No, no, no, no, no, no, no, no, no, no, no.

That horrible, vacant expression overwhelms her, and with how still she perches herself on the bed, I almost fear that I'm looking at her corpse. It is only then that I remember what she had shared with me in confidence, her one, singular fear—loss. And here we are, our lives transpiring in the path of her worst, remaining nightmare: that right when she allows herself to love, I will be snatched away from her.

But then, I sense her devastation begin to dwindle, replaced by the familiar fire that courses through her veins. Determination. The kind that contorts her face into the portrait of pure, impenetrable hatred.

"I won't let them take you from me," she resolves.

And though I do not normally question Venus's judgment, the pressing matter of life or death makes it hard to see the depth of her resolve. "How?"

Venus looks at me like she's just hatched a plan from our mutual hell. "By letting you go." My feet rush towards her, reaching for her with the motives of changing her mind. But Venus shakes her head in dreaded comprehension. "Yes, that's it. Because if the assassins are apportioned to each heir, as long as *I* don't endanger them, they won't kill me. But I heard what Victor had propositioned you with at the docks, and if

Slater's coming with the knowledge that you interfered with his wants . . . you can't be here. If he's leading the charge, I can be a worthwhile distraction and—"

"No," I intervene.

Her eyes narrow and her arms cross tightly over her chest. "What do you mean *no?*"

"I mean *no*. I will not have you subject yourself to his whims just to keep me alive."

She pauses at that, as if I just threw a wrench into all her scheming, and the gesture only makes me feel more disturbed.

"You cannot be serious. Venus, please tell me you are not actually considering being with him as a bargaining tool after you and I just—"

"You think I *want* to be with him?" she stammers. "You think I want to cast you out of the castle right when we've started to figure things out. No, I do not. But I have no choice. My Blessing can draw him in, so if this is going to work—if you're going to survive this—I cannot push him away"—she swallows hard—"under any circumstances."

The thought of her with him, of her forcing a smile for him while she's dying inside, makes me go feral. Worse, the idea of living with the mental image far away from her reach . . .

Then, as she strides towards the door, I catch her wrist within my hands. She looks at me with true pain welled within her beautiful eyes. "Don't make this any harder for me than it already is," she pleads.

"I don't mean to." And foregoing any self-control, I press myself up against her, slowly backing her into the corner of my room. Venus only briefly fights my advances before acknowledging what we both wish to savor before this impending separation. She slowly exposes her neck to me, and I stoop lower to kiss the spot I learned she loves the most. A soft sound escapes her lips. "I know better than to change your mind. But let me show you what you're missing."

After we both were spent, I longed for her to sink into the mattress with me, to breathe in our shared air until she drifted off into sleep and forget all about the idea of sending me away. In the end, she only stayed for an hour, and I do not care to relive the emotional desolation of those final moments together.

Venus departed ten minutes ago with a strict agenda, and as I lace up my shoes, she returns with Tolcher in tow, of all people.

"You've got to be shitting me."

"Unfortunately, not," Tolcher says uncomfortably, still managing a wise-cracking smile.

"I don't need a babysitter," I insist, baring my teeth at him. "If anything, I need you to make sure that Slater and Diana—"

"It's already been decided," Venus cuts in, her words stiff. Reluctant but firm. "I'm not sending you out into the open alone, and the only person I know how to trust anywhere near as much as I trust you is him. Let's go."

Cold as ice, she turns from the doorway and hauls her feet forward, and before Tolcher makes a move to drag me out by the collar of my shirt, I follow after her. As we cut through the halls, my soul finds a tinge of warmth at the fact that Venus no longer struggles navigating her way through Broadcove. She leads us along, refusing to turn around, and the slight view of her face as we turn a corner reveals that she's fighting the urge to sob.

I want to tear Ardian limb from limb for it.

Suddenly, sunlight streams from the massive windows that border the foyer, and as Venus pitter-patters down the grand steps, I get the sinking feeling that things will never be as they are right now. That even if I live to crawl my way back to Broadcove—back to her—the fruition of Venus's fears will haunt the rest of her days, and I will not have the means to ever apologize for it. Treasonously, my feet keep moving even as my head spins and my mind recognizes how wrong and unfair and brutal this is. There are ways out of this. I know there are. Hell, I could hide here. I could face Slater and his pack of confederates and die with dignity rather than cower into a carriage and watch Venus disappear over the hills.

But when we cross the threshold onto the front drive and Venus looks back at me with a fixed resilience, I know that putting my trust in her—in whatever crackpot plans she's cooking up in that pretty little head of hers—is the safest bet.

If anyone can save us, it's her.

Venus' eyes instruct Tolcher to board the carriage, and with a surge of sudden conviction, he wraps his arms around her and tightens his grip for a beat. She whispers something in his ear that I don't quite catch, to which he responds, "Whatever it takes." Then, he bows his head in response—a gesture that does not go unnoticed by me. He does not smile, but even knowing their private friendship, I would've considered beating him to a pulp if he did.

When he's out of earshot, Venus stares daggers at me. "While I went to find Tolcher, you didn't speak to anyone, did you? Not even Ardian?"

"No."

"Or my sisters?"

Guilt floods me thinking about Genny and the baby—that things may not progress fast enough for me to be there with Venus when she gives birth. "No," I say.

"Good," Venus reasons, more with herself than with me.

"Where are we going?"

"I'm taking care of those arrangements," Tolcher cuts in pleasantly.

Since he seems to be answering for Venus now, I turn my head towards Tolcher. Irritation eats away any decorum and respect I could shape my face to hold. "Then how is Venus supposed to stay in contact with us?"

"She won't be," Tolcher answers plainly.

My head snaps back to Venus, who avoids direct eye contact. "And why not?"

"I will not risk compromising your location," she defends diplomatically. "If my efforts fail, I do not want them to torture any information out of me."

"*Torture* you?" I bellow, heat filling my entire body. I'm overcome with the urge to make someone hurt, to make them writhe at the mercy of my will. But Venus knows what she must risk. Just from the look on her face—the brutal proof of painful acceptance for what lies in store—she stands ready to face any hell Slater or

Diana or their wretched assassins could give her. Tough as nails. So beautifully brave. I use whatever willpower I have left to let my gaze soften upon her own. "Promise me one thing."

And before Venus can resist me drawing near to her, my hands pull her towards me, my mouth aligning with the level of her ear.

"When I come back—and I will come back, even if I have to crawl across the continent to get to you—promise me that we'll pick up right where we left off."

Venus presses her hand against my chest, and the pounding there seems to slow right as the trembling in her fingers starts to still. It hurts how much I already miss the way we quell the chaos within each other. "Remember what I told you last night?"

It's me and you against everyone, my love.

"Of course, I do."

"Good. Remind yourself of that when you're out there. And take some deep breaths. What's happening right now is merely . . . precautionary."

But we both know the kind of danger we're equally up against, and I hear it in her voice; the words are becoming painful. Her sentences shorten. Her gaze breaks mid-phrase. A glaze falls over her eyes.

I'm out of time, and I choose to spend this moment kissing Venus like I'll never get the chance.

It's hungry and sloppy and passionate and wild. The kind of kiss that makes your hair stand on end and draws the sweat from your pores. I try not to fold into her as her fingers rake through my scalp, stirring up foul, delicious thoughts of what we'll be doing if we live to see one another again. It's my last semblance of control—to kiss her like I'm pouring my very soul into her own. One last act of being in charge before I'm carted away from the one person I would give my life up to protect.

Tolcher clears his throat, and it makes me want to punch the bastard in the face.

Still, I force one foot onto the carriage step, and the moment my body suspends upwards, I pivot, facing Venus fully. Hands braced on either side of the doorframe, I fight off the urge to cradle her in my arms again and never let go. "How do you expect me to leave you in the hands of twenty assassins and three vicious heirs?"

Tears stream down her cheeks, and she takes an unsteady step towards me. "Like this."

She whistles sharply to the coachman, two fingers poised between her lips, and just as Tolcher manages to pull me fully inside the carriage, Venus slams the door in my face.

52
Venus

Racked with emotion, I retreat to Jericho's room, lock the door, crawl back into the sheets we tangled up together, and weep in the cover of darkness. I do not know how long I stay there, how long my tears stain the pillowcases that capture his scent before I drag myself into the bathroom and become physically sick over it.

Yes, I fear loss, and Jericho could certainly read the proof of it in my body language as I escorted him out. But the moment his carriage disappeared from view, a new, more sickening fear began to manifest.

On top of being betrayed by the man meant to provide wise counsel to Jericho, on top of sending away my two fiercest protectors for the sake of their survival, I have to face Slater again.

Knowing now what Victor had done to Greer, I can only imagine Slater's capabilities for violence. Raised up by a man who beat his own children, Slater probably sees abuse as a means of controlling those in opposition of him. But now, hollowed out on the floor of Jericho's bathroom, I wonder which fate is worse—being Slater's enemy or being Slater's plaything.

You brought this upon yourself, my own voice scolds me. *You fucked Slater Seagrave to get a rise out of Jericho, and now, Slater believes that he has earned the ownership of you. You deserve what's coming.*

It takes people seven hours to realize that the king has gone missing, and the first person bold enough to ask me if I've seen Jericho recently is Delta.

I'm settled along the chaise in my room, reading over paperwork that Jericho had passed my way earlier this week that I hadn't gotten to yet—if only to preserve some semblance of his presence—when she searches me out and portrays her initial indifference. "So . . . been up here all by yourself?"

"Yes," I say flatly.

"All day?"

"Yes, Delta." My stomach grumbles at the end of my phrase, and I suck in air through my teeth, displeased. "Shit, I worked straight through lunch. I'm starving. What are the chefs preparing for dinner this evening?"

"Not sure." She sighs, tapping her foot repeatedly on the floor. A nervous tick. "Perhaps Jericho would know?"

I dismiss the remark without a sound, my attention reverting back to my documents. This record happens to speak on the eligibility requirements needed to take up the monarchy. My gaze lingers along the most recent phrase I left off on, which reads: *In the rare instance that a dynasty or bloodline requires immediate preservation, the cardinal member of the governing family may designate—*

"Would you happen to know where he is?" Delta finally blurts out.

"He's the last thing I want to dwell on right now," I scoff.

Her nose scrunches up at that. "That reminds me, how the *hell* did he get a hold of your dagger? I thought you always carried that thing on you!"

"The slit in my dress was rather revealing," I improvise, my tone coming out a little defensive. "I didn't want to risk him seeing it on me."

But the truth is, I hadn't been keeping the weapon on me for weeks. There was no point. In fact, I do not remember the last time I had it on my person since our stay in Mosacia. It doesn't matter, however, given that Delta buys the excuse without so much as a blink. "Yeah, good point. It's just . . ."—*here we go*—"I may or may not have wandered down his hall."

"And?" I ask stiffly.

"All the guards assigned to that corridor were gone."

My eyes widen. "Oh?"

Maybe it is the inflection of my voice, or maybe it's my overzealous demeanor at the prompt of pretending to be intrigued—either way, it shifts something in Delta. "*Saints*, how insensitive of me!" She grabs hold of my hands and invites herself onto the chaise. "I mean, shit, the last time I saw you, Jericho had a blade against your throat, and yet I'm too busy asking you if you'd know where he is I'm totally disregarding how scary last night was for you—"

The second person I've seen in the last seven hours arrives—Calliope. She instantly rolls her eyes at Delta. *Nosy bitch*, I hear her internally comment. But the urge to giggle doesn't last.

Not when Calliope alerts me that, "We have visitors. In the boardroom."

The last time I saw Slater Seagrave was the night of the Menagerie.

I remember forcing him to chew on the blueweed he had arranged in a bouquet for me, saving his life after Jericho threatened to damn his entire dynasty in the name of male jealousy. His guards escorted him to the infirmary, and while Slater had said nothing to me following that interaction, my divine connection heard his thoughts scrambling to figure out his next point of action. It wasn't until I'd heard Victor conversing with Jericho about possibly aligning us in marriage that I realized Slater had fallen in love with me.

In any normal scenario involving foreign politics, I could not have boarded *Crystal Wrath* back to Urovia on better terms.

But each additional step towards the boardroom is another step closer to death. My blessing has only brought me doom—and somehow, it's my job to try and flatter my way out of the mess Ardian created for me. To convince Slater and Diana and their pack of killers that Jericho is the true enemy, even though their presence on my doorstep implies that they are the ones who possess ill intentions.

So I find it a small mercy that the first face I see when I enter the boardroom may be my only potential ally.

Misty grey eyes pierce through mine, and her mouth, lined with rosy paint, once again remains sealed shut. In fact, I certainly would not be surprised if Greer hasn't said a word to anybody since the last time she spoke to me—since revealing the contents of Merrie's final letter. In our split-second, silent exchange, I try to peer into her mind to uncover what little context they have for coming here. Instead, I hear a warning.

You better hope Jericho is far, far away from this castle.

Despite Greer potentially coming to aid me, her presence comes with an additional ten guards—ten more than I was anticipating. Her cluster of men linger with the other two groups of guards, all of them armed with swords and sharp knives situated in holsters along their waists. Upon a thorough examination, I begin to pick out which ones I have met previously. One of the men designated to Greer's safety was the jester I spoke to before entering the Menagerie. And one of Diana's men looks to be the clown who offered me the sugary treat in the circus tent.

Diana is the only member seated as I enter the room, arms crossed over her chest, staring at me through her bangs with no ounce of the friendliness she first welcomed me with across the Damocles—assessing me. I silently thank Merrie for the blessing she instilled upon me, because at first glance, Diana's look of death certainly promises downfall. But with a closer look and enough focus, her mind shares with me her concern. Diana is looking for marks of violence. Bruises, gashes, cuts, scars—any indication that Jericho has done something violent enough to warrant their retaliation.

"Hello, Venus," a familiar voice croons to my left.

My concentration on Diana blinded me from seeing Slater advance towards me, and I turn to find him no more than five feet away from me. I jump back, startled by how towering his height is compared to my own. Slater reads it as a defensive reflex. "It's okay," he assures me, even when I know deep down, this is the beginning of a horrible, downward spiral. "It's just me. Not him."

I suppress the feeling of disgust and alarm before I force a shivered response. "W-what did they tell you about what happened? H-h-how much do you know?" I touch a hand against my throat feebly, just as Diana's studious, invasive glance shifts there.

"Ardian told Mother everything," Slater says, ticking his head to the side in indication. That's when I spot Ardian in the room, too, perched in a chair towards the window. Unmoving and quiet, eyes downcast in shame. *Good.*

"So brave," Slater murmurs, placing his fingers at the base of my chin and raising my head so I can look nowhere else but into his eyes. "And so wise, being able to see through Jericho's façade and calling him out for his atrocities, even with death on the line."

Nausea begins to work within my stomach. "I didn't want my sisters to see me die," I choke out. "I didn't know he was going to kill the other Holymen. I thought he was . . . going to kill me—"

Slater whispers my name to me over and over before jailing me within a tight embrace, one that ought to provide me comfort but instead fills me with dread. Shushing my frantic recollections of that night, he rocks me back and forth. So fatherly—I wonder what else he's learned from his own father. I try not to dwell on the image of the paperweight he hurled at me.

Just barely over his shoulder, I make out Calliope's face, contorted in displeasure, even as Delta practically swoons at her side. And then, an all-knowing smile dimly cracks towards me. Split-second and brief.

Calliope doesn't buy my distressed damsel act for a second.

Suddenly, the Dial Line rings, and Slater's shoulder muffles my genuine scream. I had not been informed what sound was programmed into the system, and I certainly hadn't been warned about how *loud* the alarm would blare. Shielding my ears from the intensity, the sound sending shivers up my spine, the shrill, repetitive chatter threatens to shake the floor. Somehow, the thirty assassins stand undeterred, while Greer and Diana grit their teeth.

Ardian storms across the room, tearing the receiver off the hook if only to rid the sound from the room. "Jericho Morgan's Head Council speaking," he says by way of greeting. Seconds that feel like several minutes pass by in suspended silence, and just as I begin to revert back to normalcy, Ardian whispers, "Congratulations to the both of you. I trust that the babe is healthy?"

Diana grins from ear to ear, clasping her hands in delight, even as Greer looks like she may pass out next to her. I brave a glance up at Slater, curious to unearth his opinion on the arrival of the newborn heiress. No surprise, his soul silently gives away the farce that his touched smile portrays.

Another girl. Let's hope this one is at least normal. When I take Father's place, I'll marry her off the first chance I get.

My belly fills with rage and my blood sings with the urge to launch myself on him, to claw his eyes out for such a nasty view on his own sisters. Ardian continues to gab about how the present Seagraves in Broadcove are wishing them health and happiness and some other bullshit people say when celebrating a new baby. Delta rushes over to hug Diana, intentionally avoiding touching Greer, even with her garments. And in the brief moment I'm afforded to look back at Calliope, I see that she's stepped closer to me, eyes wary and vigilant.

Slater feels my sister's impending presence, and gently guides me further away from her as Ardian ends the call, only drawing further suspicion and disapproval from Calliope.

"All is well in Sevensberg Palace," Ardian reports mildly. "The rest of the children will get to meet her tomorrow once the doctors deem it safe to allow visitors."

"And what about the state of affairs here," Slater asks diplomatically. "Did you care to mention anything to them since your frantic inquiry?"

Slater's harsh tone does not go unnoticed or ignored. "We're still trying to decipher them ourselves," I respond, hoping my tone comes out more soothing than I know it sounds inside my head. "I do ask that you give Ardian and I some grace as we navigate—"

"Which reminds me," Diana interrupts. "It's come to our attention, Lady Venus, that you are no longer

Councilwoman, but Jericho's Right Hand. Is that true?"

I nod my head against Slater's broad chest before peeking my head out towards her. "Yes. He bestowed the honor upon me when we departed Sevensberg," I return. "A reward for successful negotiations. For earning his trust."

Diana's eyes harden. "And yet he made an attempt on your life."

Slater's grip on me tightens, and I feel vaguely ill at the intensity of his touch. *I don't need protection. Least of all from you.*

"That's certainly what I had assumed he was doing. I thought that he was going to slit my throat in front of my sisters and wreak all kinds of havoc on the world I'd leave behind. But . . ." and to the best of my ability, I try and draw tears to the brim of my eyes. "He was just using me. All I ever was to him was *bait*."

"For what?" Ardian dares to inquire.

My connection reaches out towards him, coaxing out the incentive behind his unexpected questioning, and I detest what I find there—because beneath his curiosity, there's a deep-seated bitterness.

How could you Jericho? Right as Venus was starting to make you better, how could you go and ruin everything? How are you so good at destroying everything good.

And I resent it. I resent the jaded, limited perspective he holds for the man he's provided counsel and company to amidst the passing of his parents and their throne. In all the growth Jericho underwent, Ardian's takeaway shares the likeness of those who have always been out to get Jericho—and I will have none of it.

"To test you," I finally bring myself to answer, wrath simmering within my bones. "Jericho confided in me about believing a spy was in Broadcove spreading false intel about him. I didn't believe him, and he nearly killed me for it." I raise my voice, spit flying out of my mouth to make the lie seem credible. "But after specifically instructing you not to use the Dial Line, you called on the Seagraves anyway. You *betrayed* him."

If Ardian had felt ashamed before, the sheer dishonor that overtakes his posture multiplies tenfold.

"If Jericho had killed me, my death would've been on your hands! This fear that I live in, now, is your fault!" I shout.

Slater finally releases me, no longer able to contain my female fury. Everyone takes a step back away from me, save for Delta. "Venus," she pleads, fearing for the fate of her uncle, and rightfully so. "You know him. He's been nothing but good to you. He would never intentionally try to—"

"GUARDS!" I scream, knowing what must be done next.

Every King's Guard member within three halls of us flock into the boardroom, some of them rushing in, swords drawn. I try not to ache in regard to the absence of Tolcher among them. "Yes, Madam Right Hand," one of them salute reverently.

"Take Mr. Asticova to the penitentiary," I instruct coldly.

"*No!*" Delta chokes out. Diana must restrain Delta to keep her from groveling at my feet.

"I want an around-the-clock watch on him to ensure

that he remains contained. Do not grant him visitation. Do not grant him leave. By my authority—"

"Your authority?" Delta scoffs, frantically lashing out against Diana's steadfast hold. "Venus, you can't do this!"

"Actually, I can," I square off against her. "And I will. Your uncle nearly cost me my life, and according to the laws of this land," I say pointedly, flicking my fiery gaze towards the woman holding her leash. "If the ruling monarch is not present to govern, the duties fall upon their coronated spouse, then to their most trusted officer, and then to any children they have in biological order." A horrified expression falls over Delta's face, recalling the stack of paperwork I was reading over when she approached me earlier on. "Jericho has never taken a wife, and with my title, I outrank your uncle."

And with a surge of power and twisted elation, I announce to the room, "Therefore, I now serve as interim monarch of Urovia." I offer up a sidelong glance to the King's Guard unit. "Take him away."

Ardian doesn't meet my eyes, nor does he fight my soldiers as they forcefully remove him from the boardroom. He meets their unified pace and proceeds towards his less desirable fate, and when he is gone, three new guards enter the room, flanking my back.

"It is very noble that you have all ventured here to ensure my safety," I drawl amicably, my voice carrying a strategic poise. "I am grateful for your concern and am charmed by how deep our diplomatic relations run in times of crisis. However, let it be known, the King is nowhere to be found, and as Right Hand, it is my responsibility to take up his duties in his stead."

I align myself equidistant from each individual in the room save for my three guards, eyeing each one of them like a hawk, making sure they do not have the gall to step near me as I speak. "Slater, Diana, Greer. You are welcome guests and will be treated as such. Your . . ." and Saints, I surely press into the part of me flooded with genuine fear as I say, "security detail, however, is rather unnerving. If Jericho were here, he'd consider their presence to be a threat. Perhaps even an act of war."

And with all the strength I have, I pour my entire being into ensuring my connection pulls at Slater's heartstrings. "I don't want anything bad to happen to your family," I croak.

Slater raises a cautionary hand in my direction. "You've been under great duress these last couple of days, and even so, you're still looking out for us. We appreciate your kindness. But these men," he gestures gently, "are merely here at my request, to protect you if Jericho intends to cause you any harm."

If he comes crawling back for his crown, and he will, I feel Slater revel.

"Their presence here is unnecessary," I alter, "when I already have you to protect me."

His ego swells with pride, but I sense lust simmering beneath the surface. "I will not take my chances when it comes to your wellbeing," Slater murmurs sweetly, possessively stroking the side of my face. "Rest assured," he whispers, pressing the faintest, claiming kiss against the slope of my neck, "I'll keep you safe."

53
Venus

I spent the better part of yesterday catching my sisters up to speed. I told them everything, sparing no detail whatsoever. Though Genny knew I had my sights set on killing Jericho in the beginning, I explained how the desire faded and remorse swept in. I shared all that happened in Mosacia, everything with Slater, and the night of the Menagerie. Then, I explained what had happened the evening of my birthday—how Jericho uncovered my plans to kill him and put me in a dangerous position only to lure Octavian into the light.

I had full intentions on skipping over the sex part, but Genny apparently read it all over Jericho's face the next morning. Calliope squealed like a little girl as I eventually caved and provided a full rundown on that, too.

And finally, when we all settled down, I found the nerve to tell them the deepest, darkest parts. Father's plan to sell me out to Jericho if he got caught for his conspiracies. Greer and every haunting discovery in

Harriet's gallery back in Sevensberg. My Blessing and all that transpired in the cathedral regarding the ritual.

It was all very cathartic, truthfully. It bonded us, and after sealing our discussion with a loving embrace, I figured all would be well in the world again. But now, the following morning, Geneva watches indifferently as Calliope berates me with no refrain over breakfast.

"I cannot believe this shit, Venus." Calliope practically stomps as she paces about, fingers tearing through her hair and forsaking her omelet. "I cannot *believe* that this vindictive, handsy prince has taken up lodgings here and brought his herd of weapon-bearing mutts—"

"I had no choice. If I don't play nice or if I make it seem like I'm sheltering Jericho, they won't just kill me to get to him. They'll kill both of you."

Calliope grumbles in frustration, plucking out the pins in her hair just to have something to throw at the wall. "*Argh*! What loose screw in your head ever made you think, 'Hmm, let me charm the pants off this guy so I can rile up Jericho,' and did you ever consider the possibility of it backfiring like *this*?"

"Cali, that's not a fair thing to ask," Genny pipes in.

"I mean, *bleh*! I nearly vomited watching him touch you like that in the boardroom. And you just *let* him."

"You're making my eggs taste bad," I complain.

"Have you become so good at stringing men along with your feminine wiles that you're immune to your own stupidity?"

"*Calliope*," Genny snarls. "That's enough!"

There's a deep, unspoken history in her scolding, and the temperature of my blood rises to an unholy, hot level.

"Need I remind you that back in the marshes, my *wiles* are what kept us fed and alive."

"Well, turn them off, Venus! Find a will and a way to turn them off and send Slater and the rest of them back to their own territory. Tell Jericho to come out of his hiding place and face Slater like a man. Slater cannot call on his assassins if it will lead to war. He wouldn't be that stupid."

I'm laughing, but the sound is not joyful—it is unhinged and mocking. "You don't get it. Oh, you do not even *begin* to understand the problem here, so you need to shut your mouth and listen to what I'm about to say. You weren't there. You did not sail across the Damocles and see the size of their palace or stronghold of their wealth. I am a mere speck of dust compared to Sevensberg, and that's not even counting the vast land and multitudes of people who live beyond the gates." My teeth are chattering, and I grab Calliope by the bodice of her daygown and hiss the words through my teeth. "Urovia is outnumbered and weak. Our military forces have been depleted by poor alliances and our people fear their own leader—and Slater knows it. He plans to capitalize on our pitfalls, meaning if Jericho resurfaces, Slater will kill him." I bite down on the inside of my lip, focusing on the pain there rather than the one stirring in my heart as I picture the worst fate imaginable. "He'll butcher him, knowing damn well we're too small of a nation to go against Mosacia . . . and believing that he will claim me among war spoils."

She shakes her head, stumped on what else to assess other than, "How long do you think this will go on?"

"I DON'T KNOW, CALLIOPE!" I roar, slamming my fist onto the frame of my bed and instantly yelping at the sting. Genny prepares to rise from her chair, likely to examine my hand, but I wave her off. "I'm fine," I snarl. Bruising or bloody knuckles are the least of my worries, now.

Genny's eyes engulf me in pity. "Do you at least know where Jericho is?"

"No." I sigh. "I didn't want to risk compromising his location if I'm tortured."

"*Tortured?*" Calliope gulps.

"You don't know Slater like I do," I remind her. "He may be handsome and complimentary and interested in me, but beneath that pleasant exterior, his cruelty eclipses Jericho's by a landslide."

"Do they know that?" Genny asks, sitting up straighter.

"Who?"

She smiles, her mind already tinkering. "The people of Urovia."

No words come to mind, because the truth is, I do not know.

In fact, I'm not sure if any publications of the *U. Herald* discussed the Seagrave family or their massive territory. Likely not, given the bad blood between the two nations when our Urovian ancestors broke away from Mosacia. It would not surprise me if the only communication between the two territories came from Broadcove Castle and Sevensberg Palace. Hell, I knew nearly nothing of Mosacia other than its location in reference to us before Jericho brought me here.

Genny revises her question, mischievously pleased

with my silence. "Do people know there's a vile prince from a foreign nation trying to subdue Broadcove Castle and make an attempt on King Jericho's life? Do they know the Jericho that you have come to care for?"

Finally, my mind recalls the name of someone who might be able to help, someone who just so happens to have a very personal tie to these sudden circumstances. "No . . . but they certainly should."

The first thing that comes to mind as my sisters and I approach Ivanna's doorstep five miles from Broadcove Castle, my stomach gurgling in hunger, is how I'd promised Tolcher that I'd have a meal with his family when I returned from Mosacia. How I'd sworn to give my friend that simple courtesy, and now, he and Jericho are Saints-knows where and stuck there for Saints-knows how long. Betrayal keeps me from knocking on the door, so Calliope jolts the knocker on my behalf.

Geneva's soft hand loops around my forearm, drawing me near in the hopes of providing me minimal comfort. "Perks of being friends with the kitchen servants," she murmurs, "is that they turn a blind eye when I decide to slip in sleep-inducing herbs into the communal soup."

Saints bless Genny. No wonder she insisted we leave Broadcove exactly thirty minutes into Slater and his assassins' dinner.

Ivy and moss line the wooden doorframe, and as my eyes evaluate the humble porch, I note that potted assortments of blueweed and peonies help add some vibrancy to the row of desaturated brown mulch. The colors evoke a sort of solemnity within me, the duality of motherly love of male pride, and perhaps the additional reminder of Genny nearing the delivery of her baby. Two latches creak from the other side of the door before Ivanna swings it open.

"Lady Venus." Ivanna grins, her eyes politely and quickly scanning my sisters. "And you brought company."

"Ivanna, these are my sisters. Calliope"—I gesture, and Calliope stiffly nods her head in greeting—"and Geneva."

Ivanna swoons, eyes full of joy and warmth as she takes in Geneva specifically—most people's typical response when standing before all three Deragon girls. She reaches out to take Genny's hands in her own. "Oh, do come in! I've got some stew on the stove, but I can easily roast something. Are you ladies hungry?"

"Famished," Genny blurts, her free hand at the base of her belly.

Almost too caught up in the exhaustion in my sister's voice, I shake out the cobwebs, finally remembering to ask Ivanna, "Is Nadine in?"

"Just upstairs," she replies over her shoulder, leading my sisters inside her home first.

Genny happily lets Ivanna lead her to the food while Calliope takes up the protective older sister duties. As far as she is concerned, I've brought them into the den of a lunatic—but the scent of steaming vegetables hits too close to home and her feet carry her after Ivanna, despite her preconceived notions. I peel off to my immediate right and quietly ascend the stairs. Nadine hears me coming, though, and peeks her head out of the hallway overhead.

The first thing I notice about Nadine are her dimples, more pronounced than her wild, red hair and more striking than even her rounded spectacles. I easily understand how Tolcher fell in love with her, at least where appearances are concerned. Happiness is sure to delay her aging down the line. Nadine practically skips towards me as she matches me to whatever description her husband provided her of me. "Henry has told me so much about you!" she squeals, waving me into the sitting room and promptly flopping down onto the somewhat dusty couch. She coughs as specks of it rise in the air, then giggles. "Sorry. We don't get visitors much."

"That's quite alright."

"How are things at Broadcove?"

My nose scrunches. "They could be better."

"I figured as much." She sighs, and I finally find the will to settle down onto the neglected sofa cushions. "Henry hasn't shown face around here since before the Violet Ball, and my inside sources informed me that there was . . . a scene."

I try not to dwell on the sentimentality of my party being named after my mother—likely Jericho's intentions—and focus more on her mention of sources. "That's right. I forgot that you write for the *U. Herald*."

"I find that hard to believe, Lady Venus," she says sweetly, reading right through me. "I figured it would be the job of the king's Right Hand to know every writer involved with the *U. Herald's* publication process." Where I anticipate being met with negative energy and well-concealed calculation, Nadine's words are spoken with respect. Genuine assumption.

"Something like that," I concede.

"And while I know you have found favor with my mother's blooms and share a friendship with my husband, *I* am merely a stranger to you. Which means you want something that involves my position with the paper." Nadine props her bare feet up on the accessory table at the center of the seating area, strapping in for whatever long story I mean to divulge. "And I'd like to know what that is."

I shrug, choosing to put the truth bluntly. "Your husband and King Jericho are not in Broadcove anymore. The Heir Apparent of our opposing territory came to the castle with his sisters and thirty men trained to kill Jericho if they find him, so I asked Tolcher to take him somewhere safe. Somewhere they'd never think to look for him." I bite my bottom lip, remorse overcoming me. "I'm not sure when they'll be back, and worse, if they find them . . ."

Her eyes widen in shock, and I brace myself for any ugly cry that could destroy her perfect, jubilant face. Instead, Nadine leans in, pieces of her hair falling over her face as she whispers in awe, "So my husband is heading up a secret mission . . . with the *King*?"

I nod, oddly surprised by how well she's taking her husband's foreseeable absence and ever-present danger. She practically gushes. "That's incredible! I shall miss him until he comes home, of course. But my, what an honor to be the only guard entrusted with the King's life!"

I try not to let her excitement cover me in guilt for being unable to see Jericho's absence as a positive thing.

That's when she comes back down to earth, reading the discomfort in my face and slightly scolding herself for getting caught up in her own head. "Right, you were coming to me for help. My apologies, Lady Venus. You and Ardian must be under a great deal of pressure attending to the King's tasks in his stead. What can I do for you?"

What Nadine doesn't know about Ardian won't hurt her, and the last thing I need is for information on his current location to be shared with the masses. "I need you to explain the process you undergo to have your writings published in the *U. Herald.*"

Nadine smiles a little too mischievously. "There's not much to tell. The only person who had the authority to override or alter any of my stories is dead, now." Her eyes widen, filled with revelation and delight. "And with the credibility of the Holymen now debunked, it seems that the regulation of publications falls upon . . . you, Venus."

"Including its distribution locations?"

She nods.

I cross my arms over my chest, afraid I'm testing my luck. "Then here's what I need."

"Anything."

Just then, an obnoxious slurping sound floats through the air up to where we sit, followed by satisfied noises of full mouths and happy taste buds. I think I even hear Calliope swear after finishing a spoonful of what I can only assume is Ivanna's stew. I can only hope that my sister's unladylike table manners do not sabotage my request.

"Have the other *U. Herald* writers take a sanctioned leave of absence, by order of the king."

Nadine's head tilts at that. "Oh?"

"You are in charge now, and will submit every story to me for final examination."

"As honored as I am by your faith in me, Madam Right Hand," she begins formally, "I must inform you that I cannot be everywhere at once. I am a fair writer, but I merely draft my articles on information that our hired scouts provide me—"

"You won't be alone, Nadine." I smile. "You'll have my sisters, who just so happen to have a front row seat to what's occurring in Broadcove Castle. I can assure you, Calliope and Geneva—or should I say, your unnamed sources—will certainly help craft the precise stories we need to flush these Mosacian shits out of our territory."

Nadine doesn't move, as if coming to the grand realization that her husband isn't the only one carrying out a covert operation. And it makes her simmer with satisfaction.

"Your promotion in exchange for my agenda," I pronounce. "Do we have a deal?"

Nadine laughs, low and soft, leaning in as if disclosing some ghastly secret. "Saints spare us. I'm in."

54
Jericho

After living here for the last week, my only semblance of gratitude for this place rests in the fact that Tolcher wasn't torturous enough to hide us within the marshes. And I suppose Tolcher should be happy, too, because if he did station us there, I'd bludgeon him to death for it.

I know when to admit my faults—rare as they may be—but the first one was pouting in the carriage all the way here. On top of being dragged away from Venus, leaving her and Broadcove Castle in imminent danger, I visibly expressed my displeasure with how modest our traveling vessel was, not to mention the coachman in rags. Tolcher ignored me up until we crossed the final fork in the forest-lined path, at which point he told me to stop bickering and shut the hell up. I wanted to fight back, but my eye caught something out the window.

We'd just crossed beyond the Noble District, towards the heartland Venus and her sisters dwelled within her whole life. I started to consider groveling, threatening, and bribery all at once. Begging Tolcher to take us back home. Bribing the coachman to turn the carriage around. Threatening to kill both of them and run like hell. And then, I saw it—the line of wet laundry drying in the sweltering sun. Children fetching pails of water from the nearby pond to stay cool. Apples discarded on the ground, bitten all the way down to the cores with no pickings left for even a rodent to nibble on.

And I entered into a shame spiral.

From what I read among our long-standing family records, the Morgan Dynasty always ruled out the obligation to protect and sustain Broadcove. The Royal Domain existed as a spectacle, as proof of the Saints' favor when we decided to forsake Mosacia long ago. Therefore, Broadcove was meant to be honored with riches, the trading ports in Honeycomb Harbor, and housing the monarchs. Urovia's purpose was always to keep the beating heart of the territory alive . . . but at what cost?

The cost of every other citizen's well-being if they were not fortunate enough to be born to the one woman destined to carry the next governing royal in her womb? The cost of my own citizens scorning me for neglecting them? The cost of not understanding Venus's roots or her past struggles?

And yet . . . and yet these people—starved and sweating and tired from a hard day's work—all seemed to have smiles on their faces. I didn't understand it. I still don't. I'm not sure that I ever will. But it unwound something within me. It got me to stop resisting this fate and trust Venus's instincts.

If she could survive a place far more decrepit for twenty-three years, I can survive this, too—however long I have to.

"Your Majesty," Tolcher calls to me, emerging into the dark seating room. "I think it's time that you got some fresh air."

I said I'd survive here, not choose to thrive. "Pass."

Tolcher rolls his eyes. "It's a beautiful day outside, Jericho."

"Too hot."

"Ah, see, I tricked you," he grins, pointing a finger at me. "It's actually raining outside. See?" And with a near theatrical yank, he throws open the curtains and exposes the window at my side. Rain and storm clouds aside, I still find myself squinting at the surge of brightness filling the room. "You'd know that if you . . . oh, I don't know . . . *went outside.*"

"Why bother going outside in the rain?"

He sucks in a sharp, annoyed breath. "My King, you've kept yourself cooped up here since we arrived. I understand that these circumstances are not ideal, but they exist for the benefit of your survival. I think it would be in your best interest to go outside, even if only for five minutes. Clear your head."

"Piss off, Tolcher."

He scoffs. "Suit yourself, but I'm not going to get you dinner while I'm out until you do."

The humble townhouse we've filled has a kitchen, but one that Tolcher insisted we not stock in advance. With the mediocre amount of money he got to stash for the two of us in such a rushed period of time, he believed it was safer to not spend it all in one place. I've never had to ration food, or money for that matter, so this arrangement definitely stung in the beginning. But now, having Tolcher *bait* me like this—

"You know," he offers up as a means of smoothing things over, "Venus loves the rain."

"*Don't* say her name."

"She never told me directly," he continues on, "but just looking at her, I knew she was that kind of person. She had to be. Because rain would heal the dry soil, water the wilting plants, and shield her from the harsh sun when she worked herself into exhaustion."

I glance through the cottage window and sigh, unfortunately seeing Tolcher's point.

The rain gave her hope.

Saying nothing, I rise from my chair and stride past him without meeting his eye. Because I do not want to be with him. I haven't wanted to be near him to begin with. I've only ever wanted to be with Venus—and if this is as close as I am afforded, I would be a fool to resist.

Sliding the screen door to the house and letting the humid, summer air hit me almost feels like escaping a jail cell. Damn me to hell, but Tolcher was right. I feel better already. It smells like peace and restoration—a scent of reassurance against the constant rhythm of fat raindrops on the wooden deck. My senses become overwhelmed with ease, as if all the anguish in my personal world slowly melts away, making my breathing less labored. I shut my eyes, trying to hone my clairvoyance towards her, reaching and reaching. To an onlooker, I probably appear constipated or in the beginning stages of a stroke, but inside, I'm soaring through the pathway Tolcher led us through to get here, retracing my steps at the speed of sound until I'm on Broadcove's doorstep. In the foyer. Running up the stairs. Down the halls and rounding corners.

Venus leans casually against the doorframe of a room I know gives way to a guest suite, a seductive feline smile plastered across her painted lips. My insides gurgle at the foul presumption my mind instantly generates, and in devastation—unrequited desperation—I try and beseech her to keep from knocking on his door. Or perhaps I'm just praying to the Saints, who tend to have selective hearing where I'm concerned.

Please don't do this.

But she feels it. Somehow, she senses my voice down the invisible tether between our two blessings. I see it in the way the thought manifests in her eyes, how she realizes that the words are not spoken in her own voice. "Jericho?" she wonders out loud, a hand weakly going to cover her heart.

And then, Slater opens the door.

I refuse to watch him make a cuck out of me, and I urge my eyes to reopen.

Just then, a little girl, one with several similar attributes to Venus and her sisters, catches sight of me from the front porch. I mean to give her a meek smile, maybe even wave hello, but the child drops all of the items in her hands. Her lips tremble. She takes a step back, then bolts in the opposite direction.

That girl looked at me as if witnessing a monster from

her nightmares in real life.

"Tolcher," I growl, storming back into the house. "We have a situation."

My guard merely looks at me and waits, as if thinking to himself, *You dumb bastard, what did you do this time?*

"I've been recognized."

"By whom?"

"A child. Someone I likely rounded up when I first tracked down Venus."

He rolls his eyes. "Easy fix." Without another word, he saunters off into another room, and for all I know, Tolcher could be fetching a gun to kill me for not being cautious. I suppose that alternative would be a lot more desirable than what I imagine comes next, as Tolcher returns from the bathroom with a broad smile and a set of clippers.

"Are you out of your fucking *mind*?" I yell, my hands reaching for my head instinctively. "You cannot possibly be serious."

"Kids have the widest imaginations," he says in a way that makes me wonder if he has kids at home. "I mean, this young girl claims to have seen King Jericho in her small village out of formal uniform, with no guards or carriages accompanying him?" He shakes his head in playful disapproval. "I mean, *everyone* knows King Jericho has stunning, onyx waves of hair. Or does he?" he asks, raising the clippers again.

My mind clutters up with profanities and hatred, but I know better than to fight or scream or shatter furniture that doesn't belong to me. So instead, I remind myself of what proves to be at stake. Survival. My survival.

Tolcher's survival—well, I don't necessarily care all too much about that. But *Venus's* survival . . .

It's the only thing that allows me to sink submissively into one of the kitchen chairs and block out that stupid giggle in Tolcher's throat as he begins to shear off my hair.

I had been told once by someone long forgotten that hair holds memories—and while Tolcher likely considers me incredibly vain for sulking the entire time he shaves down my hair, I mourn the memories that go to die on the kitchen floor. The sleepless nights I spent rolling around alone after Delta first showed me Venus sleeping on the floor of an old office. The first time Venus raked her fingers through my scalp when we collided in the cathedral, how the feel of my hair finally unchained her. The secret optimism I felt rush inside of me as I combed it down before the Violet Ball.

I fear that we'll never get the chance to make new memories together, and that in an effort to stay hidden, I just erased all of ours.

"All done, Your Majesty," Tolcher announces before turning off the clippers and setting them on the counter.

I rise from my seat, vaguely catching a glimpse of this new me in the mirror.

A devious smile blooms across his mouth, and I dread what prompts it. "You know what, sir? You're right," Tolcher says. "If the young girl you encountered remembers your face after all this time, perhaps others will, too. Which means that your hair was a start, but it needs a finishing touch . . ." he ponders. And for all of a few moments, I consider how troublesome it may be to grow facial hair. *A beard? No. But perhaps a mustache might prove to be—*

Lightning sharp pain reverberates in my skull, sending stars across my vision.

It seems Tolcher's brilliant solution is to punch me in the face, and I don't fully process it until he deals the second blow.

55
Venus

The only saving grace that comes with playing the fool for so long is that Slater seems to pity me like one.

He has certainly started pushing his sexual advances, but they seem to dwindle every time I voice the possibility of Jericho lurking nearby, watching me. I tell Slater in every heated moment he initiates, "What if Jericho is waiting for you to make a move and strike once we've become distracted with one another. I want to be prepared when he shows his face again." And it works. Any time Slater's hands fumble with the ribbons on my day gowns, the mere mention of fearing Jericho's counterattack forces him to rest his hands idly on my waist again.

I just do not know how much longer the excuse will hold up.

A footman by the name of Eli—Tolcher's stand-in for all sakes and purposes—knocks on my open door and bids me good morning. I nod back, and he proceeds to hand me an assorted stack of papers. Unmistakably, I recognize one of them—the weathered texture and wider dimensions—as Nadine's newest *U. Herald* publication. "I trust that no other Broadcove eyes have observed this document."

"Yes, Madam Right Hand," he assures me. "Even I, myself, have not spared a glance at the papers."

"Thank you." I breathe. "That will be all, then."

Like a ghost, Eli vanishes within seconds, his steps silent and soft as he returns to his post. Chuckling to myself, I flip through the disjointed pile. Accounting records for the staff, licenses from local vendors wishing to do business in the marketplace In private satisfaction, I dare a glance at the title Nadine penned for today's distribution. The smile that meets my lips is almost menacing.

After nearly two weeks of tactically crafting the most intentional and provoking article we could—especially for recipients in areas where distribution became nonexistent—Nadine and my sisters had done it. And as much as I want to revel in it, to read it until my heart soars above the clouds, I choose to stand from the chaise and bury the article beneath the cushions. Discarding the other postage and spreadsheets, I find that there still remains one last envelope. My name is scrawled in an unrefined penmanship, and the absence of my title in any form makes color flush against my neck and collarbone.

This is a personal, *private* message.

I make quick work of the seal, tearing it apart as quietly as possible, constantly scanning the doorway or listening for footsteps. Then, when the coast feels clear, I dare a glance down, expecting to be sucked into a long-winded letter. Instead, I find a short message in Greer's handwriting.

We need to talk. Whenever you can get away. I'll come find you.

"Venus?"

"Shit!" I sputter, dropping all of the papers onto the chaise. Conveniently, Greer's note hits the cushion first, sinking to the bottom of the large pile, and I glance up to find the very person I least desired to see. But while I'm too late to fight back the shiver that runs down my spine like ants, I'm just lucky enough to have Slater view my misery in a concerned light.

"Oh, Venus," he croons, though I do notice how he hasn't begun strolling towards me yet. In fact, Slater does not even fully stand beneath the doorframe. He lingers in a way that makes it look like he's been peeking in, eavesdropping. My heartbeat quickens for all of two seconds before a voice in my head—one that I hope and pray belongs to Merrie—calms my nerves. *He knows nothing.* "How cruel it must be to not only assume Jericho's duties, but to remain on edge about his return every waking moment."

I nod my head emphatically, feeling my eyes grow bigger from within my head. "It's torture," I whine.

Still unmoving, Slater makes a sad face at me. "Poor doll. Perhaps we should help make you feel a bit more protected."

Saints, no, I think to myself, already accepting another

painful defeat. *Please don't stick one of your grisly assassins on me. I already feel suffocated enough.*

But he puts his fingers to his lips and whistles sharply, and at that wordless command, an odd, gurgled sound floats in from down the hall. Distantly familiar, and yet, I have a hard time tracing it back to its origin in my mind. Then, the noise is soon followed by footsteps click-clacking in a frantic rhythm. No, not one set. *Multiple* feet. Feet somehow adorned in material that scratches the shimmering floors—

Diana emerges first, and as she grimaces towards something on her left, a dark, coiled bracelet catches my attention on her wrist. Then, I see that the strand of it extends out beyond the doorframe. No, not a bracelet, I realize, but a leash.

As my eyes fall upon the precious tiger cub I'd met after the Menagerie, the world stills.

For the first time since Jericho escaped, my heart swells with unbreakable happiness to the point where I do not need to force tears to the brim of my eyes or purposely stumble over my words. The young cub, now slightly matured and baring its fangs in a childlike smile, coos in recognition, and I feel my knees hit the floor. "I just . . . how did you . . . Slater I—" but the words die in my throat as Diana releases her hold on the leash.

The female cub practically gallops across the room and into my awaiting embrace.

Her fur nestles softly against my skin as I wrap her into my arms, and while the animal cannot experience human emotion, it still feels as though she hugs me right back. *I needed this*, I find myself silently telling her, knowing she cannot understand me or hear my thoughts. In the liminal space of our embraced reunion, I try not to think too much about it. The absence of Jericho, his touch, his scowl, his smile, his presence.

I think I needed you more than I realize, I amend, breaking away to cup her whiskered cheek in my hand.

"See, Venus?" Slater chimes in again, and for a moment, I forgot he even remained in the room with us. "So long as you and Pax stick together, you have no reason to fear for your safety."

My brows scrunch at the name. "Pax?"

"Named after the Goddess of Peace," he says proudly. "Fitting name, don't you think, given her purpose is to alleviate fear and restore tranquility in your life?"

"I think it's . . . lovely," I lie through my teeth.

Of course, Slater had to go and name her after one of the goddesses he and his territory worship. Worse, he named her after peace—which certainly is not his motivation for his presence here. Feeling the annoyance simmering in my blood, I look into the cub's eyes once more. *When that egomaniac leaves us alone, I'll give you a new name. A better one. I promise.*

"She's five months old, according to her handler," Diana tells me, and my eyes go wide at the detail. Not-Pax looks big enough to eat a small dog. "The most passionate one amongst her kind back home. With that said, Menagerie performers did wish for me to inform you that within the next year or two, Pax will adapt an independent mindset and perhaps even reach her sexual maturity. Meaning if she is not well trained, she may become volatile—"

"Jericho's coin will surely fund the finest of keepers," I decide spontaneously, and I swallow hard before stomaching the mention of her name again. "Only the best for my darling Pax."

Not-Pax herself even scrunches her nose at her own name. Yes, that shall be the first thing attended to once we have a moment together. Diana flashes a knowing look to Slater before she tells me, "You two make a great pair."

I only hope Diana references that in the context of me and the tiger. "Well, she's beautiful," I reply tactfully. "Truly, I thank you both for remembering how much I adored her, and for thinking of me in these current state of affairs. It's just been so . . ." *Lonely, stressful, hard as hell, obnoxious having you here.* I finally land on, "Challenging."

Diana nods, appearing to understand the weight of what I'm working through—but not Slater. No, because in the high of making me gush with happiness, Slater rushes towards me, practically pushing the tiger aside to get to me, and plants the most violently affectionate kiss square on my mouth.

The crush of his lips against my own, merged with the crash of his muscular frame almost knocks the wind out of me—the kind of kiss that makes you have to monitor your breathing to make sure you don't suffocate. His hands run in a straight line from my spine down to its base, fingers inching lower, likely to grasp me. A small gasp escapes me, and while the sound comes out fearful, I know that Slater is twisted enough to believe it comes from a deep lair of longing.

"What do you say we kick Diana out of here?" Slater

whispers huskily for only me to hear, and despite my best efforts to save face, I fear I may retch.

A low, menacing sound pours into the room. It takes me a moment to glance past Slater's shoulder dipping down to meet my shorter stature to see Not-Pax grimacing and growling, her posture poised into something that promises revenge for being sidelined moments earlier.

Or, perhaps more curiously, the cub felt my anxiety and reacted in kind.

Does my connection work on animals, too?

"Eeeeeasy there," Slater tries to instruct soothingly with one hand. "Good kitty." But just as the cub begins to settle down again, he tests the waters and lets his lingering hand pat my backside. Just once, and I try and laugh teasingly through the knot in my throat—if only to keep the tiger from shredding him. "Perhaps I should let the two of you get acclimated with one another first," he suggests. "Lunch in my rooms today?"

I hate the person I've been forced to portray. Always apologizing. Whimpering. Fawning. Playing nice. Acting far more submissive and disinteresting than I know I am at my core. When I find the will to respond brightly with, "Sounds perfect!" the taste in my mouth reminds me of tangy blood, like biting down too hard on my lip and sucking on the wound. I smile at him without showing teeth, and Slater takes my expression as a finality. He begins to walk towards the door, and Diana waits for him to catch up before picking up the cub's leash once more and chucking it at me like she cannot wait to be through with it. As they file down the hall, I vaguely hear Diana grumble, "Breakfast was dreadful. How much longer do you expect us to stay here in this—" and I thank the Saints she drifts out of earshot, because if I had heard the end of that insult, I may have considered telling Not-Pax to charge after her.

"Speaking of which," I say aloud, driving my focus back to my new friend. "You need a new name, don't you, little one?"

She makes a trilling noise in response, one that sounds like the beginning of a roar that still needs a few months of development. I pat the chaise cushion, inviting her up to sit with me, and she obliges. Her fur tickles my face as she nuzzles herself against my shoulder, and I find myself baby-talking to her, cooing and grinning and scratching the back of her ear with a crooked finger.

That precious growl-purr returns, and she smacks her lips, licking over her fangs as if she couldn't be more content in life. My fingers move to massage her cheeks, delicately running across her whiskers if only to draw out that bashful, happy sound.

The fully grown tigers at the Menagerie had roared amongst the likes of lions and bears, but not her. It sounds choked off and giddy—more rah than roar. I mimic the sound, baring my teeth at the end of the word, and it hits me.

"How about . . . Roxie? You like that better than Pax?"

The bristly, wet lick up the side of my face is answer enough. Truth be told, I did like the X sound in her previous name; but naming a wild beast after a goddess of peace seemed to clash. I forsake her leash on the ground and beckon her to follow behind me as I head for the door. "Well then, Roxie, what do you say we take a tour about your new home?"

Despite wanting to avoid Slater at all costs, I attempt to turn Roxie around before she discovers the gardens and keeps me out past my intended rendezvous time with him. However, Calliope catches sight of her from beyond the grand doors, and any possibility of untangling myself from conversation goes out the window.

While my older sister practically launches herself on Roxie, Geneva appears rather cautious. Scared, even. But as she musters up the courage to draw near to her, Calliope discovers some kind of magic spot along Roxie's belly to scratch that has her rolling around and purring like a damn housecat. The rest comes easy, though nothing prepares me for the overload of preciousness when Roxie gets a true whiff of Genny and senses something special about her specifically, something she instantly grows protective over.

Feeling worn out from all the love and adoration, Roxie sprawls out on the sun-warmed footpath. Then, Geneva takes the time to provide me with a rundown on what's been going on with Nadine and the communications for the *U. Herald*. "Nadine says she's ready for another article whenever you have something up your sleeve. You have anything in mind?"

"Not yet," I admit, but a smile stretches over my lips as I recall the scribbled note from Greer. "I might have something by tonight."

"Good. Distribution for the first exposé should already be underway, and if I'm not mistaken, Eli should have provided you with a proof copy per Nadine's request."

"He did," I inform.

"Excellent," she continues, but instead of proceeding with the rest of her debriefing statements, she pauses to assess Calliope's curious blush. "Something funny over there?"

"Not particularly," she says, feigning neutrality.

Although Eli's post requires him to come at my beck and call, he has been particularly fond of checking in on "Genny" given Calliope is always with her. Just this once, I choose not to badger her about it—but not Genny. No, she decides to go for the jugular. "You liar. I heard you and him giggling in your suite late as hell last night."

My eyes go wide, my head snapping towards Genny for the juicy gossip. "Do you mean . . . *giggling*?"

Her blush gives away her hand. "You two are insufferable." Calliope groans.

It takes an hour or so of girl talk, sprinkled with minimal business discussions, before I successfully pry Roxie away from my sisters. Still, I find a decent enough excuse as something shifts in my peripheral vision— something like a blurred silhouette against the glass walls of North Star. Roxie trots behind my quickened pace, her claws scratching against the pavement, and it's only until I practically body-slam into the entry door that I remember Roxie may sense my distress. I spin around and crouch before her, my voice gentle. "Friend. We are meeting another friend."

But Roxie walks on past me, nose low to the ground as she creeps through the door—the same one I hadn't realized Greer had opened while my back was turned. I try not to leap out of my skin at the surge of surprise. She merely waves me in before shutting us inside of North Star. I almost worry she has descended into her previous silence, that is, until her eyes wistfully wander along the property's horizon. "The gardens are beautiful," Greer says quietly. "You did all this?"

"Back when Jericho and I were at each other's throats," I say, and just saying his name makes my heart sink into my stomach. "I'd spend every waking moment out here, avoiding him. At the time, I convinced myself I could spite his cold heart with pretty flowers and lush greenery."

"And now?" she asks.

I laugh bitterly. "Now, all that work amounts to dust. It feels like nothing, nothing compared to this. Compared to having to water what he left behind." The silence that follows tells me that Greer understands that the statement applies to more than the flowers in North Star.

Then, a warm, phantom breeze brushes along my arms. The familiar presence I always experience in this space begins to soothe me, coaxing out the truth to where I do not entirely realize what I'm confessing to Greer.

"I've always been a fixer, or at least the person that *thinks* they can fix it all. Things. Myself. Others." I shut my eyes to keep them from stinging. "People told me I could fix Jericho, and my prideful mindset allowed me to buy into that flattery. My rage soon became replaced by the selfish pursuit of how I could *change* Jericho." Overcome and feeling weaker with each word I speak aloud, I find my way over to the stone bench, just before the fountain. "But I was wrong about him. I was wrong to waste my time finding ways to rile him up, to instigate his temper to prove that his anger was all that he was composed of. All the fun I had in making Jericho detest me fills me with disgust, now. Because . . ." and it takes two long inhale-exhale patterns before I can bring myself to sincerely look towards Greer again. "Because I *miss* him. Because the games I played with your brother have come back to haunt me, and now, because of me, Jericho could lose his kingdom. He could lose his *life*."

Greer takes up a spot next to me, and her hand floats across the space between us, softly settling along my thigh. I feel her soul pause, listening. *This is not your fault,* I hear her silently insist.

I wipe my eyes and shake out the cobwebs. "What did you wish to discuss with me? Your note seemed urgent."

Greer gulps, eyes downcast as she picks a peony from the dirt. "You're in danger."

"Seems about right," I sigh, hoping to remain indifferent. "What kind of danger are we talking about, here?"

"Diana called our father on the Dial Line."

Son of a bitch, nothing good has come from that damned line.

"And told him what, exactly?"

The light in Greer's eyes darken. "That if Father has any chance of overtaking Broadcove and repossessing Urovia, he needs to strike. Soon."

I nearly snort out a laugh. "They won't find Jericho. He may as well be dead."

But that provides her no reassurance. If anything, the room becomes more suffocating. "Venus," Greer tries again, staring intently into my soul.

The gesture immediately hits home—makes me believe that my blessing is not in the unspoken connection with others, but in the revealing of dreaded secrets. Because in the voice of her conscience, Greer tells me, *They're not coming for him. They won't have to. Because when they kill you, they know Jericho will come running.*

Death has stood beside me so long in life that I've almost become numb to its presence. It nearly took me in sickness, it almost bestowed itself upon me by my father's intended designation, and it condemned me the moment Jericho put the blade against my throat. Even now, in debating who will draw their weapon, or which trained killer will smother me in my bed, I feel numb to the growing prospect of it.

But to know that my death will draw Jericho out from his safe harbor, whether to defend my honor or defend his crown . . . I cannot have that. I *will not* have that.

"How much time do I have?"

Greer shakes her head. "Unless you can find a surefire way for Slater to order the men with us here to stand down . . . maybe another day. Two at most."

Shit.

I'm doomed.

Something shifts beneath me—cutting through the tension in the atmosphere—and I realize that Roxie's eye has caught sight of something intriguing to her. Her soft tail wraps around my ankle as she moves, rising onto her hind legs to drape herself along the stony planter's ledge. Her head bobs up and down as she inspects the different flowers there, ultimately settling on one of the peonies. Her teeth snap at the stem's center, and rather than consume the peony whole, she brings it to me as a gift. I try not to laugh at the mental picture my mind presents me: of Roxie bestowing the flower to me as a gift while I'm alive rather than a token upon my grave.

My . . . grave.

Greer sees the understanding of something profound fall over my face. "What is it?"

My mind's made up in the blink of an eye. "Head to my rooms. Before you make it there, you'll be approached by a guard named Eli. Work the word violet into conversation—it's our designated code word, so he'll know you can be trusted to provide him tasks and information. From there, tell him to release Mr. Asticova from his holding cell."

Her eyes flare. "What?"

"Inform Eli to endow Ardian with the duties of Acting Monarch until further notice."

"*Venus* . . . what is going on?"

The fear in her voice is hard to look past, but I press on. "Then, I need you to find Slater. Tell him that I am meeting with a handler for Pax," I quickly adjust, "and that I likely will not return to the castle until after nightfall. Have him wait for me in my rooms, as I need to speak with him about something urgent."

Greer looks like she may become ill, silently filling in the gaps for herself. Unsure whether her assumptions are correct or not, she still manages to nod in acknowledgement. "And after that?"

The numbness returns. "Pray that you're not caught in the path of my destruction."

56
Jericho

The sun has finally set on another horrendously dull day of staring out the window, icing my swollen eye sockets courtesy of Tolcher's fists, and being agitated by everything in existence.

The kitchen chair creaks when I sit? I'm pissed off.

The overhead fan gives way and the summer heat begins to swallow the cottage whole? Livid.

The only upside to each day occurs when Tolcher and I pursue a later supper in the cover of darkness.

At this hour, most places have long closed for the day, meaning each night, Tolcher and I rotate between the three local pubs and the few food shacks the town has available. Today, we return to the ricketiest option of the lot, a patio venue called Sour Maiden—affectionately titled by the owner who slurs his speech whilst sharing his origin story I never asked to learn. "I wanted a place where I could avoid my wife and drink myself to deaf."

"You mean, to death?" I ask disinterestedly.

The owner-bartender seems tickled by the correction. "No, I mean *deaf*! I'm sick of her yapping! Y'know the feeling?"

His accent is thick, almost thicker than the one Venus carries from the marshes. The thought makes me think of her, and it takes the wind out of my sails. "No, I don't," I answer half-heartedly.

He blows a raspberry and takes a swig of the drink he served me not even five minutes ago. "Lucky bastard." He hiccups.

"*Don't* call him a bastard," Tolcher says, his tone unforgiving.

The man takes a step back—not particularly interested in a drunken fight tonight—and it gives the female server behind him a chance to set our plates of food down in front of us. She says nothing, just smiles like she's having the most miserable shift in her life. Given how appalling our meager entrees were the last time we frequented here, Tolcher opted to get us their coveted pork loin. Looking at it now, my stomach gurgles in apprehension.

"I want to know where we are, Tolcher," I say, force-feeding myself a bite of the overcooked beef with my eyes shut tight. I miss my bloodied steaks and creamy potatoes—I miss sharing said meals with Venus and her sisters. Damn, who knew I'd even come to miss *Calliope*?

"So picky and dramatic," Tolcher merely responds, snickering.

"You know, you kind of owe me, considering you got not one, but two free swings," I say, pointing at the hideous bruise. "I could technically have you executed for that."

"You wouldn't," he says calmly, shoveling down his food like it's the finest cuisine he has ever tasted. "Because if we make it out of this shithole town and back to Broadcove in one piece, I'll let you get even. Two swings." He pauses, mulling over something, and then adds. "It doesn't have to be in the face."

It's pathetic, knowing that his offer provides me a small glimmer of hope in the form of a grin. "Deal."

Tolcher shakes my hand, and then, he glances amongst our surroundings. Leaning in towards my ear, he tells me, "We're in Cheratowe."

A vague memory rushes over me. A previous vision followed by vicious complaints from my King's Guard about the road hazards they ran into in pursuit of someone I foresaw. Even Ardian had a few choice words to say about the travel conditions, so I eventually threw a sack of coins at them and told them to level out a path and rid the area of what had them bickering so relentlessly.

Sure enough, when my neck cranes towards the back left side of Sour Maiden, the only decent looking trail juts straight on until a far-out turn hooks out of view. "How far is that from Broadcove?"

Tolcher flashes me a stern look that reads a lot like *don't push it*, and I choose to fall back instead of lay in. It is too hot out and I'm too tired to press on, that is, until I hear the faint yet familiar jolting and rustling of something down road. It almost reminds me of . . . wooden wheels? The neighing of horses? *Am I going crazy, or is there—*

"NEWS FROM BROADCOVE CASTLE!" a coachman hollers just as a carriage comes into view.

My coachman.

"Holy shit, Tolcher," I gasp, grappling him by the shoulders and forcing his vision to match my own. To see what I'm seeing. "Someone is here! Do they know we are here? Are they here to take us back—"

And then, realization grabs me by the throat, choking off the rest of my question.

News.

That's when I notice the contents of the carriage's full belly: piles and piles of papers stacked against the right half of the carriage, leaving just enough room for an inside rider. The coachman continues to yell, *"NEWS FROM BROADCOVE CASTLE"* like the outcry is the only complete sentence in his vocabulary, and people begin to flock out of their homes. Even the sleazy owner of Sour Maiden seems jolted not only by the arrival of a royal carriage, but the resurfacing of many citizens, many of which were likely winding down for bed prior to this moment.

The carriage ultimately halts in the middle of the road, and the passenger kicks open the door. Out comes a woman with striking red hair and a gumption about her that radiates through the entire village. She manhandles a massive stack of folded papers as she stomps into the center of the square, barking, "Broadcove Castle needs your help. The King needs your support. Urovia needs your bravery."

My stomach lurches. "What the hell?" I find myself hiss-whispering to Tolcher. "Why is the *U. Herald* being dispatched beyond the Royal Domain?"

But Tolcher's muscles have gone slack. "Nadine?"

Despite sitting relatively far from the woman drawing everyone's attention and even as she becomes swamped with strangers' hands as they reach for a copy, she turns her head towards Tolcher at the mention of her name. Her eyes nearly surge out of their sockets. Then, they flick towards me, and she releases a held breath, as if relieved to see the both of us alive. I catch Tolcher faintly touching his wedding band to keep from running towards her and realize the depth of their connection. "Go on," I say quietly, even as the envy I have for Tolcher getting to briefly reunite with his girl begins to eat away at me. Tolcher practically springs out of his chair.

"Broadcove Castle needs your help!" Nadine repeats her proclamation, firmer this time. "The King needs your support! Urovia needs your bravery!" All the while, she chucks papers to anyone on the outskirts of the growing crowd, and bodies scramble everywhere to get their hands on the first update from Broadcove they've seen in a long time.

Tolcher catches one of Nadine's lobbed copies, smiling sweetly in her direction before going back to pretending she is a stranger. He's mid-read as he stumbles back into Sour Maiden, and just shy of our dingy table, he freezes—swears.

He chooses not to stifle his growing smile. "Get a load of this, Jericho," he insists, shoving the *U. Herald* into my hands.

The headline threatens to split my heart in half.

⚜ U. HERALD ⚜

Written by Lady Venus Deragon - Right Hand to the King   2 JULY

KING JERICHO VANISHES AS ASSASSINS INVADE BROADCOVE CASTLE

Our territory has been betrayed from inside Broadcove Castle, and now, the Heir Apparent of Mosacia, and a handful of King Victor's armed assassins have arrived in Urovia to lay claim to our land. In an effort to ensure the King's survival, I have sent him to an undisclosed shelter, and am running the kingdom-making one last ditch effort at alliances to keep them from pursuing violence. So long as King Jericho lives, this country can never be theirs.

But I assure you, they are looking for him. They will destroy your homes to get to him. And if they do, if they bring about the fall of the Morgan Dynasty, things will never recover. Do not fool yourselves, because under Mosacia's rule, we will not be provided for. This land will be laid to waste as punishment for our ancestors' resettlement, and we will live in perpetual suffering.

I implore you all to take action. I beg of you to band together and find a will and a way to help bring down this enemy of ours. Help save our home, and in exchange, I will promise to do far more than stabilize your villages and redistribute the territory's wealth. I will burn Mosacia to the ground.

Outside of Sour Maiden, the low build of grumblings turns to jeers. Orbs of flame lick up several torches progressively being lit across the grassy expanse. The sound of children stomping, of women chattering something I cannot quite make out from within the glassy, restaurant walls, of men beating their chests and stepping towards Nadine and the carriage. Fists fly in the air, taking up a pattern among the masses as they whoop a united message.

"It's happening." Tolcher chuckles. He stands from the table, overcome with amazement. "Shit, it's really happening."

"*What* is happening?"

Tolcher yanks the *U. Herald* out of my hand, but only for as long as it takes him to flip to the back and smack his index finger over an old photograph. Thousands of troops suited up and standing before their designated ships in Honeycomb Harbor.

And then, another headline. A war cry.

Written by Lady Venus Deragon - Right Hand to the King   2 JULY

HAIL TO THE HIVE

The words bellow out of the crowd beyond the door right as I read over them.

I feel the earth's center of gravity shift, jarring me where I sit. I throw down the paper and bail out of my seat if only to not feel so confined and cramped all of a sudden. The rumblings outside turn to screams, and no matter how hard I jam my fingers in my ears, I cannot banish the sound.

"Jericho," Tolcher examines me in confusion. "Stop." When my unsettled state does not dissipate at his instruction, he crouches down to my level and points. "Look at them out there! This is a *good* thing! Venus is uniting people."

But I shake my head, unable to banish the sick comprehension in my mind—one that has nothing to do with the Hive. "Something's wrong."

My stomach knots up and my eyesight starts to spot. Everything spirals—

Tolcher watches my pupils dilate, and he suddenly comes to the grave understanding of what comes over me. "Shit," he breathes, reaching for me before I go limp in the chair. "Nadine!" he yells. Over and over. "*NADINE!* NADINE COME HELP—"

Slinking onto the sticky, linoleum floors, I shut my eyes and let my body give way to whatever horrors the Saints wish to show me.

In the cover of darkness, Venus emerges from one of the dips in Broadcove's sloping hills. The moonlight reveals her bloodshot eyes, and while I pray that they're from the lack of sleep, I know deep down that they're from crying.

No blood on her, no scratches, and no bruises. There aren't even signs of a struggle shown in the upkeep of her fabrics. For the first time in a long time, she dons her gardening clothes—the linen overalls, her wear-and-tear boots, and a long, dark undershirt. But I cannot ignore the phantom presence of her tears. Something unspeakable has happened—or is about to happen. I search her soul for any sort of indication as to what it could be but am met with silence. It makes me want to burn the world to ashes.

Slowly, I recognize her location: just outside of Zayanya Cathedral. Any second now, she should hoist herself up the stairs and push her way through the double doors—

Suddenly, in a jerking motion, Venus angles her body away from the front of the cathedral. Instead, she trudges along the side cobblestone path. Eyes narrowed in focus and in fury, fists clenched as she pumps her arms forward, she looks prepared for an unknown battle—as if approaching death itself. Undeterred by what lies in front of her at the end of her mysterious journey, she stands in waiting—gathering her thoughts.

Venus stands before my mother's tombstone, muscles tense and eyes lined with silver tears. "I'm sorry," I hear her rasp. And for all of two seconds, I believe that she's paying her respects.

That is, until Venus grabs a shovel.

And begins to dig.

PART III
CATASTROPHE

57
Venus

The clock booms, signaling midnight's swift approach. With as little of a scene as I can make, I haul ass back to Broadcove, slipping in through the footpath I helped line through the back gardens. My boots track through dry mud, matching the dirt from Merrie's grave that has crusted beneath my nails and coated my hands in dark dust. Calliope waits at the doors, motioning me into the castle as her eyes dart back and forth for any sudden changes.

Once inside, she drapes a shawl over me to disguise my disarray. In chilled silence, Calliope escorts me through a discreet stairwell before hanging a hard right and promptly shoving me into her and Geneva's joint apartments.

Genny staggers to her feet at the sight of me, eyes wide and filled with worry. "You're late."

I toss the shawl onto the floor and begin stripping off my overalls. The sweat on my body beneath all the fabric makes the act far more difficult and time-consuming than I intend for it to be. "You try digging up a grave sometime," I huff, still trying to catch my breath. I wipe my brow with the side of my forearm, but all it does is smear the droplets beading out of my pores. "That was the hardest shit of my life."

"Bath's all set," Calliope calls out from the other side of the room, her hand dripping from where she tested the water's temperature. "I added salts and soaps, too. Scrub is on the ledge."

"Thanks," I blurt out as I remove the last of my clothes. I rush to the porcelain bowl, immediately feeling relief from the grime and earth clinging to my skin.

Geneva holds the base of her belly as she paces the room. "Venus, I love you, but sometimes, when you come up with an idea and you don't share it with anyone, it genuinely scares me."

"Oh, I'm terrified," I admit. "But this one might just be bad enough to work."

"And . . . what if it doesn't?" she asks tentatively. "Not to doubt your intuition, but—"

"Then you and Calliope will be the first ones escorted to safety outside of the castle. Promise," I tell her, then dunk myself completely under the milky white bathwater. The heat makes my face burn, and I emerge from the water with a gasp, immediately reaching for the scrub and going to town on my shoulders. "Where's Roxie?"

"With Greer," Calliope assures me. "You sure we can trust her?"

"I'd risk my life on it. Where's Slater?"

"In your rooms."

"What time did he get there?" My scrubbing intensifies, and Genny flashes me a look that worries I'll rip my skin off.

"Three hours ago. He snagged some books from the library to keep him busy."

"And Ardian?"

Calliope stiffens at his name. "In the Boardroom."

I give myself one last glance over, and when I finish my cleanliness assessment, I step out of the tub and let the water pour off me. Genny throws me a towel, and as I dry myself off, she comes in behind me with another rag to help squeeze the added moisture out of my hair. The silence is palpable, and the sensation feels beyond constricting. To all of us.

"Calliope." I finally sigh as I slip into a rather slinky nightgown.

"Yes, Venus?"

I wordlessly direct her towards the pile of my dirty, discarded clothes. Indicating the deep, side pocket as if worried that the walls have ears. I watch a peculiar expression settle over her features as Calliope feels something stashed there. Upon removal, she finds the very thing I went digging for. "What . . . what is this?"

"It's the last letter Merrie ever sent to Harriet," I say, my voice hushed. "Buried away with her body."

Geneva stares at it in Calliope's hands, still and cold as the statues in Sevensberg Palace.

"Read it," I instruct them as I tie my wet hair into a bun and pad towards the door. "And then, I want you to publish it in the *U. Herald*. I will not rest until every eye in Urovia has seen it."

An oval hallway mirror grants me one, final look at myself. No glimmer of joy, no color in my cheeks, no remnant of assurance in myself. Looking at my reflection, all I see is a girl living on a prayer, unsure of whether or not she'll see the sunrise. Despite being in better physical health, I witness the mental distress all over me, and it only worries me further to know that *this* version of myself is the one that must pull off a miracle.

"Venus?" Slater says hoarsely, standing in the doorway of my room.

Escaping the hurricane of my racing heart and clouded head, I snap my attention towards him. His eyes instantly turn hungry as they rove over me in the nightgown, slightly wet in the spots that the towels didn't quite dry—an intentional detail. "You waited up for me," I hum sweetly, closing the gap between us in a matter of steps.

"Of course, I waited," he answers, his voice rough. "But . . . gods," he lets out a ragged breath, as if one look at me equates to running three miles without rest. "You look exactly how I picture you when I'm alone, touching myself," he gets out.

An innocent grin meets my lips, but Slater charges towards me, erasing it with the crush of his mouth.

His hands run down the length of my spine as he traps me within his kiss, and against my best effort, I go to war with my conscience. On one hand, I can try and imagine something else, anything else to make me forget what I'm doing right now. Twisted imaginings like rotting fish, wounded animals, or even my traitorous father. But on the other . . . I could convince myself to be happy here. To remember that Slater and I have done this dance before, and that the only difference between then and now is how desperately I'm hoping Jericho never uncovers this.

"Shut the door," I slur, letting Slater hoist me up off the floor.

His whole torso rumbles with an animalistic enthusiasm against my front, and I only have a second to gulp down my dread before his tongue comes sweeping in. I meet him stroke for stroke, going to battle with him while he believes we're dancing, and Slater makes a show of slamming the door behind us. My nightgown bunches up around my waist, and the center of me goes stiff at the feel of his pants—of his erection pushing forward.

And just when I expect him to be selfish, he surprises me. "Tell me what you want," he whispers frantically, his voice crazed.

I pause.

"Really?"

"Anything," he says.

I feel the bloodlust smoldering within his soul as I unloop my legs from around him and climb onto the bed, waiting to see if he follows. He stands there, hesitant on what to do next until I murmur with a self-conscious smile. "I want you to marry me, Slater."

The words seem to set his mind aflame with pleasure, as if this moment is the prelude to all his wildest fantasies coming true. "*Venus—*"

"I don't want to do life here in Urovia," I lie, feigning desperation and undying love, "and I don't want to play

King anymore."

Slater licks his lips. "I bet you don't."

I crook my finger beneath his stern chin, a feature he shares with his father. "Not when I could be with you. Not when I could live somewhere that appreciates me, with someone that will bend for me rather than stand by and watch me bleed out for them."

Slater stands up straighter at the side of my bed. "Come here," he orders.

I crawl to him, watching his eyes trail down the tunnel between my breasts and his mouth parts at the sight. "I want to be adored, protected, treasured . . . *revered.*"

He's breathing hard again, his chest puffing relentlessly.

It's how I know my blessing is sinking its hooks deep into him.

Slater hums an approving laugh. "I've wanted you to be mine ever since you shed your clothes in the water lily lounge."

My smile turns sinister. "And now?"

He pulls me onto his lap, and I tilt my head back as he grinds against me. The feel of him trying to spring out of his pants is so evident it becomes punishing—claiming. "I'm fully and happily prepared to take everything from Jericho that he's ever loved."

I laugh, the sound coming out evil. "Jericho is incapable of love. I was only ever his plaything."

"That's what I told myself, too," he tuts. "But when Jericho refused my father's offer for you, I knew that you had sunk him without even trying."

Something inside of me withers at the way Slater takes pride in his father bartering for my hand in marriage—

like I'm no better than a piece of food in the markets back home in the marshes.

"So, tell me, Venus," he croons, dropping the thin straps of my nightgown off my shoulders. "Are you prepared to destroy him with me?"

"Only if I get to do so at your side," I say, baring my teeth in a beaming smile that reminds me of Roxie, a tiger flashing its fangs. It makes the hair along his arms stand on end.

"Alright," Slater confirms, taking my small face into his meaty hands. "I'll marry you."

My optimism turns devious. "Tonight?"

Slater barely mulls over the suggestion. "Tonight," he repeats. "But first things first..."

He removes his shirt with a single, overhead pull, and before the fabric hits the floor beyond the side of my bed, he's already peeling off my silken gown. Greedy. Impatient.

Still, I will myself to do as I must. I play my part— Slater's submissive, devoted fiancée.

The—almost—Heiress of the Mosacian Empire.

58
Venus

After thirty minutes of pure grunt work and over exaggerated moaning, Slater sets off to find Ardian, while I veer off to look for Delta. No surprise, I find her lingering in the hallway just shy of Diana's door, and the moment she sees me, she straightens, as if alarmed.

"Venus," she remarks brightly, "is everything alright?"

I'm kind of in the middle of something, she means.

"Is Diana there?" I ask, letting my voice lighten.

Delta studies the look in my eyes, suddenly registering the weight of my inquiry. She nods quickly, pounding on the door with her fist until Diana yanks it open with an attitude. "What happened to being *discreet*—" and then she notices me standing there. Clears her throat. "My apologies, Venus. Is there something you needed me for?"

"From both of you, actually," I clarify.

Diana's brow furrows, and she waits for an explanation. Finally, I announce, "Slater and I are getting married"—I clasp my hands together, as if unable to tolerate how happy I am about it—"in an hour."

Diana blanches. "*Married?*"

"IN AN *HOUR?*" Delta screams. "Holy shit, we have to get you ready! Do you have a gown? Flowers? How long has this been planned? *Why didn't you tell me—*"

Delta pulls me towards her face by the trim of my nightgown, and it takes Diana to separate the two of us and break her relentless interrogation. "Because they're eloping," she grinds out, her words dry in her throat.

"Is that a problem?" I ask innocently.

"No," Diana answers, but her tone is unconvincing at best. "It's just . . . if you marry Slater, you surrender your affiliation to Jericho, leaving Urovia without a ruler."

"Not necessarily. As of a few hours ago, Mr. Asticova is now Acting Monarch."

Delta's eyes bulge. "My uncle is King?"

"Temporarily," I tell her pointedly. "But once everything is official with Slater and I, we'll see to it that Jericho is . . ." A scheming laugh reverberates within me. "Taken out of the equation. And from there, Ardian will train and install Urovia's new Queen."

The two of them lean in, as if they misheard me.

The smirk that meets my lips is laced with poison. "How about it, Diana?"

A twisted sense of intrigue prickles across her skin. "Me?"

"Our ancestors were your citizens, which means Urovia *belongs* to Mosacia," I profess, circling them. "It's only fair that it returns to its rightful possessor. Wouldn't you say?"

"Yes . . ." Diana mutters, retracing the steps of time

and history. "Yes, it would."

"But with the Damocles dividing our lands, it doesn't make sense for me and Slater to go back and forth in attempts to govern both territories. Slater will have his hands full learning all he can from King Victor, and I will need to be there to support him." I try not to meditate on the thought—waiting on Slater hand and foot while he inherits full jurisdiction over thousands of people's lives, abiding in a world where Jericho is dead. "That's where you come in."

And then, with careful calculation, I turn my eyes towards the first friend I made in the castle. "You, too, Delta."

Her eyes glimmer with the faint recognition of needing to be discreet. "What do you mean?"

"I didn't see it at first," I say truthfully. "And if I'm being honest, I was starting to feel sad that you didn't spend as much time with me as you did before going to Sevensberg. But . . . of course you'd pick her, just as I picked Slater."

Delta's eyes soften, blurring with shame and remorse. "I wanted to tell you. Really, I did, but—"

"I think what the two of you have is truly special, and I know how hard it must have been to go without each other for so long. To have fallen in love with each other an ocean apart. And I do not want that for either of you anymore."

Diana's fixed expression starts to crack, giving way to a solemn softness. "No more back and forth?"

"Never again," I promise her. "Just let me marry your brother, let me find my own happiness, too."

The two of them share an exchanged look, which fades into identical, almost spider-like smiles. "It's sure to be an honor," Diana formally proceeds, dipping into a curtsey, "to see you transform the world, Heiress."

Diana ran off to find Slater in order to call Harriet and Victor on the Dial Line and tell them the good news. Meanwhile, Delta snagged me by the wrist the moment Diana turned the corner and led me to her room.

Delta had always come and kept me company in my own suites—and drinking in the sight of everything, I understand why.

Her walls are painted periwinkle blue, and a massive pile of letters in multiple stacks litters a desk that appears to be collecting dust. Letters I presume are from Diana. A netted canopy hangs over a mid-sized bed that is dressed in crème quilts, and on her nightstand lies a picture of two strangers I imagine are her parents. I know better than to ask what happened to them, to unearth an entire sob story I do not need to invest in right this second. Instead, I choose to ask her a more worthwhile question as she returns from her bathroom with a few loose hair pins. "What is something I may not already know about Slater? Something that I should know before binding myself to him forever."

A faint smile falls over her lips. "Funny you should ask, because before you came into the picture, *I* was set to marry Slater."

I certainly didn't see that coming. "You and *Slater*?

Delta laughs at the mental image, sectioning off my

hair into the desired number of pieces for an elegant braid. "Silly, right? Well, the whole arrangement came together because Jericho refused to be betrothed to Diana, a failed attempt to align our territories through marriage rather than exchanged Advisors. But Merrie . . . she raised me like a daughter. I may as well have been her daughter." Her eyes soberly flick back to the framed photograph. "So Slater and I were her and Queen Harriet's compromise."

Her hands rapidly weave in and out from one another, and when she reaches the end of my hair, she ties off the end with a small band. "Slater has his strong suits, don't get me wrong," she prefaces, "but there was something about Diana that captivated me. Her friendship set my heart on fire. Thinking of her made me homesick for a place I barely got to grow up in, and every letter she signed *'With love, Diana'* made me reevaluate what a life with Slater would be like."

No devotion.

No spark.

Only responsibility and ego.

"I couldn't bear to be married to him when my heart forever wandered after her," she says, her words grave. Then, she looks at me through the mirror. "Thank the Saints that you showed up, though! The moment I told him about you, he was sold. Broke our engagement right then and there."

Something pings in my head. "Told him about me?"

"When I'd write to Diana about you," she tells me like it's obvious, and my eyes drift back to the cluttered desk of messages. "I'd tell her about how you survived standing up to Jericho. How you matched him blow for blow—pushed his buttons. I think Slater became enamored with you just from reading about you. Seeing you in action only solidified his instincts."

All this time, I believed my powers carried a gravitational pull with Slater, one that always swayed him in my direction. But it appears I didn't even need to bother with all that. Slater only ever desired me because of what I was to Jericho, a prize to be possessed. "How wonderful," I say, even as the words make me nauseous. "So with Slater out of the way, you were finally able to love her?"

"Freely, yes," Delta notes. "But I loved Diana long before Slater was out of the picture."

If only to make decent conversation, I ask her, "When did you know for sure?"

Her answer comes immediately, as if instantly recalling her fondest memory. "I knew I was in love with Diana when she trusted me enough to send me Merrie's final letter."

The world inside my skull bursts into flames.

It's her.

Delta is the traitor inside of Broadcove.

She finishes pinning my hair up, then turns to a potted flower arrangement on her coffee table and fishes out a few of the small, white-blossomed sprigs. "I remember reading it and realizing that everything I knew about this place, about the people who ran Broadcove Castle and beyond, was a lie." Delicately, she sticks the stems of the tiny flowers through my hair, decorating me with them. "And then, I thought of Diana. Of the courage it must've taken her to share that with me."

Courage? This bitch's mind is warped.

"And I decided to return her affection," she says proudly just before a new emotion falls over her face like a shadow. Delta prepares to explain herself, realizing that I might not know what she is referencing—but my power sees straight through her.

The Fall of Jericho painting.

"So you . . ." I try to form coherent words, chuckling in an uncomfortable laugh. It takes my entire life force to smile at what this conversation has uncovered. "You saw me coming."

She winks at me through our reflection again, pleased to see me impressed with her treachery. "Why else would I have given you the dagger?"

Delta steps away to open her armoire, showing off her vast collections of suitable, elopement-appropriate outfits. In desperation, she searches for something white, harping on tradition and elegance. I merely flash her a knowing look, and she laughs like we're old pals again. "I hear you; I hear you," she insists, and with a wide-eyed grin, pulls out her final selection from off its hanger.

No surprise, she handpicks a blue gown.

A soft blue, however. Not the dark, aggressive blue that Slater put me in the night of the Menagerie. The hem of the dress falls at a tea length, and a tulle underskirt helps pronounce the belled shape of it. The strapless bodice cuts straight across my chest, giving it a conservative touch, and perhaps my favorite aspect, it feels . . . childlike. Lace swirls and embellishments run throughout the dress, curling along where my breasts would fall, tiering down past my waist—and at the base of the skirt, horses prance in a wrap-around pattern. Not wild horses, though, but the kind that rise and fall while a carousel spins. Forever chained to the rhythm of a force they cannot control. How fitting.

She holds up a pair of white, heeled shoes, and I concede to her insistence on showing at least some formality. "Let me help you with the buttons," she offers.

"Wait," I dare to voice, eyes downcast and heart pounding. "I . . . I have to tell you something. It's important."

Delta stares at me like she is about to uncover a hoard of gold and get filthy rich. "You can tell me anything, Venus," she assures me, her voice enthusiastic. "I'm here for you."

Her hand burns the skin on my shoulder, and I swallow my retch as I confess to her, "I know where Jericho is."

Delta looks at me in disbelief, stuttering over her next question. "Y-You do?"

"Yes," I reply. "That's where I was all day when I left Ardian in charge. One of my guards was tipped off by someone, so I went looking for him. I just didn't want to endanger the kingdom if I found him and he lashed out."

The subtle suggestion of something deeper makes her mouth faintly fall open. Salivate. "He's dead. Isn't he?"

"A wedding gift," I whisper, my smile venomous. "You think Slater will like it?"

I wait for her response, knowing that it is her last chance at self-redemption. For Delta to truly prove to me that she hasn't fallen too far from grace. That even if she brought about the death of Queen Merrie—a woman she described as a mother to her—in favor of a deranged relationship with Diana, she still knows how to own up to her poor decisions. To move past them.

But Delta's eyes flick back towards me from beneath her dark lashes, a damning look on her face. "You're a mastermind."

"I'm glad you think so," I say, standing up as she attaches the final hair pin in place. "Because I want you to see him for yourself."

Abandoning the powder blue gown on the edge of her bed to keep from potentially getting blood on the fabric, I usher Delta and I down the stairwell furthest from the Boardroom and the Dial Line. *The path of least resistance*, I insist. *That way we do not spoil Slater's surprise or scare any of the staff that might still be awake.*

Casually, as if discussing the weather, I bullshit my way through an explanation for where we're going. Something about killing Jericho in the gardens, being seen by a guard who promised to stash the body in the tunnels, and me fleeing the scene before an outside witness discovered us. Jericho told me sometime during the night of the Violet Ball, after commanding everyone to take shelter, that they likely holed up in the underground tunnel passages that stemmed from a trick door in the kitchens. The memory of him explaining its location as he kissed my neck and shoulders may be the only thing keeping Delta from growing suspicious about our journey there, especially at this time of night. Whether she realizes that I have no idea how to guide my way through this dark maze or not, only time will tell.

The air quality hits me the moment Delta opens the trick door and I grab a lantern, its golden flame dancing in the dim breeze. It's the kind of hot that feels sticky, even though the darkness would make one assume that the cold would kill them. Unlike what I envisioned a royal castle's tunnels to be—wide and cavernous and littered with hanging tapestries detailing Urovia's rich history—the ceilings here are maybe two feet above my head, made of jagged rock, and its walls are bare. A distant bat screech sounds off beyond one of the forks in the road, and Delta practically trembles with fear. Knowing how pestering and loud the bats in the marshes were, I press on without concern. "Stay close," I instruct, and Delta instantly draws near. "I don't want to get separated."

"Here," she says, stopping me in my tracks to dig something out of her dress pockets. Moments later, the dagger she originally gave me glimmers faintly in her hands. She shoves it towards me with a shiver. "I'll hold the lantern if you'll take care of whatever the *hell* that was."

Aside from being a gossip and a traitor, I discover another one of Delta's signifying traits: not having a spine.

We reach our first split passageway, and just as I mean to veer left, Delta's body leans towards the right, and I catch myself before completing my damning step. "I only know the correct turns up to a certain point, so let's hope the guard you spoke to thought to meet you halfway."

A new noise filters through the catacombs, one far less menacing than a lost bat. Slow-dripping water. There's something taunting about it, though—water in a place so dry. Sweat begins to bead along my hairline, and I try not to think about how badly I need a drink, not having had one since before digging up Merrie's casket and entertaining Slater. The idea of thirst, however, quickly becomes second priority to my present rage as Delta asks me, lantern held at face level to display her innocent smile, "How fast did he fall?"

"Sunk like an anchor," I tell her, trying not to imagine the scenario to keep from wincing.

She shakes her head. "Weapon?"

It only takes a split second for me to think of a suitable murder device. "Rock."

"Damn, you're *far* more committed to your role than I thought you were."

You have no idea.

"Since you told me the moment you knew you loved Diana," I say to keep the spooky silence from eating the both of us alive. "Tell me about the moment you knew you hated Jericho."

Her smile quirks to the side. "I *always* hated him."

I chuckle, but the sound doesn't seem believable when it falls upon my ears.

"When I got old enough for Ardian to explain my true heritage, every part of my Urovian upbringing felt like a lie pressured upon me—every last one. A crimson and black coat of arms lining halls that should bear hues of silver and blue. A quiet castle with a contentious king rather than a palace full of children I *should* have grown up in. But no." Delta laughs morbidly. "It was just me and Jericho. And perhaps that wouldn't have been such a bad thing, you know, if Jericho wasn't a clone of his father."

Delta snickers to herself at her own remark, and I feel my anger beginning to simmer deep within me, like boiling a kettle of tea. It's only a matter of time before steam spews out of my ears. "What was King Ronan like?"

"Deplorable," she drawls, and given what little I've picked up on about him in the vague details Jericho has provided me, I'm inclined to trust her description of him. "For as fair and lovely as Queen Merrie was, I do not know what she ever saw in Ronan. She was sociable, he was reserved. She was slow to anger and gentle with people, while Ronan never hid his resentment for the world, especially vocally. But mainly, King Ronan was insecure. Everything he ever said or did stemmed from that plumbline, including what he did to Merrie."

Ah, yes. What *he* did to Merrie—although, the longer it sinks in, the more it feels like what Delta and Diana did to Merrie.

Everything changed when I dug up the casket and found Merrie's final letter to Harriet. I remember reading it with my back propped against the accumulated pile of dirt and earth, too tired from exerting myself to read it within the privacy of the cathedral. And when my eyes reached the final paragraph, I thought my mind was playing vicious tricks on me.

Because there was no way that what I was reading was true.

There was no way that Ronan was preparing to sick the Hive on Sevensberg Palace, and that Merrie was *warning* the Seagraves. There was no way that Merrie was granting them permission to retaliate against him, so long as they didn't harm Jericho, her only son and heir.

There was no way that instead of providing aid, Harriet and Victor allowed her cries to go unheard—allowed their daughter to return the letter to Delta. And allowed Delta to conveniently let it fall into Ronan's grasp.

"Did you see it happen?" I try not to grimace.

"When Ronan killed his wife?" she clarifies.

Three diversions in the road lie before us, and Delta pauses, reevaluating the path she learned. After a heartbeat or two, she proceeds straight on, forsaking the side routes. "Merrie was on one of the observation terraces, looking out at the morning sun. Ronan simply came up behind her and pushed. It was quick. She never even saw it coming. A mercy killing."

Too far. That final addition—her idea on the concept of *mercy*—crosses a line.

"What do you even think mercy is, Delta?" I stammer.

Delta stops walking then, sharply aware of the shift in my tone. As she spins to face me, the warm light flickering within the lantern reveals the harsh lines creasing along the space between my eyebrows as they tilt downward with wrath. Her breath comes out shaky. "What?"

"You said that woman was a *mother* to you," I seethe. "And yet, you had the gall to give Ronan that letter. You had the nerve to be both a facilitator and a bystander of her murder."

She looks around, realizing that we've been drifting into the darkness too long to have not found Jericho by now. Panic flashes over her eyes, and she shrinks before me. "Now, Venus, wait a minute—"

"How do you live with the knowledge that her blood is on your hands?" I snarl.

She sputters, unable to clearly articulate her defense.

"How do *you* expect mercy in return after what you've done?"

Delta realizes her mistake—the one where she handed me a blade in exchange for the lantern—but she is too late.

Too late to stop the dagger she gifted me from slicing through her own throat.

Delta means to scream, but her throat is exposed, spurting bright blood in the manner that it should be currently coursing through her arteries. She chokes violently, gagging while still managing to hold her slashed throat together, as if she could stop the detrimental bleeding. She drops the lantern, and the flame winks out as glass shatters on the stone floors. Then, her knees hit the ground, eyes flaring in grave realization. Tears well up in the corners of her eyes, and I merely stoop over her, the darkness hiding my devious smile. "Thanks for the dagger."

A gurgled curse leaves her lips, and then, there's one final cough before she and the tunnels go quiet altogether.

This kill feels different from the last.

It feels *good*.

And I wonder if there's an addictive quality to getting retribution against those who have wronged you—or, in my case, those you love. It makes me understand Jericho on an infinitely more intimate level.

Even though I know Delta cannot hear me in death, I tell her corpse only for the sake of spite, "Long live the king."

59
Jericho

Every waking moment since the vision of Venus at my mother's gravesite first haunted me continues to be a living nightmare.

All I can picture is her, sweat coating her brow as she grits her teeth and fights the dirt below with her shovel. I relive it in my sleep. I sense its remains in the way my meals taste offbeat. And now, in the silence Tolcher left me with—silence I willingly agreed to after granting him a brief leave of absence to be with Nadine—I'm left to wonder why she went digging in the first place.

All the Saints cared to show me were those first few minutes, up until Venus's rage made tears leak out the sides of her eyes. I remain unsure of why she disrupted the site, but frankly, knowing Venus's brilliance, I think that may be for the better. After all, if she felt convicted enough to go there to begin with, she must have been provoked. Must have been searching for something . . .

My insides twist into a knot.

The only thing banishing the turmoil in my head are the conscriptions.

Ever since Venus rerouted the distribution of the *U. Herald*, communicating her agenda and pushing just the right buttons of the people, the once quiet town Tolcher and I took shelter in now thrums with life. All day long, even in the hours of night when the population should be sleeping, people line up in the center of the square. They're filling out paperwork and other personal records in order to be considered for the assembling fleet. Four days, nonstop.

The clouds cast a hazy glow over an otherwise beautiful afternoon, and in the glassy backsplash reflection of another pub Tolcher and I rotate between, I notice the first signs of growth along my scalp again. Raising a hand to the spot, the soft, almost fuzzy texture makes me unwind a little bit. I haven't cropped my hair this short in ages—not since I took a nasty spill down the stairs in Sevensberg during one of our yearly visits and busted my head open. Mother was the one to buzz my hair off, alongside the sympathetic nurse stationed in the Mosacian infirmary.

Come to think of it, *Slater* had pushed me down those stairs.

"Another pint?" the bartender calls out to me, even though his back is turned to me.

"Just one more," I tell myself more than him. "Thanks."

He goes about his work again, and someone settles into the straw bar stool to my left. In efforts to stay out of awkward conversation, I try not to turn and assess him, simply ignore his presence. But the guy seems to be itching to talk to someone, because his incessant foot tapping hammers along the wooden bar below him and he laughs subduedly, as if hoping it prompts me to ask him what's so funny.

I'm not biting.

The bartender returns with my pint, the ale's heady scent rising in the summer air. I instantly sink back in my chair. *Day drinking alone and practically bald. So this is what my life has come to?*

I'm so caught up in my internal lamentations that I almost block out the voice of the bartender, who asks the patron next to me if they'd like anything. To which I hear him eagerly reply, "Your foulest shot of liquor. And one for him as well."

Slightly disgusted, I finally angle myself towards the man, hellbent on refusing his gesture. However, I end up staring into the mischievous eyes of a familiar face.

"Trust me," Chumley says over the sound of the bartender divvying out two portions of murky, brown liquid. "You look like you need it."

"I thought we agreed to pretend we didn't know each other," I say.

He merely rolls his eyes, waiting for the bartender to roam elsewhere before muttering, "I agreed to pretend I didn't know the King of Urovia. For all I know, you're a bruised, washed-up commoner."

Annoyance tugs an unconvincing smile across my lips. "Pretty much. How'd you even find me, anyway?"

"Guesswork," he admits, shooting the liquid down the back of his throat. He winces, but only briefly. "The *U.*

Herald made it sound like you got flushed out of your own home, so I figured you were hiding out somewhere. But all the people from the marshes wanting to enlist for the Hive have to funnel into Cheratowe through the main road. They're piling in by the trolley-load. In fact, I just got off one myself. That is"—he chuckles—"until I saw you here. I've never seen a so-called poor person's posture so *dignified*."

I instantly slouch, and he nods his approval. "Better."

A hysterical mother from across the square embraces her son and implores him to be safe, to which the young man, likely around Venus's age, ensures her that he will come home in one piece. Overdramatic as it appears, there's something about the exchange that makes my heart tighten within my chest. Mother would likely spiral like that woman is if she knew I was left unescorted and unprotected here. If she were still alive.

"So, you're enlisting," I say, if only to keep from dwelling on her too long.

"Enlisting?" He laughs bitterly. "Jericho, I'm the Chief Naval Officer."

My stomach lurches, knowing a role like that doesn't get bestowed to a nameless stranger. Chumley must've told them his entire life's story to be granted the title. "Part of a secret escape means keeping your existence a *secret*. Did you not understand that?"

Chumley clears his throat, the liquor having a sharp aftertaste, apparently. "I'd rather die in the Hive than in the marshes, that's for sure," he remarks sourly. "How Venus was able to run that ramshackle household *and* manages to keep Broadcove afloat with only a few months' worth of experience in your administration, I'll never know."

"She's a powerhouse," I tell him, a pleased smile blooming along my face.

"And at any rate, I want to serve my homeland," he continues. "Jericho, I advised King Victor for more than a decade, including in military preparations. So as long as these new editions of the *U. Herald* never reach Mosacia—"

"Editions?" I catch, my brows furrowing. "Plural?"

His face slackens, the color seeping out of his cheeks. "Saints," he says in a tone that most foul language comes out of. "You . . . you haven't seen it?"

"Seen what?"

"Shit," he breathes rockily. Chumley stumbles out of his seat and rushes over to the newsstand, where copies of the *U. Herald* are supposed to be stacked for public consumption, but the shelves are empty. My fingertips tinker along the side of the shot glass, my drink gradually warming the longer I avoid it, and I watch as Chumley hurriedly pleads with a herd of people gawking at what must be the newest imprint. It takes a while before they reluctantly grant him a copy, and I bet Chumley pulled rank in order to get it.

"The riders brought them in this morning," he pants, setting the article upside down on the bar top. "I'm surprised you didn't hear the response to it from where you were staying."

I scoff. "Woke me up just as I managed to get some quality rest. I chose to ignore it."

His eyes turn icy. Then, he tells me to take the shot.

"Chumley—"

"Trust me," he stiffens.

Grimacing, I try not to think too hard about why I'm compelled to obey him—that he wouldn't be offering me a way to take the edge off if what I am about to read does not have a bite behind it. I knock the glass on the counter once before tipping back my head, shutting my eyes, and sucking down the shit-colored liquor. Heat funnels down my esophagus, sparking a trail of fire from throat to stomach, and with a hard nod and a second gulp, I flip the article over.

The title hurts worse than the shot I just took.

Written by Lady Venus Deragon - Right Hand to the King   6 JULY

QUEEN MERRIE'S LAST LETTER OF DESPERATION

As if current circumstances weren't grave enough, I recently stumbled upon a document that was intended, by traitors to our territory, to stay buried forever.

Queen Harriet of Mosacia and our dear Queen Merrie, Saints rest her soul, were once political allies. Friends, even. Their bond and loyalty preserved peace between our nations. However, as King Ronan grew violent, insisting our forces stage an attack on Mosacia, Merrie wrote to her friend for aid. She warned them that her husband was preparing to bring danger upon their home and their civilians—and in exchange for this knowledge, she only asked one thing in return: not to harm her son, Jericho.

  However, rather than choosing to honor their relationship, the Seagraves returned her frantic letter, ensuring it would fall within King Ronan's grasp.

  So, let the record state it clearly: Merrie Morgan did not commit suicide. She was murdered. By her own husband and by her own friends.

  King Jericho and I need your support now more than ever. Look past your bitterness for a king given the throne out of infinite tragedy and join the fight. It's what Merrie would have wanted.

  See page 2 to read the late Queen's final recorded writings.

I barely managed to get through the preceding paragraphs, but any internal defenses I have turn to rubble upon reading the last line. My eyes rush to meet Chumley's. "Tell me it's not true," I croak, unable to convince my hands to turn the page. Unable to move or breathe.

He hesitates, unsure if mentioning this article to begin with was the healthiest thing he could've done for me. Chumley turns the page for me. "I'm . . . I'm so sorry."

For the loss I bore alone.

And for how my soul becomes shredded into scraps the moment I see my mother's familiar cursive penmanship. A photograph of the letter rather than a printed transcription stares back at me, dirt still crusting the page and the edges folded and worn with time.

This is what Venus went digging for.

My Dearest Harriet,

In all the years we've known one another, I'd like to think that I haven't asked you for too much—and that, perhaps, I've held off on doing so for a moment like this one.

It is with deepest concern that I share with you the state of my husband, Ronan. He is not well, nor in the right frame of mind. He is under the impression that your forces are drawing inland, and he is preparing the Hive to directly attack Sevensberg Palace. For the sake of your children and your safety, I urge you to prepare accordingly, or even to strike first.

And if the latter is the plan of action you choose to take, I understand that I am not at liberty to ask for conditional protection, as I am a reflection of my husband just as you are to Victor. If I get caught in his crossfires, I shall not blame you. But I urge you as a mother, please spare my son from harm.

Jericho is not his father. I try to shield him from Ronan's temper, but I know that he must learn to stand up for himself. And while that comes with facing him directly, this is a special circumstance. If it were Slater that faced the repercussions, would you not do the same?

I beg of you. Do what you must, but please, not at the cost of my son's life. Our people will look to him when the time comes. Jericho is many things, but above all, he is the crowning jewel of my life, and I would do anything for him.

—Merriweather Morgan

My eyes glaze over at the presence of her swirled signature. The sight of it brings back a wave of painful memories. The scent of her perfume and how her eyes crinkled when she smiled at me. The sound of her laugh. The way her shoulders shook as she began to cry, and how she'd force them down again when she heard me lurking behind her. How I'd ask her how she was, and her voice would softly soothe me with her murmur, *"I'm doing great now that you're here, Jericho."* Even as I watched her cover the bruises on her arm with her free hand.

She died for me—she paid the ultimate price for the sake of ensuring my safety.

He is the crowning jewel of my life, and I would do anything for him.

In the pit of my stomach, rising up to combat the grief for her absence, I recognize that there is someone else that is prepared to do the same thing Mother did, to die on my behalf in the name of love. And I cannot lose her, too—I wouldn't survive it.

"My King?" Chumley asks feebly, the ghost of his hand reaching to rest on my shoulder and reassure me. I do not even realize that I'm crying until I nearly choke on a ragged breath. "I'm sorry you had to find out this—"

I throw myself onto my feet, tears raining from my eyes and down my face as I kick the barstool out of range. Smashing the shot glasses against the backsplash, shards flying everywhere, I sink into the depths of my rage and pay no heed to the people around us staring with gaping mouths.

Chumley wraps his arms around me, trying to pull me away from the damage I've created. "Jericho, please," he yanks me backwards. "I know this is difficult to learn—"

"I already knew, you moron!" I shout, kicking my feet

like a child. Chumley's embrace feels nothing like my mother's—restrictive, not comforting. "But no one believed me. Not my staff, not Ardian, not anyone. My father made sure of it, always chastising me for trying to explain that I have visions when all he ever told me was that I had a screw loose and couldn't be trusted."

Chumley says nothing, but his grip on me doesn't let up.

"Then, one night, the Saints showed me what Father did, and when I confronted Father about it, he laughed. He didn't even *try* to deny it. So I killed him for it. I'd never killed anyone before, and I remember making myself physically sick over it. I murdered him knowing it wouldn't bring her back to life, but at least it would even the score—except using violence to calm the storm in my head didn't stop there."

The words come tumbling out, if only because I know that *somebody* is listening, now. "Convinced that I wasn't going mad, I read every book I could find on the Saints and the history of their rituals. Eventually, it led me to Zayanya, to the altar, to my Patron Saint who confirmed what no one had believed to be true: I had visions, just like Mother did. It was the only aspect of her I had left to cling to, and I ran with it. So I pledged my undying loyalty to the Saints, and in return, they kept giving me visions of people who were hungry, who were grasping for power, scheming for money, fighting for control. People who were wronging others for selfish gain, and it made me think to myself: having vowed to uphold their truths, why would the Saints be sharing these visions of injustice with me if I wasn't supposed to amend them?

"So one day, I set out to make sense of something I had foreseen: a disruption in the middle of the Noble District. The vision was vague, but it reminded me of the way people flock to watch a brawl between two people take place. I brought two guards with me, just in case things got hazardous, but when our carriage pulled up, I discovered that the disruption I dreamt of was not a present conflict, but my arrival into their town."

My body caves within Chumley's hold, and he lowers us to the ground, desperately trying to shush me into a state of ease as I sob my guts out. "They cursed my name. Threw food at me and my guards. Mocked me to my face when I tried to explain how I could see into pockets of the present and future." I steady my breathing, eyes barreling into the ground as I reveal to him, " T h e y told me that I would never compare to the kind of rulers my parents were—that I was too weak to be Ronan and too jaded to be Merrie—and that I should have done Urovia a favor and perished with them.

"And that's when I came unglued. I remember grabbing both of the swords from my guards' holsters and just *swinging*. There was no calculation in it at all, only the hellbent mission to forever silence the voices of those who spoke against me.

"I could never be like Mother, not when I was also raised by Ronan Morgan. I knew that. But for people to have the *audacity* to speak of Father's vindictiveness as if it were a strength, and then to write me off for not instantly conforming into that image after his death—I just snapped. No, I wouldn't be like Ronan. I'd be *worse*. I'd be a menace, a monster, a nightmare.

"I would cut off all contact with Mosacia, refuse to show my face in their palace, and ignore every attempt at reconciling the strained relationship Ronan cultivated between our nations before he died. I'd hole myself away in Broadcove Castle and wait for my guards to bring me those whom my visions had condemned, ensuring that people would never see my face again unless they were coming to die. They'd speak about me in whispers. Parents would warn their children about me as if I were the subject of a centuries-old ghost story. But most of all, they would learn to fear me, because it became very clear that it was better to be feared than be seen as their fool."

People have started to awkwardly venture elsewhere, convincing themselves I'm some mindless drunk unable to control myself. "And it worked for a while," I tell Chumley, surprised that he still hangs around. Most people tend to leave me at this point. "I grew accustomed to being coldhearted, even if it meant that my life was consumed in loneliness. But . . . ." I'm unable to suppress the knot in my throat and the way my voice begins to give out. "But then I met Venus. Or, I dreamt of her, rather, and for the first time, my visions sent me something that gave me hope. Something that didn't require mediation or punishment. Instead, the Saints showed me a girl who was just as hurt and angry and unruly as I was, and I wanted to learn why. Vain curiosity and divine intervention brought us together, and while I expected love to catch up with us eventually, I didn't know . . . that love would be what separated us."

The heartbreak inside of me shifts at the thought of her, hardening into fury. "Not being with her, it feels like someone is stomping on my ribs, crushing me beneath their full body weight. Not being there to stop whatever horrors are happening back at home, and knowing Venus is caught in its epicenter . . . it makes me want to unlearn all the good things her love has taught me. It makes me want to turn my enemies to ash. It makes me—"

My words cut out, and Chumley fears I've gone mute, my voice supernaturally sucked out of my body. His eyes enlarge and the muscles in his face wither with empathy, aging him. I can barely look at the man, his pity downright gruesome—and I choose to stand to my feet. Wipe off the earth and blades of grass that cling to my clothes.

And march my way to the front of the conscription line.

Rebuttals bubble up from the four of five people closest to the registration table, one of them daring to grip me by the shoulders and trying to spin me around. I stand my ground. "The hell's your problem?" the guy barks.

"There's a line," the man at the table tells me numbly.

I mean to respond with something snide, but Chumley's tall frame casts a shadow over me and half of the enrollment table. "I don't advise you to send him to the back," Chumley insists smugly.

The man recognizes Chumley's face and his casual demeanor jerks into something edgy. "Oh, he's with you? My mistake, Chief. Of course." He quickly reaches for a document with hundreds of names listed in a descending stack, his pen trailing to the bottom margin. Then, his attention flicks back towards me, more alert this time.

"What's your name, son?"

Chumley and I only look at each other with a secret, shared smile.

60
Venus

Slater and I have been married for a week, which means as long as no one goes in the tunnels, no one will be arrested by the rotting smell of Delta's equally-as-old carcass.

By the mercy of the Saints, immediately following the private ceremony, Diana and her delegated guards boarded a ship for Sevensberg to show Victor and Harriet proof of the marriage documents and all licensing approving Ardian's Acting Monarch status. Too consumed by responsibility and the fantasy of ruling a land that isn't hers, she didn't think once about saying goodbye to Delta. And Ardian was so out of it that he believed Delta went with her. I find myself chuckling at the thought.

What's not so funny, though, is the fact that Diana returns tomorrow.

With her father in tow.

If each *heir* gets ten assassins, I can only imagine

the hell I'm in for when Victor shows up. Forty trained guards? Fifty? Saints, my odds of making it out alive are dwindling by the day.

All I knew to do with my anxiety was write—write down all the shit that hit the fan in the last seven days and wait for Nadine to meet with me and collect the pages. And boy, was there a lot to tell. If this publication in particular doesn't stir the pot, I'm not sure what will. I all but kicked open the door to my new marriage and invited them in. That, and pronounced the timely death of the Broadcove Castle traitor.

But Nadine is late.

She's never late.

Pacing through North Star, racked with nerves, I find my only relief in lecturing the invisible presence of my boyfriend's dead mother. *Boyfriend? Lover? I still don't know.* I suppose Jericho constitutes as my sidepiece, considering I'm a married woman, now. Whatever, that's beside the point. "You could've told me," I groan after Merrie spent the last several minutes outwitting all my rationales for why she should've told me the true manner of her death.

"I'd rather not dwell on the past," she replies quietly.

"Then tell me about the present," I switch gears, conceding. "How is he? Is Jericho . . ."

The air near my neck and shoulders warms, and I picture her smiling at the inquiry. *"He's alive, if that's what concerns you."*

I do not bother hiding my vivid reprieve, releasing a held breath. "Thank the Saints, I was so worried." And then, a chord of revulsion strikes in my chest. "Has he seen your letter?"

"Yes."

The idea of not being there to comfort him in that moment makes me sick with guilt.

"But I assure you, Venus, Jericho is okay. In fact—"

Nadine nearly shatters the glass door as she barges in, her breath hot and jagged as she gasps for air. She cuts right to the chase, her scarlet hair falling over her face in a heap. "You want the good news or the bad news first?"

"Well, shit." I rub my temple, feeling the early signs of a massive headache building. I bite the inside of my cheek; glance passingly at the papers I have ready for her. "Bad news," I finally settle upon.

"Henry lost Jericho."

My pulse quickens and I fight the urge to swear. "How?"

That's when Tolcher himself enters the greenhouse, and any restraint over myself vanishes as I launch myself at him.

"YOU *PROMISED* TO BE WITH HIM!" I shout, hands digging into his biceps in attempts to throw him around. Nadine rushes away from the brawl, while Tolcher dukes it out with me. He hisses as my nails sink into his skin. "How could you leave him—"

"He let me go," he interjects, wincing as I draw blood on my second, deep scratch. He bares his teeth. "Nadine found us in Cheratowe when the first article was distributed, and he let me leave with her. I meant to only be gone for a day, but we got distracted."

My eye twitches with rage.

"By the way," he adds, clearing his throat briefly. "Great work."

"Flattery won't earn you forgiveness. Especially after you get a load of what I've been waiting on Nadine to publish," I sneer, pressing the pages of writing firmly against his chest.

They only need to inspect the title to know what has happened since the *U. Herald* last reported anything. "Bloody Saints," Nadine gasps.

Tolcher, on the other hand, looks like he may shit his pants.

"You *married* him?"

I only shrug, not willing to read deeper into any judgment he may have about it. "What other choice did I have?" I ask, but my voice clearly carries pain.

"I'm . . . I'm so sorry, Lady Venus," Nadine says in a tone that almost sounds fearful, like she may very well grovel for mercy in the next few moments. "If it helps, you still need to hear the good news."

"What could possibly make any of this better?" I grumble.

"Your sister, Geneva. She's having the baby."

Greer stands outside the door to the infirmary, waving me over when she catches sight of me at the end of the hall.

"How is she?" I pant, still mid movement when I ask about Genny.

"She's been contracting for hours," Greer whispers. "Shouldn't be too much longer."

"Where's Slater?" I ask, knowing if he's in there with Genny, my first responsibility will be to promptly expel him from the room.

"As far away as he can get from here," she chortles. "The man cannot handle blood."

Of course not.

I push through the double doors, instantly assessing the sliding tray of tools and other supplies needed for Genny's immediate care. Some of the utensils are enough to make me shiver, especially in the context of sticking them—

"Where the *hell* have you been?" Genny snaps, one hand reaching to soothe an ache in her side and the other situating the cold towel draped across her forehead.

I swallow. "Taking care of a few things," I answer nervously. "But I'm all done, now, and I'm not going anywhere."

"Great," Calliope huffs, moving from Genny's bedside to trade spots with me. She nearly shoves me up towards her. "*Your* fingers can take a turn being crushed by her iron grip."

I willingly accept my fate, knowing that in these last seven days, I've been through much worse than having my bones crunched. For starters, Slater has wanted only one thing from me practically nonstop since I officially became Heiress Apparent. The feeling of triumph swept away any rational thought his head could hold. And while I complied to his whims, I had to admit to myself, I feared this new person marriage had made him become. Now that he had possession of me, there were only two things that made him happy: having sex and berating me about how long it'll be before we find Jericho.

"I mean, shit, what's the issue?" he griped, referring

to the latter in conversation with me two days ago.

"Jericho's tricky," I say flatly. "Our guards are doing their best—"

"Well, their best *sucks*, Venus. My men would've found him by now."

I tried stroking his arm. "I understand your frustration, but—"

"Father wants proof you got to Jericho," Slater told me, his voice laced with venom. It was a miracle I didn't rip into him about always interrupting me. "So if you cannot provide me with a body, he's going to call me a fool for believing you could hold up to your word. Do you *want* my father to think you're an embarrassment?"

As Slater spoke the words, his large hands grappled against the soft skin on my arms, the movement so forceful I yelped. He did not budge. "You will answer your husband when he asks you a question."

I wanted to spit in his face. "No."

"No, *what*?"

When I didn't immediately answer, Slater yanked my arm out of socket, and the sound that came out of me—shock and sudden pain—reverberated through the hallway. Eli came running, and it took all the strength inside of me to insist he stand down. "No, sir," I said stiffly, not thrilled whatsoever to give Slater the satisfaction of respect.

"Fix your own damn arm," he snarled before throwing me off him.

I wonder if my sisters sense it yet—the slow dissipation of hope and confidence in my system that is steadily being replaced by anxiety. Because if anyone can sniff it out, it's them, but in Genny's hour of need, I cannot allow things to gravitate around me. I refuse to draw focus away from the arrival of my niece or nephew, even if times are grim. Even if my arm still aches from Eli attempting to reset it in my room before anyone else saw.

A midwife comes scuttling into the room, cooing about how *it won't be too long now* or *you're doing great, precious. I just need to check on the little one.*

The woman nearly nose-dives beneath the towel draped over Geneva's legs and center, and Calliope nearly shoots backwards, squawking in horror. Meanwhile, the midwife looks incredibly pleased. "Excellent progress, dearie! Do you feel the urge to push?"

To her credit, Genny appears to maintain her composure, even as she whimpers, "I don't think I can do this."

"You can," Calliope says from the corner, still shielding her eyes.

Geneva groans at the throws of another contraction.

"You must," the midwife chimes in clarification, examining her again with a cheery smile. "And darling, I have a feeling this won't take too long."

Genny pants, and I go to blot the washcloth over her glistened forehead again, drawing a feeble smile out of her. "Forgive me," she whispers frantically.

"For what?" I almost laugh.

And as Geneva Deragon begins to push, she screams violently enough to remind me of a person under gruesome torture.

I resurface from my twenty-minute mental blackout at the first sound of her newborn's cries of life.

Calliope has been sobbing for the last six series of ten-second pushes, nearly choking on her tears as Genny drew in each separating breath before her next pass—all sweat and sorrow and pain. But a new kind of weeping overtakes her as she watches the baby finally break through into the real world. Not one of horror or discomfort at the amount of blood smeared around the child's fresh, wiggly body—but one of overwhelming joy.

Before the midwife raises the baby up for Genny and I to take it in directly, Calliope wails with happiness. "You have a daughter, Genny! It's a girl!"

Frozen in time and space, I watch as the midwife confirms Calliope's great delight, and all at once, I unearth a new appreciation for life—a better understanding for what it is I'm fighting tooth and nail to keep safe.

Trembling within her bed, Geneva reaches for her newborn babe, cradling her with the exact precision an experienced mother of four would have. The moment her fingertips unite with her daughter's fresh skin, her cries emulating the bleating of sheep, Genny looks . . . like life makes sense. Like every let down and heartbreak finally have their explanation. That it was all for the sake of running towards this moment—towards this beautiful, remarkable little baby.

Calliope traps the midwife in a grateful embrace, tough enough to draw a grunt of surprise out of the kind woman, while I watch as Geneva whispers unintelligible sweet nothings into her daughter's ear, ensuring the first words to fall upon her ears are loving.

Saints, I have a niece now.

I feel genuine solace watching Genny soothe my newborn niece, swiping her thumb gently over the baby's left temple. It seems to relieve some individual tension that only Genny could sense she was experiencing, and in efforts to keep a sob from gathering in my throat over how treasured this all is, I find myself asking my sister, "Have you thought of any names yet?"

Genny barely has the strength to shake her head. "No. All I've really determined is ..." and she swallows hard. Shuts her eyes tight, as if a phantom pain jolts within her at the thought. "Cali, you want to tell her for me?"

Calliope's joyous smile falters, melting into something wounded.

"Tell me," I say softly, letting a hand rest gently on Genny's shoulder.

Calliope slowly walks towards me. "She wants the baby to bear the Deragon name."

My head tilts to hers sharply. "Genny, are you sure?"

I do not dare to mention Kurt's name, not when I can only imagine how hard it must be to experience this day, this moment, without him. And even so, Genny smiles faintly. "Kurt was wonderful, and I certainly had a soft spot for him. Truth be told, I wanted so desperately to love him, and maybe I did . . ." she says, and before she continues, the midwife takes her daughter from her arms and out of the room, setting off to clean her up and jot down her measurements.

"But Kurt made it clear the way he wanted me," Genny explains. "He loved how I was his best-kept secret, and I complied with his wishes for privacy because I thought if

I waited long enough, he'd change his mind. He'd want to share me with the world. But truthfully, I wonder if his death gave me the mercy of never having him break my heart. I mean, what if our daughter . . . what if her existence spoiled his secrecy and he wanted nothing to do with her or me?"

Calliope and I both want to offer her some sort of rebuttal, but the fact is, Kurt never showed face in our home, nor did Geneva ever speak of him aloud. Sharing a room with her, I saw the signs of a covert romance, but never pried further than that. "I'd like to believe," I begin to say without really recognizing it, "that he would've been overjoyed to be a father."

"I'll never know either way," she simply replies, and then, I watch as something turns her soft eyes ice-cold as they angle towards mine. "But I do know this. If I bestow her father's name upon her, I will be deliberately hurting the man you love every time he looks at her."

A wave of sadness crashes over me, and I mean to take a step back, but Genny's fingers loop through my own. Her touch provides bittersweet comfort. "I learned to find forgiveness for him a while ago," she continues. "But the moment I realized what Jericho has become to you, what *you* have become to him—"

My voice cracks as I whisper her name, a last-ditch effort to keep me from splintering. And Geneva finishes with, "I knew I wanted to honor that."

I shut my eyes, shake my head in disbelief, but Calliope comes over, running her hands down my arms before enveloping me in a nurturing, safe embrace—and I come undone entirely.

"I just know," I choke out, a teardrop falling onto Calliope's honey-brown skin. "That Jericho would've wanted to be here for you today. I . . ." Everything in my soul hurts as I tell her, "I can *feel* it."

Calliope nods against my shoulder as the door to the infirmary reopens, revealing Genny's daughter swaddled in fresh linens, no longer crying. The midwife says nothing, understanding the gravity of the conversation she has walked in on. Handing Geneva her baby, she reaches for a handkerchief stashed away in her pockets and extends it to me. I do not bother refusing her, wiping at my eyes as they continue to leak.

"I thought . . ." Genny murmurs, even as her undivided attention falls upon her little girl, eyes slowly wilting with sleep. "I thought you'd like to name her."

I instantly balk. "Genny . . ."

"You gave me a life I never dreamed could be possible," she says sternly, even as the volume of her words remains soft and tender. "And I know Calliope feels the same. Sure, Jericho played a part in it all, too, but where it really counted, it was all you. I won't hammer you over the head with what we all know you did for our sakes, but in most scenarios, you willingly took on too much—and I only hope that my daughter grows up to be even half as resilient as you are, Venus."

Unable to dwell on my past too long without shattering internally, I instead look at my niece, now dozing peacefully in the arms of my little sister. And while I do not wish to be in Genny's role, I take heart in having this consolation piece of motherhood. To get to watch from the wings as Genny excels in raising a child up from the roots of adversity and into a life of love and security.

"Pandora," I say.

Calliope and Geneva give each other a knowing look, as if something forever shifted in the atmosphere. "Pandora . . ." she says weakly, then glances down at her newborn babe once more. "I've never heard that name before, but . . . it's beautiful."

"It's elegant," Calliope adds. "It reminds me of music somehow."

"Pandora Deragon," Geneva sighs, as if her daughter's name is a song. "I love it."

There is no need for me to bring Slater's story into this moment, nor any word of the danger setting sail across the Damocles as we convene together. For now, I'm fine with letting my sisters go about their lives believing her name is a figment of beautiful imagination. I shall gladly go to my grave knowing that my niece was named after a myth—or, in some way, after her Aunt Venus.

The girl who unleashed hell on the natural world.

61
Venus

Ardian and I take a hastened breakfast together, both of us eating a plate of eggs and two sausage links that go cold the longer we stare down one another. With Slater on his way to meet his father and Diana down in Honeycomb Harbor, I know that we have minimal time to iron things out—and by that, I mean that he has minimal time to interrogate me on what the hell I'm up to. He comes right out and verbalizes it in that manner, too. To which I merely reply, "Cutting to the chase so soon, are we?"

"You locked me in the interrogation cells," he reminds me, his tone blunt. "*You* did that."

I disregard his frustration. "No, *'Good morning, Lady Venus?'* Not even a polite *'hello'*?"

Ardian sets his fork down right as I have the gall to grin at him, taking a taunting bite of my eggs. "I thought you wouldn't stoop to his level."

I nearly fly out of my chair, hands white-knuckle

gripping the boardroom table. "*Whose* level?"

Ardian refuses to speak Jericho's name. Instead, he asks a far more fascinating question. "Why did you make me Acting Monarch?"

Without letting Ardian see it too clearly on my face, I use my powers to search his soul for any deceit or duplicity. Anything that would make him an unreliable protector of my secrets—and while I should be flooded with relief when I find nothing condemning, the revelation of true curiosity and innocence begins to make my insides shrivel up. "Because you're the only one that I trust to keep Urovia safe from the Seagraves, even if you were the one to get us into this mess to begin with."

"Am I supposed to believe that despite you being all too eager to drive Jericho out and marry a man he despises, *I* am to blame?"

"He told you not to use the Dial Line. You directly disobeying his order means that you don't trust him or properly observe his authority. *You* betrayed him, not me."

"You are the Heiress of Mosacia," he pushes back, his voice gruff and unforgiving. "You want me to keep Urovia safe from the Seagraves, and yet, *you* are a Seagrave, now."

The words hit me like a blow. I knew what I was getting into when I started on this trail of treachery, but the way Ardian words it now, I realize how deep this really runs. Yes, I took the title of Slater's counterpart, but I also took his name. I am the very thing I swore to myself I would destroy.

"So which way is it, Venus? Whose side are you really on?"

"The side that keeps Jericho alive, no matter what

it costs me," I hiss, laying all my cards out on the table. "The fact that you even have to ask me that proves that you may not be the man I thought you were to him. Jericho specifically told you not to do one thing, and instead, you called up our enemies and willingly brought them into our home."

"For the last time," he stiffens, preparing to yell at me. "Mosacia is *not*—"

But I merely slam down the folded editions of the *U. Herald* I've written since Jericho has been gone, and despite his irritation, Ardian picks them up with pursed lips and begins reading.

"I hope that when you finish these," I sneer, "you're ashamed of yourself. Because yes, I did what I did—every last bit of it—but I did it for Jericho. So I'll leave it up to you. You can rat me out to Victor and tell him that my marriage to Slater is a sham, or . . . you can prove to me that you're not another slimy cowardice traitor and help me fix this. You get ten minutes to decide."

Departing from the boardroom, I return to my rooms to dress, fishing through the sea of hangers and fabrics. Eventually, I find the last blue dress I haven't worn yet, and for good reason. It's practically sheer, with minimal lining and blue-tinted pearls dotted across spots that will land ironically when I put the garment on. Thin, cerulean gloves of a similar material pair well with the provocative dress—which, the longer I look at it, strikes me more as a functional piece of lingerie.

No excuses. Let's finish this.

Moments later, Roxie and I coast through the grand foyer and emerge into the daylight of the morning.

My eyes examine the grassy terrain beyond the massive doorway and make purchase on a sleek, obsidian carriage—the same one Jericho had ridden into the marshes when he first came to find me. Wheels rattling against the sloped trails leading up to Broadcove Castle's raised elevation, I secretly hope the stark change in altitude upsets their systems, anything to delay the inevitable.

Sensing the unease in me, Roxie nuzzles the side of her face against my shin, and I briefly bend over to stroke the fur along the top of her head. "Be a good girl, okay? We don't like any of them, but we must pretend."

Roxie trills in response, which I only hope counts as faithful acknowledgement. I shoot a passing glance down to Honeycomb Harbor, if only to provide myself the passing mercy of not watching the carriage draw near. *Crystal Wrath* tosses faintly on the waves, still rocking from the arrival of Victor's and Diana's vessel, its name too small to detect from this vantage point. Otherwise, the Harbor lies vacant, a peaceful contrast to—

"Saints," I breathe, clapping a hand over my mouth to muzzle my shock. My heart thunders with sudden, unexpected hope.

Honeycomb Harbor is *empty*.

"Quite the getup," a sly, female voice comments from behind me.

Despite my best efforts to ignore her remark, I recall her saying something similar before standing at my side, as Diana did for Slater, while I prepared to pledge my love for Slater during our wedding. Every repetition was a deeper, more traitorous lie, and Calliope and I both knew it. Even so, Calliope never budged, nor did she speak up when Ardian offered her the chance to disapprove and derail the ceremony. And perhaps that allows me to learn something about her—that she trusts me. That I can trust her. With everything.

I reveal to her with a conniving smile, "The boats are gone."

Her brow crooks. "What boats?"

"Every last boat dedicated to the Hive's operations."

Calliope's attention darts towards the docks below, but only for a moment. "Holy shit," she chuckles, grinning ear to ear. "We did it."

"We did." I beam, letting the familiar wind of Merrie's lingering presence cast warmth over my dry skin. A silent symbol of her gratitude, just enough to soothe me as the dark carriage clanks against the cobblestone path and finally parks under the awning.

The coachman hops down from his perch, and Calliope straightens out her spine, clasping my hand in hers one last time before the door opens. Diana steps out first, taking the coachmen's extended hand with a gentle smile. Behind her, Slater resurfaces from the carriage, his golden hair tied off in a knot along the back of his head. I curse the way it makes him almost look handsome, and he senses my attention poise along the side of his face. His eyes veer towards mine, then cast downward. He does not bother to hide his snide satisfaction, and casually walks towards me. Pressing a kiss to my neck, he whispers in my ear, "You're lucky my family's here, or else I'd do unspeakable things to you in that dress right now."

Anxiety curdles up in my belly, and to my horror, Calliope pieces together what she managed to hear and stifles a gag.

And then, King Victor emerges.

From what I know about Victor's and Jericho's political relations, Victor hasn't set foot in Urovia in at least three years, so I certainly anticipated his entrance to be big. I imagined a navy cape flowing five feet behind him as he walked, his obnoxious crown sparkling in the morning light, and maybe even a silver scepter in his hand that he'd use as a walking staff. But this version of Victor is unexpected.

His typical regalia has been swapped for an indigo button down and dark slacks. Shined, black loafers click against the pavement, and despite his salt and pepper hair, his wardrobe makes him appear younger, like this is a leisure trip as opposed to a legal gathering. No crown, no cape, no extravagance. Just himself, a refreshing reality. Still, I bow before him. "Welcome to Broadcove, Your Majesty"

"Hello, Venus," he says with a smile that could shift gravity. "I must admit, seeing you on my son's arm is a sight for sore eyes."

As opposed to Jericho's, I hear him think but conveniently leave out.

"It's a refreshing feeling," I assure him. I cling tighter to Slater's bicep, and he flexes at the touch, puffing himself up. I know the gesture makes him look further like a buffoon given the giggle Calliope isn't quite able to hide, which earns her a glare from Diana. The sudden movement also draws Victor's attention towards her. "My apologies," I quickly blurt. "Where are my manners? King Victor, this is my older sister, Calliope Deragon. Calliope, this is my father-in-law."

Although I manage to say his relational title to me with a bashful newlywed's grin, Diana instantly tenses up. Calliope catches it, too, and gregariously curtseys. "It's an honor."

Wow, this one's even lovelier than Venus, I feel Victor contemplate.

While I always grew up knowing I bore my father's hard angles and alluring stare, my sisters all took after our mother. And in Calliope's case, she inherited one of her specific traits that I understand instantly draws Victor's approval—her softer complexion. It makes me want to snap the bones in his arms with my bare hands.

"How is Queen Harriet?" I try to make pleasant conversation.

"Fine," Victor shares plainly, not particularly thrilled to have the attention be taken away from himself and not wanting to elaborate further. "We can discuss more about her and the children later. Might we attend to these documents first?"

"Gladly," I oblige.

"Lead the way," Diana grunts, hauling her baggage into Calliope's hands as if she were the help.

Prissy, spoiled bitch, I hear Calliope shout into the walls of her mind, even as she shifts her weight to properly carry Diana's luggage. Or maybe she is merely collecting her balance so she can launch her belongings back at her. A tug from Slater careens my sights away from Calliope and back towards the castle, an arm hooked across my lower back and his hand lazily stroking the side of my hips. My heeled shoes click against the gilded flooring of the entryway as we press onward. "Where's my *other* daughter?" Victor calls out from behind me, he and Diana trailing us. "I only noticed after my two oldest set sail the first time that she was . . . a stowaway," he finishes carefully.

"Probably sulking somewhere, not speaking to anyone," Slater chortles.

"I know she's enjoyed walking the gardens now and then," I defend gently. "There's a greenhouse out there where she likes to sit."

Diana's silence chills me to the bone, and I reach my power out towards her as seamlessly as I can manage. *Merrie's greenhouse?* she wonders calculatedly to herself.

All I think about is violence. If Diana so much as mentions wanting to visit it herself—

I force myself to shake away the thoughts. "Is her presence required for this gathering?"

"Not at all," Victor says casually. "In fact, her presence will not be anyone's dilemma anymore, because she has been written out of the Seagrave family records."

That makes all of us stop in our tracks, me especially. "I beg your pardon?"

King Victor amusedly watches how sharply both Slater and I turn around to check if he's serious. "She's of no use to me," he says plainly, even as I hear his conscience whisper to me, *She is traitorous filth to this family and nothing more.* "Disobedient, stubborn, pathetic."

There's a nasty emphasis on the final remark, one

that makes spit fly off the edge of his mouth. The only thing keeping me from lashing out on all three of them is the fact that no one laughs in response. Slater forces my feet to turn back towards our original direction, and we pass through another hallway before Ardian conveniently resurfaces. "Your Majesty."

"Mr. Asticova," Victor says, his voice uncharacteristically bright. "It's good to see you."

"Likewise." Ardian's weary eyes drift towards Diana. "You as well, Princess. Glad to—"

"Here we are," I cut in sharply, not particularly interested in hearing false flattery from Jericho's Head Councilman—especially for the likes of Diana. He only curtly nods, understanding his place, and I swing open the doors to the banquet hall.

62
Venus

It saddens me to have not utilized this space while Jericho was still here. I spent so much time griping at him or avoiding him entirely to ever have supper with him here, a room not quite as formidable as the ballroom, but a stronghold, nonetheless.

Whereas the ballroom has stunning paintings lining the ceilings, these ones hang low, giving me the perception that the banquet hall is shrinking by the second—or perhaps that is because all thirty of Greer, Diana, and Slater's assassins are already situated in their seats. To my great relief, however, no new faces seem to circulate amongst the space, meaning Victor was foolish enough to come here without his own set of protection. Worried my eyes may be lingering too long on some of the threatening faces lined along the table's edge, I let them quickly pan towards the walls, where ornate scribblings look etched into its construction. Rather than have everyone face inward at a circular table, the one we approach in silence is rectangular, with two solitary heads on either side of a sea of people.

As Victor and his children file into the banquet hall— the enormous dining table set for a company of forty-five according to my headcount—I dash briefly into the kitchen's revolving side door. I do not bother to check my surroundings beyond ensuring I did not smack into any of the staff when I burst through the door. I just need a moment, a split second to breathe deeply, let my guard down—

"Don't tell them I'm here," a timid voice whispers.

Greer stands huddled in the corner, motionless amongst the many cupboards, but alert in a way that reminds me of a cat sensing its looming predator. I fight the knee-jerk reaction to gasp, swallowing hard on the sound. "I don't think that will be an issue."

Greer frowns at me, more confused than anything else.

"He wrote you out of the family," I blurt, immediately unsure if telling Greer the truth was the right thing to do.

An ancient form of anger flashes over her eyes, wrinkling the harsh scar that spans across her face. It is obvious in this moment that as much as Victor's decision to sever ties with her frees her, it hurts her just as strongly. "Meaning Mother agreed to it," she whispers through her teeth.

I hadn't even thought about the possibility of her being involved. But, then again, they rule jointly, and with the arrival of a new baby girl . . . she probably saw Emmaline as a future replacement for Greer. It makes me sick to my stomach. "Greer, I'm sorry. I just—"

"Everything's set, per your request," she manages to inform me, unwilling to discuss the matter further. I watch as the muscles in her arms twitch from where they rest crossed against her chest—a last ditch effort to protect herself. "I'll have the servants bring everything out shortly. Now get out of here, if you're gone too long, they'll start asking questions."

I slip out as quickly as I entered, resurfacing into the banquet hall where, just as Greer predicted, Slater and his father eye me curiously. "Just checking on the preparations. The staff is uncorking the champagne as we speak."

Victor nods in approval and as he sinks into his chair first, the fleet of guards rises from their own—a sign of respect for the guest of honor. Ardian follows. Then, Diana and Slater, and I follow suit at his side. One of Slater's designated guards pushes me further towards the table, mannerly and dignified, and only after I'm completely settled do the rest of those present feel comfortable returning to their seats.

"I'd like to thank you all again for being here," Ardian begins from the far end, his voice pronounced enough for all of us to distinguish clearly. "Crossing the Damocles and giving up the comforts of Sevensberg Palace to convene with us is no small ask, and this gathering is a semblance of our gratitude."

Right on cue, a line of Broadcove staff file into the room, their gloved hands braced beneath circular trays of glittering champagne flutes. Stars fizzle within the golden liquid, and a unique sunshine quality about them winks at me in vague recognition. I smile as they sporadically set the glasses down before our guests.

"And a celebration," Victor chimes in, positioning his glass to his liking on the table. "In honor of my son finally taking a wife, safeguarding the future of our empire."

Diana bristles at the implication that her works mean nothing. All her scheming and secrecy and indirect killing: what did it amount to if Victor never felt inclined to acknowledge it? "Marriage is simple," she remarks under her breath. "Anyone could do it."

"Yet here you are. Single—unaccounted for by a suitor," her father notes bluntly, having heard every word out of her mouth.

To her credit, Diana bottles up her intended response, and I try not to chuckle at her foul choice of language that only I can hear. Still, Victor feels the need to further comment on her insolence and disruption. "My children exist to protect my legacy," Victor bellows. "The longer you avoid settling down, you endanger me," he says, then realigns his gaze towards me. "But the moment Slater tied himself to you in marriage, you ensured my legacy. More so, by uprooting Jericho, you ensured the growth of the empire, and I'd like to reward you for your efforts."

Something about the word reward makes my heartbeat quicken, and I feel the mood of the room shift into something expectant. Diana practically white knuckles the edge of the table, and I'm not entirely sure that Ardian draws breath.

"There's a great deal to be said about a woman who can charm not only a prince, but a king," Victor drawls, his voice carrying a tone that typically pairs well with pacing about the room. It almost terrifies me how still he is as he speaks to me. "The world is changing, and meek women endanger themselves the longer they play nice. But you . . . you are a paragon of intellect, and surely prove to be a worthy recipient of my wife's crown."

He removes a pen from his pocket, snapping the tip upward with a singular click.

"Father," Diana snarls. "Not now. Not like this."

Even Ardian seems lost. "Would someone care to explain what's going on here?"

"I never wanted a seventh child," Victor says quietly, and I cannot clearly read if he exudes sorrow and grief or eternal annoyance. "But Harriet kept hounding me about wanting to bring more lives into the world, lives we didn't need when we already had the two of you," he says, offering some sort of softness towards Slater and Diana. But it only lasts for a passing moment. "When she became pregnant again, I resented her, considering the last two times she had given birth, one child was born with permanent deficiencies and then the twins nearly killed her. Frankly, we were too old to become parents a seventh time, but Harriet didn't care."

In silence, Victor Seagrave begins to deconstruct the pile of documents and licenses, and for the first time ever, I seek Slater's comfort in order to prepare for the inevitable.

"Emmaline passed three days in," Victor states, "and without the baby to distract her from the blood loss she experienced from delivering, Harriet succumbed soon after."

Tears fall down Ardian's face freely, but he seems to be the only one truly distraught by the news. As shaken as I am internally, I save face for Slater's sake, who seems to be taking in the concept of his mother's death with fresh ears.

"But you won't," he cuts back in, Victor's sharp glare once more poised on me. "You've never succumbed to weakness, Venus. And neither has my son."

Then, Victor passes the top piece of text-covered parchment to Ardian for further assessment. "So it is, therefore, my right to grant ownership and governance of the Mosacian Empire to you and Slater effective immediately."

Ardian guffaws, clearly in disbelief as he reads his copy of the agreement. I fight the urge to echo his sentiment. "However," Victor continues, "I'd like to make an addendum to the agreement, one that reads—"

Ardian raises from his seat, reading the transcription aloud. "Should Venus survive Slater, I, Victor Seagrave, being of sound mind and body, endow her with the responsibilities of ruling the Mosacian Empire . . . in solidarity."

I realize in the span of a few short moments that the document Ardian reads from is a copy of what Victor has set before him—a document he now inks into the page with a flamboyant signature.

Even if Diana or Slater had a rebuttal against the document, his name on the bottom line refutes it forever— and I masquerade my sinister delight as honorable surprise.

"A toast," King Victor proclaims, and every guest at the table rises to their feet. We universally reach for our champagne. "To the groom and his bride—the new rulers of the Mosacian Empire!"

Everyone cheers—even the hired herd of lethal muscle—and clinks their glasses together before taking hearty swigs of the golden liquid. So consumed with the realization of what has just transpired, I cannot find the means to even sip my own drink, meanwhile, nearly everyone else at the table shoots their entire celebratory champagne down the backs of their throats. Considering how sobering of company the Seagraves are, it certainly would not surprise me if the guards are rarely afforded alcohol, especially the kind of quality that this bottle holds.

At the sound of merriment, two King's Guard members enter the room—Eli and Tolcher. They smile at me as nonchalantly as they can despite knowing the gravity of this moment. Ardian, too. He flashes me a knowing look as he folds up his copy of the document and hands it to Eli, who then tucks it away within one of his uniform pockets. In turn, Tolcher whispers something in Ardian's ear, something that makes his face change into an emotion I cannot read. He raises his glass towards me in unknown acknowledgement, and as his lips touch the rim, he stops—puts the drink down.

Something's off.

I know it instinctually, my powers shifting at the unspoken apprehension coursing through the veins of the man sitting across from me. First, his eyes begin to twitch, and he rubs at it with his index finger before dismissing the sensation. Then, I see him place that same hand over his chest, as if experiencing the kind of heartburn that interrupts you mid-sentence. "Somethin' wrong, mate?"

the guard next to him inquires, but just as steadily, the same symptomatic response begins to overtake him, too.

My eyes scanning the room, I begin to realize that every guest here that carries a weapon has begun to sweat. Severely. The two gentlemen closest to Diana even begin to fan at themselves, desperate for cooler circulation.

And then, the first guard I noticed struggling begins to cough up blood.

Diana screams, jumping back from the table. Slater grabs me, pulling me away from the scene in a way that makes me believe he is more worried someone will stain my dress in their distress than about the people themselves. Ardian, all the while, watches from his seat at one end of the table, immobilized by his horror as more of the guards begin to sputter. Clutch at their chests.

Eyes wide with panic, I watch as people experience the crippling sensation in different stages. Some are only beginning to feel their body heat spike, some cannot seem to catch a full breath, and others begin to have tears leak from their eyes.

No. Not tears.

Blood.

I shriek, clinging to Slater, who instinctively tells me to close my eyes and stay behind him—but shutting my eyes only makes the cacophony of pain and misery grow louder and more precise. I hear every drop of fluid hit the table or spew from their mouths or remain lodged in their throats, yet it doesn't compare to the newest sound entering the room and reverberating along the walls.

The sound of people slumping onto the table and staying there.

Hiding most of my face behind Slater's massive build, I dare to peek out at the scene, unable to look away any longer. The dining table is painted scarlet with blood and littered with bodies that, moments ago, fought to gasp for air. It's almost too much to comprehend.

It's just as I intended.

King Victor stands to his feet, though slightly off kilter. His rage is diffused by the fear taking over his eyes. "Sabotage," he manages to say.

And then, his knees hit the floor and his full weight crumples into a heap on the ground.

His eyes remain open in death, a single, bloody tear proof of the poison his guards consumed alongside him.

Diana's horrified screams are shrill in our ears, and another cluster of King's Guard members stationed throughout the nearby hallways come rushing in at the sound. Ardian retches, and in between the ghastly sounds of his body coming to terms with such turmoil, he stops. Eyes me from across the room.

What have I done, I hear Ardian shudder in his mind.

My responding grin is vile.

Thank you for your service, Head Councilman.

Ardian balks at the words he hears in his head but does not see spoken from my mouth. He almost scuttles out of the room, his brain coming to terms with too many things at once—my blessing, but more so, his unknown responsibility in my latest scheme.

The moment he understood the magnitude of what Delta and the Seagraves had done; he became consumed with sorrow—guilt. In his haste to get some air, he assured me that he'd do whatever I needed him to do in order to get us out of this hostile situation. However, knowing Ardian's track record with detesting vengeance and bloodshed, I chose to be sparingly with the details. All I required of him was to find Greer and have her gather a bundle of Belladonnas from North Star—assuming that Ardian did not know shit about flowers and gardening.

I was correct.

"*You* did this," Diana accuses, boldly pointing a manicured finger at me.

"No," a new voice says from where the kitchen door lies. "I did."

Greer stands, fists clenched at her sides, with a disgustingly satisfied smile on her scarred face. As desperately as I want her to take off and run from the scene, I feel empowered by the way she takes back her confidence in the eternal absence of her father's violence.

"You *talk* again?" Diana gasps.

"I do a lot more than talk," she gleams, and then, Greer reveals an all-too familiar dagger, still stained with blood.

"Where the hell did you get that?" Diana gasps, retreating from her presence long enough to unsheathe one of her deceased guards' swords.

"From Delta's corpse," she reveals, simmering with anticipation. Greer's magnetic eyes stare down Diana in defiance. "Tell me, sister, do you want a face to match mine?"

"Get her out of here!" Ardian bellows.

I figure that the gathering crowd of King's Guards are going to barrel down towards Greer or split the two women apart from one another. Maybe even restrain

Slater.

But instead, Eli and Tolcher rush for me, yanking me away from Slater, whose vision has become clouded with rage that cannot be diluted or redirected. Greer stands prepared for a fight, for a life-or-death altercation, and as a few of the guards draw their weapons, I hear Ardian instruct Tolcher and Eli, "Take her to the interrogation chamber."

The interrogation chamber?

I kick and scream, trying to fight their hold on me, but Tolcher hisses at me to stop resisting even after we're out of the room. The pace of my heart rate skyrockets, dangerously so. "We have to save her!" I try to rationalize, if only to get a moment to break free from their unrelenting grip.

"Our instructions are to keep you out of harm's way. Not her. And considering Greer chose to break her silence to cover for you," Eli adds pointedly, "I am pretty sure she doesn't want outside intervention."

"But they'll *kill* her—"

"It's a *diversion*," Tolcher tells me, hefting me forward.

Time slows. "Why would she risk her life for the sake of a—"

Eli throws open the door to the interrogation room, and not having comprehended how close the cells were in correlation with the banquet hall, I suddenly feel the need to fight harder, dirtier. I scrape my nails across the skin on Tolcher's neck, but even as he yelps in pain, Eli hooks his arm around my middle and hurls me into the room, shrouded in darkness.

Before he can shut me within the tomb-like space, I

brace my hands against the door and struggle to push my bodyweight against Eli's formidable muscle. "I'll make sure your sisters are safe. Pandora, too," he tries to assure me, as if his words will make me let up.

I gain an inch of ground, but Tolcher finally overcomes the initial sting of his deep scratch. "Go in willingly, or I'll have to lock you inside."

"Don't you dare—"

Suddenly, an invisible force snakes its phantom arms around me, pulling me backwards into the darkness. I watch in horror as Eli and Tolcher slam the door in my face, and before I can emit a cry for help, a hand covers my mouth. "You're in trouble now," a male voice whispers in the dark, almost dementedly happy.

That *voice*.

Slowly, as if worried I'll scream fire, that unseen hand moves away from my mouth, reaching out to turn on the lights in the room.

And in the exact moment the mirrored walls cast multiplied versions of me once more sheltered in Jericho's arms, I come apart entirely.

63
Jericho

Venus tackles me onto the marbled floor, and I'm too enchanted by the long-awaited luxury of holding her again to care. I refuse to hold back, knowing I spent the last week fearing she was dead, that someone discovered the *U. Herald's* she published to slander our enemies and punished her for it. So I take this time to run my fingers along her back, smell the scent of her hair, brush a kiss along her neck.

The moment she pulls away, looking over me as if to convince herself I'm real, Venus's eyes line with tears. "I thought I'd lost you."

"Not a chance, Venom," I assure her, stroking the side of her face. "You'll never get rid of me."

She laughs as our mouths crash together, all teeth and tongues and desperation. Kissing Venus feels like having a glass of water after days of endless thirst, like a lifesaving antidote coursing through veins poisoned by distance and time. Venus climbs onto my lap, the lacy gloves along her arms tickling my chest as she tugs open my shirt. "If one of us should be getting out of their clothes, it's you," I whisper, casting my eyes down her dress. "I'm sick of seeing you wearing their colors."

"Then do something about it," she sneers, grinding her hips against me as she guides my hand towards one of the straps. Then, her fingers crawl up my scalp, trying to find purchase on hair she can no longer grapple. "Why'd you—"

She gasps as I draw my tongue up the column of her throat. "It'll grow back."

I pull her closer to me by the length of her hair, hiking her upwards. She gasps, but still leans back enough to let me whisper in her ear, "Keep that attitude up, and I'll put you back in chains."

Suddenly, the door violently swings open and I move to cover Venus with my body until she can manage to fix the bodice of her dress. Not bothering to glance up nor wanting to go into a full-fledged lecture, I merely huff a breath, sick of being cockblocked. "We're in the middle of something Tolcher—"

A hard shove throws me off balance, and I go rolling across the marbled floor. I hit my shoulder before coming to a stop, and I'm damn near ready to sock my fist into Tolcher's teeth for it when I hear a smack against skin and Venus's sharp hiss of pain.

My head rockets upward in time to see Slater draw back his hand, aiming to strike her face again.

"You better fucking *not*," I sneer, already launching to my feet.

Venus holds out a hand, silently urging me not to

move.

She thinks he's armed. Worse, she thinks I cannot defend myself.

Meanwhile, Slater doesn't look the least bit concerned about me. Instead, his attention focuses wholly on Venus. "*What* do you think you're doing with him?"

When she does not answer him immediately, Slater grabs Venus by the throat hard enough to bruise her.

"*LET HER GO!*"

Venus struggles against him, not strong enough to pull his massive hands away. I can see her eyes bulge, blood vessels popping along the inner corners. "I thought you said he was taken care of," he seethes.

"You told me to produce a body," Venus chokes out, still staying true to her character one last time. "You didn't specify that he had to be dead. Here he is."

"At what cost, Venus? Whoring yourself out to him?"

I've never seen Slater Seagrave so enraged in my entire life. And I sense it within her, in the way Venus's glare shifts as she stares Slater down—the roleplay isn't worth it anymore. Not when he's got her in a chokehold and hitting below the belt.

"It's what I had to do to sink you," she finally sneers.

And in signature Venus Deragon style, she spits in his face.

Slater practically rips the substance out of his eyes, his red-hot anger making the room feel sweltering. He huffs heavy breaths like he may very well combust, but then, something shifts over his face, and I soon realize what it is: humor—realization.

"Your brilliance truly knows no bounds." Slater

laughs. "I mean, poisoning all those guards? Killing Father? Having *Greer* take the fall for you? That's stooping to Jericho's level, sure."

And then, lowering himself to her level, Slater draws Venus close, a claiming action. I mean to make a run for him, to rip his eyes out of his skull, but then, he tells her, "But marrying me to keep your ruse intact? That's a new kind of evil."

I think I may be sick.

"You . . . " I say for no reason at all. "You're his *wife*?"

Slater finds great amusement in knowing how clueless I was, but Venus isn't focused on how blindsided and disturbed. She refuses to break eye contact with her husband. "You killed Greer?"

"She was easy prey, and *you* set her up for her own slaughter."

Wrath wrinkles Venus's lovely face, casting a shadow of death over her hazel eyes. "Funny," she grinds out, her voice guttural. "I figured you would watch Diana do the grunt work of killing her for you. She was always far more pragmatic than you."

Slater only chuckles. Just once. "Nah, I took care of Greer. But rest assured, Diana's doing her part. I think she heard your niece crying. Maybe she went to check on that."

Something within Venus snaps entirely.

Venus, he's bluffing. He's testing you. Do not listen to him. There's no way Eli would let Diana get close—

But my words are lost to her, and Venus begins to scream.

It's the most gut-wrenching, terrifying, awful sound

in the world. It's anguish and all-consuming fury. It's the blatant threat of her darkest fear, and Slater capitalizes off it. I do not know how Venus possibly draws enough air to scream her lungs out when her air supply is constricted by his hands, but something about the sound unhinges Slater enough to where his concentration buckles.

I side-swipe him, launching my entire weight into Slater and assaulting him onto the floor. Venus crumples into the ground, her throat clawing for air and coughing hard enough to puncture her lungs. Slater and I crash into the ground, his temple taking the brunt of the fall, and he shouts out in pain. The sound of bone fracturing makes my stomach turn, and I watch as blood begins to leak from the side of his head.

And then, I'm wailing on him.

Punch after punch, pummeling Slater into the ground as if he could sink further into it. Gashes open across my knuckles with each violent slam, and I do not care. I do not care that he flails his feet in attempts to kick me off. I do not care that Slater gnashes his teeth and says vile things about Venus in attempts to rile me. I've gone deaf to his cries and blind to his agony. My clenched fists land across his face and his foul words begin to morph into calls for a ceasefire, perhaps even mercy. Soon, I hear him gag on one of his teeth that have flown to the back of his throat.

My body thrums with electricity, my soul recharging.

I'm going to kill him.

He begins to slip away from consciousness, and I smile like nothing has made me happier in this lifetime. But then, I feel Venus's gentle touch on my lower back, and I stop long enough to look at her. Her eyes are closed and her lips purse with concentration. "Move," I barely make out from her lips.

Slater starts to regain control of himself, and I jam my knee into his groin to knock him down again. "What?" I ask her.

That's when a monstrous, blood-curdling sound echoes through the hallway, getting closer with each passing second—

"*Move*," she yells, practically crawling away from Slater's frame.

I only let up in time to separate myself from Slater right as a fucking tiger enters the room, pounding across the marbled floor and launching onto Slater like a hunk of meat.

"HOLY SAINTS!" I scream, rolling away from its path, doing my best to shield Venus from the unknown beast in case it decides to turn its ravenous hunger towards us.

But the creature buries its maw into Slater and thrashes him around like a lifeless doll, digging its sharp fangs into his intestines. Slater makes no sound, likely already gone from the world, and as the beast moves upward to detach Slater's head from his body, I look back to see Venus . . . grinning.

"Good girl," she whispers aloud, and I realize that she and the animal know one another.

Slowly, she rises from the flood, bracing both hands on the floor to help regain her balance. It's like watching a doe learn to walk without the help of its mother, but in Venus's case, a maniacal sort of power radiates within her, like a phoenix rising from the ashes. Even with her neck lined with dark bruises and her dress slightly disheveled, Venus has never looked more dominant. More majestic.

Venus reaches for her other hand, removing what I now realize is a massive, sapphire wedding ring, and drops it onto the ground. It skitter's towards Slater's body, a final forsaking. And yet, my traitorous tongue still forms the words, "I cannot believe you married him."

Venus has always been smart enough to know where my words come from—how these words, now, come from a place of hurt for her and the things she has gone through since I've been away.

Then, Venus walks towards me, carefully taking my face within her shaky hands. "I loved you every moment you were gone, Jericho. And I knew, even if the Saints never let me see you again, I'd do anything for you. Anything to make you proud." She brushes a tender kiss over my mouth. "So I married Slater Seagrave, and then, I killed my way to his crown—for you. We kill Diana, and there's no one left to stand in our way," she tells me in a hushed tone, "when we lay the Mosacian Empire to waste."

As we lurk through the halls, guarding each other's backs as we drift along, I come clean about all that has occurred since she sent me away. Living with Tolcher in squalor, hiding from the public, eating like a prisoner. I tell her about the night that Nadine brought the first edition of the *U. Herald*, and how I became overcome with the vision of her digging up my mother's grave. And then, I share with her how she single-handedly revived the Hive, how conscriptions littered the mainland and permeated through the districts.

"Chumley is an officer?" she says with delightful intrigue.

"Traded Sevensberg intelligence for the honor."

"I noticed the ships weren't in the harbor today. When did that happen?" she inquires. Slowly, a deeper understanding casts a shadow over her stern features. "Wait, where is the Hive now?"

Even Venus's tiger—who Venus had called Roxie while playfully reprimanding her about the sloppy way she devoured Slater—halts her steps at the question.

"They're crossing the Damocles as we speak," I inform her softly. "Poised to strike Sevensberg Palace the minute they reach the shoreline."

Despite the wake of bloodshed she has created for herself, Venus blanches at the thought of the Hive destroying a palace full of orphans. She places a hand on her forehead, blatantly overwhelmed. I can hear her mental spiral. *Annabelle, the twins.* "And there's no way to contact them?"

"Not the fleet, no."

We get the idea at the same time, and pivot in order to sprint back for the boardroom. Arms pumping, we race down every corridor, up every staircase. Sweat brews along my brow, but not Venus. She's so locked in on the singular objective of saving those kids that any efforts of softening her steps as we stampeded through the castle vanish entirely.

I know this is going to get messy when we discover the

boardroom door is already open.

There are no guards, but there is one person shielding the crimson receiver from view.

Ardian.

I step towards him, hand extended in warning. "Last time you used the Dial Line," I remark, "all hell broke loose."

His dim smile fills me with warmth somehow. "It's good to have you home in one piece."

Venus doesn't bother with small talk or formalities, weaving around Ardian altogether to get to the Dial Line herself. She picks up the receiver, knowing it takes a few moments for the line to ring on their end. Moments pass like years. "Pick up . . ." she whispers delicately, dwindling hope in her voice. "Please pick—Hello?" she begins, pacing briefly as she waits for a reply. "This is Venus Seagrave," she then informs the responder carefully, and the addition of Slater's surname makes me wince. "Slater and I—" she pauses, slight babbling emerging from the other line. "Yes, thank you. But I must urge you to do me a favor, as your ruling Queen."

I lean inwards, but only enough to distinguish the person Venus communicates with as a soft-spoken female—likely a governess or a ladies maid. "Is something wrong?" she replies.

"Is there anyone in the palace that knows how to steer a ship?"

The woman goes quiet for a moment, racking her brain for someone that can do the job adequately. "I can certainly find someone—"

"Find them. Put the children on a ship and sail away

to . . . anywhere else."

"Your Majesty—"

"That's an order. They do not need to be cooped up in a house where their mother has perished."

She promptly hangs up the receiver, and as Ardian scans her in confusion, Venus merely shrugs. "If I warned them outright, they'd anticipate an attack. But those children don't deserve to pay for their family's treachery. They're too young to understand."

"You did a good thing," Ardian says calmly.

She gulps, as if wanting not to open the wound of asking the question, but still pushes through the word, "Greer."

Ardian shuts his eyes. Shakes his head.

Venus shudders, going to battle against the urge to weep, and while I do not know the full extent of Greer's help, I piece enough together to know that she betrayed the Seagraves and Mosacia on more than one occasion. At the very least, she trusted in Venus more than her own family. At most . . . she assisted in the chaos and death that Venus orchestrated.

"My sisters?" she croaks.

"Eli and Tolcher are guarding Geneva and Pandora," Ardian answers.

"What about Calliope?"

My Head Councilman says nothing, and just when his silence is answer enough, Venus's body goes stiff, sensing something uncertain. "Venus?" I exhale. Even Ardian suddenly seems on edge just looking at her. "What's—"

"*Jericho!*" she shouts, dashing for me with terror taking over her eyes.

I do not realize that whatever causes her concern lingers behind me, and in absolute desperation, Venus shoves me out of the way.

For being a smaller woman, the strength she exhibits to push against me is incredible, and I'm so caught up in it that my astonishment nearly masks the sound of steel swinging through the air.

Catching my breath, I see Diana, coated in what must be her sister's blood, carrying a sword from one of the guards. She looks to Ardian with hate smoldering within her green eyes. "Did Venus have the guts to tell you that she killed your niece? Not Greer?"

For the first time in my existence, I watch as Ardian draws his own weapon against another person. "Knowing what the two of you did to Merrie, I say it's well deserved."

She finds Ardian's disloyalty and understanding of the situation to be eternally amusing. "It's a shame those Urovian bastards drained the Mosacian blood right out of you, Mr. Asticova. You could've—"

But the words die in her throat as something yanks her backwards.

No, not something—*someone*.

Calliope doesn't bother giving a menacing speech before twisting her hands sharply around Diana's neck, snapping it. She's dead before her body hits the floor.

I ought to reevaluate every preconceived notion I ever held towards Calliope, now, but a wild sense of realization sweeps over her eyes. Pupils dilated and brows raised in horrified concern, I take a cautious step towards her. "It's okay, Calliope," I tell her, unsure if the understanding of her first kill is sending her into an internal panic. "It's going to be—"

"Jericho . . ." she says, the color seeping out of her face.

I trace her gaze back towards Venus and find her smiling at me. But then, it gives way to a painful grimace.

That's when I notice her hands laid flat against her stomach, and the fresh blood that seeps through her fingers.

Her knees weaken, and my body moves—no, *sprints*—to catch her before she sinks. Ardian moves fast, too, stripping off his top layer and chucking it at me. "Apply pressure," he commands shortly. "I'm going to find a nurse."

Calliope hasn't moved aside from letting her lip quiver.

I take Ardian's clothing, crumpling it up and pressing it firmly against her bleeding stomach. I almost wretch at the way blood spreads out across her dress like branches, and the second I begin pressing my weight into the wound, Venus groans, her eyes shutting tight enough to contort her entire face. "Calliope, go find Eli and Tolcher."

When she doesn't move, frozen in space and time while watching her sister hemorrhage, I finally scream, "GO! *NOW*!"

She weeps as she exits, running at top speed to fulfill orders, leaving Venus and I alone together once more.

"I couldn't . . ." Venus forces out, her lips darkening with blood, ". . . let it be you."

And that's when I remember that the last time I laid eyes on her before this moment was when I watched her shove me out of the path of Diana's stolen sword.

Venus took on my death blow.

She sputters her words again. "It's bad, Jericho."

"That's enough. You're going to be fine," I stammer, beginning to grow angrier.

Still, a depressing acceptance settles over her, and she tries to hold her head up. "We were . . . so . . . close."

"No, Venus," I try to encourage, even as my voice gives away my distress. "You did it. You took their empire. You made them pay, and you brought me home."

She gives her best attempt at a smile, but it instantly falters. My own composure begins to splinter as more blood gathers along Ardian's garments, soaking through the first crumpled layers. Her hand captures the collar of my shirt, tugging me lower, and my heart shatters into a thousand little pieces as she cries without making a sound. "I—" she tries, blood gurgling in her mouth. "I wanted to rule the world with you."

"And we will. I promise," I swear.

Her mouth now full of liquid, Venus reaches out towards my mind. *I love you*, she reminds me, unable to form the words aloud—and the familiarity of this confession is not lost on me. Its reprisal, however, makes this moment feel all the more dire. Final.

"Don't give me that shit. This isn't the time for goodbye."

I refuse to shed a tear and trouble her. I refuse to let Venus think that I'm scared for her, or worse, how terrified I am of the prospects of her leaving me here alone. I try to hide the tremor in my voice, trying to convince myself more than her. "You're okay, Venus."

But her eyes begin to flutter shut, as if being lured into blissful rest, and it snaps something in me.

"*Venus*," I press, gently tapping my hand along the side of her face that doesn't sting from Slater's attack. "You . . . you need to stay awake—"

But it's no use.

Venus's head falls back, neck extended and limbs limp.

And were it not for me already holding the love of my life in my arms, I'd use my hands to tear the entire world to shreds.

64
Venus

There is no blood here. No pain.

But there is also no joy.

Even though I remain in Broadcove Castle, now nestled under a canopy of beautiful wisteria in the middle of an observation terrace, my otherworldly senses comprehend Jericho's absence. And not just his—everyone's.

Ardian, Calliope, Geneva, even little Pandora feels worlds away—like none of them ever existed to begin with.

"I find it interesting," Merrie's comforting, feminine voice says from behind me, "to see that your soul has brought you here first."

I suppose it is rather fascinating, given I haven't dared wander here since the morning I threatened to leap from it into the depths beyond—a last ditch effort to get Jericho talking. As time passed and tensions between him and I transformed into something more than resentment, I silently came to terms with how manipulative it was, and so unkind given my previous assumption of how Merrie met her end. Coupled with what Delta divulged about Ronan, too, I figure this would be the last place I'd ever want to revisit, even in spirit.

I turn on a heel, expecting to converse with the open air and prepare to offer her some falsified excuse—but when my eyes fall upon Merrie Morgan in her full, physical glory, I find myself dipping into a reverent curtsey.

"That's not necessary," she tells me, extending a hand that insists I return to an eased posture. Without a care in the world, Merrie strolls to the stone banister, draping half of her body over the ledge. "I remember the day you and Jericho met," she recalls, her face neutral. "At one point, I believe he asked you what you'd want to be remembered for."

The haunting memory makes my eyes burn.

At the time, all that my identity ever was, or wasn't, existed because of my family. I wasn't the talented sister or the pretty sister—I was the outlier. The sister that didn't match the pattern of genteel, pleasant daughters. And yet, when my family needed me, I was the one who took on my father's load. I was the one to do appalling things for basic survival necessities—because I knew that Geneva and Calliope wouldn't.

That kind of thinking followed me for the remainder of my life, and it made me cast this helpless perception of them. Made me believe that when Father died, I needed to become their parent, their provider. But now, understanding that their lives will go on without me, I realize they didn't need me after all. I mean, Genny is a mother, fully prepared to raise a child on her own. And

Calliope, she proved me wrong for all the years I believed she was soft. The moment she snapped Diana's neck, I witnessed how strong she really was—able to protect her own just as well as I could.

And without the duty of worrying about them, no longer having the means to interfere or even be in their physical company—I realize what really motivated me to stay alive.

The prospect of someday finding a partner who intimately understood me and the parts of myself I couldn't bear to come to terms with. Someone who wanted to help me through them. In the parts of my soul that I did not like to shed light on, I know that I longed for a companion not just for the sake of being cared for, but for the opportunity to finally unwind. Someone to share the burden of life's responsibilities with.

And with Jericho, I found infinitely more than that.

I found a love true enough to kill for.

"I do not want to be remembered," I say with gritted teeth, trying hard not to fixate on the loneliness settling within me. "I just want to be with them again."

Merrie's smile withers at the words. "I know it's hard at first—"

"No. You don't understand. I was sleepwalking through my life, and your son woke me up. How is it fair to have put myself through so much suffering just to miss out on the life I so tirelessly worked to build for us?"

The late queen's prepared response falls silent on her lips, vanishing entirely.

"I don't care to be remembered as the woman who unraveled a dynasty," I say. "Truthfully, I do not care if the world forgets Venus Deragon ever existed to begin with. But if history must say one thing about me, let it be that I loved so fiercely, I destroyed myself. That I took the fall for Jericho when fate believed that I'd be the one to blame for his demise."

Merrie lays a gentle hand over my own, staring out into the Beyond. "As a mother, I will never be able to thank you enough . . . for giving him more time."

I shake my head, unwilling to accept her affection. "I do not know how time passes here as opposed to there," I whisper, my breathing turning shallow. "Every hundred years there could very well be a minute here, but I do not want to wait around for my loved ones to get here. I just want . . ." I sniffle, wiping at my eyes. "I want a lot of things, really. Revenge. Victory. Power. Seeing my sisters safe and cared for. But mainly, selfishly, I just want to be alive in the same universe as Jericho Morgan. Even if I must sacrifice the chance to be together again, knowing we coexist on the same planet will be enough."

Suddenly, I realize that all those times on earth when the phantom feeling of warmth would surround me, it was Merrie's way of embracing me beyond the realms of life and death.

She holds me with such tenderness, like the way Genny enveloped her newborn daughter, and the sensation makes me want to disintegrate altogether.

"It gets easier," she vows.

"I don't want it to get easier. I just want to go back."

65
Jericho

Even after I knew Venus was gone, I stayed with her—kept applying pressure to the wound. It wasn't until one of the nurses told me it was time to let go that I gave in, too weak to tell her to leave us be.

But there wasn't an us anymore, there was just me.

And while some would consider it torture, remaining with her body until I couldn't bare the absence of her breathing anymore felt like a small mercy from the Saints. Like they extended me time as a parting gift—time I never got to take advantage of when Mother died, as well as answers.

Because Mother left the world as a mystery, but Venus left as my champion.

No news of Venus's death has been broadcasted, and yet, all of Urovia feels like it has fallen asleep. Somehow, even the sky seems to mourn her, hot rain weeping onto the sloped plains beyond Broadcove's doors. The summer storm clouds roll slowly through the atmosphere, but in the distance, pockets of daylights break through. It's cruel, and it forces me to find brief respite in the darkness of my room.

I know that I need to break down—to set something on fire and scream until my lungs dry out—but I do not think my brain is ready to process the loss I just experienced.

So I strip off my clothes, aiming to change into something that isn't covered in blood but finding that the dark scarlet remains have stained onto my skin, too. I sulk as I try not feeling guilty for showering off the last evidence of her I have, and my efforts amount to nothing. Still wet, I throw on a ribbed sweater in the middle of summertime and aimlessly pad through the halls again.

It's not like I have anywhere to be, anyone to talk to. Everyone is likely off in their respective corners grieving in their own ways. I just . . . I don't think I can function alone right now. The silence is deafening. My soul feels empty. So distracted by how grim my reality has become, in fact, that I do not notice Calliope until our bodies collide as we both turn from our respective hallways.

"I'm sorry," she murmurs apologetically.

"You're not to blame," I tell her, truly meaning it.

Bloodshot eyes unable to meet my own, Calliope shakes her head, and I realize that my passing remarks sinks its claws far deeper in her than I intended.

"I thought Venus could take her," she confesses dryly, her face the portrait of personal misery. "And when I saw Diana's sword slice through my sister, I got so mad that I just . . . broke."

"I do not care what brought you to that point," I say. The woman had it coming, and I had to admit, I *cherished* seeing Calliope deliver her comeuppance. "I'm just grateful you did it."

"I just . . ." she says, biting her lip to keep from breaking. "I never thought I'd be like her."

The idea doesn't make sense. "You're not like Diana."

"No, not her," Calliope clarifies solemnly. "Venus." Embarrassment and shame flushes color within her cheeks. "For so long, I never imagined being the one to draw a weapon, let alone use it. And I'll admit, I cast judgment on Venus for being able to do so. I saw her as irrational, violent, hot-headed. But the moment Venus began to bleed out, and I knew who was to blame . . . it finally made sense to me, how a person can express love through cataclysmic violence."

And while the sentiment is out of character, especially with Calliope, I find myself reaching a hand towards her own. We barely have the strength to hold hands, to accept this reality. "It's how she and I loved one another," I whisper, the words like rocks caught in my throat. "And now, with everyone dead, there's no way for me to avenge her."

Calliope's fingers grasp gently along mine. "Maybe avenging her is not the point. Maybe we're just supposed to . . . exist again. Search for a new kind of happiness—"

"Happiness does not exist for me without her."

The words were not meant to be harsh, but her responding silence reminds me that while I may have lost the love of my life, Calliope just lost her sister. A love with different stipulations than mine, but one we both resonate with.

Calliope squeezes my hand in a manner that pulls a

corresponding heartstring. "What if you could have a living piece of her?"

I see so much of Venus within Geneva's daughter that it makes me want to weep.

"She's beautiful," I say, unable to articulate further as I watch Genny cradle her with such devotion and softness. I think of Mother in her younger years, holding me in the same manner—tighter, even. "What's her name?"

Genny blushes. "Pandora."

I've only ever heard of one other Pandora, infamous and well-known across the Damocles for causing mayhem. If this girl grows up to be anything like Venus, I suppose her namesake is a rather perfect fit.

Still, I take note of how proud Genny seems to be in voicing her name, blissfully unaware of its origin—and I certainly do not feel like spoiling her only remaining joy now that Venus is gone. "That's a lovely name."

"You think so?" she asks, a fragment of joy in the words.

Pandora seems to coo in response, squirming within her mother's hold. Genny giggles. "Where are your manners? Why don't you say hi to Uncle Jericho," she babbles, playfully moving her tiny hand in a waving motion.

I almost think my ears deceive me. "Uncle?"

Genny's eyes burn into my own, silver tears lining the rims. "I think we all knew you were well on your way to the title. As far as I'm concerned, you'll always be that for my daughter."

I have a niece.

I'm an uncle.

And it only hits me now that I'm automatically going to become the main father figure in this little girl's life.

Genny's statement kicks down a door I'm not sure I'll ever be able to close—and the emotion it overcomes me with begins to take over my body. My hands tremble, the skin along the back of my neck beads with cold sweat, and my stomach heats in the way it does before becoming violently ill. I cannot distinguish whether my vision goes blank or if I'm shutting my eyes as I backpedal out of the room. Genny and Calliope both try to reel me back towards them, but anything I could voice in response would surely be gibberish. There is only enough time for me to shut the door behind me and stumble into the hall before my weeping brings me to my knees.

The only word I can form in my language is her name.

Over and over.

I've only done life without Venus for two hours, and yet the pain feels aged and unrelenting. I may as well have been the one Diana gutted with her sword. It's not just tears streaming down my face, now. It's sweat and snot and something more somehow. And as disgusting as it all is, I let it happen undeterred, knowing the agony is proof to the world that hated me that I had a heart all along.

"My King," a meek voice reaches out towards me between my gasps of grief.

My insides twist at the use of my title, knowing no one in my personal circle would address me in this manner at a time like this.

I glance up to lock eyes with a man I've only seen a few times before—the last time being the day I interrogated the Holymen before the ball. Unremarkable face, but the symbol strewn on a chain around his neck remains unmistakable. It consumes me with wrath. "Are you here to tell me that if I had prayed more, she'd still be here?"

Despite my vicious intent, the Holyman before me lets the words slide off his shoulders. Empathy wells within his kind eyes. "On the contrary. I'm here because I think I know how to bring her back."

66
Jericho

I have no time to consider whether this is all some elaborate, cruel joke to poke fun at my defeat, not when each passing minute is another minute further from a miracle. A miracle I'm somehow choosing to believe is possible for me. For *her*.

"The boardroom is this way," I tell the Holyman as mildly as I can manage while remaining instructive.

"She's not in the boardroom," he merely responds.

Ardian must have asked the nurses and the guards to help relocate her and clean up the mess we left in the boardroom. So we walk on, my expectant, unnerved inner dialogue on the verge of spiraling up until we approach a familiar room, the door already propped open.

My mother's abandoned study only held a haunting quality about it whenever Venus first started sleeping there, insistently forgoing her mattress for the merciless carpet. I remember the night I first saw her dozing peacefully on the floor, her hard exterior softened in slumber. But in death, Venus's features are defined in harsh angles, a still capture of how she spent her final moments fighting for her heart to keep beating.

Whoever attended to her after I departed did a fair job of cleaning her wounds and removing her delicate frame from that ridiculous blue dress. Her hands situated gently over her middle, she dons a sheathed, black gown with minimal trimming, but the absence of her gloves reveal a trail of fresh bruises—marks that make me wish Slater were still alive just so that I could murder him myself.

A reverberating growl catches our attention from the side of the room, and as the Holyman takes in the sight of Roxie, he leaps back in terror as he clenches his medallion and begins muttering ancient prayers. If he reopens his eyes, however, he will see that the creature poses no real threat to him, Venus's beloved tiger stepping pitifully over towards her body, settling down behind her, and rubbing her whiskered jaw along the edge of her unmoving face. Protecting her.

"We're not going to hurt her," I tell her softly, easing towards her slowly so that she knows we can be trusted. "Isn't that right . . ."

"Clemence," he answers, daring to open one eye, then following suit.

Taking Roxie's nonverbal cues, Clemence and I move as one, slowly lowering ourselves towards the ground. Once poised over Venus's still frame, I look to him for answers and find his eyes darting back and forth. *Stage fright? Guilt? What's going on?*

"I've . . . never shared this with anyone," he eventually

begins, eyeing me with the kind of seriousness that sends chills down your spine. "Because I didn't want anyone to use me for it or turn me into some kind of supernatural tool—"

Now it all makes sense. "You're one of the Blessed."

Clemence nods briefly. "When I got approved to become a Holyman, I was so sure they only wanted me for my gifts, even though I had worked all my life to remain unnoticed in those regards. But they never mentioned it, and thank the Saints for that, because even though I'm here with you now," he tells me truthfully, "I didn't want to spend my life at people's bedsides, saving strangers from the brink of death."

A healer.

Clemence is a *healer*.

Just as my hope begins to resurface from the depths of my despair, he holds up a single finger in warning. "I need you to know, Your Majesty, that I've never successfully raised the dead, nor have I previously made any attempts to do so—"

"Wanting to help me at all is honorable enough," I tell him, unable to dwell on anything other than the mere possibility of having her back in my arms again. "Just tell me what you need me to do."

Rather than voice his needs aloud, Clemence lets a soft smile fall over his features and gathers Venus's hands before settling them within the cradle of my own, wrapping my fingers over top of them. He then mimics the posture of a servant, kneeling down and resting his weight on the back of his legs, and silently encourages me to join.

He stoops over to let his Saint's Symbol emblem hover over her frozen heart. "Let's pray," he finally says, bowing his head.

Ashamed to verbally acknowledge my lack of true faith up until this moment, I decide to offer up something more reverent than any prayer I've made before. An intimate vow I hope Venus hears from whatever dimension her soul now abides in.

"Forever and Always and Forever and Always and Forever—"

Somewhere between my pathetic attempts at saying a prayer and Clemence commencing his work, my conscience brought me here.

Mother's art gallery casts a sense of peace over me the moment I stroll in. Natural sunlight pours in from the looming windows, illuminating a canvas littered with greens and darker tones—at least from what I can see of it from over Mother's shoulder. Her perfume permeates the room, and as I inhale the nostalgic, forgotten scent, she hears me and shifts her weight along the stool. "Come in, sweetheart," she coaxes without looking up from her work.

Stepping lightly towards her, Mother turns around to finally meet my gaze. She looks just as beautiful as the day I lost her, and it only reminds me how much I've missed her, more than I care to express. "It's good to see you again." I sigh.

Mother beams a bright smile, as if the joy in our brief reunion might render her speechless. It takes her a moment before remembering what she meant to say originally. "I want to show you something."

The look on her face tells me that she's up to something devious, and as she steps aside, giving me full access to her artwork, I finally understand the depth of her Blessing—the very one she passed down to me.

It's Venus.

Scattered across the canvas, Mother has captured all the versions of Venus I've grown so fond of. At the top, her overalls fold along the pattern of her body bent over a fresh flower bed. Different still captures of her facial expressions line the left side—her infamous scowl reserved solely for me and the lovestruck blush I saw flood her cheeks the night of the Violet Ball among them. In the center, a reverent depiction of Venus dressed in black, a wraith's grin plastered on her maroon-painted lips. It's the same thing she wore to the concord back in Mosacia. In the bottom corner, Venus stands with a knife held behind her back, eyes assessing her surroundings—and upon reading the painting's official inscription, I find myself unable to breathe evenly.

Mother knew Venus and all her intentions before I ever did.

"How did the Saints reveal her to you?" I dare to ask.

A laugh bubbles up in her throat as she looks over the canvas again. "Conflicting images," she answers. "Each vision of her I received never stayed congruent to the one before."

"How often did you see her in your head?"

Mother falls quiet for a moment, gearing her eyes upon my own. "Weeks. Maybe months," she confesses, tickled by the concept. "They were all so different, I was convinced the Saints were messing with my mind, showing me different people. One moment, she was kissing her sister's forehead and helping make dinner, and the next, she'd be working herself to the bone, her face etched in exhaustion after hours in the fields. Some nights, I saw her bartering in the Makers District, negotiating with men that were gruff and unrelenting for the sake of finding food, and on others, I'd watch her dance by herself in her room, her windows thrown open to faintly hear a fiddle being played in the streets."

I think of how strong Venus was in the time I knew her, so bold. But to imagine what my mother saw as Venus danced alone, it shatters my soul. It makes me realize just how young she was. How she only lived enough years to barely make up the number of hours in a single day, and it makes me want to riot.

"How come I've never seen this painting?"

"Because it was taken away from my gallery, hidden away in Sevensberg Palace after I left."

My stomach knots up, my sadness melting into molten rage.

"But you should know . . . the vision I experienced that made me want to paint her," she begins, suddenly stumbling over a hitch in her breathing. A lump in her throat. Mother shuts her eyes. "It was the moment Diana prepared to kill you. When she swung her sword."

And Venus pushed me out of the way.

"You knew . . . you knew that Venus was going to die for me."

The words are not formed in a question.

"Yes, Jericho," she whispers with heartbreaking softness. "I knew."

The chosen title of this artwork never meant to warn me about Venus's plot to take me out, nor did it insinuate the love I would come to find with her.

It meant to commemorate the pivotal moment in history when even after all my enemies had been eradicated, I had been eternally defeated.

An insuppressible ache overcomes me, body and soul, and before I can fall onto my knees, my mother's steady hand goes to rest along the spot over my heart.

"Listen to me," she pleads, her voice thinning out, becoming brittle. "I knew your father was starting to grow restless, that he

was fully prepared to act on the grudges he had been holding onto, but this is why I sent the letter to Harriet. It didn't matter what happened to me, so long as I didn't have to watch you experience the most devastating loss imaginable, whether in the world of the living or within the realm of the dead."

All my soul knows to do is shatter, and she embraces me so tightly, fully bearing every sob that escapes my body. I'm so broken here . . . but it's worlds better than trudging through a reality without Venus.

"Please," I beg. "Let me stay here with you."

She lets out a heavy exhale. "I would love that," she admits, but something bittersweet lingers in the silence that follows. "But I can't."

"Why not?"

"Because someone came for her . . . and she's on her way home to you."

Still in the same spot I drifted off in, the carpet leaving a painful imprint on the skin of my knees, I jerk back to life in time to see tears shining in Clemence's eyes.

"My . . . my King," he croaks.

Then points behind me.

Somehow still believing that I'm being toyed with, I only manage to turn my attention towards his indicated direction slowly. Painfully so. I think I even shut my eyes as I move. But I hear the tiger purr, her rough tongue licking up Venus's arms.

I dare to open my eyes again and catch her fingers delicately combing through Roxie's fur.

The words and tears spill out of me. "Oh, my love—"

Her eyes haven't opened yet, but with what little strength Clemence restored her with, Venus reaches for me. I scoop her up off the floor, careful of her sustained injuries, and let her sink into my grasp and find rest within my arms. I cover her in kisses, undeterred by Clemence's presence, and as I hear her familiar, beautiful laugh, my tears of relief begin to drop onto her face.

And as Clemence runs from the room, scouring the grounds for anyone that will listen to his proclamations, I look down at Venus just in time to see her eyes gaze into my own. Surprise glimmers within them. "Does this mean—"

"Yes, Venus," I tell her without a moment's hesitation, knowing it is all that I have ever wanted. "We get to rule the world together, now."

Epilogue
Venus

S evensberg fell the moment our forces arrived on the Mosacian shoreline.

According to Chumley, who called us on their end of the Dial Line to confirm Sevensberg's capture, they needed my word to further ransack the continent—the perks of being bequeathed a kingdom I stole right out from underneath an entire family. So I had one of Jericho's King's Guard deliver all the documents Victor signed regarding transfer of power, and with it, a letter of instruction to stand down until I sent word again.

In the meantime, here on the home front, everyone felt like celebrating.

Against my better judgment, I let Jericho talk me into getting married on his birthday—which, really, didn't take much convincing at all. But in exchange, he had to promise that we'd keep the invitation list extremely condensed. He conceded, both of us knowing a formal, grandiose coronation would follow soon after.

A knock sounds on the door to my apartments. "Come in," I call out.

I expect my sisters, only to have Jericho stroll in. His hair is finally starting to curl at the ends again, and his usual wardrobe is substituted for a dark shirt and cozy, black slacks. As surprised—and ridiculously happy—as I am to see him, my attention snags on the garment bag he hauls in after him. I rise up from the chaise as he stoops over to keep it from dragging across the floor. "That looks heavy. Can I—"

"No," he insists, his voice calm. "You don't need to lift a finger. I've got it."

I study the bag again, realizing that he doesn't have one, but rather *two*. "What's this?"

"My birthday present," he grins in a way that makes me forget the kind of heartache he's endured in his life.

"I thought your present was me agreeing to be your wife," I point out.

"That's *one* of them," he says.

"Spoiled brat," I tease.

Jericho lays the garment bags on the edge of the chaise and presses a tender kiss to my lips, his hands cupping my face. His eyelashes brush the skin on my face, and the contact makes me tremble. How do I deserve this happiness?

"I know you were expecting Genny and Calliope to help you get ready . . . but I was thinking," he whispers, dotting a kiss onto the tip of my nose, "that maybe we could get dressed together, instead."

So *that* is the second bag. His uniform.

The minute Jericho and I began planning our intimate

ceremony, Calliope cared to inform me of every wedding superstition on the planet—seeing the bride beforehand being one of the biggest no-no's. But we've never been a traditional pairing, and frankly, I'd love to get him out of his clothes one more time before tying the knot. A bashful grin spreads across my lips. "Yes, that sounds nice."

A quiet laugh leaves him, and he runs his hands down my arms before moving to unzip our bags. He undoes his first, revealing the fateful crimson uniform I first laid eyes on him then. I think back on how, even as I despised him, the first thought I had in my mind was that he was intoxicating. I never stood a chance against him.

"You want to see yours?" he asks, a scheming grin on his perfect face.

Considering everything Jericho has orchestrated in the past, I had no qualms about letting him design the gown I would marry him in. All I asked was that he didn't put me in some kind of white monstrosity that made me look like a snowman. I wanted something sleek and endearing—something elegant enough for a royal wedding, but revealing enough to make him want to tear the dress off me.

I nod, watching him move to the other bag, unzipping it carefully—

"*Jericho*," I gasp, catching the first glimpse of color.

Only the king wears crimson. It's a precedent that, if Ronan didn't make it perfectly clear, Jericho certainly did. An unbreakable rule, and a sacred one, at that. And yet, there's no mistaking it.

That dress—my wedding dress—is blood red.

"I . . . I don't know what to say."

"You don't have to say anything. Just let me help you put it on."

So Jericho does, first untying the sash of my robe, then sliding it off of me. I'm bare save the slinky underwear I had meant to reserve for later, along with the garter along my right thigh. Jericho runs a hand over it, fingertips coaxing me towards particularly bad behavior. "No dagger, huh?" he murmurs against my neck.

"Don't tempt me, or we're not going to make it in time for our own wedding."

"Right," he says, resuming his earlier movements.

Pulling the gown out of the bag fully, he gathers the fabric to where I can easily step through the middle. Once secure, he weaves my arm through the satin straps, and then reaches for the ties that hang from the small of my back. Criss-crossing them in a corset's pattern, his lips hover above the dip in my shoulder, and his breath draws goosebumps to the surface.

Then, I turn and help Jericho out of his shirt, his pants. He doesn't need much assistance, and I'm perfectly content watching him methodically fit himself into his finery, but I do take pride in helping him straighten out each of his medallions.

Once he's all set, he beckons me to sit in the chair before my vanity. "How would you like your hair?" he asks gently.

The question takes me by surprise. "Since when do you know how to do hair?"

He laughs beneath his breath, the sound making my insides flutter. Still, he positions himself behind me, dragging the brush from my scalp down to my ends. "I had this moment of realization . . . while you were out," he says. "That Genny may have forgiven me, but I hadn't quite forgiven myself. Pandora was going to grow up without her father, and if I was to blame for that . . ." He stops, and I can only begin to imagine how hard it is to complete his thought through his remorse. "I wanted to be able to be a worthy stand-in when the time came."

I picture it then—the same man who's ruthlessly killed so many people, fighting with a fussy, four-year-old Pandora Deragon as he braids her hair. The thought makes me smile.

"You will be," I tell him, truly meaning it. "And I cannot wait to watch it happen."

He sighs, then eyes me through the vanity mirror. "You didn't answer my question."

"I just assumed there's a certain way you like it most."

"You're beautiful in every form," Jericho reminds me sweetly. "But . . . there is one way I'd like to see it done today, yes."

That's when Jericho reveals a splendid, golden diadem, with magnificent, glittering red stones bordered by countless diamonds.

"It was my mother's, but I added the rubies," Jericho says, his words constricted in his throat, like he's on the verge of breaking into a million pieces. "I know it's traditional for me to give you a ring—and I have one for the ceremony—but I'd be damned if I didn't do this. If I didn't find some way to honor you for all that you've done for me."

The dress was already beyond anything I could've asked for, but as Jericho settles the diadem along my brow, the truth in what the red stones signify shimmer back at me in the mirror. It's not just the king's color and Jericho's permission to let me embrace it. It also represents my sacrifices.

The people I've betrayed and fooled and killed.

The truths I've had to stomach about my father, about Kurt, about myself.

Every choice I've made for the sake of my love for him, even dying for him.

"You deserve far more than I can ever give you—more than crimson and kisses and crowns. I think it'll take our entire lifetime together to wrap the idea around my brain that you love me enough to have endured everything, but I'm grateful for it, nonetheless."

A single tear spills from the corner of my eye and cascades down my cheek. Jericho kisses the spot, pink coloring his pale cheeks as he tells me, "You look enchanting, my love." His lips brush the shell of my ear.

"I hope you know," I whisper, the words hardly manageable as I look through the mirror and deep into his fire-blue eyes. "That even though I cannot pull your own heartstrings and allow you to forgive yourself, I forgive you, for all that we have been through. And I'd go through it all again just to get to this moment with you."

Without restraint, Jericho begins to weep.

Pulling me into his chest, his arms locking around me, Jericho's sorrow and gratitude take over his body in jagged, shaky movements. His ribs crush into mine, and I simply hold him as close to me as he needs, let him feel all that he needs to feel.

I remember what it felt like to die, to feel my soul slip

away from life here on earth and into the Beyond—and even so, being on the receiving end of Jericho's unbridled emotion feels more supernatural and haunting than my encounter with death.

"I don't deserve you, Venus," he says through a painful sigh.

"If we had to marry the kind of people we *deserve*, we both would be miserable. But I'm perfectly content with binding my soul to someone who treasures me amidst all my failures. Wouldn't you agree?"

That's when I reach into my vanity drawer and pull out one last accessory—the Saint's emblem necklace that Jericho had bestowed upon me. His stunned expression barrels into me, but he still finds the strength to move, to fasten it around my neck. A soft sound escapes my lips as his fingers trace the symbol on my skin.

Jericho kisses me then in a way that is so worshipful and reverent that it nearly cleaves my heart in half. "I never really prayed before you came into my life," he whispers delicately. "But after what we've faced together, there will never be a day when I don't thank them for bringing you to me, and for allowing me to keep you."

I couldn't have said it better myself.

Clemence officiates our ceremony, North Star's glass structure and lush scenery sheltering us from the brutal July heat. Even though the guest list is condensed down to our inner circle, it's all we truly need.

At my side, Calliope holds my flowers—a cluster of peonies for Merrie accented with violets in honor of my mother—while Geneva cradles Pandora, and on Jericho's side, Ardian's weary smile gives way to silent tears of happiness despite the chaos we've endured. Everyone else remains perched on golden chairs we pulled from the banquet hall and watches us with a tenderness that I may never be able to burn from my memory. Ivanna wipes her eyes with a handkerchief, while Nadine buries her silent tears in Tolcher's shirt. I catch Eli eyeing Calliope in her dress, to which he mouths a lackluster, regretful apology, and when Clemence dares to offer the floor to anyone who may disapprove of our union, Roxie bares her teeth in the center of the aisle, ensuring blissful silence.

Our crowns touch as Jericho stoops down to seal our commitment with a kiss, and as the greenhouse and the rest of the world melts away, I try to imagine the woman I was a year ago and fail miserably. It is as though the love I found for Jericho—and the knowledge of what I would do to safeguard it—gutted me from the inside out. She may as well have never existed to begin with, and perhaps that's for the better.

The rest of the afternoon and evening is a blur. Lots of hugs from our friends, dancing, and cake—the latter of which I insist carry the exact number of candles according to Jericho's new age. We all watch him close his eyes and make a wish before blowing out the scattered flames, and while everyone applauds, Jericho whispers to me, "I need to take care of our documents. I'll come and get you when I'm done."

Of course, there's only so much paperwork that has to be taken care of. Yes, my end of it is likely a bit sticky, considering I went from Heiress Apparent to Queen

Consort of Mosacia and now Queen of Urovia in the span of a month. But he's gone for nearly an hour, and when the sun eventually falls beneath the sloping hills beyond Broadcove Castle, I almost begin to wonder—

"You didn't think I'd forgotten about you, right?" Jericho murmurs from behind, heat instantly coursing through my blood as I feel his body press against me.

I mean to say no, but I know better than to lie to him. "You were gone for a while."

"All for good reasoning," he says, pressing a kiss against where my pulse beats beneath my neck. "I think it's time we turn in for the night."

With absolutely no argument, I make my final rounds. I embrace my sisters, kiss my niece, and bid the rest of our guests goodbye as Jericho *insists* on carrying me to his room—our room. "We're a whole wing away. You don't have to do this."

"I want to," he murmurs lovingly, the words so soft and so unlike the version of him I'd first come to know.

The closer we get, the more my body and my brain come to terms with what's about to happen. Sure, Jericho and I have already had sex, but . . . I think I wanted to distract myself from the possibilities of what being married would do to me, to that aspect of our relationship. Not long ago, I truly believed I'd never marry anyone— perhaps because it was easier to believe I'd end up alone rather than fear the possibility of it. But now, here I am, sheltered in Jericho's arms, being whisked away to whatever our wedding night holds.

And I'm suddenly terrified by how much this man has come to love me.

Jericho stops just before the door, a childlike smile on his face. "Promise me you won't laugh."

The request has me making a face. "Laugh? Why would I—"

Shifting my weight into a better grasp, Jericho uses his free hand to turn the knob of his door and swing it open, revealing the room drowning in candles.

"It occurred to me last night that I never proposed to you," he says as he closes us inside.

That's right, he didn't. Frankly, we were both so relieved that I made it back to the living realm that we couldn't have been bothered to think twice about him getting on one knee and formally asking me to marry him. We figured that was a given. All we really cared about was that we would have each other until the end of our days, and we wanted that chapter of our lives to start as soon as humanly possible.

"It's beautiful." The words come out so dry, so faint. My eyes begin to well up. I've never been the kind of woman who imagined being romanced by anyone. "But you don't have to—"

"Stop telling me that I don't *have* to do things for you. Like I've said before, I *want* to." I can tell he's irritated, but not enough to truly get worked up about it. "Can't you just accept the fact that I don't know how to do anything else now other than ensure you understand my affection for you?"

I blink away the hot tears that start to brew. "I'll try."

Jericho takes my hand, gently squeezing it before he drops to one knee.

I've seen Jericho on his knees before, but not one

knee. In fact, I had always thought that seeing him beg and grovel would be enough to satisfy me forever—but witnessing him like this . . . I feel a shift in our shared atmosphere. Like my center of gravity will never be rectified, and I'll forever be tipping towards him no matter how hard I try and stay away.

"Venus Deragon," he says. "The Saints smiled on me the day they brought me to you."

And then, he digs into his jacket for something, pulling out a folded piece of parchment. Unlike the yellowed documents that litter his desk, this page is almost white— fresh and perhaps infinitely valuable.

"And ever since I found you," Jericho continues, his eyes solemn and his lips trembling as he speaks. "My life has been getting better. Little by little, your devotion and your mischief and your infectious nature have helped my wounds heal over, and while I can't ask you to marry me, because you've already graced me with the act of doing so, I figure that . . . that this could be a start. A token of my appreciation for the positive change you've put into motion in my life."

A singular sob leaves him, and with trembling hands— one in mine and the other holding the paper—he offers the parchment to me. I read the penmanship carefully, my eyes tracing each individual letter.

CERTIFICATE OF MARRIAGE

UNITED TOGETHER IN THE BONDS OF LOVE

HER MAJESTY, VENUS DERAGON,

AND HIS MAJESTY, JERICHO MORGAN DERAGON

"You . . ." I release a strangled breath. "You took my name?"

"I took your name," Jericho whispers, a joy in his voice that could sever me.

I refuse to believe it. I scale the certificate over again, just to make sure that my eyes didn't deceive me. But Jericho stops the frenzy in my movements before I can escape the room in a flash of bare skin and confusion. I drop the document on the floor.

"Why would you do that?" I ask, a shaky hand moving to cover my mouth.

But Jericho catches it within his hold, forcing me to lower it and look at him so brazenly that I fear I may implode. "Why wouldn't I?"

"I don't think you understand what this does," I start to panic, my eyes going wide. "The Morgan lineage has held a stronghold here for over a century. And, Saints, that means . . . you just threw away a *dynasty*," I mumble, bracing my weight against his desk. "You—"

I don't even feel him pull me down to him, only that his lips crash into mine, hard and demanding and silencing. "Stop," Jericho gasps against me, even as he presses us tighter together. "I didn't ruin anything," he insists, his hands slowly lowering to my hips. "I made something better. Something new."

Jericho presses a suggestive, lingering kiss along the column of my throat. "It's the name both territories will bow to."

My temporary guilt is eclipsed by the concept of such indomitable power, and I lean into Jericho's touch. Glancing at the certificate once more, I realize that the document has a crimson, foiled border—dragons in flight, with red flames licking up towards the corners.

"It's part of our new coat of arms," he whispers. "History aside, I've always loved Urovia's crimson and black, but it was missing something. It was missing you and your fire."

Deragon is not a far stretch towards *dragon*, I realize.

I don't bother hiding my blush. "I love it."

"I love you," he tells me again, and he carefully sets his crown on the floor, sliding it far from our reach, before cradling my face between his hands and kissing me in a manner that tells me it's time. "Nothing in life will ever compare to loving you."

After enough time with Jericho, I began to distinguish exactly which dreams were my own and which were his. Mine always felt like I was drearily walking through my waking world, to the point where I couldn't tell I was dreaming until my body throttled me from sleep. Whereas Jericho's dreams always had this enhanced vibrancy about it, the clarity of every detail so vivid it was unmistakable. His headspace always proved to be more detailed and compelling than mine ever was or could be.

But this dream exists somewhere between those two distinct realms, and it deeply unsettles me.

Everything within my line of sight is on fire. Trees, prairies, villages, monuments, even people—all up in flames. The smoke begins to fill my lungs as if I've leapt through time and space to witness it firsthand, and my body tries in vain to rid itself of the fumes. The pain is horrible, weakening my ability to stand, and my nose and mouth seek shelter from the ash that litters the plains before me in my shirt.

I look to both sides—fearing that the smoke is overtaking Jericho's system, too—but he's not there. I'm alone in the midst of a warzone. But that can't be. Jericho wouldn't dare leave me to my own devices in a place like this . . . unless . . .

Just then, staggering from one of the nearby houses, a mysterious figure cloaked in black appears—perhaps Death itself—and while I do not see their eyes from where I stand, I know their gaze is fixed on me.

But I can see into their heart, their soul. A black, inky abyss of hatred seeps into me like poison, and it makes me stagger away from him for a brief moment. I am almost certain they mean to draw a weapon—their hands clutching something behind their back—but something tells me that what they hold will cut me far deeper than any sword ever could.

The smoke is unbearable, but it lets up enough for me to see the strange figure reveal their mystery object.

Jericho's crown—broken down the middle.

I mean to scream, but I do not have enough air to draw in to form the shrill sound. My mind mirrors the devastation around me, and even through the tears that instantly brew within my eyes, I start to make out where I am. The hills I drop to my knees within are all too familiar. The heat has sucked the rivers dry and made kindling of the bridges that once arched above them. Honeycomb Harbor is a wasteland in the distance.

And Broadcove Castle has been utterly destroyed.

I throw myself awake, unable to fight the heaving breaths that overtake me.

I violently cough, as if the smoke will come out in a

cloud, and put a hand to my forehead. Yes, I'm sweating. Hard.

Is this my dream or Jericho's?

Panicked, I drink in the sight of the bed, the walls around us, and the way that Jericho seems undeterred by my nightmare and sudden movement. He dozes peacefully beside me, and while I wish to shake him awake and ask if what I just witnessed is something he's foreseen before, I refrain. I let him seek his rest—a mercy he once gave me—and make sure the top quilt of the bed covers him enough to stay warm before I silently slip out of our room.

Tiptoeing down the massive hallways, I make my way to the boardroom. Still mentally recovering from what happened the last time I occupied the space, I don't look towards the spot in the floor my blood still stains, gearing my eyes only towards the crimson receiver of the Dial Line.

I pick it up with unyielding conviction.

It rings once. Twice. Then, the line scratches briefly before giving way to Chumley's eager voice. "Hello?"

My throat is painstakingly dry when I go to speak. "Chumley?"

"My queen," he says, his tone hinting at surprise. "What hour is it there? Is everything alright?"

"I have your official orders," I say stiffly.

I hear him clear his throat over the line, adjusting sharply. "You have my attention."

The mental image of my world—my home—taken away from me simmers within my mind. It heats up my entire body to where I feel like I could catch fire, and all at once, I realize just how lonely Jericho must have felt all these years. Seeing visions of violence and treachery, tirelessly paying the toll for the lives he took with his soul. Did he ever know peace?

If I give the order, *will* he ever?

"Your Majesty?" Chumley says, his voice cutting through the silence between our two lands.

The ghost of my hurt in seeing Jericho's shattered crown—the proof that I'd lost the most treasured person in my life—awakens something within me. Something vile and ugly and monstrous. It turns my blood to venom, charrs my skin from the inside out, and forms unseen, impenetrable scales around my heart. It courses through me like lightning piercing through the atmosphere, like I could bend the whole sky to my will or crack the earth with my fists.

It's love.

Love so dark that it burns like hatred.

So forget peace.

Forget goodness.

Forget diplomacy.

Forget sanity.

Forget everything that could leave room for weakness— because I will not risk this life I killed my way to attain. Even if I go down in history as a madwoman. Even if it means I create a mountain of bodies, high enough to eclipse the one my husband created over the years of his reign—I will do it.

I will murder and scheme and battle and betray and bring endless ruination upon *anything* that could separate me from my home.

From my family.

From Jericho.

"Strike them while they sleep," I hiss, undying love and endless vengeance swallowing me whole. "And if they don't surrender, erase every trace of them from history."

Acknowledgements

First and foremost, I'd like to thank my Heavenly Father for calling me into a career that sets my soul aflame with joy. I'm not perfect, but I am continuously grateful for His sacrificial love.

Secondly, thank you to my husband, Houston, for always rooting for me and rooting for this book. You're the most treasured person in my life, and I'm so grateful for your constant encouragement as I keep creating new things. I love you (with no ulterior motives).

A massive shoutout goes to the three women that helped set this book over the top of anything I could've done all on my own. To Caitlin, my editor and personal champion. Your hand in this story is so impactful, so present, and so appreciated. I am grateful to have gotten to work with someone so dedicated to ensuring this story is a success and someone so compassionate in the process of making corrections. To Bianca, my cover designer, for helping embrace my vision of what *The Fall of Jericho* is at its roots. Your work is stunning, and I'm consistently blown away by your art. And to Farrah, for helping the right eyes see this before the rest of the world did, and for exuding kindness all the while. Thank you for making this launch successful and exciting!

Now, for some of my special people! To my most loyal reader, Makayla—from reading chapters from my first few books at the high school lunch table, to now—I'm so grateful for your constant love and support. To Heather, for being this book's first pair of outside eyes: eek! I cannot believe we're here! To Corinne, for making this book a reality with me. Thank you for not thinking I was clinically insane for wanting to write a story littered with villains and kickstarting this awesome journey that fateful Friday the 13th. To my parents, for never belittling my dreams of writing and providing me an environment growing up that allowed me to find solace in storytelling. To my friends who cheered me on, all of you mean the world to me.

And lastly, thank you to my readers. Whether you knew me before this book, you found me on social media, or you simply decided to take a chance on this story without knowing anything about me, I value you beyond words. Thank you for allowing my passion to amount to something more than just personal enjoyment. I'll never take that for granted.

About the Author

Sydney Applegate is a lover of comfort food, Taylor Swift, all things purple, and feel-good literature. She graduated Magna Cum Laude from the University of North Texas where she studied Media Arts and English, and when she's not writing, she can be curled up on the couch with her husband and their cat, Shiloh.

Sydney has dreamed of becoming an author nearly all her life, and is thrilled to have *The Fall of Jericho* stand as her debut novel. Connect with her on social media @authorsydneyapplegate or visit her website at www.booksbysydney.com to stay up to date on all her upcoming projects.

If you enjoyed *The Fall of Jericho*, please consider leaving a review on Amazon and/or Goodreads, as it would help support the author's work and allow more people to discover it!

Amazon

Goodreads

Visit Sydney's Author website to learn more about her upcoming projects, events, and more! Scan the QR code or visit www.booksbysydney.com